INSTINCTIVELY, BETH BACKED UP TOWARD THE DOOR.

"There's no way I can remain in the same room with you without loathing you!"

"Really?" Jake said, amused. "Then I'll be quite interested to hear your response to the proposition I have in mind."

"Save your breath—I accepted a proposition once from you, and that was enough."

Jake grasped Beth's shoulders and pulled her into his arms. The provocative scent of her perfume was like an aphrodisiac, a tantalizing reminder of that long-ago weekend they had shared.

"How badly do you want your railroad back, Beth?"

Suspicion flickered in her eyes. "What do you mean?"

"I have an offer for you—and I'll make this as succinct as possible." He returned to his desk, where he divided the railroad stock certificates into two piles.

"Here's my proposition, Beth. These two piles are equal: one of them is yours if you'll marry me."

ANA LEIGH—Winner of the
Historical Storyteller of the Year Award
from *Romantic Times*

Other **AVON ROMANCES**

THE MACKENZIES
JAKE

ANA LEIGH

AVON BOOKS · NEW YORK

This is a work of fiction. Names, characters, places, and incidents either are the product of the author's imagination or are used fictitiously. Any resemblance to actual events, locales, organizations, or persons, living or dead, is entirely coincidental and beyond the intent of either the author or the publisher.

AVON BOOKS, INC.
1350 Avenue of the Americas
New York, New York 10019

Copyright © 1999 by Ana Leigh
Inside cover author photo by Fantasies Photography Studio
Published by arrangement with the author
Library of Congress Catalog Card Number: 99-94777
ISBN: 0-380-79339-3
www.avonbooks.com/romance

First Avon Books Printing: August 1999

AVON TRADEMARK REG. U.S. PAT. OFF. AND IN OTHER COUNTRIES, MARCA REGIS-TRADA, HECHO EN U.S.A.

Printed in the U.S.A.

WCD 10 9 8 7 6 5 4 3 2 1

To Mike,
one of the few real heroes in the world

Prologue

Cambridge, Massachusetts
1877

Moonlight gleamed on the Charles River as Beth MacKenzie sat on the hill with her knees drawn up under her chin and her arms wrapped around her legs. Music and laughter carried up to her from the grassy bank below, where a group of students from Harvard had gathered for a lobster boil with some of her classmates. One of the students had brought back a new instrument called a ukulele from Hawaii, and it was creating a sensation among them. But Beth had no heart for the gaiety. She was homesick for the Roundhouse. She missed her father, Angie, Giff, and Middy. And she especially missed Thia.

Only a year separated their ages, and they were as close as sisters could possibly be. They had come east together two years ago to attend Wellesley, but Thia had quit school two weeks before and sailed to Europe.

At twenty-two most girls her age would be dreaming about getting married, but Beth's dream was that of her father: building a railroad linking Denver to Dallas. She knew she had to remain in

1

school to get an education, and as soon as she finished college, she would become part of that effort.

"Hi."

When Beth looked up at the speaker, her heart lurched to her throat. Tall, with dark hair and bronzed face, he was barefoot with his trousers rolled up to just below his knees.

"I'm Jake," he said. Plopping down beside her, he stretched out his long legs. "I bet with that hair of yours, you're called Rusty."

She reached up self-consciously and touched her head. "Thank goodness, no—I hate the color of my hair. My name's Beth."

"Beth's a nice name, but Rusty suits you more. I think your hair is beautiful." For a long moment his steady gaze remained fixed on her face. "If you don't get down there soon, all the lobster will be eaten."

"That's okay. I'm allergic to seafood anyway."

His warm chuckle tickled her spine. "So why did you come to a lobster boil if you can't eat lobster?"

"I don't know. I guess I was lonely, so I tagged along with some of the girls in my dormitory."

"I'm glad you did."

His grin was devastating, and she hugged her knees tighter, hoping to quell the fluttering in her stomach. No man had ever had such an effect on her.

She felt his gaze fixed on her face again. Blushing, she finally asked, "Why do you keep staring at me?"

"Because I think you're beautiful. Do you believe in love at first sight, Rusty?"

The intimacy in his deep voice was so compelling that it shut out all awareness of everything else. Beth swallowed and took a deep breath. Then she looked directly into his dark, mesmerizing eyes.

"Not until now," she said, sinking deeper into their depths.

Beth awoke alone in the bed Sunday morning. For several seconds she was confused. Where was Jake? At the thought of him, a floodtide of happiness swept through her. Stretching out in languorous contentment, she recalled the ecstasy of his kisses and the thrill of being held against his warm, strong body.

She slipped out of bed and began to gather up her discarded clothing. Catching a glimpse of herself in the cheval mirror in the corner, she moved closer to it.

With bright sunlight streaming through the window, she took a longer look at her naked body. Surely it had to have changed! Yet she saw no difference in it from that of the blushing virgin who had entered this same room Friday night. Wantonly she spun in a circle. She had never felt so alive. The feeling went far beyond a physical desire for Jake—she was in love with him.

Back home in Colorado she had had her share of beaux, but she had never even kissed one of them, despite the several who had tried. No man had ever known her body until now—until Jake. Now he knew every curve and hollow of her better than she did herself. His erotic exploration had uncovered every pleasure spot, every sensitive area, arousing her to exquisite heights she had never suspected she'd be capable of scaling, much less enduring.

She could still feel the delicious touch of his hands and mouth. Heat surged through her like fire. Turning away hastily, she finished collecting her clothes. She didn't want to miss church, particularly on this Sunday—she had a great deal for which to be thankful.

The service had lasted longer than she anticipated, and by the time Beth descended the church steps, she had less than two hours to return to school. But she couldn't leave without speaking to Jake. He would be graduating in a week, and all she knew about him was that he was from Texas. They still had so much to talk over. They hadn't discussed anything about their future: when they'd get married, where they would live—even when they'd see each other again.

As Beth hurried across the park toward his room, she was delighted to see Jake up ahead. But he was not alone: a circle of four other fellows surrounded him. She slowed her step, uncertain if she should interrupt their conversation.

"So you did it again," she heard one of them say.

"Don't forget, fellows, our leader's got a reputation to maintain," another said. Laughing, he slapped Jake on the back. "And he came through again with flying colors."

"I don't know how you do it," one said.

Beth was confused. Did they mean Jake, or were they talking about someone else? But a suspicion of the truth was already gnawing viciously at her stomach.

"Yeah, only Jake could meet a girl on Friday and convince her to spend the weekend in bed with him. You did us proud, buddy."

Another round of laughter followed the comment.

Oh, God, they were talking about her!

"I've got to go, guys. I'll see you all back at the frat house," Jake said.

"Ah, come on, Jake. You can't leave without filling us in on all of the juicy details. Was she any good?"

Beth felt nauseated. Her body had turned to ice and felt numb, except for the stabbing pain in her chest that hurt so severely she thought her heart had burst. Then he turned his head and saw her.

"Rusty!"

Somehow through the agony of her despair, she heard him call her name, and she became dimly aware that she had become the center of the group's attention.

"You gonna introduce us, Jake, or must I do it myself?" one of the fellows said.

"Jake, I don't understand. Is what they're saying true?" she asked in a voice she barely recognized as her own.

"What do you think, Blue Eyes? He's got a reputation to maintain. Congratulations, you've become a member of an exclusive sorority."

"Shut up, Randy," Jake snarled.

Still stunned, Beth looked at Jake, hoping he'd deny it all. He looked angry—and so guilty that the truth was undeniable.

The sound of the men's laughter invaded her nightmare. She wanted to scream herself awake, but she couldn't get the sound out. Jake took a step toward her and put his hand on her arm. The movement somehow galvanized her into action.

"No! Don't come near me! Don't come near me!" She struck out at him like a cornered animal fighting for survival, and managed to jerk out of his grasp. Then, sobbing, she turned and sped away, blinded by tears.

Chapter 1

Dallas, Texas
1880

As Michael Jacob Carrington entered the foyer of his family's mansion, the butler appeared to take his coat and hat.

"Good evening, sir," he said.

"Good evening, James." Shedding his outer garments, Michael handed them to the man.

"Madam is waiting for you in the library, sir."

"What's Grannie doing up this late? It's past her bedtime."

"I'd appreciate your reminding her of that, sir."

"I'll do that, James," Michael said, amused. James had been the Carrington butler for the past twenty years and he revered Rachel Carrington, the matriarch of the family. He would never presume to censure her.

Michael paused in the doorway of the library to smile fondly at his grandmother, who was dozing in the chair. Despite the fire on the hearth, a knitted afghan covered her lap and legs. He went over to her and gently closed and put aside the novel that lay on her lap.

She opened her bright blue eyes, whose merry

gleam had not dulled despite her eighty years, and removed the pince-nez glasses perched near the end of her nose.

"About time you showed up, young man."

"Why aren't you in bed, darling?" Leaning over, he kissed her on the cheek, then knelt on the rug at her feet.

"I waited up to talk to you." Her wrinkled hand clasped his. "Is it done?"

Michael knew at once what she meant. "Yes, Grannie, it's done."

"That's good. It's too bad your father didn't live to see this day. It would've meant so much to him."

In the years since his father's death, Michael had put a lot of time and money into this goal. Now that he had succeeded, he should have felt elated. Instead, he felt like a damn, stinking sneak.

He stood up. "Come on, Grannie, it's past your bedtime. I'll help you upstairs." Grinning, he swept her up in his arms.

"Put me down, you young whippersnapper!"

"Now, Grannie, how often do I get a chance to carry a beautiful woman up to her bedroom?" he asked as he climbed the stairway.

Her eyes twinkled. "A handsome young devil like you? Humph—too often for your own good, I imagine! It's time for you to find yourself a decent woman, settle down, and start having some young ones. Why aren't you at that ball right now? Stephen and Millicent went hours ago."

He set her down on the edge of the bed. "I haven't decided if I'm even going. Dressing up in a costume is asinine, as far as I'm concerned."

"Nonsense! Of course you're going. It's New Year's Eve: go out and have yourself a good time." She reached out and caressed his cheek. "You work too hard, dear. From the time your father died, you've carried all the company's burden. Before you know it, life will have passed you by and you'll have nothing but a pile of money to show for the passing." Her eyes deepened with sadness. "It's a poor substitute. I'd give up every dollar I have just to be able to spend one more day with your grandfather ... to hold his hand ... to hear his laughter."

Her chin locked into the resolute position he had witnessed often through the years. "Time is a fleeting enemy," she warned. "The time two people in love have together is always too short. Find yourself that woman. Do what you must to get her—give up whatever is necessary. If she's the right woman, you'll never regret it. The only regret in true love is the short time you have to spend together."

" 'Whatever is necessary' sounds pretty extreme, Grannie. You're saying the end can justify the means?"

"Yes, when it comes to love."

A light tap sounded on the door, and a maid poked her head into the room. "Are you ready for bed, Mrs. Carrington?"

"Yes, she's ready, Bertha." He kissed his grandmother on the forehead. "Good night."

"Remember what I said: don't wait too long. Once you find her, do whatever's necessary to keep her. You hear me, son?"

"I hear you, Grannie."

By the time he reached his room, Michael had already pulled off his cravat and shirt collar. His jacket and waistcoat quickly followed. Then he shoved his foot into the bootjack and removed his boots. In stocking feet, he crossed the room to the bed and with a disgusted glance shoved aside the costume laid out for him. Stretching out on the bed, he tucked his hands under his head. His grandmother's words rang in his ears. Grannie was right. If he had any sense at all, he'd forget the railroad business and go live on the ranch. But as much as he loved the serenity of La Paloma, he knew he'd miss the business world. He liked the role of an entrepreneur. It had nothing to do with money or power—it was the challenge of making something out of nothing. And the satisfaction of doing it honestly and ethically. His face sobered. *Until now, that is.*

This time he hadn't played fair from the beginning. His only concerns had been for the Lone Star and revenge, and in the end he had deceived people whom he liked.

He sat up sharply. That was just business, wasn't it? His father had always warned him that business was no place for the weak and vulnerable. And vulnerability had destroyed his father. *Well, Father, at last your death's been avenged.*

To hell with it! He wasn't going to lie here and battle his conscience. He got to his feet and snatched up the costume. Grannie was right. This was New Year's Eve; he might as well go to the damn ball.

As soon as Michael entered the ballroom, he saw her. He watched her remove the mask that covered her eyes and peer at her image in one of the floor-to-ceiling mirrors in the opulent ballroom.

He knew what the reflection would disclose: incredible, dark-lashed sapphire eyes set in an oval face blessed with a delicate nose, the high cheekbones of her Scottish parents, and a sensuously inviting lower lip. She was dressed as Queen Guinevere, her tall, willowy figure clothed in a long-sleeved white crepe gown, unadorned except for a gold-braided girdle belted loosely at her waist. A sleeveless purple velvet robe fell in folds to the floor. An imitation-jeweled crown capped the white gauze wimple that covered her thick auburn hair and draped beneath her dimpled chin. He was obsessed with that face—a face etched on his mind like a tattoo.

You look ridiculous! Beth thought. The serenity in her eyes belied the turmoil that churned within her as she leaned forward and spoke to her likeness in the mirror. "Good Lord, how could I have ever let Thia talk me into this insanity?"

Replacing her mask, she turned away from the mirror and scanned the crowd of painted clowns, rogue pirates, horn-helmeted Vikings, bewigged Marie Antoinettes, and equally beruffled King Louises—and at least a dozen Davy Crocketts! They all appeared to be having a grand time.

Am I the only one here facing a crisis?

She was at her wit's end. No matter how she tried, she couldn't put aside her nagging worries and get into the spirit of the party like these others gathered to welcome in 1881. With all sources of funds exhausted, construction on the railroad—her father's dream—had come to a stop. Some of the crew had already sought other jobs.

On Monday morning she had an appointment with Lucas Walters, the president of the bank that held the largest note against the Rocky Mountain Central. Not only would she have to tell Walters she couldn't make the payment due on the note, but she had to ask him to increase the loan. He'd turned down her request for more money six months earlier but had been kind enough to waive payments to give her a chance to raise some capital. She knew the banker's patience and benevolence had a limit, but she was desperate enough to try again.

Well, she'd had all the revelry she could bear. She'd inform Thia and Dave she was leaving and take a carriage back to the hotel. Her gaze continued to sweep the room until she spied Cynthia in the crowd.

Her vivacious sister attracted men like flame the proverbial moths. Tonight was no exception. Several men were clustered around her and appeared entranced by her every word. Dressed as a cancan dancer, Cynthia glowed with vibrancy from the bright red plume topping her dark hair to an appealing set of dimpled knees peeking out of the front slit of her ruffled gown. Beth couldn't help smiling, for despite Thia's audacity—a role her sister embraced enthusiastically—her arm was firmly tucked into that of her handsome husband, Dave Kincaid. This evening he'd forsaken the working garb of jeans and plaid shirt, which he usually wore as the chief engineer of the Rocky Mountain Central, in exchange for that of a French sailor.

As Beth moved toward them, an inebriated George Washington, complete with powdered wig and tricorne, stumbled against her.

"My apologies, little lady." Even his drunken slur couldn't disguise his thick Texas accent. Attempting to bow, he fell against her, shoving her into a tall man who swiftly reached out to prevent her from falling.

Texas George doffed his hat in apology, then staggered away as Beth turned to her rescuer.

One glance and her mouth broke into a smile. "It can't actually be Sir Lancelot to my rescue! This is too much of a coincidence to believe."

The man was dressed as an Arthurian knight. A full mask covered his face, and the hood of his short cape covered his head. A heraldic cross was blazoned across the front of his white tunic, which had a low, boat-shaped neckline and fell in scalloped points to the mid-thigh of long, muscular legs clad in black tights.

With a graceful sweep of his arm, he bowed. *"Puis-je danser avec vous, mademoiselle?"*

Beth shook her head. "I'm sorry; I don't speak French."

Sir Lancelot nodded toward the waltzing figures. "Dance?" he asked, demonstrating with a whirling motion of his hand.

Though she was anxious to leave, it was the least she could do to show her gratitude for his rescue. Smiling, she gave him her hand.

When his hand clasped hers, pleasant warmth spiraled through her as the tall man led her to the dance floor.

The moment he took her in his arms, she felt a sense of security and quickly discovered that Sir Lancelot was an excellent dancer. Relaxing, she surrendered to the melodious strains of the Strauss waltz.

Because of the language barrier conversation between them was impossible, but she could feel his intense stare searching her face. Occasionally she glanced up and smiled but generally kept her gaze fixed over his shoulder. Finally she closed her eyes, shutting out everything except the music.

Lost in its beauty, Beth remained in his arms after the dance ended, still hearing the music playing in her head. When she opened her eyes, she discovered Sir Lancelot was silently staring at her. Whatever he was thinking remained shrouded behind the mask that covered his face.

"I'm so sorry." Blushing in embarrassment, she began to pull away. "I didn't mean to . . ."

To her further distress, the maestro suddenly began the countdown to midnight. Within seconds people would be unmasking and kissing each other to welcome in the New Year. She couldn't bear that. The fairy tale had ended with the dance, and the relentless worries that had plagued her now swirled again through her head, which only moments before had been filled with the lovely melody.

The orchestra began the strains of "Auld Lang Syne," and as her partner started to unmask, Beth turned and fled like an alarmed Cinderella. Her escalating anxiety began to overpower her, and her heart seemed to bludgeon her chest. She had to get out of there!

Panic-stricken, she pushed through the crowd, seeking the nearest exit. Seeing a door ajar, she sped through it and found herself on a small concrete balcony.

The cool air was a merciful caress to her heated brow. She pulled off the mask, then the crown and wimple, and lifted her face to the night's soothing touch. Gradually her breathing slowed to normalcy.

What had come over her? She was the calm and clearheaded sister—of the three MacKenzie sisters, the one who remained levelheaded in any crisis. Thia and Angie often let their emotions get in the way of their judgement, but not her—not Elizabeth Ann MacKenzie! She'd only been eleven years old when her mother died, but being the eldest, she had naturally taken over the responsibility of guiding her sisters. And when her father had passed away the previous year, she had accepted the equal responsibility of completing the railroad trunk linking Denver to Dallas. It had become her dream as much as her father's—and now she knew she had failed.

Dear God, please help me. What shall I do?

In total despondency, she lowered her head as the strains of the song and voices of the singers drifted through the gap in the door.

"Happy New Year, Rusty."

Beth's head jerked up. Her heart knotted in her breast. Only one person had ever called her by that name: the one man she had tried to forget but never could. Didn't she have enough to cope with without having to confront him, too?

Squaring her shoulders, she turned around to face Michael Carrington.

"So it was you behind that mask. Your French had me fooled."

"I believe Lancelot was a Norman, wasn't he?" He chuckled. "Besides, you'd never have consented to dance if you'd known it was me."

"You certainly have that right. Hiding your real character behind a mask is your forte, isn't it?"

He made a courtly bow. "You wound me, my lady."

"I can only hope it hurt. Don't you think disguising yourself as a knight who rides to the aid of damsels is overly hypocritical, even for you?"

"You looked so troubled that your loyal knight could do nothing less than come to the aid of his beloved queen."

"If you sincerely want to help me, please leave. The sight of you turns my stomach."

He threw back his head in laughter. "I could never walk away from the pleasure of being with you."

"I don't find it difficult at all. Happy New Year, Mr. Carrington."

She started to walk past him, but he grasped her

arm. "Please don't leave. We have to talk."

"I'm not interested in hearing anything you have to say."

Her look of contempt would have been enough to make a lesser man withdraw, but Michael had waited too long for this opportunity.

"Why won't you let me explain—"

"I don't know how much clearer I can be to make you understand that I'm not interested in an explanation for something that happened years ago. It no longer matters. I have more to worry about right now than mistakes of the past."

"It wasn't a mistake, Rusty."

"Not for you—your actions were very calculated."

At the pain in her voice, he found himself struggling with his conscience. "Rusty—"

She lashed out angrily. "My name is Elizabeth. I am not the family pet, so please refrain from addressing me as if I were your loyal companion, trotting at your side. I suggest you get yourself a dog."

Her incredible eyes burned with loathing, and the passion of that emotion challenged him. Lord, she was the most exciting woman he had ever known! The only one who could excite him cerebrally as much as she did physically.

She gasped when he pulled her nearer and fingered several strands of her auburn hair. The moonlight glistening on the silken strands changed them into copper. "You know why I call you Rusty," he said in a husky murmur.

"And *you* know why I never want to be reminded of that time again."

"Rusty, fellows in college make up stupid stories about each other's prowess. The reality never lives up to the legend."

"Oh, really, *Jake*? They appear to make up stupid names, too. How many more aliases do you have, Michael?"

"As the Bard would say, 'What's in a name?' For tonight, just think of me as Sir Lancelot."

"Well, Sir Lancelot, as the Bard would also say," she parodied, "a rose by any other name *still stinks*! So please take your hand off me."

He complied, saying, "Before we part, remember this *is* New Year's Eve." He slowly lowered his head. "For the sake of auld lang syne, Rusty."

Michael had intended the kiss simply to be light and gentle, but at the feel of her warm, moist lips his hunger for her shattered his intentions. Crushing her to him, he devoured the softness of her mouth in sweet remembrance, until breathlessness forced him to reluctantly release her. Raising his head, he saw the shock and confusion in her eyes and suspected his own bewilderment was just as plain.

"We haven't lost it, have we, Rusty?"

"I don't know what you're talking about."

He looked at her seriously. "I think you do. You can't forget how great it was between us any more than I can."

"Wrong again, Michael—I forgot a long time ago." Her eyes mocked him as much as her words. "All that kiss did was to confirm what you said: the reality just doesn't live up to the legend, does it, college boy? Furthermore, I don't need you to slay my dragon, Sir Lancelot. I did that myself a long time ago."

She strode away with royal hauteur.

For a long moment, Michael stared at the door. Lord, she was one hell of a woman! That kiss had reignited the fire that had been smoldering within him for over three years. He had definite plans for

Elizabeth MacKenzie. She'd had the last word to-night, but tomorrow belonged to him. And revenge could be sweet. Michael grinned. But was it sweeter than her kiss?

The drone of conversation at the breakfast table the next morning barely penetrated Michael's consciousness as he sat deep in thought. He had lain awake most of the night wrestling with a decision—should he or shouldn't he carry his revenge one step farther?

If he decided to go on, it would mean disposing of practically everything he personally owned. He'd never before risked his personal wealth, but he had a Midas touch for making money—and money *could* buy an awful lot of happiness. It could also buy a lot of revenge.

As soon as he finished breakfast, he had a private talk with his grandmother and told her of his intentions. He not only needed her approval, he respected her advice. Then he left the house and headed for the bank. If he was going to start disposing of his assests, that was the logical place to start.

Chapter 2

Why had she let Michael Carrington get close enough to kiss her? That question continued to plague Beth as she entered the bank. She had tossed and turned the past few nights, her thoughts shifting constantly between the scene with Michael Carrington and what the outcome of her meeting with Lucas Walters would be today.

Normally Charles Reardon would be with her, but due to ill health the faithful family retainer had not accompanied her on this trip to Dallas. Dear Charles. If only he'd put the railroad's troubles out of his mind and concentrate on getting well—but he blamed himself for the current crisis. In their independent efforts to raise money for the railroad, they had inadvertently put up all the Rocky Mountain stock as collateral. His blame was no greater than hers, but the dear, loyal man would not accept that argument. If she could persuade the bank to increase the loan, it would buy her time to find a new source of credit and maybe ease Charles's worry.

And, as if it wasn't bad enough that she had to weather this meeting without Charles at her side, encountering Michael Carrington on Friday night had certainly not helped to ease her own anxiety.

He was like a force of evil—a leering messenger of impending doom.

"Good morning, Miss MacKenzie," Lucas Walters said when she entered his office. As he offered her a chair, she sensed his nervousness. After sitting down behind his desk, Walters withdrew a folded white handkerchief from his pocket and wiped at the thin sheen of perspiration on his brow.

"Can I get you anything? . . . A glass of water, perhaps?"

"No, thanks, Mr. Walters."

Any hope she might have had sank, along with her stomach. She could tell that the worst lay ahead and wished he would just get on with it. Obviously it would be a waste of words to ask him to lend her any additional money. The question now was what he intended to do about the past-due note.

Walters patted his forehead again, then cleared his throat. "Well, Miss MacKenzie, I imagine you're quite upset with me, but I hope you understand it was not my decision."

Frowning in confusion, she said, "I don't understand what you mean, Mr. Walters."

"I'm referring to your loan note. I had no choice but to sell it."

Beth jumped to her feet. "You sold it!"

"Please sit down, Miss MacKenzie," Walters said, mopping his brow yet again.

"How could you *do* that, Mr. Walters?"

"You were six months delinquent in your payment, with another payment due the beginning of this year. What did you expect us to do?"

"But you told me you'd waive the payment due date until I could raise some capital!"

"Miss MacKenzie, I don't own this bank. I am accountable to the stockholders and their wishes."

"What about the Rocky Mountain Central stock that we put up for collateral?"

"We surrendered it, of course."

Beth gasped in shock. "Whom did you sell it to? And why wasn't I properly notified at the time of this exchange?"

"The transfer was handled by the law firm of Randolph Bowing."

"And just who is Bowing representing?"

"That information will come from his firm. I would expect your lawyer has received a notification by now and will inform you."

"Mr. Walters, your bank sold twenty-five percent of the Rocky Mountain stock, which was intended to be merely held as collateral, to someone else without giving us the opportunity to settle the loan. The least you could have done was to allow me to talk to your stockholders. I might have convinced them to do otherwise."

"I doubt that. Mr. Carrington was—"

"Carrington! Michael Carrington?"

"Yes, of course. I assumed you knew the Carrington family owned this bank."

Beth paled. "Well, now everything is clear to me. No wonder your bank was so quick to dispose of the note."

"Did you raise the capital, Miss Mackenzie?"

"That's beside the point."

"That *is* the point. Did you bring the two payments with you today?"

"No," she said in a subdued tone.

"Then the outcome was inevitable. You're merely splitting hairs, aren't you, Miss MacKenzie?" He reached for his handkerchief.

If she had to watch him mop his brow one more time, Beth knew she would scream aloud. She got to her feet. "Where is Mr. Carrington's office located?"

"Why, in the Carrington building, directly across the street."

"Thank you, Mr. Walters, for your time." She walked out before he could get the handkerchief to his forehead.

From his office window, Michael watched Beth leave the bank. Smiling, he sat behind his desk to wait. It didn't take long. Within minutes, his secretary tapped on the door and stepped into the office. "Mr. Carrington, Miss MacKenzie wishes to see you."

"Show her in, Howard."

Michael rose to his feet when Beth entered. "Good morning, Beth."

She didn't waste time with amenities. "You are the most despicable person I have ever met!"

As she launched into a tirade, Michael sat down and patiently waited until she finished.

When she spun on her heel and headed for the door, he bolted to his feet. "Sit down, Beth. You've had your say; now it's my turn."

The command halted her in her tracks. She pivoted to face him. "I am not interested in anything you have to say, Mr. Carrington."

"I suggest you listen just the same."

"Why? More explanations for your lies and deceit? You can hardly pass off this latest duplicity as just another college prank."

"I don't intend to try—although it was just as calculating as my seduction of you."

Her eyes rounded with curiosity. He had caught her attention—there was no doubt about that.

"Are you ready to sit down and listen now, *Miss MacKenzie*?" He pulled back a chair for her, and when she sat down stiffly, he leaned over and grinned broadly at her. "Would you like a cup of tea or something else to drink?"

"Get your gloating face away from mine," she declared. "I realize your immaturity knows no bounds, but I'm hardly in the mood for it this morning."

Returning to his chair, he faced her across the desk. Beth sat with her head high, those gorgeous sapphire eyes never wavering from his.

"I must say, Beth, you're taking this whole situation very admirably."

"Did you expect me to grovel, Michael? So you own twenty-five percent of my railroad—I suppose I can live with that, if I must. After all, I'll only have to tolerate your smirking face once a year at the stockholders' meeting."

"I'm afraid it's not quite that simple." He opened a desk drawer and pulled out some papers. Tossing them on the desk, he leaned back in his chair as she slowly picked up one after the other, her expression changing from haughtiness to shock, then finally despair as she realized the full ramifications.

"You've bought up *all* the Rocky Mountain's outstanding loans."

"It was careless of you to put up all your railroad stock as collateral."

"It must have been quite a task, ferreting out our creditors."

"Not really. After your unfortunate disaster at the end of last year, it became much easier. You were so desperate for money that you didn't take the proper precautions to check out the sources: the Lone Star was behind most of those loans."

"Still true to character, aren't you, Michael? Sneaking and manipulating is your forte."

"If you recall, I once made you a generous offer

to purchase your railroad, but you refused. If I couldn't acquire it one way, it was necessary to do so another. You left me no choice."

She sparked to life like a smoldering ember in a windstorm. "No choice!" Her eyes glowed with anger and loathing. "You're even more despicable than I thought. My family trusted you. You came into their home, accepted their hospitality, and pretended to like them, when all the time, you were scheming to get their railroad."

"I do like your family. I like them very much."

"You admitted earlier that what you've done was calculated."

"It was, but it has nothing to do with how I feel about you and your sisters."

"Of course," she scoffed. "Big, powerful Michael Carrington finds it necessary to gobble up his competition—no matter how much perfidy he has to stoop to in carrying out that goal. Congratulations; you succeeded: you now own the Rocky Mountain Central. Your record remains unblemished, your crown intact. Enjoy your reign, Michael."

She was halfway to the door before he could respond. "My motive had nothing to do with business either. I did it for revenge."

Beth paused with her hand on the doorknob and turned to look at him. The misery she was feeling had begun to take over; her eyes had lost their glow of anger and her shoulders were slumped. She was vanquished, but he felt little satisfaction in the victory.

"Revenge? For what? What did I ever do to you?"

"Actually, you did nothing. I was merely fulfilling a promise I made to my father before he died." She frowned in bewilderment. "Sit down, Beth.

Don't you want to hear the whole story? I would, in your position."

As much as she wanted to march out of there, he could see that her natural curiosity prevented her from leaving.

"Did you know my father had attempted to get the rights to build that same track? When Matthew MacKenzie won it, my father was devastated."

"That's unfortunate," Beth said, "but business is competitive. The best man won."

"It wasn't a fair fight. Your father won with bribery."

"That's a lie! How dare you make that kind of accusation about my father? He was an honorable businessman; he'd never resort to such a tactic. If that's all you've got to say, then I'm not interested in listening."

"Beth, I investigated it myself. Your father bought the votes of two congressmen."

She shook her head. "There's no limit to how low you'll sink to justify your actions, is there? Is this how you purge your conscience of guilt? You can tell yourself whatever you wish, but don't insult my intelligence. You're pathetic, Michael," she said contemptuously.

He felt the rise of anger. He'd allowed her to vent her shock, but enough was enough: it was time she opened her eyes.

"Listen, honey, you played with the big boys and you got yourself burned. If anyone is trying to purge their guilt, maybe you ought to look in the mirror."

"You didn't—"

"I didn't do anything that anyone else wouldn't have done in the same position. The only difference is, I did it out of revenge. When my father lost the rights to build that track, it broke his heart. He died shortly after—but before he did, I promised him I'd get the Lone Star that railroad. And I did! I don't owe you an explanation; and frankly, Beth, I'm tired of your accusations and name-calling."

"Then I'll relieve you of my presence, because there's no way I can remain in the same room with you without loathing you."

He walked around his desk. Instinctively she backed up to the door. "Really?" he said, amused. "Then it'll be quite interesting to hear your response to the proposition I have in mind."

"Save your breath, Michael. I accepted a proposition once from you, and that was enough."

"As enjoyable as that incident was, I think you might find this one just as appealing."

"Appealing is *your* description of it, not mine."

He grasped her shoulders and pulled her into his arms. The provocative scent of her perfume was like an aphrodisiac, a tantalizing reminder of that weekend they had shared.

"How badly do you want your railroad back, Beth?"

Suspicion flickered in her eyes. "What do you mean?"

"I have an offer for you, and since you have a tendency to bolt, I'll make this as succinct as possible."

He returned to his desk, where he divided the stock certificates into two piles. "Here's my proposition, Beth. These two piles are equal: one of them is yours if you'll marry me."

Chapter 3

❦

Beth shook her head in disbelief. For nearly four years she had harbored anger toward him over what she'd believed to be a cruel college prank, when in truth he was clearly a very sick man.

"I suggest you seek medical help, Michael," she said in a controlled tone that belied her feelings.

"Sit down, Beth, and hear me out. I can tell you think I'm mad, but stop and think how you can benefit from being my wife. On the day we get married, I'll sign over that stock to you."

"I'm not so dedicated to completing my father's railroad that I'd prostitute myself for it," she snapped.

"But enough to *martyr* yourself," he said. "I'm betting that you believe no sacrifice is too great to fulfill your father's dream. Besides, I said I want you as a wife—not a mistress. As such, you'd be wined and dined by Dallas's finest families."

"There are more private wifely obligations that go along with that role."

He looked at her boldly. "Of course: companionship, attending social functions, hostessing, traveling with me on business trips—"

"You left out an obvious one."

26

"I will not force you to be sexually intimate with me, if that's what you're concerned about. But I will expect you not to become involved with any other man, either."

She was thoroughly perplexed. He sounded serious, but why would he make such an offer? He already owned the railroad, so why marry her? There had to be more to it than he was telling her. She finally sank into a chair.

Michael chuckled. "I can see by the confusion in those blue eyes that you haven't quite figured it out."

"I think I'm beginning to. Revenge again—right, Michael? You want to keep me under your thumb and watch me suffer. The cat playing with the mouse. That's it, isn't it?"

"You guessed it, sweetheart. By martyring yourself, you keep your father's dream alive—which shouldn't be too difficult for you. Isn't that what you've dedicated your life to doing?"

The accusation in his voice riled her. Considering what he had stooped to for the sake of *his* father, who was he to accuse anyone? She lashed out angrily, "Is that any worse than you dedicating your life to seeking revenge?"

"Then my plan should bring satisfaction to both of us. You get your railroad; in return, I get to make you miserable. *Quid pro quo.*"

Dare she even consider such a bizarre arrangement? Everything she had worked relentlessly for in the past few years was lost if she didn't. Not only this trunk line, but the whole Rocky Mountain Central. All she had to do was agree to his insane offer and she could gain back some of the loss. She owed that, at least, to her sisters and Dave. Half a railroad was better than none at all. But if she agreed, she was literally committing herself to an emotional prison.

She closed her eyes as the vision of her father filled her head. She could see him, hear the love and pride he felt for his railroad—his dreams for it. *Oh, Daddy, I can't bear to fail you.*

Beth opened her eyes and met Michael's stare. For a moment, the triumphant look in his eyes made her falter. He knew she was going to say yes. Her stomach felt as if it were being gnawed from within. If only she had the courage to laugh in his face and walk out of there—but she knew as well as he did that she couldn't say no. There was too much at stake—too many people who would be affected by it, too many dreams that would be lost.

"Will the MacKenzie name remain on the railroad?"

"That all depends on you, Beth. I have an additional condition to offer." He opened a drawer and pulled out a single certificate of Rocky Mountain stock. "I've divided the shares equally, but whoever owns this share will have the controlling interest. It's yours if you'll share my bed."

Her heart seemed to flip to her throat, and she couldn't swallow. For a moment she had actually believed there'd be no strings attached.

"You said no sexual intimacy."

"What I said was that I would not *force* you. I've never had to force myself on any woman—I prefer the subtlety of seduction."

"Your arrogance is endless, Michael. Surely you can't believe that I'm still *that* naive."

"And I hope you don't think that I'm naive enough not to know that once we wed, you'd haul that pert little rear end of yours back to Denver—with stock in hand—to tuck yourself contentedly into the Roundhouse. No, my dear, that would be too easy. I don't want you to forget for one day why you married me. The only way I can be sure of that is to have you share a bed with me."

He pushed the certificate closer to the edge of the desk. "There it is, Beth—for the taking. The control of your railroad back."

She didn't have the willpower to refuse. Grasping at straws, she sought an excuse to try. "I'd still be accountable to your Lone Star stockholders."

"No, you wouldn't. Other than your family, I'd be the only other stockholder. And since you and your sisters would own the majority of the stock, I'd easily be outvoted on any issue."

"But you said the Lone Star bought up our outstanding notes—doesn't it own this stock?"

"I intend to purchase it from the Lone Star with my own money. I've broken my cardinal rule of business: never operate on your own money. That's the mistake your father made when he started this trunk line. But that's how much I want this marriage, Beth." He grinned at her obvious shock. "Do we have a deal, Miss MacKenzie?" he asked, rounding the edge of the desk.

She could barely whisper her reply. "We have a business arrangement, Mr. Carrington." Her heart thudded in her breast as he slowly drew her into his arms. "What do you think you're doing?"

His hand cupped her neck and his breath mingled with hers as he lowered his head. "I'm thinking about kissing you."

"I consider that intimacy."

"Afraid to trust yourself, Rusty?"

"Of course not," she said, hoping she sounded confident.

"You don't believe that, any more than I do." He lightly traced her lips with his tongue.

Oh, he was lethal! His nearness assailed her

senses, intimidating, seductive. Shoving up her false bravado, she tried to resist what was coming.

He covered her mouth with a hard, possessive kiss. Hot blood rushed to her temples and pulsed as she fought the persuasive demand of the kiss. When he finally released her mouth, she managed to appear indifferent despite the fact that her legs were trembling. Only his arms holding her firmly in his embrace kept her on her feet.

"A handshake would be more professional," she snapped.

His warm chuckle ruffled the hair at her ear. "Then next time think of it as a handshake, my love, because I intend to kiss you a great deal. This is going to be the most enjoyable business arrangement I've ever ventured into."

"I must be as insane as you are to agree to it."

"No, you're a good businesswoman who recognizes what has to be done to get what you want."

"That's exactly right, Michael. I'm getting half of my railroad back—debt free—without it costing me one dollar. I guess that makes you the real loser: you're giving up half of the Rocky Mountain Central just to keep me miserable. That isn't sound business acumen to me."

He took her arm and led her to the door. "Don't be too certain. I have a reputation for having a Midas touch, and I rarely lose in any business . . . arrangement. Would you like me to take you to lunch to celebrate our engagement?"

"Don't be ridiculous."

"I'll accept that . . . for now. I'll have Howard hail you a carriage."

"That won't be necessary. I prefer to walk."

"Then I'll pick you up at eight o'clock tonight."

"What for?"

"Didn't Cynthia tell you? We made a dinner engagement the other night at the masquerade ball. I can't wait to tell her our exciting news."

She jerked her arm out of his grasp. "Oh, how I'd love to scratch that smirk off your face."

He lightly ran a finger back and forth across her brow. "I, on the other hand, would love to kiss this scowl off yours." He kissed her cheek. "Until tonight, darling."

Beth fumed all the way back to the hotel. Why had she ever allowed herself to agree to such an outlandish arrangement? She reached deeply inside her mind and heart for the answer. Was she really doing it for the sake of her father, or for a more complex reason? Could it be out of pride? She had failed the railroad miserably, and this *was* a way of redeeming some victory out of defeat. Michael certainly had outsmarted them all on this one. How could she have been so careless? What could she have done differently?

What will be, will be. If your destiny is to face the future married to a madman, nothing you might have done would have prevented it.

Entering the hotel, she caught a glimpse of her pinched frown in the lobby mirror. Good Lord, was she going to walk around looking like this the rest of her life?

When she stopped at the desk, the clerk greeted her with a wide smile. "Howdy, ma'am. Sure is a mighty fine day, isn't it?"

Despite her mood, she returned his smile. "Yes, it is. May I have my key?"

"Yes, ma'am. This wire came for you while you were gone," he said.

"Thank you," Beth said, picking up the key and telegram from the desk.

"Now, you have a pleasant day, ma'am."

"I certainly will try," she said.

Though I've got as much chance of that as a snowball has in hell, she thought as she crossed the lobby to the elevator.

The carrot-topped elevator operator, a lad of no more than seventeen or eighteen, greeted her with a smile wider than the desk clerk's.

"Howdy, ma'am. Sure is a mighty fine day, isn't it."

"Yes, it is," she replied. This time her smile was considerably more forced than the previous one.

"Watch your step, ma'am," he warned, then began to whistle "The Yellow Rose of Texas."

Next time I'll take the stairs, she thought as the cage jerked and shuddered up to the third floor.

"Here we are," he said cheerily when the elevator wrenched to a stop. "Watch your step, ma'am, and if you need anything, you just let me know. Tim Mahoney at your service, ma'am. Now you have yourself a good day, Miz MacKenzie."

"Thank you," she said, stepping out with relief. The friendliness of these people was beginning to wear on her frayed nerves. From the moment she had arrived in Dallas, she seemed to be at odds with these gregarious Texans—especially one particular man.

Once in the privacy of her room, she opened the wire and discovered it was from Cynthia.

FORGOT TO TELL YOU MC IS JOINING US FOR DINNER STOP THE MAN IS CRAZY ABOUT YOU STOP THIA

"He's crazy, all right," she mumbled. It was a good thing she had talked to Michael Carrington, or she'd never have guessed whom the MC was in Thia's cryptic message.

She knew Thia was fond of Michael, and it distressed Beth to think that, despite her sister's worldliness, the conniving reprobate had fooled even Cynthia.

Tossing aside the wire, she removed her bonnet and mantle and kicked off her shoes. Then, rubbing her aching temples, she stretched out on the bed. Beth had just started to relax when there was a rap on the door. She opened it to be met by the carrottop's wide grin. This time he was holding a crystal vase filled with red roses.

"These came for you, Miz MacKenzie."

"Thank you," Beth said, stepping aside for him to enter.

"Where would you like them, ma'am?"

"The table will be fine."

"Is there anything else I can get you?"

"As a matter of fact, there is. I have a headache. Would you mind getting me some fresh water?"

"It's as good as done, ma'am." He grabbed the ewer and scurried off.

Beth picked up the small white card that had come with the flowers and read the message. *Until tonight, my love.* The roses could only have come from Michael. Disgusted, she tossed the card aside. Good God! Did the crazed man actually intend to woo her?

By the time the bellboy returned with a pitcher of water, the flowers' pleasant fragrance had begun to permeate the room.

"Thank you . . . ah, Tim," she said, reaching for her handbag. Opening it, she extracted a quarter for him. "You've been most helpful."

As soon as he departed, Beth poured herself a glass of water and withdrew a small pillbox from her bag. After swallowing an analgesic she laid back down on the bed, and within seconds drifted off to sleep.

The persistent knocking at the door penetrated the haze of slumber. Whoever was at the door was determined to wake her, Beth thought, as she slowly forced herself to return to wakefulness.

It wasn't until she got to her feet that she realized the room was dark—she had slept away the afternoon. All those sleepless nights had finally caught up with her.

"I'm coming," she called out in irritation when the pounding continued.

Unlocking the door, she swung it open. Michael Carrington scowled down at her as he took in her disheveled hair, her wrinkled gown, and her stocking feet. He, on the other hand, looked elegant in a fitted overcoat and silk top hat.

"Is that what you're wearing to dinner?" he asked.

"I'm not going to dinner."

"And why is that?" he asked calmly.

"I have a headache."

"I see."

Actually, she had slept the pain away, but it was the first excuse that popped into her head. "Please extend my apology to Thia and David."

"I have no intention of doing that." Gently moving her aside, he stepped into the room and closed the door.

"What do you think you're doing?" she asked, folding her arms across her chest.

Ignoring her question, he lit a lamp, then walked over to the wooden clothes cupboard set against a wall. Riffling through her dresses, he pulled one out, grabbed a pair of shoes, and tossed them on the bed. "Get dressed."

How dared he storm into her room and start issuing orders! "Who do you think you're talking to?"

"We have an agreement, remember? I expect you to make yourself available when I'm entertaining."

"Oh, for heaven's sake! It's only my sister and brother-in-law. They'll understand."

"Family or not, they're my guests. And I expect you, as my wife, to show them the same courtesy you'd extend to the president or the governor."

"Don't be ridiculous, Michael. It's not necessary for me to put up a front for my own sister, whether she's your guest or not."

"I'm aware of that. What I won't tolerate is your using family as an excuse to get out of dining with me."

"I told you, I have a headache."

"And I don't believe you."

"Then, Mr. Prosecutor, I suggest you ask the bellboy. I had him bring me some water earlier in order to take a pill for the pain."

"Did it help?"

Annoyed at being trapped, but too honest to lie, she replied, "As a matter of fact, it did."

She waited for him to gloat at his victory, but he simply picked up the gown and held it out to her. "So, are you going to get dressed, or must I do it for you?"

Angrily she snatched the gown from his hand and stepped behind a Chinese silk screen. "If you think I'll continue to tolerate this type of bullying, Michael Carrington, you are mistaken," she declared, flinging her discarded dress over the top of the screen.

"It won't be necessary to *bully* you, Beth, as long as you honor your end of the bargain."

"Which appears to be subservience to your

wishes. Am I to have no rights in this arrangement?"

"Of course you have rights," he said, coming around the end of the screen.

Dressed only in her corset and unmentionables, Beth clutched the gown to her bosom. "Please stay on the other side of the screen," she snapped.

"That's ridiculous. I've seen you naked before, and you're far from that now." His bold glance dropped down to her red cotton hose. "I see those legs of yours are as beautiful as ever."

"I'm not your wife yet, so kindly get back on the other side of the screen where you belong," she ordered. It was a moot point, but there was a modicum of satisfaction in issuing him an order for a change.

After he retreated, Beth quickly donned the red sleeveless gown he had chosen, annoyed to realize it was the same one she would have selected. After struggling with the buttons, she stepped out from behind the screen.

Michael got up and returned the paper he'd been reading to a pile on the desk.

"I'd thank you not to snoop in my business papers, Michael."

"I've already seen those figures."

"Of course—how naive of me. Is there any of my personal business of which you're unaware? I'd hate to think of you entering this marriage blindly."

She walked over to the dressing table and sat down to fix her hair. He came up behind her and put his hands on her bare shoulders. The warm pressure of his hands brought a tantalizing sensation she'd believed had long been exorcized.

"Have you had a lover since me, Beth?"

For an instant her hand froze in motion as she

glanced up and met his eyes in the mirror. "You tell me, Michael. Apparently you're aware of everything I've done over the past three years." She resumed brushing her hair.

"The Pinkerton Agency knows of no such man."

She slammed down the brush and once again met his mirrored stare. "You had me followed!"

"I didn't want any unexpected surprises, Beth—especially from the woman whom I intended to marry."

Shocked by the statement, she shakily resumed putting up her hair.

He opened several buttons at the back of her gown. "You missed one," he said, rebuttoning the gown. Then he pressed a kiss to her bare shoulder.

"How . . . how long have you had me followed, Michael?" she finally managed to ask.

"From the time you left me in Massachusetts," he said. Turning away, he removed a knee-length black pelisse from the closet. "You look lovely, my dear. Shall we leave now?"

Still stunned by this latest revelation, Beth pulled on elbow-length gloves, then stood up and slid her arms into the coat he held open for her.

She didn't believe she could ever loathe anyone as much as she did Michael Carrington.

Chapter 4

Michael had a carriage waiting, and Beth remained silent on the short ride to the elegant ballroom he had chosen for dinner. As they crossed the floor, his hand lightly rode the small of her back, steering her to their table. She could feel the stares of the diners and overheard a whispered comment of "Who is that woman with Michael Carrington?"

Cynthia and David were already there. David stood up and the two men shook hands.

"Sorry, we're late," Michael said.

Cynthia greeted them with a wide smile. "Well, don't the two of you look friendly."

"Appearances can be deceiving, Thia," Beth said under her breath.

"Hi, Beth," David said, giving her a kiss on the cheek.

Michael reached for Cynthia's hand. "You light up the room, Cynthia," he said, bringing her hand to his lips.

"I'll never wash my hand again," Cynthia said soulfully. "I haven't seen such continental manners since I left Europe." She grinned wickedly at David.

"In the future, would you prefer a kiss to your

hand in lieu of your lips?" David teased.

Giggling, Cynthia patted his hand. "No, darling. I don't want *you* to change a thing."

As soon as they sat down, a waiter hurried over to them. After Michael exchanged several words in French with him, the man rushed off.

"I hope you don't mind, but I took the liberty of ordering for all of us. I've a great deal to celebrate tonight."

"I suppose you could say that, since Beth finally consented to go to dinner with you." Cynthia laughed lightly. "How did you ever convince her, Michael?"

"You'll be surprised to hear what else I've convinced her to do," he replied.

Despite how much Cynthia liked Michael Carrington, Beth knew that given the facts, her sister would not be so amused. And their chitchat now was only adding to her irritation. "Would the two of you prefer I leave, so you can discuss me less cryptically?"

Michael grasped her hand and squeezed it. "Sorry, Rusty."

"Rusty? Where'd that come from? You've really piqued my curiosity," Cynthia said. Her glance went from Michael to Beth, then she looked at David. "Do you have any idea what's going on here?"

"Not in the least, but I can see you're on the verge of bursting with curiosity, Miz Sin."

"Then I'd better put you out of your misery," Michael said.

Just then the waiter returned, and they waited while he popped a bottle of champagne and filled their glasses. As soon as he departed, Michael picked up his glass. "Will you all join me in a toast?"

Knowing what he intended to say, Beth reluctantly picked up her glass. As she did, she glanced at Cynthia, and from her quizzical stare Beth knew her sister sensed something was amiss.

"Thia and Dave, you're the first to know that Beth has consented to become my wife."

Cynthia gaped in surprise.

"Close your mouth, Thia; it spoils your image," Beth murmured.

Cynthia swung her startled glance to Beth. "Did he say *wife*?"

"That he did," she replied in a cool tone.

"Congratulations," David said, apparently as surprised as Cynthia. "I think that's great."

Et tu, Brute? Beth thought, with a woeful glance at her loyal chief engineer.

Cynthia had managed to regain her composure. "I was unaware . . . I mean, isn't this rather sudden?"

"Not really," Michael said. "I've thought about it for a long time. I just had to convince Beth."

Cynthia arched a brow. "My guess is that wasn't an easy task. We all know Beth is already married to the Rocky Mountain Central." She put down her glass. "Oh, how clumsy of me. I've splashed some champagne on my hand."

David handed her his napkin, but she brushed it aside. "Thanks, but I'd rather wash it off." She smiled apologetically. "So sticky, you know. Why don't you come with me, Beth?"

Once out of the room, Cynthia turned to her sister. "Okay, what's going on here? A couple of days ago, you couldn't bear the sight of Michael Carrington."

Beth regretted never having told Thia of her affair. They had never kept secrets from one another, and carrying this one around for years only gave it a greater importance than it deserved. If their roles had been reversed, Thia would have brushed it off and gone on with her life. But Beth never could be as lighthearted; she'd carried it around like a deep, dark sin. Out of shame—or was it pride?

Cornered, Beth tried to fib her way through. "I've had a change of heart."

"Yes, I'm sure," Cynthia said skeptically. "I know you too well, Beth—you're miserable. I want to know right now just what this is all about."

"All right, Thia; it's about a railroad—the Rocky Mountain Central, to be exact."

"I don't understand."

"Simple economics, dear sister. We ran out of money and had to borrow heavily to finance the construction. In so doing, we had to put up the stock as collateral. Michael bought up the bank loans. His wedding gift to me will be the return of half the railroad stock."

Beth waited silently as Cynthia analyzed the explanation. Finally Cynthia took her hand and pulled her over to two high-backed chairs in the corridor.

"Are you saying you're selling yourself to save the railroad?"

"Not exactly. Michael said he won't force me to be intimate with him."

Frowning, Cynthia held up her hand. "Wait a minute, slow up here. This is getting more confusing by the moment. In truth, Michael now owns all of the railroad's stock, but he's giving you half if you'll enter into a sexless marriage with him. Is that what you've just said?" When Beth nodded, Cynthia asked suspiciously, "Why?"

"For some reason, he's obsessed with me."

If Cynthia suspected that Michael was doing this out of vengeance, she'd do everything in her power to prevent the wedding—and Beth well knew that Cynthia MacKenzie Kincaid was a force even the conniving, manipulative Michael Carrington would find difficult to handle. But this was Beth's battle, and she'd fight it without dragging her family into it. As it was, she had already told Thia more than she'd have liked to.

Leaning back in the chair, Cynthia crossed her legs. "Sooo, just how long have you known Michael, *Rusty*?"

"A couple of years."

"Uh-huh."

"All right! I met him right after you left for Europe."

"You mean at Wellesley?"

"Yes."

"And you had an affair, didn't you?"

Dammit! Cynthia's instincts were uncanny. Beth sighed deeply, then replied, "Yes."

"I figured there was something between you two the first time I saw you together."

"So, you were right," Beth snapped. "I think we'd better get back to the table or the men'll wonder what's keeping us."

"I doubt that I fooled either of them for a moment. And you aren't fooling me either. Under any other circumstances I'd advise you to tell him to take his stock and . . . well, take it and keep it. I don't like the idea that he's dangling something in front of you that he knows you can't resist. On the other hand, if he's in love with you, I can't blame him for trying. And my gut instinct tells me that although you may have convinced yourself that you're marrying Michael to get that stock back, I think you care more for him than you're willing to admit. A lot of women would love to be in your shoes right now, Beth. Michael's handsome, wealthy—and obsessed with you. Sounds kind of romantic. You get what you want, and Michael gets what he wants.''

''That's the same thing he said,'' Beth said, exasperated. ''And you must be as crazy as he is if you can find anything romantic about this situation.''

''Aha, dear sister, that's where you and I differ—because I'm convinced that love will win out in the end.'' Cynthia stood up and tucked her arm in Beth's. ''I suggest we get back to those two handsome darlings before some other women get designs on them.''

''I don't think you have to worry. Dave has eyes only for you, Thia.''

''And from what you just told me, the same can be said about Michael for you.''

Relieved to get out from under her sister's questioning, Beth thought it best to leave Cynthia with her romantic illusions.

As soon as they returned to the table, David smiled broadly. ''Michael just told me the good news.''

''What good news?''

''About the railroad: he said we can resume laying track tomorrow. Your meeting with the banker today must have gone well.''

With a quick exasperated look at Michael, Beth replied, ''Not exactly. Actually, Michael is financing us.''

''That's a surprise,'' David said. ''Last I heard, Michael, you were trying to buy out the railroad. You two planning on merging the two lines?''

Michael shook his head. ''The Lone Star's not involved in this transaction. I'm backing you with my own money.''

Dave chuckled. "Sounds like you're mixing business with matters of the heart."

"It worked for us, didn't it, Kincaid?" Cynthia interjected.

"I'm sorry, Dave. I know you're in charge of the operation, but everything happened so fast this afternoon that I haven't had a chance to explain it to you," Beth quickly said. "I thought I would ride out tomorrow and fill you in on all the details."

"I'm just glad to hear I can tell the crew to go back to work. I hated to lose any more of them."

"Can't we forget railroad talk for the rest of the evening and concentrate on celebrating the engagement?" Cynthia complained. "Tell me, when's the wedding day?"

Beth shrugged. "We haven't set a date. After all, it takes time to plan a wedding."

"I thought we'd get married immediately," Michael said. "That was part of the deal."

"Deal?" David asked, perplexed.

Michael quickly revised, "I suppose that was a poor choice of words. I meant to say Beth's promise to me. If I give her too much time to think about it, she might change her mind. We'll have a quick marriage here in Dallas."

"I can't do that; I want to get married at the Roundhouse. I couldn't consider getting married without Angie and Giff present, or Middy, String, and Red. Besides, I've got to get back to Denver and order some supplies to get the crew moving again."

"Have you thought of doing what Angie and Giff did?" Cynthia asked. "They had a quick marriage in St. Louis, then remarried at the Roundhouse."

"That's an excellent idea," Michael approved. "How about tomorrow?"

"Tomorrow!" Beth gasped in shock. The man was truly insane. "That's much too soon," she protested. "Besides, I told David I'd ride out to Tent Town tomorrow."

David looked at her solemnly. "Beth, are you certain you want to get married?"

"Of course she does, David Kincaid," Cynthia declared. "All brides get nervous before their wedding. It's called bridal jitters."

"I guess when we got married, I was concentrating so hard on trying to get out of that stranglehold you had on me that I never noticed yours."

The two men broke into laughter, easing some of the tension.

"I don't have bridal jitters," Beth insisted. "I just need more time to prepare for it."

"Beth, you don't need any preparation to get married at City Hall," Michael said firmly.

That wasn't the point. Beth needed more time to *mentally* prepare herself to marry him, but she couldn't make such a confession in front of Cynthia and David.

"The judge is a close friend, Beth. I know he'd cut through any red tape as a favor to me."

"I have a simple solution," David said. "Tomorrow you could go back to Denver, have your quick marriage there the next day, and order whatever is needed to get the railroad rolling again. It would certainly be easier than trying to deal with the railroad from here."

"That's not a bad idea, Dave," Michael said.

"What about your family?" Cynthia asked. "Would they object?"

Michael shook his head. "The only one who'd care would be my grandmother, and she'll be so happy to hear I'm getting married that she won't care where."

"What do you think of the idea, Beth?" David asked.

At least it gave her one more day of freedom and a chance to get back to Colorado—on her own range. "I guess that'd be the wisest thing to do," she agreed, still overwhelmed by the speed of the whole situation.

Cynthia grasped her hand. "Honey, since Dave and I are staying in town tonight, we can all leave together in the morning," she suggested.

Beth looked at her gratefully. "You mean you'll go back to Denver with us?"

"Of course we will, Beth," Dave said. "We wouldn't miss your wedding. Will this cause you any inconvenience, Michael?"

"Not in the least, if it makes Beth happy," Michael said. "I was going to take my private car, but we can just as well go in yours. So we agree: we leave for Denver in the morning." Michael raised his glass. "Shall we drink to that?"

Beth downed the champagne in a toast to the brief delay before she'd begin serving her prison sentence.

But it was difficult to remain in a disgruntled mood for too long with Cynthia there. Her sister had such a capacity for enjoying life that it bubbled over and affected those around her. As the evening lengthened, Beth finally managed to relax.

Listening to the repartee between Cynthia and Michael, Beth realized that he'd probably been truthful about liking her family. They did get along famously, and it was clear that he held David Kincaid in high regard.

Later, as Michael waltzed her around the dance floor, he said, "I imagine you had to explain to Cynthia the reason for our sudden engagement."

"I did tell her about our stock agreement and

admitted that we'd met in college. I didn't tell her your real motive for marrying me. She has the romantic fantasy that you're in love with me."

"Maybe I am, my love. Maybe I am," he said lightly, smoothly leading her in a twirl.

Chapter 5

It was late by the time he'd left Beth and the Kincaids off at the hotel last night. Despite that, Michael had risen early this morning, packed for the trip to Denver, then dressed in a shirt and Levis and gone downstairs to wait for his family to assemble for breakfast. He wanted them all present when he made his announcements—particularly Stephen. He anticipated that his cousin would hit the roof, since Stephen had a tendency toward histrionics when confronted with unexpected situations.

Michael considered Stephen a thorn in his side—and a real pain in the ass. They'd never liked each other even when they were younger and Stephen's dislike had escalated after Michael's father had died, when the reins of the company had fallen to Michael instead of to Stephen. Petty and spiteful, Stephen constantly voiced trivial objections against anything Michael proposed, even though the company had prospered under Michael's leadership. His cousin's jealousy was magnified by the fact that their grandmother, Rachel Carrington, who was the principal Lone Star stockholder, lined up with Michael on most issues.

"Good morning, Millicent," Michael said, when

his cousin's wife entered the dining room.

"Good morning, Jake," she said, with a slight smile. She sat down and folded her hands in her lap, awaiting her husband's arrival.

Michael knew that any further attempt at conversation would be useless. Blond and small of stature, his cousin's wife was an attractive woman whose beauty was muted by her timid nature. Millicent's lack of confidence in herself had been further nurtured by a failure to produce a male heir in the twenty years of her marriage to Stephen Carrington. Their only child was a seventeen-year-old daughter at a finishing school in the East.

Michael liked Millicent and felt a deep sympathy for her. Despite the way Stephen belittled her with his pretentiousness and sarcasm and the common knowledge that he kept a mistress in the south side of the city across the river, Millicent remained steadfastly loyal to her husband. Her grandfather, Elias Wallace, had been one of the early investors in the Lone Star, and upon his death he had bequeathed the stock to his only grandchild. Considering the little affection and even less respect that Stephen bestowed on his wife, Michael suspected that the hope of getting his hands on the stock was the only reason his cousin had married the unfortunate woman.

Stephen joined them and said gruffly, "Millicent, I told you to wait for me before coming down to breakfast."

"I'm sorry, Stephen, I didn't hear you." She dropped her glance to her folded hands in her lap.

Michael was disgusted, but he had given up coming to Millicent's defense years ago since it only led to bitter exchanges between the two men, and Stephen would then turn his bad temper on his wife.

Grinning, he thought about Beth and her independence. She'd really shake up the breakfast table if he ever tried such behavior with her.

Just then his grandmother entered the room on James's arm.

"Good morning, Grandmother," Stephen said quickly.

"Good morning, Grandmother," Millicent parroted.

"Morning, Grannie," Michael said.

As soon as James seated her, Rachel's glance circled the table. "And good morning to all of you. Jake, it's a pleasure to have you join us for breakfast again." Her eyes twinkled with devilment. "To what do we owe this honor two mornings in a row?"

"I wanted to catch you all together, because I have several announcements to make. Since it concerns the Lone Star, I thought this would be the best time to do so."

"If it concerns the Lone Star, I think it should be discussed at a board meeting," Stephen said stiffly.

"If I thought that, Stephen, I would have called one. Since you're all family, I wanted to tell you that I've sold the shares of the Rocky Mountain stock that the company bought up."

"To whom?" Stephen asked. "I hope it wasn't a rival."

"Really, Stephen," Rachel declared, "I would think that anyone buying a railroad would naturally become a rival."

"I sold them to myself," Michael said.

Stephen tossed down his napkin. "You had no right to do that without consulting the rest of us."

Exasperated, Michael shook his head. "Stephen, you know as well as I that, as the executive officer of this company, I do not need stockholders' approval to transact any business other than that directly relating to Lone Star stock. Even so, I did mention my intention to Grannie and she saw no objection."

"Grandmother, how could you agree to this?" Stephen asked, turning an accusing eye on her. "Jake will be our competitor now."

"Good Lord, Stephen, do you actually believe Jake would do anything that would hurt the Lone Star? Aren't you carrying this petty rivalry to an extreme?"

"I see. Once again I'm at fault and your precious Jake is right."

"Stephen, dear," Rachel said kindly, "you're both my grandsons, and I love the two of you dearly. I'm certain Jake has a good reason for his actions. He's guided the company successfully so far."

Michael saw no reason to try to withhold the truth. "I have to admit, Grannie, my motive this time is not necessarily for the good of the company. It's entirely personal."

"See—what did I tell you!" Stephen exclaimed, jumping to his feet.

"Sit down, Stephen," Rachel commanded. Clearly agitated, Stephen flounced back down in his seat. "We're all Carringtons here—family. Let's resume our meal and discuss this calmly." She transferred her penetrating stare to Michael. "Just what is your reason for wanting that stock, Jake? Perhaps I should've asked when you mentioned your intention to buy it."

"I intend to present half of it to my bride on our wedding day."

"Wedding day!" Stephen snorted. "And just when will that so-called wedding day occur?"

"Tomorrow in Denver. I'll be leaving shortly."

The cup she'd just raised to her lips slipped through Millicent's fingers and bounced on the table, splattering tea stains everywhere. The clumsy action would normally have brought a chastisement from Stephen but went ignored as he stared goggle-eyed at Michael. His grandmother showed no reaction other than the barest glint of amusement in her eyes.

"Jake, dear, you never cease to surprise me," she commented. Her mouth curved into an expectant smile.

Michael winked at her. "I took your advice, Grannie. I'm hoping that you'll want to give us a small reception to announce it after we return on Saturday."

"It'll be my pleasure, Jake. Since you're leaving town to get married, I can safely assume you're not wedding that odious Diane Bennett, despite all her efforts to entrap you."

"That's right, Grannie."

Stephen taunted, "I see you're already dressed for the occasion. A shame we can't attend. Will this be some kind of backwoods ceremony?"

Michael fought the urge to land a punch in the center of his cousin's smirk.

"Do tell us, just what *is* the name of this fortunate bride with such a generous groom?" Stephen jibed.

Michael relished the moment, knowing he was about to put the torch to a bomb that would explode in Stephen's face. "Her name is Elizabeth MacKenzie."

The bomb went off with a blast. "Matthew MacKenzie's daughter!"

"The very same. A coincidence, wouldn't you say?"

Concerned, Millicent grasped her husband's arm.

"Stephen, are you ill? You're all flushed."

"I'm fine," he snapped, shaking off her hand.

"I have the impression you don't approve of my selection of a bride, Stephen."

"Well, I do," Rachel declared. "Matthew MacKenzie's daughter, you say. Time we got a real railroader into this house again. No offense, Millicent, dear." She cast her eyes heavenward. "Ah, Jacob, I can feel you smiling, darlin'."

"I doubt that Uncle Mike is, though. He certainly had no love for the MacKenzies. Have you forgotten your dying father's wish, Cousin Jake?" Stephen asked contemptuously.

"Not at all, Stephen. I accomplished what he asked me to do."

"And now you're handing the railroad back to a MacKenzie."

"Correction, Cousin Stephen. I'm not handing it back until she's a Carrington." Michael shoved back his chair. "Now, if you'll excuse me, I have to leave."

"When will we get to meet your bride, Jake?" Rachel asked.

Michael bent down and kissed her cheek. "Beth has some business in Denver, Grannie, but we'll be back Saturday for the reception. Then I intend to take her to La Paloma for a week."

Rachel patted his cheek. "I'm happy for you, dear."

"You'll love Beth, Grannie."

"I'm sure I will." She looked deep into his eyes, as if to probe his soul. "But the important thing, Jake, is that you love her."

What had she meant by that? Had the wise old woman guessed his motive for marrying Beth? He was saved from wrestling with his conscience when Millicent said timidly, "I wish you happiness, Jake."

Michael stopped at her chair. "I wish the same to you, Millicent," he said gently. He paused at the doorway. "No congratulations, Stephen?"

"I'll congratulate your wife. She's the one who deserves them."

James had the open carriage packed and waiting for Michael. A team of matched mahogany chestnuts was harnessed to the high-backed two-seater, which was upholstered in morocco leather.

"Congratulations on your forthcoming nuptials, and have a pleasant trip, sir," the butler said, handing him the reins.

"Thank you, James. And take good care of Grannie while I'm gone. Don't let her exhaust herself."

"I shall do my best, sir."

With a slight flick of his wrist, the well-trained team trotted forward. Michael grinned, exhilarated by the prospect of seeing Beth again.

Beth and the Kincaids were waiting when he drove up to the hotel. As soon as Michael jumped out and tied the reins to the hitching post, he pulled Beth into his arms.

"Good morning, darling," he said, and covered her mouth with his own for what he intended to be a long kiss. She ground her heel on his toes, and he pulled away.

Beth smiled sweetly. "Good morning, *darling*," she replied, fluttering her eyelashes outrageously at him.

He grinned. He could see that after a night to sleep on their arrangement, she had no intention of going down without a fight. He shoved his Stetson off his forehead and folded his arms across his chest.

" 'Pears like you ain't takin' to the saddle this

mornin', honey," he said in an exaggerated Texas drawl. "Reckon my little filly's got a mind to fight the bit."

"You've got that right, cowboy. Nobody's putting a saddle—nor a brand—on this little filly."

"Reckon we're just gonna have to see about that," he said. "Might have to get me a bigger pair of spurs."

He lifted her up as if she were weightless and plopped her down on the passenger side of the front seat. "Hope you notice who's handling the reins."

"Don't be surprised when they slip through your fingers." Seated, she was now eye to eye with him, and her gaze remained unflinching.

"Is that a challenge, Beth?"

"I believe it's considered throwing down the gauntlet, Sir Lancelot."

He dipped his head in a bow. "Then I'm at your service, my queen. Morning," he said to the others, turning away and limping back to where Cynthia was directing Dave's loading of the luggage.

"Good morning." Dave put his hands on his hips and threw a disgruntled glance at the remaining trunk on the ground. "I don't understand why women have to bring so much clothing when they're just visiting for a couple of days."

"To aggravate their husbands, my love," Cynthia said, winking at Michael.

"You succeeded," Dave grumbled.

"Oh, what are a few trunks to a big, strong husband who's used to tossing iron rails around as if they're straw?"

"There—that does it," Dave said, squeezing in the last piece of luggage.

"Then let's get going," Michael said.

"You're limping!" Cynthia exclaimed, following behind him.

"Nothing serious. In the future I just have to learn to be more fleet-footed."

Chapter 6

After riding for a while in silence, Michael asked, "You comfortable, Rusty?"

"Bow wow," Beth replied.

"Beth, why are you imitating a dog?" Cynthia asked. "Is that why he calls you Rusty?"

Beth shook her head. "No, just the reverse."

"Is that true, Michael?"

Beth added, "And he continues to do it because he knows it irritates me."

"Don't listen to her, Cynthia," Michael refuted. "The first time I saw that gorgeous hair of hers, the name popped into my head."

"Bow wow."

Michael gave her a sidelong grin. "Not that I'd object to an affectionate little puppy who'd jump up on my lap to lick my face."

"Not to mention an occasional wiggle of the tail," David remarked.

"I would appreciate it if you two men would contain your obscene conversation until you're in a saloon, where it belongs," Beth declared.

"Obscene? I don't understand what you mean, my love. David, what do you suppose is on the mind of my blushing bride at this moment?"

"Going for your jugular, no doubt," Cynthia in-

57

terjected. "And rightfully so, after those comments. May I point out, David, that dogs wag their tails, not wiggle them."

"I stand corrected, Miss Schoolmarm."

"Furthermore, you both should be ashamed of yourselves," Cynthia added. "My advice is to change the subject quickly, because I haven't fully recovered from my incident with a rabid dog and have no wish to witness another attack right here in this carriage."

Close to laughter, Beth turned to look at Michael. "Thia's right, Michael; your throat looks very tempting right now. Besides, you're confusing me: perhaps I should practice neighing instead of barking. I don't know if you'd prefer a pet dog or trained filly."

He turned his head to look at her. "I'd settle for a loving wife." In a lighter tone, he continued, "As long as we're on the subject of nicknames, since we'll all soon be related, you should start calling me Jake. My family does."

"Jake. Jake," Cynthia said, rolling it around on her tongue. "I like it. How did that come about?"

"My full name's Michael Jacob—I was named after both my father and my grandfather. Since my father was already called Mike, my grandmother started calling me Jake. I worshipped my grandfather, so I consider it an honor to carry his name." He leveled his glance at Beth. "And among those I care about—or who care for me—I go by Jake."

"Then Jake it will be," Cynthia said. "Right, Dave?"

"Sounds fine," he agreed.

This time Cynthia breached the silence that ensued as the two antagonists continued to stare at each other. "Jake, did you know that Beth is named after our mother?"

Michael broke their locked gazes. "Is that so?"

"Daddy always called our mother Betsy, so he came up with a different nickname for his daughter."

"I think that Rusty fits her just as well."

Beth's mouth curved into a smile of satisfaction. "Perhaps to you, but among those I care about—or who care for me—I go by Beth."

"And it's a lovely name," he said gallantly.

Beth smiled, satisfied that she'd made it clear that any pleasure he'd glean from his revenge wouldn't come easy: it would be a double-edged sword.

She closed her eyes and rode the remaining miles to Tent Town in a dozy state twixt sleep and wakefulness, the flow of conversation between the others a comforting lullaby.

Tent Town was the name applied to the group of tents and railroad cars that housed the crew building the railroad and their families. With construction halted due to lack of funds, some of the men had sought work elsewhere; those who remained were a large colony of Irish, steadfastly loyal to David Kincaid and the MacKenzies.

The freight train was waiting for them there, and as the luggage was transferred to the private car coupled to the train and the others boarded, David stopped to give Sean Rafferty, his crew boss and right-hand man, some final orders. As soon as David boarded, the train pulled out for Denver.

Looking around, Michael saw that Matthew MacKenzie had spared no expense when he'd built the lavish private car that had become the living quarters of Cynthia and David. Elegantly decorated with upholstered furniture, rich draperies, and walnut paneling, the long car offered not only a comfortable sitting room, but a bedroom, bathroom, and a kitchen with a refrigerated compartment. Once underway, Beth and Cynthia went into the kitchen to prepare a meal, while Michael and David stepped out on the observation deck to enjoy a cigar.

"You build a good track, Dave. How much more do you figure it will cost to finish up?"

"Roughly just under a hundred thousand."

"Beth shouldn't have any problem raising that."

"What do you mean? I thought she said you were financing us."

"I think Beth would rather explain it herself."

Dave tossed away his cigar. "What in hell is going on here? Is the Lone Star taking over the line?"

"No, my company's out of it."

"So you said. So why the mystery?" Dave asked, bristling. "This whole thing has smelled funny from the beginning. Beth suddenly announces you're engaged, but the two of you sure as hell don't act like two people in love. Thia hit it on the head today when she said it's more like she's going for your jugular."

"Well, friend, if you can keep a cool head, I'll try to explain it." Michael drew a final drag on his cigar, then tossed it away. "I don't have to tell you that this trunk cost a lot of money to build."

"Of course not. I've worked with those costs daily for the past four years."

"So you know how deeply the Rocky Mountain went into debt—to the point where any government sources as well as private ones were exhausted."

"Yeah, Beth mentioned she'd put up some of the stock to back the loans."

"Between her and Reardon, they put it all up. I

think it was a case of the right hand not knowing what the left one was doing."

Dave shook his head. "God! That's the very thing the Chief wanted to avoid," he said glumly. "That's why he sold all his assets to buy back all the outstanding stock from his investors before he started this project."

"And that was Matthew MacKenzie's big mistake," Michael said. "By buying back the stock from the original investors and selling off his other holdings to do it, he drained his own sources of cash, which ultimately forced Beth to go to strangers for money. It's amazing she got this far. With both Beth and Reardon attempting to raise funds, they got careless and inadvertently lost control of the railroad. The Lone Star saw what was happening, and we began to buy up those notes to acquire the stock. Half of the time we even put up the money. As the legal advisor, Reardon should have checked out who was behind some of those loans. We ultimately ended up owning it all."

"Congratulations," David said bitterly.

"If you remember, I made Beth a good offer for the railroad when her father died. She knew then that they were running out of money, with only two hundred miles of the track completed. She should have cut her losses and sold out then."

David flared angrily, "This trunk was Matthew MacKenzie's dream. If you really knew and understood Beth, you'd know she'd never give up without trying."

"I understood her completely. That's why I didn't show my hand. You see, I wanted more than just the railroad—I wanted Beth, too."

David clenched his fists. "You son of a bitch!"

"Hold on, Dave, before you start throwing any punches. The moment Beth and I are married, I'm signing back the controlling interest of the Rocky Mountain Central to her."

"How can you? The Lone Star owns the stock."

"I bought it from them."

For a long moment David stared out at the scenery flashing past. Finally he turned back with a cold stare. "So that's the reason for this sudden engagement. Beth's marrying you to gain back control of the railroad. I ought to kick your ass off this train right now."

"I know what you're thinking, and you're right. But before you do, answer me one thing: if you were in my place, would you have done less to get Cynthia if she'd refused to marry you?"

"Don't give me that bullshit! Thia and I are in love."

"Beth was in love with me . . . once. I don't intend to go into the details, but we met in college."

"And you figure she still loves you, is that it?"

"I'm gambling on it."

Michael knew he was stretching the facts a bit, especially since Beth currently hated the sight of him. He only hoped that Dave wouldn't question him about his feelings for Beth. He liked and respected Dave Kincaid and preferred to keep him as a friend rather than an enemy.

"A pretty costly gamble, isn't it? It's costing you millions of dollars."

"I know. I'll be practically broke by the time I finish disposing of most of my holdings. But the Rocky Mountain Central is debt free, so as I mentioned, Beth should have no problem raising the funds to finish this trunk." Michael extended his hand. "Still friends, Dave?"

David smiled and shook hands. "Still friends. All things considered, I reckon the gamble's pretty cheap, considering the damn fine woman you're getting." Then he sobered. "But I'm warning you, Jake: if the girls are hurt in any way by this, you'll have me and Pete Gifford to reckon with. And most likely those three MacKenzie cousins of theirs as well, if they get wind of it."

"How can the girls be hurt? They're getting their railroad back."

"Indirectly so am I. I don't know if you're aware of the terms of the Chief's will, but if I finish this trunk, I receive five percent of the Rocky Mountain Central. But I guess five percent of half of the stock is better than nothing at all."

"Dave, you have my word that whatever you get from them, I'll match."

"That's very generous, but why would you do that?"

"Because I have an offer to make to you. I think you're one of the best railroad engineers in this business, and I was hoping that when you're through here, I could persuade you to come over to the Lone Star as chief of engineers."

"Sorry, Jake, I already have a job with the Rocky Mountain Central. But thanks for the offer."

"I figured you'd say that. I think Beth was right when she said I'm the real loser on this deal. If I'd let the Lone Star take over your railroad, you might have ended up working for me." He shook his head. "This gamble's already cost me the chance of getting my hands on a damn good engineer."

Dave slapped him on the shoulder. "Look at it this way, Jake: you may have lost an engineer—but you're gaining a brother-in-law."

Laughing, the two men went back inside.

Following dinner, the women squared off against the men in a game of whist and trounced them soundly.

"I think they cheated, Dave, don't you?" Michael said, feigning annoyance.

Dave nodded. "Probably used secret signals that they've been practicing for years." He tried unsuccessfully to restrain his grin.

"Poor babies!" Cynthia teased. "We really whupped the pants off you fellas."

"We let you win," Dave denied. "And get your face out of mine or I'm gonna—"

"Gonna what, Kincaid?" Cynthia arched a brow.

"Gonna kiss that smirk right off your face." Grabbing her, he covered her mouth with a smacking kiss.

"I just dare you to try that again," Cynthia teased.

"Oh, no! They're at it again." Beth had tolerated enough of the loving couple's play. It only made her feel guilty for trying to deceive them about her own marriage. She shoved back her chair and stood up. "I'm going to excuse myself and go to bed. I appreciate your giving up your bed tonight, Dave."

"How about a breath of air before retiring?" Without waiting for a reply, Michael grasped her hand. "That'll give these two lovebirds a chance to say good night without our prying eyes."

Cynthia rolled her eyes. "And what will you two be doing out on that deck when Dave and I are saying our good night?"

"Breathing the fresh air," Beth replied, allowing Michael to pull her along.

Once outside, Beth did take a deep breath. The night air felt good. As luxurious as the car was, she'd always found its narrowness confining. Folding her arms to ward off the chill, she gazed up at the myriad stars twinkling overhead and was tempted to make a wish for some miracle to get her out of the predicament. Her mouth twisted in a wry smile. She might as well wish for the moon.

Pensively she stared out at the darkness flashing past and wondered if she really could go through with the marriage when the time came. But she didn't have any other option if she wanted to keep her railroad. Would she have to begin and end every day with that reminder? At the thought, a shiver rippled through her.

"Cold?" Michael asked. She stiffened her spine when he wrapped his arms around her and pulled her back against him. "Just think, Rusty, tomorrow at this time, we'll be man and wife," he murmured.

"I can hardly wait."

Her indifferent tone produced a chuckle from him. "You know, the joke would be on me if you ended up enjoying our marriage."

"That's such a remote possibility that I wouldn't waste time considering it."

He turned her in his arms. "You might even start savoring my kisses," he whispered, just before he claimed her lips. Beth continued to hold herself stiff and unresponsive.

He raised his head and smiled invitingly. "You could enjoy this if you tried."

"Attempting to enjoy your pawing would be more exhausting than simply enduring it, Michael." She stepped around him to the door.

There was no sign of Cynthia when they entered the car.

"Thia went to bed," Dave told them.

"And that's where I'm going," Beth added.

"Jake, how about a nightcap and a game of backgammon?"

"You're on, pal."

Beth gave David a quick peck on the cheek. "You're a darling to give up your bed, Dave."

"No problem. Gotta watch Thia, though: she hogs the blanket."

"I will. Good night, Dave."

Beth went into the bedroom without a backward glance at Michael.

When the door closed behind her, Dave shook his head and poured some brandy into a glass. "So you're convinced she *really* loves you, huh?"

"Uh-huh. Wasn't it Shakespeare who reminded us about protesting too much?" For a long moment he stared at the closed door. "It's just going to take a little patience."

"No, friend, it's going to take a *lot* of patience." Dave handed Michael the glass.

Several hours later, they abandoned their game. David curled his long body along the circular sofa in the center of the room, and Michael sought the comfort of one of the large, plush chairs.

When he awoke to bright sunlight, the car was parked on the turnaround at MacKenzie Junction.

Chapter 7

Morning sunlight rolled across the snow-capped peaks of the Rockies, streaking the towering stands of pine and aspen with gold. The temperature had remained unusually warm for January, but the air still felt crisp and invigorating to Beth as she waited on the observation deck of the train. She drew several deep breaths, like a drowning woman snatched out of the sea . . . or paroled from prison. Being home again was like being given a second chance at autonomy.

"Good, here comes Giff now," Cynthia said, beside her at the rail.

They stepped off the train and joined the men, who had the luggage piled on the station platform. Located on the fringe of the MacKenzie ranch five miles north of Denver, the private depot consisted of a tiny log station house and a small roundhouse, where their father had kept his railroad car.

Pete Gifford climbed down from the buckboard, and the men went through the ritual of handshakes and slaps on the shoulders. Beth waited impatiently, anxious to get home. There was so much to be done before she was forced to return to Texas.

After kissing and hugging Cynthia, Giff turned to her. When his arms closed around her, she knew she was home. *Hold onto me, Giff. Don't let go*, she pleaded silently.

Pete Gifford was foreman of the Roundhouse, and six years older than she. Beth loved him like a brother. His father had been the former ranch foreman, and as they grew up together, Giff had guarded her and her sisters zealously, fought their battles for them, been their confidant, and nursed them through the heartache of the loss of their parents. Both she and Thia had harbored brief girlhood crushes on him, but Giff had wisely weathered them out, remaining their steadfast pal until the girls outgrew them. When Angie was eighteen Giff had fallen in love with her, but knowing she looked upon him as a brother, had kept the secret to himself. Beth and Cynthia had guessed his feelings and knew that Angie was just as much in love with him. Unfortunately, it took Angie longer to realize it, and both Beth and Cynthia had breathed a sigh of sisterly relief when the couple were finally married the previous summer.

Giff stepped back, and his grin carried to the corners of his clear blue eyes. "So you're getting married, Beth. I'm so happy for you."

If you knew the real truth, you wouldn't be, Giff. Unable to meet his trusting stare, she lowered her eyes.

"Hey, what's bothering you?" He tipped up her chin and looked deeper into her eyes.

"I never could fool you, Pete Gifford, could I?" She forced a weak smile. "I just hate to think of leaving the Roundhouse, that's all."

"You sure it's nothing else? Something to do with the railroad, maybe?"

"Michael's taking care of the railroad for me."

"You mean he's taking it over?"

"No, I mean he's . . . ah . . . Well, actually Michael's—"

"Beth, I thought we agreed from now on everyone's to call me Jake," Michael said, joining them. He put an arm around her shoulders and pulled her against his side. "My family calls me that, Giff, and I was hoping Beth's family would do the same."

"Sure . . . sure, Jake," Giff said. But his concerned gaze remained fixed on Beth.

She smiled weakly. "We'll discuss this later, Giff, when we have more time. Let's just get back to the house."

As soon as they came in sight of the homestead, Beth saw Angie racing toward them on the back of her dun stallion. Beth caught her breath as horse and rider vaulted a fence with the ease of steeple-chase champions.

"Magnificent jump," Michael murmured in awe, seated beside Beth and Cynthia. "Does she do that often?"

"All the time," Cynthia groaned. "It scares the life out of me. Giff, can't you make her stop doing that?"

"I'd have a better chance of stopping a charging bull with my bare hands," Giff grumbled.

"Look at that gal ride," Michael exclaimed. "Has she always been that accomplished on horseback?"

"From the first time the Chief let her ride alone. By the time she was ten, she could outride her sisters—and by the time she was twenty, any hand on the ranch," Giff said with flagrant pride.

"Hi," Angie yelled as she rode up. "Seems like we just got rid of all of you," she teased, "but it's good to see you back." She wheeled Calico and smiled mischievously at Giff. "Race you back to the house."

"No, you won't, 'cause it takes two to make a race. Dammit, Angel, slow down," he yelled after her as she galloped away.

Angie was waiting on the porch when they drove up. The front door slammed, and the housekeeper, Middy McNamara, came out to join them. Joyously Beth hugged and kissed the older woman, who had been like a second mother to her and her sisers.

Angie moved excitedly from one to the other, her dark curls bouncing on her shoulders. Amidst her hugs and kisses, congratulations, and declarations of how she knew Beth and Michael would be happy forever, she managed to squeeze in the information that the wedding was set for seven o'clock the following evening.

"Why so late?" Cynthia groaned. "We won't have much time to celebrate, since we'll be leaving early the next morning."

"How much celebrating do you plan on doing, Miz Sin?" David teased.

Beth couldn't have been more pleased, hoping that the longer the wedding was delayed, somehow a miracle would occur to prevent it from happening.

"There was no other way," Angie explained. "Mary Henderson passed away, so Pastor Williams has to officiate at the funeral in the afternoon."

"Why not have a quick marriage in the morning?" Michael suggested.

"That's not necessary. Tomorrow evening will be fine," Beth replied, with a pointed look at him. The mention of the woman's death was a grim reminder to her of how sick Charles Reardon had been when she left. "Angie, how is Charles doing?"

The sparkle left Angie's eyes. "There's been no change in his condition. I visited him yesterday and told him you were getting married. He was pleased, but unfortunately he's too ill to attend."

"I wouldn't expect him to. I'll go to see him later today. I wouldn't want to leave again without seeing him."

"Oh, are you leaving on a honeymoon?" Angie's eyes glowed with excitement.

"Not exactly—Michael and I will be returning to Texas on Friday."

"There she goes again," Michael said, joining them. "Angie, I've been doing my darndest to get your sister to call me Jake, but she keeps forgetting. I hope you won't have the same problem."

"If that's what you want, Jake."

The sight of adoration on Angie's face was almost too much for Beth to bear; her younger sister had worshipped Michael from the time he had arranged for the sale of several of her paintings.

"Jake's an easy name to remember, Beth," Angie said.

"But so much easier to forget," Beth replied. She smiled at Michael and walked away, but paused before going into the house and looked back. Even Middy had fallen under the charm of the manipulative, scheming, low-down, conniving demon: the white-haired housekeeper was glowing with pleasure as Michael hugged her. *Good Lord, am I the only one who can see through his manipulations?*

When Michael glanced over and saw her watching him, he kissed Middy on the cheek and came over to her.

"Tell me, Beth: I can't determine by your expression if you're hoping I'll be boiled in oil, or merely hung by my thumbs."

"Hung by . . . something, anyway."

Michael burst out laughing. "I love it! A bawdy-minded wife! You know, that remark is very reflective of what's been on your mind lately. Have you had some restless nights, honey?"

"Oh, you are disgusting! I'll tell you what's been on my mind lately: the fact that this is all just a game to you, Michael. You enjoy deceiving my family. You think you've got them wrapped around your finger. Just how long do you think they'd tolerate you if they knew the truth?"

"Beth, whether you believe it or not, I'm genuinely fond of your sisters and brothers-in-law. And believe it or not, I actually liked your father as well, after I met him."

She saw the cold look she'd seen before come into his dark eyes—a look many of his business rivals must have faced time and again across a table.

"Our arrangement is between you and me, Beth, and it's my intention to keep it that way. You have the choice of making our marriage easy or difficult for your family to accept by whatever you decide to tell them. But let me make one thing clear: I don't give a damn who likes it or who doesn't. If you want your railroad back, we *will* get married tomorrow evening at seven o'clock."

He grasped her hand. "Now, how about walking me to the barn like a loving fiancée? As much as I hate to go, I must leave you for now; I have some business in Denver to take care of before the wedding."

"I believe my official obligations toward you don't begin until seven o'clock tomorrow evening."

His mouth curved in amusement. "You don't intend to give an inch, do you?"

She laughed derisively. "Did you expect me to?"

"Beth, I think you'd be shocked by my expectations." He raised her hand to his mouth and pressed a kiss to the palm. "Until tomorrow, my pet."

"Bow wow," she replied, and entered the house.

Beth hurried up the stairway to her bedroom, relieved not to have to talk to anyone. From the sounds below, she could tell the others had come inside. She knew she'd have to join them, but she wanted a few moments of solitude first. Keeping up a false front on the trip for Cynthia and Dave had been a strain.

Walking to the window, she gazed out at the panoramic view. How many times had she stood in the same spot and done the same thing before? How she had taken its precious beauty for granted. To have to leave it now . . . the people she loved . . .

Beth closed her eyes and forced back her tears. She dared not dwell on memories or regrets. Self-pity drained one's strength. She had made a choice, and in the days ahead she'd need every ounce of strength she had if she were to survive.

And I'll do more than survive, Michael Carrington. I will thrive.

She was about to turn away when Giff and Michael came out of the barn. Michael was leading a saddled mount and now wore a sheepskin jacket that he'd apparently borrowed from Giff. Had she not known better, he could easily have been taken for one of the ranch hands.

As they neared the house, she started to draw back to avoid being seen. Then she thought the better of it. She wasn't going to start hiding behind drapery or cowering in corners to avoid him. They were at war—and warriors openly faced one another in battle. So she stood in plain sight at the window. If he looked up, he couldn't miss seeing her.

She watched as the two men exchanged a few

words and shook hands; then Michael swung up into the saddle. As if sensing her stare, he glanced up and saw her. Smiling, he doffed his Stetson.

Beth remained motionless.

He squared his hat firmly on his head and galloped away. She watched until he disappeared from view before leaving the room.

As soon as Beth joined the two couples in the parlor, the wedding became the topic of conversation.

"I hope you didn't invite a lot of people," she said to Angie. "This is to be a private ceremony."

"There'll only be our family, String, Red, and our godfathers: Uncle Jim and Uncle Willie. I've already mentioned that poor Uncle Charles is too ill to come."

Beth nodded. "Yes. I intend to ride over to see him later. I appreciate what you've done on such short notice. I know it put a burden on all of you here at the Roundhouse."

"It wasn't any trouble, Beth. We were glad to do it," Giff said.

"Dave, I think we should go with her," Cynthia said. "Uncle Charles is my godfather, and it'll be my only chance to see him before we go back to end of track. As soon as we get back, Angie, you and I will work on the wedding arrangements."

"What arrangements? No arrangements," Beth declared firmly. "Pastor Williams can marry us, we'll have a quiet dinner, and that's it."

"Exactly what we have in mind," Cynthia agreed. However, the meaningful glances her sisters exchanged left Beth with an uneasy feeling.

As soon as they finished lunch, Beth and David disappeared into the den, and for several hours they worked out what had to be ordered immediately to get the crew moving again. Dave drove them to town, and while he sent wires to the necessary suppliers, Beth and Cynthia went to the home of Charles Reardon.

That evening Beth had little appetite when Middy announced that dinner was ready. The visit with Charles had left Beth heavy-hearted. The family lawyer had tried to put up a brave front with her, but there was no doubt that he was gravely ill. It was only a matter of time before his weakened heart gave out completely on him.

"Aren't we going to wait for Michael?" Angie asked as they sat down at the dinner table.

"You mean Jake," Cynthia corrected.

"Oh, I forgot! I've got to get used to that."

"He won't be returning tonight," Beth said.

Dave snorted. "The night before his wedding?"

"Maybe he's superstitious about seeing the bride before the ceremony," Cynthia said. "Remember, I tried to explain it to you fellows the morning Angie and Giff were married."

"To no avail, I may add," Giff replied, winking at Dave. "Actually, Jake told me he's meeting with a potential buyer for the house he owns in Denver."

"Oh, that's right," Cynthia said. "I'd completely forgotten he bought that Stanford mansion last year."

"Aren't you excited, Beth?" Angie sighed blissfully. "Imagine marrying a man who owns houses all over the country."

"Apparently he'll own one less quite soon," Beth answered flippantly. "I hope it won't be too much of an inconvenience to the poor man to have to get along with one less twenty-room mansion."

"I don't think that's fair, Beth," Cynthia said. "Jake probably needs the money, considering how much it must have cost him to bail out the Rocky Mountain Central."

"What do you mean, Thia?" Giff asked.

"Thia, that's railroad business," David advised. "So why don't you keep out of it."

"Oh, excuse me, my lord and master. And who owns one-third of that railroad?" Cynthia snatched a biscuit from the platter and began to butter it.

"Well, I'd sure as hell like to know what's going on here," Giff said gruffly. "I realize I run the ranch, and the railroad's none of my business, but I thought we were all family here."

"We certainly are!" Angie declared, now making her voice heard. "And, David, since I'm a part owner of the railroad, it's my business, too—and anything that concerns me concerns my husband."

"See what you've started!" David directed an accusing glare at Cynthia.

"I didn't start it," Cynthia declared, her eyes flashing angrily. "I just don't like how Beth is acting. She's making Jake sound like some kind of a spoiled dandy just because he's in love with her and willing to put up a fortune to help her. Frankly, she's beginning to sound like a cold-hearted shrew!"

"Thia, you're starting to say things you'll be sorry for later," David said sharply.

"You're as bad as Beth, Kincaid. As long as it concerns the railroad, anything goes. The trouble with you and Beth is that you're both married to that damn railroad!"

"Thia, the railroad was Daddy's dream," Angie said, subdued. "Beth and Dave are just trying to fulfill that dream for him."

Cynthia turned her anger on Angie. "We all have dreams; some come true, some don't. But dreams and obsessions are two different things. Furthermore, Angie, you know you don't care any more about that railroad than I do. Your life is Giff and this ranch."

"That's not true; I do care about the railroad. You're the one who doesn't," Angie asserted.

"Let's just drop the subject," Giff said.

"That's what I say," Dave agreed.

Suddenly the door to the kitchen flew open and Middy stomped into the room.

"Shame! Shame on all of you!" she cried out, shaking a balled fist at them. "I've served this family for nigh on twenty-five years, and I ain't *never* heard the likes of such fussin' under this roof. Your pa said you gals weren't never to sit down to a meal together and quarrel amongst yourselves. Them was his words, and that was the example him and your ma set for you. You're disgracing their memory, and I'll not allow it. Do you hear? I'll not allow it." Her voice trailed off into sobs as she tramped from the room.

"I'd better go and make sure she's okay," Giff said. He got up and hurried into the kitchen.

After a long moment, Cynthia said, "I apologize to all of you. Dave was right; I didn't know when to shut up."

"Neither did I," Angie said. "I'm sorry."

"I'm the one who needs to apologize to everyone at this table," Beth said. "Thia's right; I have been acting like a shrew. I guess I've been taking my bridal jitters out on Michael."

"Jake," Cynthia corrected with a giggle.

"Jake," Beth echoed, laughing. "And after dinner, Angie, I'll explain everything to you and Giff. I never intended to keep the two of you in the dark."

"Middy's fine now," Giff said, returning to his seat. "She's threatening to wash all our mouths out with soap if we raise our voices to one another again."

Beth picked up her water glass. "We'll never do it again. Agreed?"

They all raised their glasses. "Agreed," they said simultaneously.

Beth looked around the table at the smiling faces, her heart bursting with love—but her conscience burdened with guilt. These were the most precious people in the world to her. Not one of them would ever consider letting her go through with the marriage to Michael Carrington if the truth were known. Right now the men respected and liked Michael, and her sisters were so in love with their husbands that they believed everyone was in love. She would let them keep that illusion, because the railroad was at stake here. It was within her power to save it, and that's what she intended to do. As much as she hated to deceive them, she vowed that from this moment on, she would never allow her problems to come between any of them again. In the future, whatever she personally thought of Michael Carrington would remain between her and him.

Chapter 8

After finally falling asleep long past dawn, Beth was awakened by Cynthia's voice out in the hallway.

"The foyer looks beautiful from up here. Do you think we should run flowers all the way up the stairway?"

"No, the stairs look lovely just as they are. Too bad we took down the Christmas tree," Angie replied.

"I think by now everyone has had enough of Christmas decorations. Besides, then the foyer would be too crowded. Let's get back downstairs and finish."

What were they up to? Curious, Beth got out of bed and pulled on a flannel dressing gown.

Cynthia and Angie were at the bottom of the stairway studying the dozens of red and white poinsettia plants banked around its foot. A bower, its base also immersed in poinsettia plants, and decorated with evergreen boughs woven with white satin ribbon and bows, had been set up to form an archway in the opening between the foyer and parlor.

"Good morning. What's going on here? And where did all these plants come from?" Beth asked, carefully avoiding the ones that had been set on several of the lower steps.

Angie smiled broadly. "Good morning, sleepy-head, and we got the plants from the church. Pastor Williams loaned them to us for the wedding."

"You mean these are the same ones used to decorate the chancel at Christmas?"

"Yes, aren't they lovely?"

"Angie, those plants were donated to the church by the parishioners. Don't you think it's improper for us to have them?"

"Good gracious, Beth," Cynthia declared, "we're just borrowing them. Besides, if it were improper, Pastor Williams would never have consented to loan them to us."

"Now go eat your breakfast and get it over with," Angie said. "We ate hours ago. Middy has started preparing dinner for tonight, and she doesn't want us near the kitchen for the rest of the day."

Dave and Giff came in toting more plants.

"Okay, here's the last of them," Giff said.

"My goodness, you all certainly have been busy this morning." Beth couldn't believe she had slept through all the activity.

Dave chuckled. "Haven't you heard? There's going to be a wedding here tonight. We thought maybe you intended to sleep right through it."

"What time is it anyway?"

"The wedding or right now?" he asked with a grin.

"Now will do," she said.

"Nine o'clock."

As if to reinforce Dave's reply, the clock set in the corner of the foyer began to chime the hour.

"Good Lord, why didn't someone wake me sooner?"

"We figured you needed the sleep."

"Yeah, you probably won't get much tonight," Giff added, glancing at her as he walked past. "Let's get out of here, Dave, before these women find something else for us to do."

"Not so fast, you two," Cynthia said. "You're not through yet. Will you move that deacon's bench out of here so we'll have more room? Then you can set up the folding chairs for the guests."

Beth groaned. "Plants! Bower! Chairs! I thought we agreed there'd be no fuss—that we'd keep the wedding plain and simple." She frowned at Angie. "Please don't tell me you've invited half of Denver."

"No, we didn't. Just those whom I mentioned." Angie nudged her toward the kitchen. "Now go and eat. It's bad enough you're already in a huff, without getting Middy that way too."

Beth sighed deeply. She had to get a hold on herself. "All right."

"And as soon as you finish, we'll go upstairs and decide what you're going to wear," Cynthia said.

Beth turned her head to utter a protest, but at the sight of the wide, eager grins on her sisters' faces, the objection lodged in her throat. She shook her head, unable to hold back her own grin. "You two—what am I going to do with you?" Tears glistened in her eyes. "And what am I going to do without you? I'm going to miss you both so much."

"Hey, no crying before breakfast," Cynthia scolded. She gave Beth a light swat on the rear. "Go eat, then the three of us will have a good cry together."

Middy was busy at the sink and turned her head to look at Beth when she came into the kitchen. " 'Bout time you got up, gal. Thought we'd have to wake you for your own wedding." She drew a handkerchief out of her apron pocket and blew her nose.

"Middy, you're crying!"

" 'Tain't so. I got me a cold, that's all." She turned back and resumed beating a cake batter. "You want me to fry you an egg?"

"No, I'm just going to have a piece of toast and a cup of tea. I can get it myself."

"That's how I earn my keep around here, so I'll do it. You just sit."

"Middy, you've got enough to do today. I'm not helpless, you know."

"Who knows that better than me, gal? I've already set the tea to steepin'." Then to Beth's surprise, Middy blurted out, "He'll be taking you away, won't he? To that Texas place." Once again she pulled out the handkerchief.

"Oh, Middy, you are crying!" Beth rushed over and put her arms around Middy's shoulders. "I'll be back often. I could never stay away from the Roundhouse." She brushed aside her own tears, and in trying to give comfort, she drew comfort from just holding the beloved housekeeper in her arms.

"It ain't gonna be the same around here without you. Seems like I was just swaddlin' you gals; now you're all three grown and married, with talk of leaving."

"Once the railroad's finished, it'll be easy to travel between here and Dallas. I'll be able to visit often, and you know Angie and Giff will never leave the Roundhouse."

Middy raised a wrinkled hand to Beth's cheek. "Angie's my baby, but you're my eldest, honey."

For a long moment Beth gazed at her. Each wrinkle and crease on the aged face represented a tribute earned for a life dedicated to unselfish love and devotion to others. Beth led her over to the table. "You sit down here and we'll have a cup of tea together. We haven't done that in a long time."

"And this ain't the time for it now. I ain't got time for dawdlin', and you ain't either."

"We'll make time." Beth brought over the teapot and another cup and saucer, then pressed a kiss to the top of Middy's gray head.

A warm twinkle emerged through the moisture in Middy's eyes. "Well, if that's the case, you might try looking in the bread box. Wouldn't be surprised if you'd find a couple of fresh-baked scones." She grinned. "And there's strawberry preserves in the icebox."

The stolen moments with Middy stirred poignant memories of the uncountable mornings the two of them had spent together. Half an hour later, Beth left the beloved housekeeper, and with a heavy heart went upstairs to dress. Then, facing the inevitable, she started packing. After two trunks she stopped, intentionally leaving a great deal of her clothing behind as an excuse to return soon.

Having no desire to get involved in the wedding preparations that Cynthia and Angie were attacking with such enthusiasm, Beth decided to get some fresh air. Unobserved, she slipped down the rear steps to take a walk.

Often by this time of the year they'd be hibernating, surrounded by two feet of snow; but a mild winter, fanned by westerly breezes, had pushed the temperature up to almost fifty degrees, and it felt more like a spring day than the first week of January.

Beth climbed up on a rocky bluff and sat down to enjoy the view. In the distance the melting snow formed dozens of tiny waterfalls as it streamed down from the higher slopes. Gazing at the mountain splendor, she regretted how little of her time in the past few years had been devoted to enjoying the beauty that surrounded her. What she had seen of Texas could never compare to this testament to God's artistry. If only she had Angie's skill to capture it on canvas, she could have taken it with her.

To the south she caught sight of String and Red driving some strays back to the herd. A smile softened her face. The two brothers had ridden for the Roundhouse for over twenty years. They were rugged men, who had herded Roundhouse cattle through bitter cold and scorching heat yet never lost their kindness or gentleness. Now on the verge of leaving them and Middy—people she loved but had always taken for granted—their presence took on a precious meaning to her.

Sadly she stood up and brushed herself off, then returned to the house.

She had just resumed packing when Cynthia and Angie burst into her room.

"All right, it's time to pick out your wedding dress," Cynthia declared. "Which gown are you planning to wear?"

"I thought maybe the black one I wore at Christmas."

"Black!" Cynthia exclaimed. "This is your wedding, not your funeral." When Beth arched a brow, Cynthia threw up her hand. "Oh, no," she warned, trying not to laugh, "don't you dare say what you're thinking."

Cynthia riffled through the remaining gowns in the clothespress and pulled out a fashionable cream-colored crepe gown. The bodice laced in the back, and a narrow blue velvet band bordered the low, square neckline. Similar bands ringed the wrists of the long sleeves, which were puffed at the shoulders, and another velvet band draped diagonally in front and rear from the right waist down to the left hip. Free of any bustle, flounces, or bows, the skirt dropped to a full hem that trailed a short train.

"This dress will be perfect," Cynthia said. "I've never seen you in this; it's lovely. And the blue velvet matches your eyes."

"Well, la-de-da!"

"You aren't taking this seriously, Beth, dear. Is this new?"

"No, it's a couple of years old."

"So this can be the 'something old' you wear at your wedding," Cynthia said, which produced a giggle from Angie.

"I think I still have an old blue velvet gown that will match the velvet in this," Cynthia said.

"I know I have one," Angie said excitedly. "I wore it to the governor's ball, remember? You must wear this gown, Beth."

"I don't care what I wear."

Cynthia hung up the gown. "Good, that's settled. Now, what can we find for you to wear on your head?"

"How about my hair?" Beth murmured facetiously.

Cynthia cast an exasperated look at Angie. "Pumpkin, do you feel like we're dealing with a child here?"

Angie nodded. "And I thought I was the baby in the family."

Beth sighed. "I *am* being childish, aren't I? I know you two are trying to make my wedding very special for me, and I must sound very ungrateful. I'm sorry." She clasped a hand of each of them and pulled them toward her. "Let's forget the wedding for a short time and just relax and talk.

Who knows when the three of us will be able to get together to do it again?"

Cynthia smiled in understanding. "Okay, honey, let's do that."

As they had been doing since childhood, the three women crawled onto the bed and sat down in a circle, their legs tucked under then. With heads together, they chatted and giggled about love, life, and old times—and let their love flow between them.

However, Beth could not stop the clock, and it finally became time to dress for the wedding.

Where had the day gone? She added a final dab of powder to her nose. It seemed that just a few hours ago she still had ten hours of freedom ahead of her; now the clock below seemed to toll the hour as if for a funeral, and the dreaded hour of reckoning could no longer be postponed.

After a final look at herself in the mirror of the dressing table, she rose and left the room. Her step was steady and unfaltering as she walked to the top of the stairway.

Below, a candelabra of tall, flickering candles added a romantic aura to the piano strains of the Chopin nocturne Angie was playing in the parlor.

Beth's gaze swept the dear, familiar faces assembled and waiting. With Bible in hand, Pastor Williams stood beneath the pine-scented bower. Cynthia, David, and Giff were seated in the front row. Behind them sat String and Red Bean, Middy, dabbing at her eyes, and Slim Collins, a former ranch hand, beside her. Angie's godfather, Dr. James Fielding, had taken a seat behind them, and her own godfather, Sheriff Willie Joe Benteen, was beside him. Beth smiled. Uncle Willie looked like he'd be more comfortable with a Colt revolver in his hand than with the lighted candle each guest had been given to hold during the ceremony. To catch the dripping wax, Angie had made candle rings of cardboard decorated with pasted-on clusters of cut-up poinsettia blossoms.

Her smile dissolved when her gaze came to rest on Michael Carrington. Candlelight flattered him. He looked exceptionally handsome dressed in black evening clothes.

The Devil wears many disguises.

As Angie finished the piece and took a seat beside Giff, Michael walked over to the stairway and smiled up at her. Strangely enough, she had never felt so calm as she took the first step that would change her life forever. Her gaze remained locked with his, and as she neared the foot of the stairway, he reached out a hand to her and led her to the bower. With a fatherly smile at her, Pastor Williams opened his Bible.

Numbed, she stood at Michael's side—a spectator more than a participant—and remained unmoved by the emotional depth of the vows they repeated. Yet Beth knew that every moment, every word of the ceremony, would remain etched on her memory forever. The ceremony was as short and concise as she'd hoped it would be. Almost before she realized it, Pastor Williams pronounced them man and wife, and she was looking up into the eyes of her husband.

"Michael, you may kiss your bride," the pastor said.

For a fleeting moment, as if Michael suddenly realized the full consequences of his actions, she saw in his eyes bewilderment—even penitence—instead of the mocking gleam of the past few days.

But in a blink it was gone, and Beth thought she must have been mistaken, because his expression narrowed as he murmured, "*My* bride."

Then he claimed her lips possessively.

Chapter 9

Beth managed to keep the smile on her face as she got through the congratulations and well-wishes when the guests converged on them. The strong smell of extinguished candles drove everyone into the parlor, where Angie provided pleasant background music at the piano as they awaited dinner.

Fortunately, Michael was kept occupied in discussions with the men, so Beth succeeded in remaining a safe distance from him. The glass of champagne she sipped seemed to calm her, so she reached for another one when Cynthia came around with a tray.

"How are you doing, Mrs. Carrington?" Cynthia asked, taking a generous gulp from one of the glasses.

"I'll just be glad when this whole affair is over."

Cynthia arched a delicate brow. "The best is yet to come," she said, and moved on.

Beth pondered the remark. Now that the wedding ceremony was over, how *would* she get through the rest of the night? She had to share a bed with him—that was a condition of the arrangement if she wanted to control the stock. And even if he held to his promise not to force her to be in-

timate with him, the thought of being alone with
him . . . lying beside him . . . It was ludicrous!

She raised the glass to her mouth and drained it.

Middy had hired two young town girls, Emmy
Lou and Prudy O'Shea, to serve the dinner, freeing
herself to turn out the special meal she had insisted
upon preparing herself. Once they were all seated
for dinner, the conversation flowed primarily between the men with talk of cattle, railroads, stock
market, and politics.

Beth welcomed the exclusion from the conversation. Even though it gave her more time to dwell
on what the night would bring, it also prevented
her from having to answer questions about her future plans.

Because she had none! She had absolutely no
idea what Michael intended. She knew his home
was in Dallas, but that was all she knew about him
personally—other than the fact that he was a low-
down, crawling-on-his-belly snake in the grass.

Of course, nobody else believed that. It would be
comforting if she had one ally in the household,
but no, she seethed silently, everyone appeared to
think that Michael Carrington caused the sun to
rise in the morning!

Absorbed in her reverie, she gradually became
aware of Michael's stare, and looked at him. His
compelling dark eyes were regarding her like a
greedy cat eying a bowl of cream. *You can look, you
strutting black cat, but don't start licking your whiskers
too soon, because you're not going to taste!* Tilting her
head back, she purred at him. He lifted his brows
as a gleam of amusement flashed in his eyes, then
he turned back to the conversation.

Beth glanced at Cynthia, who was seated between Dave and Uncle Jim. Discovering Beth
watching her, Cynthia raised her glass and nodded.

The best is yet to come. How could Thia say that? She knew that they had agreed not to become intimate, so why did her sister imply they would be . . . *later*? Because *everyone* believed Michael Carrington could do no wrong. So of course, grateful Beth would fall obediently into his bed, thankful for the opportunity to pleasure him.

"Hah! Hell will freeze over first!" she mumbled. Picking up her wine glass, she gulped down the contents.

Michael leaned over and whispered, "Beth, wine is best savored if sipped slowly."

"I'll keep that in mind on my next glass, *Jake.*" Turning her head, she motioned to Emmy Lou. "Will you refill my glass, dear?"

The men continued to talk as if the women weren't around, so Beth, Cynthia, and Angie started a game of silently toasting one another, which soon had them giggling. By the time the men became aware of the game and their neglect of the three women, dinner was through.

Dr. Fielding and Sheriff Benteen excused themselves to return to Denver. String and Red decided to ride with Slim and spend a long weekend in the city. As soon as the dishes were washed and the O'Shea girls had left, Middy retired for the night.

Pleased with her own cleverness, Beth had reached a solution to her problem: she would not retire at all. She'd sit up all night, and Michael could have the damn bed to himself. After all, she could sleep on the train tomorrow. Fortunately, her sisters appeared to be of the same persuasion and followed her into the parlor. By the time their husbands joined them, Cynthia had opened another bottle of wine.

Without any warning, Beth's head started spinning. "I've got to sit down." She plopped down on the floor on the very spot where she'd been standing and buried her head in her hands, certain it would fly off her body at any second.

"Someone must have put something in that wine," Angie said, sitting down beside her.

"I think it comes that way," Beth replied, trying to recall how many glasses she had drunk.

Cynthia came over with the wine and joined them on the floor. "I sure am having a good time at your wedding, Beth. Thank you for inviting me."

"You're welcome." Beth groaned. "Thia, stop bobbing up and down; you're making me dizzy."

"I think we should have a toast," Cynthia said.

Angie shook her head. "Can't have a toast without glasses."

"Who needs glasses when we have this?" Cynthia held up the bottle. "We can take turns." Raising it in the air, she declared, "To us, the MacKenzie sisters, who God hath joined together, so let no man try to put us asunder—or something like that." She took a swallow and passed the bottle to Beth, who took a drink and then gave it to Angie.

"Now what should we drink to?" Cynthia asked, when Angie handed her back the bottle.

"I don't think we should have any more toasts," Angie said, wiping a drop of wine off her chin. "We've all had too much to drink already."

"I think you're right," Beth moaned. "The more I drink, the faster the room spins."

"My dearest shisters . . ." Cynthia paused to hiccough. "I have dined with earls and dukes, duch . . . dushesses, and even a prinshess, and never"—she paused for another hiccough—"never have I overindulged."

"I think you're drunk as a skunk," Angie said.

Cynthia looked at her and started to giggle. "I think you're right."

"I think we all are," Beth said.

The admission set off more giggles.

"Say, shisters, did you notice something unusual about all the men here tonight?" Cynthia asked.

Frowning, Beth tried to concentrate. Finally she gave it up. "No. What was it?"

"They're all exceptions to my theory," Cynthia said with a triumphant nod.

"What theory?" Beth asked, wondering why Cynthia had abandoned bobbing up and down to take up weaving back and forth.

"I'll tell you." She cocked a finger to motion them to come closer. Beth and Angie leaned forward until all their foreheads were touching. "Men are all bastards!"

Angie drew back in affront. "Giff isn't!" she declared, with a toss of her curly head.

"Of course he isn't. Neither is Dave," Cynthia said. "Dave is sweet and loving. And he's smart. Jake's really smart, too."

"You don't have to include him on my account," Beth remarked. "Did you stop to think that if Michael's so smart, maybe he's got you fooled?" Beth was now convinced that it was the room that was spinning, not her head.

Cynthia thought seriously for several seconds, then looked bleary eyed at Beth. "No, Jake's smart. " 'Cause I'm *too* smart to be fooled."

"Thia, why do you think that most men are bastards?" Angie asked.

"Because most men's brains are between their legs, and that's what they do their thinking with."

"Which gives greater meaning to the expression half-brain," Beth added.

That required another round in order to quell their laughter.

Wiping the tears out of her eyes, Beth said, "Thia's right, Angie. Most men are rotten. They take your virginity by convincing you that you're the only woman they could ever love, then you find out you're just another scalp on their coup sticks. We women are fools to let them take advantage of us."

Cynthia nodded. "I agree. Take Count Roberto Cellini, for instance."

"You take him," Beth said. "You were the one engaged to him."

"Roberto Cellini took almost two years of my life!" Cynthia declared.

"But he didn't take advantage of you, Thia. He wanted to marry you, didn't he?" Angie argued.

"Sure, and if I'd married him, I'd have been bored to death. Wouldn't you call that taking advantage of me? He knew how boring he was. And worthless!" She threw up her hands in disgust. "Roberto Cellini would starve to death before picking up a knife to slice himself a piece of bread."

With a grin, Angie asked, "Well, was he a good lover or a half-brain?"

Cynthia gave the question intense concentration. "Now that I've got Dave to compare him to, I'd have to say . . ." She broke out in a big grin. "Roberto was more like a quarter-brain."

Clutching one another, the three women laughed hysterically.

"I'll tell who's a real half-brain for sure," Angie said. "A man couldn't be any worse than Edward Emory was."

Cynthia leaned over and patted Angie's hand. "That bad, huh?"

"Bad! Not only did he take my virginity with no

intention of making an honest woman of me; his so-called lovemaking convinced me I'd be content to go through the rest of my life without ever being intimate with a man again." Angie rolled her eyes. "But no one could ever accuse Giff of being a *half-brain*."

Cynthia poked Beth in the arm. "Will you listen to her brag? It's probably because he spends so much time around all those bulls."

The three women fell back in uproarious laughter.

At the latest outburst from the women, Michael glanced over, amused. "I think the ladies may have had one sip too many."

Chuckling, Dave said, "They're plain drunk would be more like it. This is the first time I've ever seen Thia intoxicated."

"I've never seen any of them ever drink to excess before," Giff said, clearly astounded. "Since Beth is the last to marry, I suppose they're a little scared that now they'll be split up. The gals have always been really close, you know."

"I gathered that from the few times I've been around them," Michael remarked. He picked up a framed daguerreotype of the three sisters, taken when they were youngsters. Smiling pensively, he gazed at it for a long moment. "I bet it was interesting watching the girls grow up. I envy you— you're a lucky fellow, Giff."

"Yeah, I know. Trouble is, I never realized it until after they were all women."

"You were good for them," Dave said, with a swat to Giff's shoulder. "I'd better put Thia to bed. I bet she won't feel like going anywhere tomorrow."

"Under the circumstances it'd be better for us to stay another day, too, but my grandmother's planned a wedding party for Saturday," Michael said.

Giff nodded. "Maybe you'd be better off staying in Beth's room tonight. When we put you in the cabin, we figured you and Beth would prefer the privacy."

"No, the cabin's fine. Besides, my luggage is there. Beth can always come back to the house in the morning to get what she needs."

"Frankly, I don't think where you're at much matters now," Dave said. " I think Beth's about to pass out."

"I'm going to try to sober her up tonight, or she'll be sicker than hell on that train ride back to Texas tomorrow."

"Cold shower would probably do it," Dave said.

"There's a stream with a waterfall a short distance from here that we often use as a shower in the summer," Giff said, "but I sure as hell don't recommend it this time of the year. There's also a pump and shower in the barn that we use to wash off the trail dust. I gotta tell you, though, the water is pretty damn cold."

"That sounds like the best thing. If the water's that cold, it'll sober her up fast."

Giff appeared dubious. "I don't know, Jake. If you try it, she's gonna be spitting venom. Sure wouldn't want to be in your boots."

Michael shrugged. "It's worth a try. Time's running out, so I don't have any other options."

"Well, good luck, pal. There's towels and whatever else you might need in the cabin. You want any help getting her out of here?"

"No, I can handle her. You fellas already have your hands full."

They walked over to the women on the floor. Angie was lying just as she fell, giggling to herself.

Cynthia was stretched out on her side with her hands tucked under her cheek.

"Come on, honey, let's get you to bed," Dave said, lifting her into his arms.

She opened her eyes and smiled at him. "Not you, sweetheart," she mumbled.

"Yes, me, honey. I'm putting you to bed."

"Roberto was, but not you. And you sure aren't a half-brain."

Dave shrugged and winked at Michael and Giff. "I'm sure there's a compliment in there somewhere. Good night, all."

Beth had remained sitting stiffly, staring blankly into space.

"You sure you want to try sobering her tonight?" Giff asked. "I still think you'd be better off carrying her upstairs and letting her sleep it off."

"No, she'll feel miserable tomorrow if I do." Michael hunkered down to her. "Beth, I want you to come with me now."

She snorted, and folded her arms across her chest. "I don't care what you want. I'm not going anywhere with you. I'm staying right here for the rest of the night."

"I see," he said calmly. Michael stood up, grasped her under the arms, and lifted her to her feet. Swaying, she fell against him, and he hefted her over his shoulder.

"Put me down," she yelled. "Giff, help me," she pleaded as Michael headed for the door.

"Sorry, Beth. Jake's your husband and he's doing what's best for you."

"Don't believe him," she cried in vain, because Giff had already closed the door.

"Settle down, Beth," Michael said, as she continued to struggle. He shifted her more firmly on his shoulder.

"Where are you taking me? And why is everything upside down?"

"I'm taking you to the cabin, and everything looks upside down because you are, my love."

"I'm not your love," she snarled, "so stop calling me that." She started to pound on his back, most of the blows falling on his buttocks.

"If I didn't know better, dear wife, I'd suspect you've been reading a de Sade novel."

He reached the cabin and tossed her on the bed, then went into the bathroom and grabbed a couple of towels. For a moment he pondered whether he should try sobering her up in the bathtub.

"I'd probably end up drowning her," he mumbled, disgruntled, and returned to the bedroom.

Beth had fallen asleep. He was tempted to let her remain that way, but the thought of the long train ride ahead the next day reaffirmed his determination.

After stripping down to his drawers, he proceeded to undress Beth. He pulled off her shoes, then her hose. He couldn't help grinning when he unlaced the back of her dress and pulled it over her head. He'd done more than his share of assisting women with removing their clothes, but this was the first time the woman had remained oblivious to it. After he removed her underskirt, all that remained was a white cotton combination. His eyes drank in the sight of her: a never-forgotten memory of firm, round breasts, long legs, and the most responsive body he'd ever known.

"That's a very functional garment you're wearing, Mrs. Carrington, but I prefer to see that luscious body of yours clothed in something more intriguing."

When he picked her up in his arms, she nestled against him. An unwelcome tightening grabbed at his loins. "I'm afraid I'm going to need this cold shower as much as you do," he told the sleeping figure in his arms. Snatching up his robe and the towels on his way out the door, he headed for the barn.

Chapter 10

As Michael closed the barn door, several horses gave him curious stares from their stalls but remained silent. After depositing Beth on a hay pile, he lit a lantern and examined the shower in the corner.

The water was pumped through piping that ran to the loft, where simple gravity dropped it to the stall below. A shutoff valve on the pipe controlled the output, which drained into a waste pipe that carried it away.

It took some strenuous pumping to get the flow of water into the shower. And it was cold! Closing the valve, he went to get Beth and found her curled up as snug as an infant in its mother's womb.

"I don't think you're going to like this," he murmured, trying to keep her propped up under the shower while distancing himself as far away from the spray as possible. Groping for the valve, he succeeded in opening it.

The cold water poured down on Beth's face, jolting her awake sputtering and shrieking.

"Let me go," she cried, struggling to free herself.

"Hold still, Beth; I'm doing this for your own good." Michael wrapped his arms around her, holding her cocooned in his embrace in order to free his hands.

"Damn you, Michael! I'll kill you if I ever get free," she sputtered as the cold water rained down on her.

She tried a backward kick and started to fall when her other foot slipped out from under her, but he managed to get her back on her feet. Locking his left arm under her breasts, he grasped the back of her neck with his right hand and forced her face up to the cold spray. Time and time again her struggles succeeded in freeing her head from his grip, and whenever she did, a string of threats spewed out of her mouth as cold as the water she tried to dodge.

"I can't believe the kind of bloodthirsty thoughts that flow through that pretty head of yours," he said. "I'd think you'd be satisfied that I'm freezing my butt off here trying to sober you up."

"Go to hell! It's warm there."

Her efforts to shake loose kept whipping her hair in his face.

"Dammit, Beth, I'm losing my patience," he said.

She managed to deliver a painful poke to his ribs with her elbow, and reiterated the invitation to visit Hades.

"Lady, I've listened to all I'm going to. There's more than one way to shut you up, and don't try to say you didn't ask for this."

Turning her in his arms, he smothered her mouth with his own.

Surprise and shock stilled her struggles, but her astonishment couldn't have been any greater than his own. He no longer felt the cold, as hot blood surged through him from head to toes. Her hungry response matched his own, and he pulled her closer, driving his tongue into the heated chamber of her mouth as their combined passions escalated with every pulse beat.

The buttons on her sodden garment flew in all directions when he shoved it down her, never relinquishing the pressure on her sweet mouth. He stroked the slick satin of her back, crushing the rounded fullness and hardened peaks of her breasts against his bare chest in a divine ecstasy that pounded at his brain and pulses until his legs trembled. He was so hard he had to have her then and there, and as he reached for the band of his drawers—the shower shut off.

The water he had pumped had run out.

Stunned, Beth looked up at him. He saw her expression change to horror as the full force of what had just transpired struck her. She stepped back as if burned and then began to shiver uncontrollably.

The moment had slipped away for her, and Michael had enough sense to know it would be useless to try and recapture it.

"You'd better finish getting that wet underwear off," he said. "I'll get you a towel."

When he came back, her teeth were chattering. Naked, she held up the wet garment in front of her like a shield.

"Beth, what's the sense? We have no secrets from each other." He took the garment and tossed it aside.

She offered no resistance when he began to dry her off, rubbing her vigorously with the towel so that the friction would help to warm her. When he felt certain she was dried thoroughly, he put his robe on her. Then he dried her hair. Beth didn't say a word the whole time; she just kept staring at him with those big blue eyes. Michael couldn't imagine what was going through her head. She wasn't the predictable kind of woman he was used to, which was probably one of the reasons why, after all these years, she still fascinated him.

He suspected she might still be feeling some of the effects of the wine, but the cold water had apparently sobered her considerably.

"Do you feel any better, Beth?"

"I'm fine," she said expressionlessly.

At the moment he felt the less said about the subject, the better; so he picked her up and carried her over to the pile of hay. "I have to dry off. It'll take a couple of minutes. You might be better off up in the hayloft; it's probably warmer up there."

He turned away and pulled off his sodden drawers. After wrapping a towel around his waist, he turned around and saw she had taken his advice and climbed up into the loft.

Michael wrung the water out of their underclothes, then spread them out on the hay. When he finished, he called up to her, "Beth, I'm ready. Let's go. I'll carry you back to the cabin." When she didn't reply, he called out again, "Beth, let's go."

Scaling the ladder to the loft, he saw her lying sound asleep amidst the straw. He crawled over to wake her, but she looked so peaceful, he didn't have the heart. There was no way he could maneuver down those loft stairs while carrying her, so he settled down beside her.

He studied the ivory softness of her face, serene now in slumber; and his thoughts spiraled back to the weekend he'd met her—when those incredible eyes had looked at him with love and laughter, not loathing and scorn, as they did now.

He'd seen a picture of her, but it hadn't prepared him that day for that first breath-robbing look of her—a mesmerizing blend of red hair and sapphire eyes. It had knocked the legs out from under him.

His pitiful mission of revenge had given her

good reason to hate him, but he had to have her again: obsession had become a greater motive than revenge. The face he gazed upon filled all of his sleeping moments—and most of his waking ones. Somehow he'd change her disdain to love. He had the rest of their lives to do it.

His gaze dropped from her face to her shoulders, then the even rise and fall of her breasts, the curve of her hips, and those long legs that could curl around a man and carry him to paradise. The wall of her resistance was much, much higher now, but he'd scaled it before, and he'd do it again.

Burrowing deeper into the straw, he pulled her into his arms and inhaled the scent of her. Within minutes, he was sleeping as soundly as she was.

Beth lay in a drowsy warmth as she slowly stirred from slumber, but her senses exploded to alertness when she realized that the pleasant warmth was generated by a hard, pulsating body. Now fully awake, she felt the very essence of him, smelled the musky maleness of him, heard the even cadence of his breathing as it stirred the hair at her ear. She didn't have to open her eyes to know who it was. There weren't enough hours in the days— or months in the years—to ever allow her to forget him.

With trepidation, she opened her eyes. He lay on his side against her, his arm flung over her chest, a bare leg thrown over hers. To her further horror he was naked, a crumpled towel barely covering that most private part of him, touching her hip.

Her bare hip!

She bolted upright to a sitting position, causing Michael to roll onto his back, and the towel fell completely away, exposing him fully. Blushing, she grabbed the end of the towel and flung it over him, saying a silent prayer of thanks that the move hadn't awakened him. Then a hot flush swept her when she saw that she was barely clothed herself, covered only by an open robe. His robe, which had obviously crawled up on her during the night to leave much of her body exposed.

She fell back in a state of abject panic. What had happened between them last night?

Beth probed her memory, searching for some clue. *Too much wine and champagne*! she realized with hindsight. A vague memory of talking to her sisters came to mind, but she couldn't remember any of the conversation. Then flashes of feeling cold . . . no, of cold water—

"Good morning," Michael said beside her.

She closed her eyes in misery. Oh, God, he was awake! Why hadn't she gotten out of there the instant she woke up?

Beth sat up again. "Don't give me any cheery morning greetings, Michael. I want to know why I woke up half-naked in a hayloft with you."

He stretched out on his side, propped himself up on an elbow, and cradled his head in his hand. "How could you forget such a night of splendor, my love?"

Beth glared at him. The only thing missing from the picture he made was a nubile maiden dropping grapes into his mouth.

"I want to know exactly what happened."

"What do you think happened?"

"It's pretty obvious: you took advantage of me, didn't you, you conscienceless cad!"

"Hardly—it was just the reverse. You were wild, my love. I could barely defend myself. Are you always that aggressive when you overindulge? Mind you, I'm not complaining; I'm just curious."

"Are you implying it was my idea?"

"Well, honey," he said, grinning, "you're the one who crawled up here in the hayloft. Can't blame me for following. Considering your . . . condition, any red-blooded man would have done the same, don't you think?"

The bravado drained out of her. She wanted to die, or at least never have to look at his smug face again. How could she have let herself get so out of control? She'd never take a sip of wine again!

"Well, even if I did, only a cad would take advantage of the situation."

"I think it was the other way around." He raised his hand in demurral. "Though I repeat: far be it for me to complain." He rolled over and tucked his hands under his head. "As a matter of fact, Mrs. Carrington, I rather enjoyed the whole evening."

Beth bolted to her feet. "Oh, you unbearable bastard! Go ahead and gloat, but I can assure you it will never happen again." Belting the robe tightly around her, she stalked away and climbed down the ladder.

The ring of his loud laughter set the horses to neighing.

Beth went straight to the house. Glancing at the clock when she entered, she saw that she had a little over an hour to dress, eat, and get to the depot before the train came through. Thank goodness she'd packed the previous day.

Fortunately, the water heater had been lit, so she drew a bath. She scrubbed herself furiously, hoping to eradicate whatever trace might have remained from the disastrous night.

Fully dressed, she went downstairs and joined the others in the kitchen. Cynthia and Angie were sitting holding their heads in their hands.

"Dave and I aren't going back with you today,"

Cynthia mumbled. "I can't go anywhere until my head shrinks back to its normal size."

"A fast night makes a slow morning," Middy declared, putting a bowl of oatmeal down in front of Beth. "I suppose you're too sick to eat this morning, too."

"Not at all. I feel fine, Middy," Beth said.

Angie groaned. "How can you, Beth? You drank even more than we did."

"I am told that not all people suffer morning effects from overindulgence," Beth advised. "Apparently I'm one of them."

Giff poked his head in at the back door. "Team's harnessed, Beth. Anytime you're ready."

"I'll be done shortly. Just give me a few minutes to get some papers out of the den."

"Sure thing," Giff replied.

After she finished eating, Beth hugged and kissed her sisters and Middy good-bye. As she hurried to the den, Michael came through the front door. "Ready, Beth?"

"I will be in a moment."

He followed her into the den. "Both of your sisters are pretty indisposed today. How are you feeling?"

"Nothing wrong that a divorce won't solve," she said, sitting down at the desk to open one of the drawers.

"No such luck, my love. I believe the court requires some legal grounds. I've been nothing but a devoted husband to you."

"Speaking of marriage, Michael, now that I am legally your wife, I haven't seen any sign of those stock certificates as per our agreement."

A momentary glint of anger flashed in his eyes. He reached into the pocket of his coat and tossed a bound packet on the desk. "There's your certificates, Mrs. Carrington—as per our agreement."

"Did I detect an edge of rancor in your voice?"

"Not at all. Business is business—and you *have* made it clear our marriage is a business arrangement."

She had no explanation for the sudden pang of guilt that coursed through her. Good grief, he was the one who had manipulated her! "Did you ever stop to think, Michael, that if you'd apologized for your actions, you might have persuaded me to forgive you?"

"Forgive me! My dear Beth, your clemency was the last thing I sought! I doubt there would be much satisfaction in a revenge that feeble. The pleasure in vengeance is punishing your adversary. Shall we go?"

She flushed but said quietly, "I'd like a moment alone, if you don't mind."

"Of course." He left, closing the door behind him.

Beth walked over to the fireplace and for a long moment gazed up solemnly at the portrait of her father.

"Daddy, I've made a mess of everything and almost lost the railroad. But I vow that somehow I shall make something good come out of this. If I allowed myself to sink so deep into this morass that I couldn't crawl out, I'd lose more than the railroad; I'd lose my self-respect. I won't do that, Daddy. I won't go down without a fight. I've made a lot of mistakes, but I've learned from them. And before I'm through, not only will I have *all* the railroad back, but Michael Carrington will rue the day he did this to us."

Her voice began to quiver, and a tear slid down her cheek. "I know it won't be easy: I'd be lying to myself if I thought it would be. Having to leave the

Roundhouse ... to spend day after day with a man I loathe ..." She forced back her tears as they threatened to choke her. "But I can tough it out if I have to; I wouldn't be your daughter if I couldn't. Michael Carrington made a big mistake if he thinks he can win this battle of wills. Good-bye for now, Daddy."

As Beth moved away, she paused at her father's desk and touched the bronzed replica of the Betsy, the railroad's first engine.

Her hand was shaking as she opened a bottom drawer and removed a box and letter. Drawing a shuddering breath, she withdrew the special gift her father had left her at his death—a diminutive duplicate of the engine that rested on the desk. The moment she'd seen it, she'd guessed the message her father wished to convey, but she had never opened the letter that had accompanied the gift.

For several seconds her fingers hovered above the letter; then she put it down. She would wait until she had fulfilled her vow to return all of the Rocky Mountain Central to the hands of the MacKenzies.

Replacing the tiny engine in the box, she stuffed it and the letter into her muff. With a final glance at the painting over the fireplace, she left the room.

Her husband awaited her outside the door.

Chapter 11

~~~~~⌒◯◯⌒~~~~~

Intending to ignore Michael on the train trip back, Beth read the novel *Ben Hur*, written and presented to Cynthia by Lew Wallace, the governor of New Mexico, on his visit to the railroad being built through his state.

Michael read, then played solitaire, and finally went into the kitchen and unpacked the lunch Middy had provided for them. He came back carrying a plate filled with tiny sandwiches, fruit, and a bottle of cider.

"Soup's on," he said, pouring Beth a glass.

When she put aside the book and moved over to the table, he grinned at her. "At last I get to see what the face looks like behind that book—and what a lovely face it is, too. Would you be interested in a card game?"

"What card game?"

"How about stud poker?"

"And what will be the stakes?" she asked, picking up one of the sandwiches.

"You name it."

As Beth ate, she tried to think of what would make the game inviting. There'd be little satisfaction in exchanging money. It would have to be something worthwhile—something that mattered to both of them. Hmmm . . .

She smiled cunningly as she sipped the cider. "Shares of Rocky Mountain stock."

"What! Are you serious, Beth? You've got control of it now. Why put that at risk?"

"Because I intend to get it all back, Michael." Smiling confidently, she downed the contents of her glass.

"And what if I win?" he asked as he refilled her glass.

"That's a chance I'll have to take."

"We could end up shoving the same shares of stock back and forth the rest of the day. I'd like to make the game a little more adventuresome. Strip poker?" he asked, popping a grape into his mouth.

"Really, Michael, what would be the point? As you've said, we've seen each other naked. Besides, what would I do with a pair of your pants?"

He arched a brow rakishly. "That would depend upon whether or not I was in them at the time." Dipping a strawberry into his cider, he offered it to her. Beth took a bite of it, and Michael finished it off.

"I have a good idea," she said. "My sisters and I used to play a card game called Truth or Jeopardy. In the truth option, the loser had to answer a question truthfully, and in the other we'd be put in jeopardy and had to do whatever we were told to do."

"Such as?"

"Oh, mucking out the horse stalls, or dumb things like riding backwards in the saddle or staying locked in the privy for an hour."

"And what were some of the questions requiring truthful answers?"

"Who was the last boy that kissed you; who

would you like to kiss—girl things like that."

"And how did you know whether it would be a truth or a jeopardy?"

"You didn't until you lost. The winner decides that."

"All right. We'll play Truth or Jeopardy, with a share of the stock as the stakes. And if the loser of the hand refuses whatever they're asked to do, the stock goes to the winner. Is that right?"

"Exactly. As long as you do the truth or jeopardy, you don't have to forfeit the stock; but if you refuse, it's a forfeit."

"All right—I'd be a fool to refuse, since you have the most to lose. You're making yourself vulnerable to a very lucky gambler, though. And remember, Beth, you set the ground rules—and the stakes could be pretty high."

"Then that makes us both gamblers, Michael."

"So, how do you play this Truth or Jeopardy?"

"Basically, it's played like regular stud poker: The first card is dealt down, the next three are dealt face up. But you don't bet on those first four cards, and before the fifth card is dealt, you have the choice of tossing in your hand or staying. If you toss in your hand, you don't lose; we simply deal another hand again. But if you stay and take that fifth card and you're beaten, you're faced with a truth or a jeopardy."

"This has some very intriguing possibilities. Remember—you've been warned."

"One more thing: if a truth or jeopardy is refused, you can't repeat it the next time. And I think the loser must be given a chance to win back the stock."

"Even if they're not willing to do either a truth or jeopardy?"

"I mean that both of us have to agree that once

a share of stock is lost, we must give the other the chance of winning it back. It's a never-ending agreement unless we mutually consent to end it. And I'll warn you now, I don't intend to stop until I win it all."

"I'm agreeable to that," Michael said, shuffling the deck. He pushed it across the table. "Cut."

Beth was dealt an eight of spades face down, then her next three cards were a king of diamonds, a four of spades, and a nine of hearts. Michael's hand showed a four of clubs, a four of diamonds, and a three of hearts.

Now she faced a decision. Her pair of eights had him beat unless he had a three or a four as his down card. Since she had one of the fours, it was very unlikely he had the remaining one, so probably the best hand he could get would be two pairs: threes and fours.

She had a pair of eights already, with the possibility of getting another eight dealt to her, a king, or a nine. Either one of those cards would beat him for sure. As she saw it, the odds of winning with just the pair of eights were in her favor as well.

"I'll stay in," she said. "Are you throwing in your hand?"

"No, I'll stay."

Surprised, she glanced at him. His expression was inscrutable, but since she had already declared she was remaining in the hand, he'd gain nothing by bluffing. Did he have a three or the remaining four already, or was he betting on catching one of them on his last card? He had a tougher poker face to read than Giff—his expression never changed as he dealt each of them the final card.

Beth couldn't keep from smiling when she saw it was a king of clubs. He had caught a queen of diamonds. She had beaten him! Triumphantly she turned over the eight. "Kings and eights," she declared.

Michael turned over the four of hearts. "Three of a kind."

Her heart sank to her stomach, and she tried to swallow. "Well, it looks like you've won," she said, with a feeble laugh. "Which will it be, truth or jeopardy?"

"Jeopardy," he said calmly.

She held her breath, waiting for him to continue. "You look like the cat that swallowed the canary, Michael. What fiendish thing do you have in mind?"

"A simple one. I want you to release that bun on your head and loosen your hair."

"That's all?" she asked skeptically.

"That's all, Rusty."

She went into the bedroom and removed the pins, and her long hair dropped past her shoulders. After brushing it out, she returned to the table.

Aglow with approval, his gaze devoured her. "Gorgeous." His eyes smoldered with desire.

Resting her chin on her hand, she stared at him, bemused. Strangely enough, it pleased her to know how she affected him. "This is really what you wanted?"

"I want a lot more, Rusty," he said in a voice made husky by passion.

Her eyes glimmered with the sorcery of Lorelei. "Yes, I know." Beth picked up the cards and began to shuffle them. "I believe the next deal is mine."

In the hour that followed, they passed the deal back and forth, neither one taking a risk on a losing hand. He couldn't take his eyes off her, and every time their gazes met, she felt a rise of satisfaction at his fascination. When she finally had a hand she felt could beat his, she bet on it, and he stayed in the game. To her delight, she won.

"So, what's it going to be, Beth?"

"A truth, Michael. You make no effort to disguise how much you want us to become intimate again." She watched the shift of emotions in his face and eyes. "When we were intimate, I'm curious to know what I did that excited you the most?"

His laughter sounded strained. "There are a lot of things about you that excite me: your mind, the way you challenge me—"

"I'm referring to the past, Michael. What physical thing excited you the most?"

"Are you planning on putting it to use in the near future?"

"The rules are that I ask the question; you are to answer it truthfully."

He thought for a few seconds, then said, "Aside from the obvious things such as kiss and touch, I'd have to say it's the way you groaned 'Jake' ... at certain moments."

"I see."

"Then shall we get on with the game?"

In a short time he won a hand and put a truth question to her. "Your turn, Beth. Same question to you. What excited you the most during our intimate moments?"

"Goodness, Michael, it was so long ago, I can't remember."

"I think you can—I think you do." He got up slowly. "But if you want, I'll remind you."

She felt like a stalked prey as he moved toward her, but she couldn't suppress the jolt of excitement that shot through her when he drew her to her feet and clasped her against his hard contours.

"Your body responds to me, Rusty," he whispered at her ear. A tremor raced down her spine when his tongue toyed with that ear. "You see, my love—you feel it already. What you'd like to deny, your body forbids you to forget." His hands roamed her back, her hips, and her spine, shivers of exquisite delight accompanying each touch. "We were so good together, Rusty. Don't try and say you've forgotten. Neither of us has put a moment of that out of our mind."

Oh, yes, she remembered; she could never forget every ecstatic kiss, every touch, every whispered word of love. She ached to feel them, to hear them again—to relive every moment of that rapture. But she fought through the passion bombarding her resistance and shoved herself out of his grasp.

"Stop it at once. I won't let you do this to me again! I forfeit. You've won the share of stock."

"So, I have control of the Rocky Mountain Central again." He smiled. "Too bad, Beth—but this game was your idea."

"You still have to give me the chance to win it back."

"Of course. Sit down and we'll play another hand."

"I've had enough cards for now."

"If it's any consolation, Beth, I would have played your hand the same way you did."

"It's no consolation," she said. She walked into the bedroom and closed the door.

She was too upset to sleep, though, and lay brooding over her foolishness for taking such a risk on a card game. But it was only one game. He wouldn't be that lucky all the time. Tomorrow night she'd win it back.

By the time they reached the end of track, every hair had been returned to a proper bun on her head.

After leaving Tent Town, Beth resumed reading

the novel, thus avoiding conversation with Michael on the ride back to Dallas. She was not looking forward to meeting Michael's family, and when he turned into the driveway of one of the stately mansions that lined Ross Avenue, Beth found herself tense and reluctant for what was ahead.

It was common knowledge that these opulent houses, the homes of many of Dallas's elite—blue blood and nouveau riche alike—offered much more than mere crystal chandeliers and Italian marble floors. Within their walls could be found any convenience that modern society offered: gaslights, centralized water heaters, refrigerators—and some even boasted battery-operated electricity for lighting.

A handsome young man not more than seventeen or eighteen immediately ran up to the carriage as Michael reined to a stop. "Welcome home, sir."

"Hello, Robert," Michael said, handing him the reins. "Robert, this is my wife, Elizabeth."

The young man quickly snatched the cap off his head. "My pleasure, ma'am," he said with a wide grin. "Welcome to Texas."

"Thank you, Robert," Beth said.

The front door opened, and an older man came out on the porch. Tall and thin, he wore his livery as elegantly as Michael did his evening wear.

"Welcome home, sir. Madam awaits you in her sitting room."

"Thank you, James," Michael said, assisting Beth out of the carriage. "James, may I introduce my wife, Elizabeth."

"How do you do, Mrs. Carrington," James said properly. "And may I congratulate you and Mr. Carrington on your recent nuptials."

"Beth, James is to our house what Middy is to yours."

"Then I'm very glad to meet you, James," Beth said warmly. She offered a gloved hand to him, but the butler had already turned away and begun to unload the luggage.

Beth dropped her hand, and Michael took her arm. "Don't be offended, Beth," he whispered as he led her to the door. "James prides himself on being very proper."

"Beyond proper," Beth murmured when they were out of earshot of the butler.

Michael chuckled. "Did I mention he's very British, too?"

Chapter 12

~~~~~~~~

As they entered the house, Beth looked around curiously. Undoubtedly the rooms were larger and the ceilings higher, but otherwise the mansion didn't appear very different from some of Denver's finer homes. Michael took her hand and led her up the wide stairway in the center of the atrium. On the landing the stairway split, with four steps on each side leading to the floor above. A painting of a dark-haired man hung on the wall of the landing, and Beth paused to study it. She instantly saw a resemblance between the eyes of the man in the portrait and Michael's.

"Is this your father?"

"No, my grandfather," he said, with undisguised pride. "Jacob Michael Carrington."

"He's a very handsome man," Beth said.

"He was up until the day he died ten years ago."

They took the stairs to the left and reached the second floor of the house. A mahogany banister with white balusters circled the open balcony that looked down upon the floor below, and a mammoth, round stained glass window in the cathedral ceiling of the atrium flooded the floor and stairway with bright sunlight.

Five doors opened onto this balcony. A long hallway led to the left, and on the other side a hallway ran to the right.

"Michael, how many live here in the house?"

"That door on the right is the suite of my cousin Stephen and his wife Millicent. The room next to it is Emily's, their daughter. Right now she's attending a boarding school in Massachusetts. The two rooms on the left are guest rooms, and there's a stairway behind the middle door that leads to the floor above. Bertha Kaul, who's been my grandmother's maid for as long as I can remember, has a room upstairs, as well as a maid named Helga Schneider, who's only been with us for a few months.

"James and his wife Mary, the cook, have their quarters downstairs in the rear of the house, just off the kitchen. Then there's Robert Harris, the groom whom you met when we arrived. He has quarters above the carriage house."

"And your grandmother?"

"Has a suite in the left wing. My suite—our suite—is in the right wing."

"What about your mother?"

"I thought you knew my mother was dead. She died when I was sixteen."

Beth did some quick calculations. "In '69?" He nodded. "That's a coincidence. My mother died the same year."

"Our mothers died the same year and both our fathers were in railroad. I would say we appear to be star-crossed lovers, Beth."

"Ill-fated, to say the least. Any brothers or sisters?"

"I did have." He swiftly took her by the arm and led her down the hallway. "You'll love Grannie."

"I'm sure I will," Beth replied, "unless she's anything like James."

"Not in the least! Grannie is just like Middy; you'll see."

The woman sitting in a wing chair made no pretense of subtlety; her blue-eyed stare boldly bored into Beth as she crossed the room hand in hand with Michael.

"Grannie, this is Beth."

"How do you do, Mrs. Carrington," Beth said.

"We're all Mrs. Carringtons in this house, so you might as well start calling me Grandmother or Grannie, as Jake does." She glanced up at him. "So, now that you've got yourself a wife, you think there's no cause to be giving your grandmother a kiss, is that it?"

"Of course not, Grannie." He bent down and kissed her cheek. "How are you, darling?"

She patted his cheek. "Glad you're home, Jake."

If Michael had any redeeming quality at all, Beth decided, it would have to be his obvious love for his grandparents.

Once again Rachel Carrington turned her penetrating stare on Beth. "So you're Matthew MacKenzie's daughter. I knew your father. Knew your uncle, too."

"Uncle Andrew!" Beth said, surprised.

"Yes. At the time, Jacob and I were living south of here, near the Brazos. Andy and a couple of his neighbors stopped to spend the night on their way to the Alamo. He was a big fella, with an even bigger grin. Handsome as sin. He had his wife, and if my memory hasn't failed me, I think he had a couple of infant sons with him. I thank God my Jacob had broken his leg the day before, or he'd have gone with them." Rachel shook her head. "When they rode away the next morning, he wanted to go with them so badly he was as loco as a wild bronco chinning the moon. The day Jacob was well enough to sit a saddle, he was packing up to go off and join them, when a rider rode in with the news that the Alamo had fallen . . . and that none of the defenders were spared."

Rachel stopped speaking, deep in reverie. Beth exchanged a quick glance with Michael. Then his grandmother said sadly, "A lot of good men were lost . . . good men." For a long moment she was silent, then she looked up and smiled. "You must forgive an old lady, Beth. We tend to spurn the present to wander back into the past. Whatever became of those two boys of Andy's? I heard a rumor they got out before the Alamo fell."

"That's true. They live northwest of here, near the Texas panhandle. Actually, there's three of them now. Kathleen MacKenzie had another son six months after my uncle died."

"Glory be!" Rachel exclaimed. "So you've still got kin in Texas." Her smile brought a twinkle to her eyes. "Jake, I think we're gonna make a Texan out of this gal before you know it."

"I think that will take some doing," Beth said. "Nothing could ever replace my love for Colorado."

"Lord, honey, you haven't seen any of it yet! There's Galveston, Houston, San Antonio—that's where your uncle spilled his blood. Texas is a country in itself. We've got the Gulf of Mexico on one side and the Rio Grande on the other, with mountains, forests, plains, and desert between 'em. All within our borders."

"You're a good advocate for the state, Mrs. . . . ah, Nana Rachel. Were you born here?"

"No, I was born in Missouri, same as my Jacob. But I'll die a Texan, same as he did." With a half-grin she tucked in her lower lip. "Reckon I've bored you enough with my talk. Here I am running on at the mouth, while you and Jake are probably tired from your trip. And it'll soon be time to dress for the party, so you young'uns get out of here and let an old lady take a nap. We'll talk again, my dear."

"I'd like that," Beth said, pleased. Perhaps she had found one person in this new life with whom she could feel comfortable.

"Save me a dance, Grannie," Michael said as they departed. As soon as they were out of the room, Michael asked, "How do you like my grandmother?"

"What does it matter, Michael?"

He started to say something, then appeared to change his mind. Pausing at the top of the stairway, he explained, "To get to our suite, you can either follow the railing around the balcony or go down these four stairs and up the opposite ones."

Beth grimaced. "Oh, dear! Must I make that decision now?"

"How long are you going to remain unpleasant, Beth?" Taking her arm, he chose the stairs.

"You're the one who set the rules, Michael, remember? Your intent is to remind me every night of my misery; therefore, my intent is to make your days just as miserable."

"It's not going to work, Beth. You'll find my will is stronger than yours."

"A joust, Sir Knight?" she asked with a brittle laugh. "I'd advise you to keep your weapon in readiness: you're going to need it."

"I'm prepared to raise it whenever you beckon, my lady. You are referring to my lance, of course."

Despite not wanting to give him any satisfaction, Beth couldn't help smiling at the innuendo.

"You see, it's starting to work already," he said, grinning.

"What is?"

"My seduction of you." He pushed a door open, and with a theatrical bow and sweep of his hand, he stepped aside for her to enter.

The sitting room was large and comfortably furnished with several upholstered wing chairs, a serpentine-back couch, and a corner desk, with the added pleasantness of several windows and a fireplace. The room led to a bedroom and a bathroom with a huge tub.

"I realize everything is pretty masculine-looking," Michael said, after she had explored the other rooms. "Feel free to make whatever changes you want, Beth."

"It doesn't matter."

"I want you to feel comfortable here."

"Michael, I'll never feel comfortable here," she said matter of factly. It was absurd for him to think otherwise.

Annoyance glittered in his eyes. "Then I'll remind you that whatever is between us remains just that. Your disgruntlement is not to go beyond this door."

His chiding tone rankled her—she was not a child who had to be told to mind her manners. "I promise only to return courtesy with courtesy, Michael. Now I think I'll take your grandmother's example and rest."

He gestured to the other room. "You've seen the bed. Now's as good a time as any to start getting used to it, lady, because that's where you'll be spending most of your nights from now on."

She had angered him, no doubt about that. But as much as she'd have liked to slam the door behind her as she went into the bedroom, Beth resisted the temptation: it would only give him the satisfaction of knowing she was as riled as he was.

She lay down on the bed and closed her eyes but made no attempt to sleep. Aware of Michael moving around her, she assumed he was unpacking. When he left the suite, she got up from the bed, realizing she had to unpack a gown to wear that evening so it wouldn't be a mass of wrinkles. There were two wardrobes in the bedroom, and when she opened one of them, Beth found that it was crammed solid with Michael's clothing. To her surprise, the other one, across the room, was empty except for one garment: the cream gown she'd worn the night of her wedding. She'd never given the dress another thought since then. Obviously Michael had packed it in his luggage and had emptied the wardrobe to make room for her clothing. She discovered he'd done the same to several drawers in a black walnut chiffonnier.

Michael returned just as she was putting the last of her lingerie in a drawer. "I see you've unpacked. That wasn't necessary; Helga could have done it for you."

"I don't need a maid, Michael. I'm used to doing things for myself."

"You're my wife now."

"That might indicate early senility, but I'm still capable of dressing myself," she declared, with a defiant toss of her head.

His hands clapped on her shoulders and pulled her into his arms. The sudden move caught her so unprepared that she responded to the intensity of the kiss before she could rally a resistance. His kiss excited her, sending her emotions whirling as the passion she had kept in check for the past years recognized and responded to his blatant need as much as his demand.

Beth was breathless and trembling when he wrenched his lips from hers. The kiss still burned on her lips, and she brought a hand to her mouth. For a long moment his dark eyes pierced her gaze.

"Every time you unleash that shrewish tongue of yours, Beth, expect the same treatment. It's the best use I can think of for that mouth." He released her.

Then, as if the last few moments had never occurred, he said casually, "There's always hot water for bathing whenever you wish. Would you like to bathe first, or should I?"

"Go ahead," she said hastily and sat down to unpin her hair, pretending to ignore him while he undressed. But he was difficult to ignore, and she was aware of his every move until he disappeared into the bathroom. Then, free of his presence, Beth drew a deep breath. She still felt shaken by the kiss and knew that she had to keep a cool head at all times, to fortify herself against the betrayal of her own emotions—and body. And if she was to avoid the kind of contact that had just occurred, she'd have to take a whole new tack. Hmmm . . . she smiled cunningly. She'd smother him with sweetness though it would take all her self-control to carry it off.

When the bathroom door opened a short time later, Beth felt confident she had a firm grip on herself—until he appeared wearing only a towel tucked around his waist. It was an instant reminder of waking up in his arms in the hayloft. It also resurrected the painful memory of a long-ago morning: of waking up in the tiny room they had shared, seeing him enter the room in only a towel, his hair still damp from bathing, their gazes meeting and the sensuous message that had passed between them, which caused him to abandon any thought of dressing, to made love to her again . . . and then . . . waking up afterwards to find he was gone.

"Better get moving, Beth. We can't be late for our own party."

His words snapped her out of her musing. Avoiding glancing at him, she snatched up her dressing gown and hastened into the bathroom.

By the time she finished her bath, Michael had left the bedroom. But to her surprise, a dressing table and stool had been set against one wall. Her brushes, perfume, and cosmetics were placed neatly on the top.

When she stole a glance out the door, she saw him at the desk in the corner of the sitting room. Beth dressed quickly, deciding to wear the cream gown she'd worn for the wedding. She was seated at the dressing table, adding the finishing touches to the chignon on the top of her head, when Michael came back into the room.

"Where did this dressing table come from?" she asked.

"We moved it from one of the other rooms. Tomorrow I'll order you a new one—and a wardrobe, as well."

That would be a welcome opportunity to get away from the house. "If you don't mind, I'd like to select it myself."

"Not at all. Are you about ready? Our guests have started to arrive."

"I just need a hand with this lacing in the back."

Devilment glinted in his eyes. "I'm well acquainted with those laces."

Applying her new strategy, she flashed him a playful smile. "Don't remind me."

He tied the strings quickly, then pulled a velvet-covered jeweler's case out of his pocket. "I have a wedding gift for you." He opened the case, and a necklace and eardrops of marquise-cut diamonds sparkled brilliantly against the black satin lining. "These were my mother's."

Beth felt a painful twist in her chest. Barely able to speak, she managed to say, "Michael, I can't accept this."

"Why not? It's a wedding gift."

She raised her eyes and met his enigmatic stare. "Under the circumstances..." She struggled for words. "You've already given me a wedding gift."

"You mean the stock?"

She nodded. "The necklace is beautiful, but it has too much sentimental meaning. It's meant to be given to the woman you love, Michael." She turned her head away. When she felt his hands on her neck, she glanced up into the mirror. The necklace now glimmered at her throat.

"The necklace is meant for my wife, Beth."

For a long moment he gazed at her in the mirror. "It looks lovely on you. I'll wait for you downstairs." He pressed a light kiss to the back of her neck, then left the room.

She closed her eyes in despair, holding back unexpected tears. She wanted nothing sentimental from him—nothing to touch her emotions. Why couldn't he just keep everything on the business level the way it was meant to be? He wasn't playing by the rules. With a heavy sigh, she put on the pendant earrings. Why, she asked herself desolately, did she expect he would?

On her way down the stairs, she gave the hanging portrait a sidelong glance. "I've noticed, Jacob Michael Carrington, that you and your grandson have the same dark eyes—with the same roguish gleam."

She surveyed the room below, overflowing with faces of strangers. She didn't recognize one person. Michael was in conversation with several women near the foot of the stairway, his back to her.

Once again, she couldn't help noticing his incredible dark handsomeness in the evening suit custom-fitted to his wide shoulders and narrow hips, his white starched collar a striking contrast with his bronzed face. A bizarre thought crossed her mind as she stared at him: how many of the women in the room were in love with him? How many had he made love to? For the first time since she'd known him, Beth felt a real sense of the mesmerizing power this man commanded over women.

As if sensing her presence, he turned his head, excused himself, then walked over to the foot of the stairway. Something beyond admiration gleamed in his eyes as he watched her descend the stairs, and when he reached out to take her hand, she sensed, despite his claim of revenge, that she held this same power over him.

Chapter 13

Michael led Beth to the couple who had been greeting guests at the doorway. "Stephen and Millicent, I'd like you to meet my wife, Elizabeth. Beth, this is my cousin and his wife."

Stephen Carrington had thinning red hair and a closely clipped gray beard and sideburns that emphasized the narrowness of his long face.

"Welcome to the family, Elizabeth," Millicent said. Despite her smile, the greeting held only a modicum of warmth.

"It's a pleasure to meet you," Beth said, purposely applying more warmth than she'd received. "I've been looking forward to meeting the rest of Michael's family. Nana Rachel is such a dear."

"How do you do," Stephen said. His eyes were ice blue as he acknowledged the introduction, then he turned to Michael. "Now that you've finally arrived to greet your guests, Millicent and I will mingle." He took his wife's arm, and they moved away.

With a fluttering hand to her breast, Beth said, "My goodness, I'm overwhelmed! If your cousins' welcome had been any warmer, I might have been frostbitten."

"I should have warned you; Stephen's an ass.

Don't even give him a second thought. And Millicent is harmless; she never steps out of his
shadow." He turned to shake hands with the latest
arrival, a short, heavyset man with bushy brows
and a dark beard. "Hello, Frederick. I'd like you to
meet my wife, Elizabeth. Beth, this gentleman is
Frederick Taylor, the Lone Star's chief of engineers."

"I vish you much happiness, Mrs. Carrington,"
he said with a thick German accent.

Beth wondered why he didn't meet her eyes.
"Thank you, Mr. Taylor."

Taylor and Michael exchanged a few words in
German, then the young man moved on. Recalling
Michael's fluent French at the masquerade ball and
later in the restaurant, she asked, "Michael, how
many languages do you speak?"

"Just four: English, French, German, and Spanish. Unless you want to include Texan, which our
critics consider to be a language of its own." He
raised her hand to his lips and pressed a kiss to
her palm. "No doubt you intend to join the ranks
of those critics, my love?"

"Why would I, Michael?" she asked, with a be-
guiling smile. "I plan to make Texas my home."
There was a puzzled look in his eyes, but before he
could question her, she said, "I noticed Mr. Taylor's English was hesitant. Doesn't that present a
problem communicating with your work crews?"

"When the transcontinental railroad was built,
Jim Strobridge with the Central Pacific didn't speak
Chinese, but that didn't keep him and his Chinese
crew from laying track from California through the
Sierra Nevadas."

Beth rolled her eyes. "I was raised in a railroad
household, too, Michael, so I've heard the stories

about how the first transcontinental railroad was built many times."

"Actually, Frederick's only been the Lone Star's chief engineer for the past year. And we do have many German immigrants in our crew. He's conscientious enough, but he's no Dave Kincaid. Stephen thinks very highly of him, though." Then, grinning broadly, he greeted a new arrival. "Oran, I'm so glad you could come on such short notice. Beth, I have the honor of introducing you to the governor of Texas, Oran M. Roberts."

"Governor Roberts, it's a pleasure to finally meet you, sir." Beth said to the gray-haired man in his sixties. "My father always spoke very highly of you; and I welcome this opportunity to personally thank you for your thoughtful wire when he passed away."

"I was sorry to hear of his passing, Mrs. Carrington. Matt MacKenzie was a remarkable man. I had the opportunity to meet your father on several occasions when the route for the railroad was being considered."

"That's most kind of you, Governor Roberts."

"With his death following just two years after that of Mike Carrington, I remember thinking what a great loss it was to the nation to lose two such titans of the railroad industry. Fortunately, both men had offspring to carry on their visions. I wish you and Jake much happiness." He rubbed his hands together. "Tell me, Jake, where is your dear grandmother? I can't wait to see Rachel."

"You'll find her in the next room, Oran," Michael said.

As the governor left, Michael took her arm. "James can handle any late arrivals; I'm hungry. Let's get something to eat."

Just then a man and two women arrived.

"Carl, glad to see you." Michael shook his hand. Then, kissing the cheek of the older woman, he said, "Caroline, you look as lovely as ever. And I don't have to tell you, Diane, that you look gorgeous as always." He lifted the mink mantle off the shoulders of the younger woman.

Observing the casual intimacy in the gesture, Beth sensed he was used to removing a lot more than just her fur wrap. The woman was stunning. Her blond curls were pulled to the side of her head and tucked behind an emerald and gold plume. She was dressed in a green gown of satin brocade which highlighted her green eyes, now fixed with icy malevolence on Beth.

Handing the wrap to James, Michael said, "Beth, this is Carl Bennett, his wife Caroline, and their daughter, Diane. My wife, Elizabeth."

"How do you do," Carl Bennett said, eying her with an intent stare.

"My dear," Caroline Bennett said, "how nice to meet you. I must say, Michael's marriage was quite unexpected."

"Yes, it was just as much of a surprise to me, Mrs. Bennett," Beth said cordially.

"Really!" Diane exclaimed. "I would think the surprise was more on Michael."

Beth turned her smile to the young woman. "Now, why would you think that, dear? You must know as well as I that when Michael sees something he *really* wants, he gets it. He's such a persuasive rogue." She tucked her arm into his and smiled up at him. "Aren't you, darling? Do enjoy yourselves," she told the Bennetts, turning to leave.

"You'd better watch whose feathers you ruffle, Mrs. Carrington," Michael whispered, amused, when the Bennetts walked away looking annoyed.

"Carl Bennett is one of the Lone Star's stockholders."

"You're so talented at bootlicking, Michael, I'm sure you'll be able to smooth any feathers I might have mussed. Most likely you'll begin with that plume on Diane's head."

"A jealous wife! It's amazing, my love, how every day I learn more about you."

"Jealous? Not at all, Michael. I could care less who you go to bed with as long as it keeps you out of mine."

"Not for long," he said with a confident smile.

Suddenly a young girl rushed across the room and flung herself in Michael's arms. "Jake!" Small in stature, she couldn't have been more than sixteen or seventeen.

"Emily!" Michael lifted her off her feet and spun her around. "What are you doing home, honey? You're supposed to be in school."

"I left school, Jake."

"What does your father say about that?"

"Father is furious with me. But I'm not going back. I hate that school. I hope you and Grandmother will help me convince him."

"Emily, you know that whatever I suggest, your father will do just the opposite. Beth, this is Stephen's daughter, Emily. Honey, this is my wife, Elizabeth."

The young girl turned a belligerent glare on Beth. "Hello."

By this time Beth had fortified herself to withstand the icy blast of Carrington hostility. "Hello, Emily," she responded graciously. "Jake and I were just about to have something to eat. Would you like to join us?"

"No, I've eaten. I'll see you later." She dashed away as quickly as she had arrived.

"Whew!" Beth said. "Why do I envision the second coming of Cynthia?"

"Emily does have a lot of energy."

They entered a grand ballroom, complete with crystal chandeliers, paneled walls, and a polished floor that glistened with beeswax.

Lining one wall of the room were several tables draped in white lace tablecloths and laden with a lavish display. Passing up several tasty-looking hors d'oeuvres, tiny sandwiches, relishes, and several hot selections in silver bowls, Beth took a small slice of ham, a deviled egg, and a potato mixture she could not identify. Ignoring slices from the six-tiered wedding cake, Beth took a small fruit-filled tart.

She hadn't realized how hungry she was until she began to eat.

"This lobster is delicious, Beth, did you try some?" Michael asked.

"I'm allergic to seafood."

He looked up. "Oh, that's right; I forgot." He forked a bite of chicken with cream sauce and held it up to her mouth. "Taste this." To avoid it dripping on her, she quickly consumed it, then had to endure several more offerings of it from him. Self-consciously she glanced around. People were watching them. He was beginning to carry his love-sick newlywed act too far.

"Michael, will you please stop this," she murmured in a low command, when he began feeding her the wedding cake on his plate. "I'm becoming nauseated."

"The food's making you sick?"

"No, you are." Laughing, he forked another bite up to her mouth. She smiled through gritted teeth. "One more bite, Carrington, and I'm shoving that cake in your face."

He popped the last bite into his mouth and was wiping a dab of frosting off her face with his napkin when Governor Roberts came up to them.

"Elizabeth, I forgot to mention that I also had the pleasure of meeting your sister Cynthia and her husband when your railroad reached Texas. I must say, your sister is as lovely as you are. I was also very impressed with that husband of hers, as I am with your choice of young Jake here." He gave Michael a fatherly pat on the shoulder.

Beth batted her eyes outrageously at Michael, who quickly said, "I expect Dave Kincaid will play a prominent part in the future of the railroad industry. I regret he doesn't work for the Lone Star."

"I'm sure you do, Michael. But it's very unlikely that will ever happen," she replied with a confident smile.

"I predict the marriage of these two families will foretell an even greater future for the growth of the railroad," Roberts said.

"At least in Texas and Colorado, Oran," Michael added lightly. "If you'll excuse us, sir, I believe they want us to lead out the first waltz."

"May I claim the honor of the second one, Elizabeth?" the governor asked.

She smiled and nodded as Michael guided her toward the dance floor lined with guests awaiting the start of the dancing.

"Now smile, darlin'," Michael warned, leading her out in a waltz. "I'm sure there's not a pair of eyes in this room that isn't watching us at this moment. So do try to show a little more adoration on that lovely face of yours."

Beth sighed theatrically. "I'm so sorry, Michael—but my sister is the actress in the family."

He chuckled warmly. "Ah, Beth, I suspect marriage to you will never be dull." He smiled down at her intimately, which appeared to please many of the spectators, who observed it with smiles of their own.

While Beth danced the next waltz with the governor, Michael chose Emily as his partner. Then Stephen did his duty by leading Beth stiffly around the dance floor. After several more partners, whose names she could not remember, Beth finally managed to slip away into a corner. As she was enjoying a cup of punch, the banker, Lucas Walters, approached her and introduced her to his wife, Patricia.

"I must say, Mrs. Carrington, no one could have been more surprised than I to hear of your marriage. I had no idea when Michael bought your note that he intended to marry you."

"Nor did I," Beth said, arching a curved brow.

"I understand you have a connection to the Rocky Mountain Central Railroad," Patricia Walters said pointedly. Obviously the banker had described in detail his version of the whole situation to his wife, and it was clear she was now prying for gossip.

Beth purposely leaned forward and whispered, "Michael's so generous. The dear man presented half of the stock to me as a wedding gift. Can you believe it?"

Flattered at what she believed to be a shared confidence, the banker's wife preened like a peacock. "Really? Isn't that romantic!"

"I thought so, too. Now you must excuse me. I see dear Nana Rachel is alone. I must go and keep her company."

"It's been a pleasure to meet you, my dear," Patricia gushed.

Beth gave her a wide smile. "The pleasure was all mine." She walked away before either one of them could get in another word. As Beth crossed the floor, she cast a backward glance in time to see the banker's wife hurrying over to a group of women.

Beth had no doubt that others in the room had the same suspicions about her as the banker and his wife. Michael's attempt to present the impression that they were in love seemed ludicrous to Beth. If his plan for revenge included making himself appear as a love-besotted victim and her as a scheming opportunist, so be it. She discarded the idea as quickly as it had entered her mind: Michael was too proud to let himself appear victimized to anybody's eyes. Glancing around the room, she saw that he was on the dance floor, his head bent attentively over Diane Bennett's. *They deserve each other*, she thought in disgust, walking over to a chair next to Rachel Carrington.

"Kind of need a spoonful of molasses to help swallow this crowd, don't you?" Rachel said.

"Oh, dear! Is it that obvious?" Beth replied with a light laugh. "And I thought I was doing so well."

"What we need is a good old foot-stomping hoe-down. We ain't had one since my Jacob's been gone. Stephen's always been too much of a stiff-neck, and Michael's gone most of the time. Wouldn't much matter though; the gals he's brought home in the past think they're too high-falutin to kick up their heels. That one's the worst of the lot," Rachel said, nodding toward the dancing couple. "Been lifting her skirt to Jake for years, hoping to corral him." Rachel leaned nearer and patted Beth's hand. "But you don't have to give her a never-no-mind, honey. She'd never be woman enough for Jake."

"Is any woman?" Beth asked.

Rachel squeezed Beth's hand. "He's found the

one who is," she said. "I can tell. You're gonna be good for my grandson."

"I'm sure most of the people in this room are convinced otherwise."

"Biggest mistake two people in love can make is listening to the naysayers. I was barefoot with no schooling the day Jake's grandpa rode up to my daddy's farm to water his horse. We were dirt-poor farmers, and Jacob Carrington was a lawyer and the son of one of the richest men in St. Louis. But that didn't stop us from falling in love." Her aged face creased into a reminiscent smile. "Lord knows, his family tried hard enough to keep us apart, but Jacob would have none of it. When he told them he planned to wed me, they said I was just marrying him for his money and they vowed to disinherit him." Her mouth curled up in vexation. "And they were spiteful enough to do it! My ma and pa warned me that when Jacob tired of me, I'd be left with nothing but a passel of kids to raise on my own." She shook her head, and her eyes sparkled with warmth. "Ah, but none of them knew my beloved Jacob like I did. None of them really understood. He told his family to keep their money. We packed up and rode west. That was over sixty years ago. We fought the wilderness, we fought for Texas independence, and we fought the Comanche. And Jacob had the grit and intelligence to make a fortune while doing it. When the day came that we had to part, he told me he'd never regretted one day we spent together." She closed her eyes. "We got to share fifty years—fifty wonderful years together, that passed as swiftly as they ended on the day he was shot in the back during a bank holdup."

Rachel Carrington was a refreshing breath of honesty in this suffocating deception. In the face of her openness, Beth couldn't bear to lie to her any longer. "Nana Rachel, I have to tell you that Michael and I are not—"

"Hush, child. I've heard the talk, and I know what you've a mind to say. First off, my grandson's too darn smart to be fooled; he's always known what he wants and how to get it. And the other thing is, I know people. I've met all kinds in my eighty years. And whatever's between you and Jake, I figure the two of you know just what you're doing."

"I'm not sure we do, Nana Rachel."

"Follow your heart, child. Ain't no one crawling in that bed at night but you and him."

"But what you don't know is that—"

"I know all I have to, girl. I trust my instincts. You and Jake just gotta hang tough, and mark my words, honey, it'll all work out in the end." She patted Beth's hand and yawned. "I think I've had enough excitement for one night. Time I get to my bed. Beth, dear, will you get James to help me upstairs?"

"I'll help you, Nana Rachel."

"Thank you, dear."

Beth assisted Rachel to her feet and led her to the stairway. James approached them immediately.

"May I be of assistance, madam?"

"She's ready to go to bed, James. I'll take care of her."

"That won't be necessary, Mrs. Carrington. Bertha and I shall do it."

It appeared to be more a declaration than a respectful request. "Thank you, James."

Taking Rachel's arm, he began to lead her up the stairway.

"Good night, dear," Rachel called out to her.

Beth decided she would follow Rachel's example. The only one who would care if she left was Michael, so she wandered through the lower hallway in search of him to say good night, peeking into rooms she hadn't seen before. She paused outside a door when she heard Michael's voice.

"Diane, it's over. We've had some good times together, but I'm married now, and it's time to get on with our lives."

"Oh, Jake, how could you marry that woman? Everyone knows you don't love her. She's nothing but a cheap opportunist who married you for your money."

"And you, of course, would have married me whether I had money or not." His tone was curt.

Beth had heard all she needed to hear. Opening the door, she stepped into the room. "Excuse me."

Diane had her arms around Michael's neck. She dropped them hurriedly and stared at Beth in stunned apprehension as she moved away.

"Oh, am I interrupting you, dear? I'll only be a minute." Beth stepped up to Michael and put her hands on his shoulders. "I just wanted to tell you I'm going upstairs now. To bed," she added in a sultry tone. She raised her head and covered his mouth with hers. Her kiss caught him by surprise, and she dragged it out until he responded and began to deepen it. Then she broke away. With her gaze locked on his bewildered eyes, she said with the bare suggestion of a smile, "Good night, Diane; it was a pleasure to meet you." Then she sauntered out of the room without a backward glance at the two stunned people.

On the way to her room, she paused at the painting of Michael's grandfather. "You know, Jacob Carrington, this is going to be more fun than I thought."

Beth had just slipped her nightgown over her

head when Michael burst through the door, a bottle of champagne and two glasses in hand.

"Michael!" Perplexed, she looked at him, the bottle in his hand, then back to him again. "What are you doing up here? You have guests downstairs."

It was his turn to look confused. "What did you think I'd do after that invitation you gave me?"

"Invitation for what?"

She flinched when he slammed the bottle and glasses down on the table, surprised they didn't break. "You know damn well for what! Anyone can figure out why I came up here—and I'm not making a fool of myself by going back down."

"I'm sorry, Michael, I didn't mean to mislead you."

"Is that right?" he scoffed. "Then do you mind telling me what *that* was all about downstairs?"

"You mean when I walked in and found your girfriend's arms around your neck? I was just trying to make it easier for you. It sounded like you needed some help to get out of the predicament you were in."

"Do you think I can't fight my own battles?"

"It looked that way to me."

"I see." She didn't like the gleam in his eyes. "And how are you at getting your*self* out of . . . predicaments?"

Beth backed up as he started to advance toward her slowly. "Truly, Michael, I had your interests at heart. Sometimes these situations are better handled by the wronged wife," she said as calmly as she could manage when he drew her into his arms.

"That wasn't the reason at all, was it?" His mouth was so near, she turned her head away, but his fingers cupped her chin, forcing her to look into his dark eyes. "You were jealous, Beth, weren't you?"

She opened her mouth in a denial and his mouth closed over hers, swallowing her words in a kiss. His mouth moved possessively on hers, and once again she felt a heated wave of passion flow through her, which seemed to grow with his every touch. She cursed her weakness to her own desire, so long denied, even as she sought more contact with his hard, exciting body.

She felt shaken when he broke the kiss. His heated stare probed the depth of her eyes. "How long do you figure you can hold out, Beth?" he asked in a husky murmur.

"Michael, you must stop kissing me," she whispered.

"A plea for mercy! Sorry, my queen—I give no quarter."

She held her breath, afraid he would kiss her again, fearful he wouldn't. Finally he released her and stepped back.

"Have a good night's sleep, Beth."

Her legs were trembling as she walked to the bedroom door, feeling his intense stare with every step she took.

Chapter 14

$\sim\!\!\sim\!\!\bigcirc\!\bigcirc\!\!\sim$

Waking early had been a way of life with Beth for too many years to break the habit overnight—and waking to find Michael asleep beside her was enough to make her want to lie back and hope it was just a nightmare. She was glad to see that at least he wasn't entwined with her, as they had been in the hayloft.

Slipping out of bed, she gathered her clothing and went into the bathroom, remaining there until she completed her morning toilette.

When she came out, Michael was sitting up in bed with a pillow propped behind his head. A sheet covered him from the waist down, but bare-chested, rumpled hair, and shadowed jaw, he looked incredibly masculine . . . and lusty.

"Good morning," he said with a broad grin. "You're up early."

When he adjusted the sheet, an appalling possibility occurred to her. "Please don't tell me you're naked under that sheet."

"All right, I won't tell you," he said, flashing the same abominable grin. "But if the thought distresses you, I'd advise you to turn your head, because I'm getting up."

"Oh, my God, that's uncivilized!" she declared

as she departed. His laughter followed her, the same way it had on her flight from the hayloft.

Preferring to have whatever protection he could offer, before walking into the lion's den, she waited for Michael to dress before going down to join the others at breakfast.

When she and Michael entered the dining room, Stephen and Emily were embroiled in an argument over her returning to school. Stephen cast a distasteful glance in their direction. His mouth tightened and he said, "I've said my final word, Emily. We'll have no further discussion on the issue."

"Thank goodness!" Rachel declared. "Perhaps the rest of us will be able to enjoy our meal. Good morning," she said, greeting them cheerily.

"Morning, Grannie." Michael kissed his grandmother's cheek.

"Good morning, Nana Rachel." Beth offered a smile to the others at the table. "Good morning, everybody." Millicent was the only one who had the courtesy to offer a faint response.

"Good morning, Millicent. Emily. Did you both enjoy the party last night?" Michael asked, pulling out a chair for Beth to be seated. "Stephen, I'd like to remind you that you didn't greet my wife when she sat down."

"Good morning, Elizabeth," Stephen said curtly, clearly vexed. "Michael, if you joined us simply to start an argument, you needn't have bothered."

Michael's steely stare locked on his cousin. "You seem to have started one without my presence. The sound of it carried all the way upstairs."

Fortunately, James put plates down in front of Beth and Michael, thus ending the impending argument. There was no further conversation as everyone concentrated on their breakfast. Back home, Beth thought, she would barely have been able to get a word in with all the chattering and laughter—but this wasn't home, as she kept reminding herself.

Rachel finally broke the silence. "Did you sleep well, my dear? So often it's difficult to fall asleep in a strange bed."

"She snored all night, Grannie."

"I don't snore!" Beth denied firmly. Then with a slip in self-assurance, she asked, "Do I?"

He chuckled. "No, but you do hog the bed."

Beth felt a hot blush. "You know, Michael, some things are better left unsaid. I think Stephen had the right idea: you do appear to want to start an argument."

"I'm only teasing, love," he said.

Beth glanced at Rachel, whose face was aglow with a pleased smile.

The meal passed without any further flare-ups. Michael left for his office, with the promise of returning to pick her up for lunch and to take her to the carpenter shop.

Beth sought refuge in her room, bemoaning the wasted time when she should have been tending to business. She was waiting for Michael anxiously when he showed up promptly at noon and took her to a quaint carpentry shop in the German section of the city. After she had picked out the style and color she wanted for an armoire and dressing table, Michael took her to lunch at a wursthaus, which he explained meant a sausagehouse. As they drank tall steins of dark beer, a Lufthansa band, dressed in leather trousers and bright suspenders, and wearing Tyrolean hats with ornamental feathers, played folk music on an accordion, bass, drums, and harmonium. The waiter put down a huge steaming plate of dumplings and thick, spicy pork sausages cooked in sauerkraut in front of her.

Beth groaned in dismay. "Michael, I could never eat all this food. It's enough to feed an army."

"Eat what you can, Beth. You'll love it," he assured her, digging into the similar plate before him.

Though the food was delicious, she barely made a dent in it. The concerned proprietor followed them out to the street, where Michael assured him that everything had been delectable and he'd bring her back to finish it.

"*Auf Wiedersehen*, Franz," Michael said in parting.

"I'm afraid I over-ate," Beth said on the way back to the house. "I doubt I'll be able to join your family for dinner tonight. I know that will be a big disappointment to Stephen."

He looked at her askance. "If I didn't know better, I'd say you did it on purpose." They both broke into laughter.

"Truly, Michael, the meal was delicious and a change from the fare I've been used to. Thank you, I really enjoyed everything: the food, the music, and—" She cut off what she had been about to say.

"And what?" he asked.

"And the company." She realized that she *had* enjoyed every minute of their lunch together. There had been no effort on her part to pretend.

"I had a good time, too. I'll bask in the satisfaction of knowing the lunch helped to put aside that lamentable breakfast ordeal this morning."

When they arrived at the house, Michael didn't come in. "Tell James we won't be joining the family for the evening meal. When I get home later, we'll just have a light repast in our suite."

After passing on Michael's message to James, Beth went upstairs. She heard a loud sobbing, and followed the sound to Emily's door. Deciding not to get involved, she started to turn away, then changed her mind and tapped lightly on the door. "May I come in?"

Emily was sitting on a window seat gazing out the window. "What do you want?" she asked between sobs.

"Is there anything I can do to help, Emily?" As unpleasant as the young girl had been to her, Beth couldn't help but feel sorry for her.

"Of course not. What could *you* do?"

"I think I know how you feel. Both of my sisters hated school, too, and left before they finished."

"I don't care about your dumb sisters," Emily lashed out. "Just get out of my room. My father told me all about you," she said scornfully. "You married Jake for his money because you were losing your railroad."

"I'm trying to be helpful, Emily."

"It's none of your business. I wish you'd get out of this house. It's your fault my father and Jake are quarreling. Ever since you married Jake, there's been trouble. You're trying to turn him against the whole family."

It was useless to try and help—she never should have gotten involved. Beth left the room and bumped into Stephen Carrington out in the hall.

"What are you doing in my daughter's room?"

"I heard her crying; I tried to comfort her." She started to walk away, and he grabbed her arm.

"You stay away from my daughter. You're not fooling me; I know you married Michael to get your stock back. As far as I'm concerned, you're nothing more than a whore he bought—and I'm warning you, keep out of the Lone Star. If you try to influence Michael in any way, you'll regret it. I'll destroy him along with you, if I have to."

Beth was shocked by the vindictiveness of his attack. "Stephen, I don't understand your animos-

ity toward me. I assure you, I have no interest in
what happens to the Lone Star. Since we are living
under the same roof, I would have preferred your
friendship, and it's a pity you aren't capable of that.
But you don't frighten me, and from what I've observed, you obviously don't intimidate Michael either."

Shrugging off his grasp, she walked away.

"Just stay out of this part of the house," Stephen
shouted after her. "You have no business here."
She didn't look back when she heard the door
slam.

Michael still wasn't home by the time Rachel
came up to retire for the evening. When Beth went
in to say good night to her, Rachel was in bed reading a book.

"Have a good night's sleep, Nana Rachel."

Rachel took off her pince-nez glasses and put
them on the stand beside her. "Thank you, dear. I
missed you at dinner. It bothers me to think of you
shut up in your room all afternoon and evening.
You have the run of this house, the same as all of
us."

Beth did not intend to air her grievances to the
sweet old woman. She smiled and said gently, "I
had a lot of unpacking to finish up, Nana Rachel."

"I know differently, my dear. I couldn't help but
overhear Stephen's cruel words. You mustn't let
him bother you, Beth. I'm afraid his parents in-
dulged him outrageously. He's always been cruelly
outspoken, besides having a streak of meanness in
him." She shook her head sadly. "Poor Stephen, he
tries so hard to impress his worth on others and
fails miserably." Her eyes twinkled. "Whereas that
rogue Michael only has to smile to win supporters.
I suspect that wears heavily on Stephen as well."
She patted Beth's hand. "It breaks my heart to see

my grandsons at such odds. I've failed them as much as their parents did."

Beth picked up the lined hand on the counterpane. "You mustn't blame yourself for the weakness of others. You're dear to all of us, myself included, and despite the differences between your grandsons, I'm sure you mean as much to Stephen as you do to Michael."

"You have a kindness, child, that's endearing. Yet I can tell you have great strength and fortitude. Your parents must have been very proud of you."

"They were proud of all their children, Nana Rachel. I hope you have the opportunity of meeting my two sisters soon."

"You miss them and your home, don't you?"

Beth sighed. "Very much." At Rachel's encouraging look, Beth told her about the contentment of growing up with Thia and Angie, the death of her mother, and her devotion to her father and his dream for the railroad. Finally, becoming aware of the late hour, she smiled sheepishly.

"Forgive me, Nana Rachel. I'm keeping you up."

"Nonsense. I've enjoyed your visit. I hope you'll come again. Without my Jacob, this house is as lonely for me as it is for you."

Beth smiled tenderly. "How would you like me to read to you for a short while?"

"I would be delighted, child. These old eyes are beginning to fail me."

Rachel settled down in bed, and Beth picked up the novel. When Rachel's eyelids began to droop, Beth put aside the book. "I think I should leave now and let you sleep. If you'd like, I'll read to you again tomorrow."

"I'd love that, Beth," Rachel said sleepily. "Good night, dear."

Impulsively Beth bent down and kissed her cheek. "Good night."

Rachel reached up and patted her cheek. "Yes, I know you will bring much happiness to my grandson."

Beth returned to her room and was writing Angie a letter when Michael came in carrying a bottle of wine.

"I'm looking forward to spending a quiet evening together, Beth—unless you would prefer to go downstairs. We could always have a whist game with Stephen and Millicent."

"Or more likely a dueling battle. Michael, your family hates me. I'm more comfortable up here."

"Well, then, shall we play a game of cards?"

"It's really not necessary for you to entertain me, Michael. I have some letters to write, and I'm sure you have something you'd rather do."

"And you know *exactly* what that is. But for the time being, I'll settle for a card game." He poured them each a glass of wine. "Come on, Beth. Don't be a spoilsport. Aren't you anxious to win back that share of stock you lost?"

She certainly did. Beth closed the book, went to the table, and sat down.

After an hour of the worst run of cards she'd ever had, Beth ended up in jeopardy. Folding her arms across her chest, she asked, "Okay, what is it this time?"

"You have to let me make love to you."

Struggling between anger and panic, she stammered a choked accusation. "You agreed that we wouldn't be intimate."

"That was the terms of our wedding agreement— not the card game."

Beth bolted to her feet. "Oh, no, Michael. You're not going to get away with that! We have an agree-

ment that no card game is going to supersede. This
game's over—and don't think I'll forfeit any stock,
either." She threw down the cards and went to bed.
She was still awake when Michael came to bed
about an hour later. She lay stiffly when she felt
his weight on the bed beside her.

"Good night, Rusty," he said.

Turning on her side, Beth moved as far away
from him as she could.

Michael had already left when she awoke in the
morning. She spent a lonely day awaiting his return and said little during the evening meal. Later,
she once again went to Rachel's room to read to
her.

After about thirty minutes, Beth glanced up from
the page and saw that Rachel had fallen asleep. She
closed the book, and before turning off the lamp,
she bent down and pressed a light kiss to the cheek
of the sleeping woman.

Beth encountered Bertha, Rachel's personal
maid, outside the door. "She's sleeping, Bertha,"
Beth said. "I've already turned off the light."

"I prefer to check everything for myself, Mrs.
Carrington."

Is everyone in this household rude? Beth wondered.
Middy's complaints were more like motherly nagging. These people were downright discourteous.

"I'm sure your conscientiousness is as appreciated by my husband as it is by me, Bertha," Beth
said graciously. "But you might better serve Mrs.
Carrington by not disturbing her rest." She was
sure the maid would do it anyway, though.

Entering their room, she saw that Michael hadn't
returned yet. It appeared they wouldn't have their
card game tonight—which was for the best, considering last night's outcome.

The young maid, Helga, tapped on the door. "Vould you like for da bed turn down now, Frau Carrington?"

"If you wish, Helga."

Since Beth preferred to dress herself, there was very litte Helga could do for her. The young woman came and went in Beth's absence, so they rarely encountered one another. And since the woman had a thick German accent, Beth found it difficult to understand her the few times they did meet, so communication between them was very limited. Beth tried to compensate with a smile, but appeared not to be making much of an impression on the maid.

When Helga finished turning down the bed, she came back into the sitting room. "Is dere anydink else you vant, Frau Carrington?"

Beth offered a smile. "No, Helga, thank you. Have a pleasant night."

"*Guten nacht*," Frau Carrington." The maid departed, her resentment of Beth as obvious as James's and Bertha's. Beth didn't understand what she'd ever done to any one of them to warrant the hostility.

Restless at the prospect of another evening confined to the room, Beth walked over to the window. In the herb garden below, the whorled leaves of columbo and pink evening primrose bathed in the glow of moonlight, and a warm breeze carried the fragrance of pine through the night air. It made her think of home—of her mother's rose garden and the scent of apple blossoms in the spring. Feeling on the verge of tears, she decided to ward off her building depression with a stroll in the garden.

She slipped quietly out of the house. At first she was tempted to visit the horses, just to bring a touch of home closer, but she didn't want to disturb Robert. Sitting on a bench in a dark corner of the garden, she wondered what Angie and Giff were up to, how Middy was feeling, and if String and Red were well. She had only been away for a short time, but it seemed like an eternity. Maybe it was because she hated this place so much. These people weren't family—they were adversaries. Rachel Carrington was the only one who made it bearable.

She thought of the home in which she'd been raised, of the laughter and love that flowed between them all. The only love exchanged freely in this household was that between Michael and his grandmother. Had Michael's father been as tyrannical to his own son as Stephen Carrington was to his child? Could that be why Michael would easily seek revenge as a motive for marriage? It made her wonder how much of his true feelings were masked behind that smile. Grimacing, she thought that at least he did smile, which was more than that overbearing cousin of his ever did, or the faint-hearted rabbit married to him. Just once she'd like to hear Millicent Carrington tell that husband of hers to go plumb to hell!

Beth got up to return to the house. If Michael arrived home and found her missing, he'd probably wake the whole household. At least her blues were gone; if nothing else, just thinking about the Carringtons roused her anger enough to shake off her melancholy.

As she rounded a hedge on her way back in the dark, she almost bumped into a couple who were kissing. Startled, she saw that it was Emily and Robert. When they broke apart, Beth heard Robert say, "I love you, Em."

"And I love you, Robert. What are we going to

do? Father says I must go back to school. I don't want to leave you again."

Beth didn't want to eavesdrop and tried to retreat, but her movement caught the attention of both. The two young people looked as startled as she, and for a long moment they stared at her. Beth could well imagine what snobbish Stephen would say if he knew his daughter was engaging in romantic trysts with the stableboy.

Robert finally broke the gaping silence between them. "Please, ma'am, Emily and I are in love. Please don't tell her father. He'll have me discharged for sure and find a way to keep us apart forever."

Beth glanced at Emily. The young girl shifted her eyes downward. Beth stepped past them without speaking and continued on to the house. She had no intention of saying anything to anyone—not that the spiteful young girl didn't deserve to be censured. In fact, Emily was so much like her father, Beth would probably have been doing young Robert a service by telling Stephen. But whatever these Carringtons did with their own was no concern of hers.

Beth had just finished preparing herself for bed when Michael came into the room.

"Hi," he said, "I'm sorry I missed our card game. I thought I'd be able to get away sooner."

She wondered what business matters could keep him so late, and for a fleeting moment, the thought of him being with a woman flickered through her mind—not that it mattered to her if he had been.

"What have you been up to all day?" he asked, tossing aside his suit coat.

"I can't remember ever being so bored, Michael. I'm used to a busy day. For the past year I've devoted all my time to raising money, at the expense of losing freight contracts. Now that capital is no longer a problem, it's time to work on profits for a change: perhaps land a government contract to ship beef or army supplies. We have a direct link with the Union Pacific, and I want to approach the Santa Fe, too. If they ever finish their trunk to California, we should be able to work out some arrangements. But I feel so frustrated—I feel like my hands are tied."

"Why don't you set up an office and hire yourself a couple of good salesmen?"

"I can hardly compete with the Lone Star right here in Dallas, Michael—especially when the hub of the Rocky Mountain Central is located in Denver."

"Then we'll have to figure something out, won't we? Tell me, did you finish that novel you were reading?"

"Why are you changing the subject?" she asked, exasperated.

"We have quite an extensive library, Beth. I'm sure if you peruse it, you'll find something you'd enjoy reading."

She took a deep breath. He had no intention of cooperating with her on this issue. "Michael, as much as I enjoy a good novel, it's a rare pastime for me. I'm used to an active day. I assume this forced inactivity is part of your scheme to make me miserable?"

"As a matter of fact, I worked late finishing up business today so that we can go to the ranch tomorrow for a few days."

Beth felt a rush of joy tinged with guilt for misjudging him. "Oh, it will feel so good to get back to the Roundhouse!"

"I mean my ranch—La Paloma."

Her soaring spirits made a 180-degree turn and plummeted straight down. "Oh."

Later, as Beth lay in bed, she was glad that at least she'd be out of this houseful of detestable people.

Chapter 15

The melancholy Beth had felt started to dissipate once she was out under a bright blue sky. It made her realize how much her attitude had begun to affect how she viewed the world. She'd gone into this arrangement with her eyes open, and if she continued to walk around hostile and disagreeable, even to Michael, she'd most likely become a bitter, disgruntled old woman. So, she vowed, even though she virtually was at the mercy of Michael's whims, she'd try to make the best of the situation for the sake of her own well-being.

As she stole a sidelong glance at him, he turned his head and winked at her. She glanced at him again, uncertain of what to make of his jovial mood. With a light flick to the reins, the devil's disciple began to whistle!

The ranch was about twenty miles north of Dallas on the other side of the Trinity River. Since Beth was used to the spectacle of the Rockies, the land appeared flat and uninspiring to her.

"The ranch is large, but as you can see, we don't run many cattle," Michael said as they drove past a small herd grazing on grama grass. "Not enough to need any ranch hands like we once did. Horses are my real love—particularly a beautiful pair of

Arabians called Solomon and Sheba. Wait until you see them. A married couple, Slim and Martha Slocum, live in a separate house and maintain the ranch. Martha does the cooking for me when I visit."

"So this is where the mighty mogul escapes to in his spare time," she said in a light, teasing tone.

"I guess you could say that. This was my home when I was growing up. Since my father died, business has kept me elsewhere." A note of wistfulness had crept into his voice, and she sensed his yearning—she felt the same about the Roundhouse.

"Did your father like ranching?"

"I doubt my father liked anything."

Beth turned her head and looked at him. He appeared to be deep in whatever dark thoughts he kept sheltered behind that friendly smile of his. She wasn't even sure Michael was aware he'd said it; but she hadn't imagined the note of resentment in his tone. If Michael harbored any bitterness toward his father, why had he resorted to such extreme means to accomplish his father's deathbed request for revenge? Half of what he'd said and done was contradictory to his threats. She just couldn't understand him. But she knew if she didn't try, she'd never win the battle of wills between them.

The ranch house was smaller than she'd expected it to be. In addition to the main house, there were several scattered outbuildings, a huge barn, and a fenced corral, where a half-dozen grazing horses raised their heads and stared with curiosity as they rode past.

Slim and Martha Slocum were at the hitching post waiting to greet them. There was nothing to distinguish Slim Slocum from most of the other ranch hands she'd seen through the years. He was lean, with skin that looked as tough as leather from years of sun and wind. His wife, Martha, was as thin as her husband, and the years of hard living under the gruelling conditions of ranch life had not been kind to her, either. Her once-dark hair had faded to gray, and she looked older than the fifty-five years that Michael had told her was the house-keeper's age.

But what readily distinguished the Slocums from the other Carrington hired help—well, maybe she could cut Robert a little slack, but he was the only exception—was their warm, welcoming smiles.

With tears misting her faded eyes, Martha hugged Michael and kissed him on the cheek. "I'm so happy for you, Jake." Then her smile turned on Beth. "And such a beautiful bride. Welcome to La Paloma, Mrs. Carrington."

Beth wanted to fling herself into the woman's arms. She could feel their comfort without even touching her. "Thank you, Martha. And please, call me Beth."

Slim had stood back, grinning. After shaking hands and offering his congratulations to Michael, he doffed his hat, revealing thinning salt-and-pepper hair.

"I'm mighty happy to meet you, ma'am. 'Bout time Jake got himself hitched up. If you don't mind me sayin' so, I'd say to a right purty woman, too."

"Thank you for the compliment, Slim."

"Sorry that I've not cleaned up, ma'am, but I just rode in. Been out roundin' up strays."

"I understand, Slim. I was raised on a ranch."

"Well, I'll be durned!" Slim grinned at Michael. "You got yerself a mighty fine woman here, Jake. Always was afraid you'd up and marry one of 'em highfalutin city gals. I'm proud of you, son."

"You stop that chawin', Slim, and let them get

settled in," Martha declared. "Make yerself useful and unhitch that team."

"Now you know who's really running this ranch," Michael whispered.

He swept Beth up in his arms. "Welcome to our home, my love. I believe this is customary," he said as he carried her across the threshold.

Once inside, he set her down. "Take a look around while I get the luggage."

Beth walked from room to room, examining the house. There was a large kitchen, two bedrooms that were clean and cozy, and a mammoth room which appeared to serve as a parlor, sitting room, and den. There was no formal dining room. An inside bathroom appeared to be an addition to the original structure.

A scattering of unique woven rugs and wall hangings gave the place a comfortable atmosphere that was soothing to the eyes and mind. Beth liked it, even though it was a far cry from the large house she'd been raised in and certainly wasn't what she'd have expected the affluent Michael Carrington to call home.

As soon as he finished depositing their luggage in one of the bedrooms, he took her hand and insisted she come with him to the barn to see his horses.

Two golden Arabians immediately attracted her eye. She'd never seen such a beautiful color. As soon as Michael approached one of the stalls, the animal began to neigh and stomp in excitement.

"Glad to see you, too, Solomon," Michael cooed, patting the horse's neck. When the horse in the next stall started to thump against the wall, Michael shifted over to it. "Relax, Sheba, you're still the only woman in my life." He turned his head to

Beth and grinned. "Sheba is very jealous of other females."

Beth stood back and watched the reunion between Michael and the horse. Unlike her sister Angie, Beth had never allowed herself to grow too fond of a horse after she'd outgrown her first pony. Of course, since her return from college, she barely rode anymore.

"Come on over here, Beth, and meet these two."

"They're beautiful, Michael," she said. "How long have you had them?"

"They were a graduation gift from my grandmother. Solomon was just a colt and Sheba a filly when I got them. I'll be shipping them up to the Roundhouse soon."

"The Roundhouse?" she asked, astonished.

"When we were up there, I spoke to Giff about buying them."

"Why would you sell them? You're obviously very attached to those horses."

"I'll be selling the ranch, too, as soon as my lawyer finds a buyer."

"But you said this was your real home."

"It is, but I need the money, so I'm disposing of whatever assets I can—except my Lone Star stock, of course."

The revelation surprised her—although considering the dollars involved, she should have expected it. "I don't doubt that. I have a pretty good idea what it must have cost you to buy up all the Rocky Mountain's notes."

He shrugged casually. "I've a Midas touch, Beth. I'll just have to start all over."

She gave him a long look. "Was it worth it, Michael?"

"What do you mean?"

"Your mission of revenge. It appears to have cost

you a great deal more than just money."

She left him and went back to the house to unpack.

Later that evening, Beth suggested a game of Truth and Jeopardy. When they faced each other across the card table, her pair of aces beat his pair of jacks.

"Most likely, my jeopardy will be walking barefoot across a bed of hot coals."

"I'm not putting you in jeopardy, Michael. I've decided on a truth question."

He laughed nervously. "Maybe I'd be better off with that bed of coals."

"It's not your choice to make, remember?"

"All right, what is it?"

"No doubt you love your father, or you wouldn't have honored his final request. But I want to know: did you *like* him?"

At first he looked shocked, then his face contorted with anger. "What kind of damn question is that?" Then he strode out of the room.

She was in control of her railroad again.

An hour later, he still hadn't returned. Beth knew Martha had left after dinner, so he couldn't be visiting with her. She told herself she couldn't care less if Michael was angry with her, but soon her curiosity won over indifference.

Beth went outside. With three-quarters of the moon concealed behind dark clouds, the night was nearly pitch black, but she saw a faint glow from the barn. By the light of the lantern inside, she saw that Solomon's stall was empty.

Was Michael's mood so black he'd endanger his own life and that of a valuable horse to ride off recklessly through the night? Beth had taken less than a dozen steps outside the barn when the sound of pounding hooves caused her to turn her head in alarm. The golden blur of Solomon's huge body was bearing down on her. Apparently Michael didn't see her. Her petrified scream caused him to rein up, and dust flew in all directions as he brought the powerful horse to a halt, so close she could feel the heat of the animal's panting breath on her face.

Almost instantly Michael's fingers bit into her flesh as he grasped her shoulders. "Good God, are you trying to get yourself killed, woman?"

In fright, she lashed out defiantly. "One of us is!" Her legs were still trembling.

"What are you doing out here at this hour of the night?" he demanded.

"Taking a walk—or do I have to get your permission?"

She started to walk away, but he grabbed her arm and pulled her back. "I asked you what you were doing out here."

She had no intention of tolerating any more of his bad mood. "Go to hell, Mic—"

He crushed her lips with his hard mouth. The kiss was punishing in its intent, and she whimpered under the pressure of it as his arms shackled hers in an embrace so tight she could feel the heat of his body course through her as if they were joined. Her head began whirling, and she felt the strength drain out of her. With a final desperate effort, she wrenched free, shaking with fury.

"I warned you what I'd do if you didn't curb that foul temper of yours," he declared.

"How dare you speak of my temper! Do you think I'll tolerate your hurting me—punishing me—whenever you don't like what I do or say?" Her retort came in ragged spurts of unleashed rage. "In truth, *you're* the one in a foul temper. I'll not allow myself to be mauled by your brutishness again. I'll leave here the next time it happens, Michael."

"So your word means nothing."

"I kept my word; I married you. And I intended to live up to my part of that bargain—but not under these circumstances."

"You understood I intended to kiss you when I chose. I made that clear to you before the wedding."

"But I did not agree to allow you to brutalize me. You want to hurt me—punish me—with your kisses."

"Do you intend to renege on the card game, too? We both agreed the game would continue until we mutually agree to end it. So the game's not over, Beth."

"Yes, it is, unless your behavior changes. Touch me in anger like that again, and I'll leave you. And yes, Michael, I'll take my stock with me. Now if I were you, I'd take care of that horse you rode so recklessly—or do you treat dumb animals as irresponsibly as you always did women?"

"For someone who claims to be over the past, you spend a lot of time dwelling on it."

"That's the pot calling the kettle black. What's the matter, *Jake*—don't you like this reminder of just how low you're capable of sinking? You and I are all about revenge, aren't we? So I'm getting mine by reminding you what a real bastard you were then and are now. That sword you're wielding is double-edged, Sir Lancelot—so don't be surprised if you cut yourself on it."

This time he didn't try to stop her when she walked away.

Michael knew he'd been wrong. He hadn't intended to mistreat her—punish her—as she had ac-

cused. But Good Lord, he'd almost run her down,
and it had frightened him as much as her. He'd
been angry with himself, but he supposed he'd
tried to push the blame on her rather than on himself. Naturally, being Beth, she didn't cower. She'd
almost been trampled, yet she still had the grit to
stand up to him. He could see that neither of them
would yield easily—yet the day was coming when
one of them would have to.

After taking care of Solomon, Michael went back
to the house. The bedroom was dark when he entered, and he moved about as quietly as possible.
When he finally settled down beside her, Michael
asked softly, "Beth, are you awake?"

"Yes."

"I'm sorry. I was angry and I guess . . . My action
tonight was wrong, and for that I apologize. Whatever you think of me—or my motives—please believe I'd never physically hurt you, Beth. That has
never been my intent. In truth—"

"What *is* the truth, Michael? I guess that's what
I really want, more than an apology."

"The truth is I wasn't angry with you—I was
angry with myself. I could have killed you out
there in the dark—and I reacted like a . . . like
a—"

"An immature bully?"

"That bad, huh?"

"That bad. But I accept your apology."

"Along with my promise that I'll never kiss you
again in anger."

"I don't suppose you'd stretch that to never kiss
me again?"

"No way, lady." He rolled over and leaned over
her. "As a matter of fact, I think we should kiss
and make up right now."

She laughed. "I'm not *that* forgiving, Carrington.

You've gotten as much out of that apology as you're going to get. Now get back where you belong." She shoved him away.

Chuckling, he lay back. "You know, Beth, I like lying here in the dark talking to you. I'd rather be doing something else, but I'm a patient man."

"Go to sleep, Michael." Her voice vibrated with laughter.

"I don't suppose you'd be interested in another hand of poker?"

She shifted to her side, her laughter muffled against the pillow. "Go to *sleep*, Michael."

Chapter 16

Early the next morning, Beth stood at the window and watched Slim walk to the corral and fill the water trough. Several horses trotted over to drink. The simple ritual reminded her of home, and she felt the stirring of homesickness in her breast.

"Martha's niece in Fort Worth is getting married tonight," Michael said, "so they'll be leaving soon for the wedding. I told them not to worry about getting back until Monday. I hope you don't mind."

She turned around as he finished pulling on his boots. "Of course not."

"That puts us on our own. I've never thought to ask—can you cook?"

"Certainly I can cook. Middy's so demanding, we've never been able to keep a cook more than two weeks at the Roundhouse. So we all learned how." She turned back to the window. "Looks like the gods are smiling upon Martha's niece; it's a beautiful day for a wedding."

"Beautiful day for a ride, too. How about it? I'll saddle Sheba for you."

"I didn't bring a riding skirt."

"Hell, Beth, this is Texas. We aren't riding to

hounds in Virginia. I'm sure Martha can dig out some old Levi's for you to wear."

"Would it be proper for the wife of Michael Carrington to wear Levi's? I'm sure it would raise a few eyebrows in Dallas."

He gave her a devilish grin. "All the more reason, isn't it, Mrs. Carrington?"

Beth grinned at the thought of how much those long-nosed Dallas biddies like Caroline Bennett and Patricia Walters would disapprove. "Get me the pants, Michael."

"Why don't we make a day of it and have a picnic?"

She laughed in delight. "I can't remember the last time I went picnicking."

"Then it's high time to go on one. I'll have Martha pack us a basket before she leaves."

As he hurried off, Beth couldn't believe she had actually agreed to a picnic with just the two of them. One would think he was courting her—or trying to seduce her! Maybe it would be wiser not to go. She was beginning to lower her weapons around him. She had to admit that lying beside him in the dark and talking last night had not been unpleasant. In fact, he had made her laugh. Oh, he was good! "And conniving enough to charm the skin off a snake!" she warned herself.

Michael was back before she had time to think of an excuse to call off the ride. "What did I tell you? Martha never throws out anything. Here's a couple of shirts and pairs of jeans that I wore when I was younger." He handed her several folded garments smelling of cedar, then followed her into the bedroom and sat down on the edge of the bed.

She pulled off her gown and stripped down to her combination. The first pair of Levi's was too short in the leg and too tight in her loin area.

"You have long legs, Beth."

"Thank you for that observation, Michael. I hadn't noticed."

"I sure have!"

"Is that good or bad?"

"Bad," he said. She felt a pang of disappointment until he added, "Because you always keep them hidden under a long gown."

The compliment pleased her, but she gave him a suffering look just the same. The second pair of jeans was longer and felt quite comfortable. "I guess these will do." Both shirts she tried on were too small. "How old were you when you wore these?"

"Twelve or thirteen."

"Too bad I'm not twelve or thirteen; they'd have fitted me."

"I prefer you the way you are now." He ducked when she threw the shirts at him.

Beth went to the dresser and found a white bodice free of any ruffles or frills. Donning it, she rolled the sleeves up to her elbows and tucked the blouse into the pants.

Michael went to the wardrobe and came back with her boots. "Sit down. I'll do this."

She sat on the edge of the bed while he knelt on one knee to put the boots on her. It gave her a funny feeling in her chest to see him kneeling at her feet, his dark head bent over intently as he worked the boots onto her feet.

He stood up, pulled her to her feet, then grabbed her hat from the clothespole in the corner and plopped it on her head. "There, now you're ready," he said, apparently pleased.

"And to think I couldn't have done it without you," she murmured drolly as she walked ahead of him out of the room. She turned abruptly when he gave her a swat on her rear.

"I beg your pardon!" she declared with a haughty glare.

"Just couldn't resist it, Beth. That little derriere of yours looks mighty pert in those pants."

"And I imagine you've done extensive research on pert derrieres, Michael?"

"Only yours, honey. I've memorized it in detail."

She gave him a backward glance, then walked away with an exaggerated wiggle of her hips.

She hadn't been wrong about the weather; they couldn't have asked for a better day for a ride, Beth thought as they toured the ranch. Sunny and pleasant, it was warm enough not to require a jacket.

Late in the afternoon, they spread out a blanket to eat the lunch Martha had packed for them. After they'd finished, Michael produced a deck of cards.

"Are you ready for a card game?"

"Of course. I have every intention of getting back as much of the stock as possible."

He dealt the hand, and after the fourth card, she had nothing higher than a nine. His hand was showing a jack, ace, and a nine also, so she threw in her hand, and he had to redeal. This time she won with three kings.

Grimacing, he shook his head. "If I hadn't dealt, I'd swear you were cheating me somehow."

"I believe there's an axiom about being lucky at gambling and unlucky at love."

"So what have you got up your sleeve this time?" he asked.

"A truth question—a simple one—so you can wipe that frown off your face, Michael."

He folded his arms across his chest. "Okay, let's hear it."

"The night we were married, did we become intimate in the hayloft?"

"What do you mean by intimate?"

"You never questioned what I meant by it before."

He gave her a long look. "Didn't I tell you that I thought a kiss could be very intimate?"

"Well, did you do more than kiss me?" she asked. "Remember, you're required to give me an honest answer or you lose the share of stock permanently."

"It *was* our wedding night. Are you asking if we consummated our marriage, Mrs. Carrington?"

"Dammit, Michael, you know exactly what I'm asking!"

He tapped his chin as if in deep thought. "Now let me see: we showered together, we kissed, and then we went up to the hayloft . . . and—"

"And what?" she asked apprehensively. "What happened then?"

"And then we fell asleep."

"You mean nothing—"

"*Happened*," he said.

Beth sighed in relief. "Couldn't you have told me that from the beginning?"

"What! And spoil the pleasure of watching you fret about it? Not on your life, lady." He handed her the deck of cards. "Your deal."

He threw in the next hand, and she did the one that followed.

"We should think about riding back—it'll soon be dark," he said. "We can continue this later." Gathering up the deck of cards, he walked back and put them in his saddlebags. Turning around, he froze on the spot. "Beth, don't move. There's a rattler right behind you."

Her heart began thumping madly, and her first

impulse was to bolt, but she knew better. "Where
. . . where is it?"

"You're doing fine, honey. Just don't move," he
warned, and removed his rifle from its sheath.

Oh, how she wanted to turn her head and see
for herself! She was breathing so rapidly, she
thought she'd black out.

"You're between me and the snake, so I can't get
off a clear shot."

"What are you going to do?"

"I'm going to try and divert its attention before
I take the shot."

"You mean to yourself?" She could barely speak.

He cocked the rifle, and when he stepped to the
side, she heard the telltale rattle behind her. She
closed her eyes, waiting to feel the fangs sink into
her. The rifle blast was deafening, and when she
opened her eyes, the remains of the snake's body
lay at her side, so near she could touch it.

Michael was sitting on the ground, clutching his
left leg. "Dammit! It got me in the leg!" He picked
up a stick, yanked off his bandanna, and made a
tourniquet right below his knee. "Beth, you've got
to get the poison out."

"Do you have a knife?"

"There's one in my saddlebags. Bring the flask
of whiskey, too."

"Whatever you do, don't move," she warned.
"You don't want that poison to spread quickly."

Riffling speedily through the bags, she found
what she was looking for, then rushed back to him.

"Lie down. I can work better that way."

"Under any other circumstances, those words
would be music to my ears." He shifted onto his
back, and she pulled off his boot and slit the seam
of his pants, grimacing when she saw the ugly fang
marks in his calf. After pouring whiskey over the

point of the knife, Beth took a deep breath and cut an X across the puncture.

"Bet you enjoy using that knife on me," he murmured through gritted teeth.

She lowered her head and sucked out the poison. Then, after spitting out the blood and venom, she wiped off her mouth with the back of her hand. "*What* are you talking about?"

"This was your chance to get free of me," he said, flinching as she poured some whiskey into the wound. "You had an opportunity to become a rich widow, and you let it slip through your fingers. All you had to do was ride off and let me try to fend for myself."

He didn't sound like he was joking, and Beth was shocked. "I don't wish you dead, Michael." She tied her bandanna around his leg.

"If you think this will make a difference, you're wrong. I'm grateful to you for saving my life, Beth, but I won't let you go. You should've left me to die."

She stood up and looked down at him sadly. "Some of us do have consciences, Michael."

After removing the saddlebags and the rifle sheath, Beth unsaddled the horses. In addition to the blanket and deck of cards, she found a poncho and box of shells in the saddlebags. When she finished, Michael had removed the tourniquet and was leaning against a tree.

Beth spread out the poncho. "You'd be better off on this, Michael."

He shifted over and lay back. She could tell he had begun to feel the effects of the snakebite: perspiration dotted his brow, and his eyes had lost their luster.

"Looks like we're stuck here for the night," he said, "unless you want to go back to the house and hitch up a wagon. There's still enough daylight left for you to make it there and back."

"We're better off right here. We've got two canteens of water to get us through the night. You'll probably run a fever, but I think we caught most of the poison, Michael."

"There's a bottle of febrifuge at the house. Martha calls it snake oil, but it's actually a good antipyretic for fighting fevers."

"I'm not leaving you alone, Michael. I doubt you'll be conscious for much longer."

"I can stay awake until you get back."

"I'm not going to argue, either, so you might as well relax."

"Where'd you learn so much about snakebite, Beth?" His voice was starting to fade.

"One day when I was eleven, I rode out and got lost. Daddy was beside himself by the time they found me. The next week, he, Giff, and Buck Gifford, who was the ranch foreman, took me and my sisters out camping for a week. They taught us every survival skill they could think of: how to tell direction by the moss on the trees during the day and by the stars at night. What to do if bitten by a snake or encountering a wild animal. How to shoot a rifle and care for your mount. What you can eat for survival, and what will poison you or make you ill. I've forgotten most of it, because I've never had to draw on it . . . until today."

"Guess I owe your father a thank-you."

She thought resentfully about his vicious accusation against her father. "No, you owe him an apology, Michael. My father was the finest and most honorable man I've ever known." She stood up and brushed herself off. "I'd better gather some firewood before it gets too dark."

Beth made several trips to accumulate enough

wood to get them through the night. Michael had drifted off to sleep, and by the time she had a fire built, twilight had slipped into darkness. Beth gathered Michael's rifle and the canteens together, then sat down beside him and leaned against the saddle.

She put a hand on his brow and discovered he was feverish, so she covered him with the blanket and put a wet bandanna on his forehead. It was the only thing she could do to try to make him more comfortable. During her vigil through the night, she remembered enough from her earlier training to gauge the time by reading the stars as she continued changing the bandanna on his forehead and feeding the fire. Michael kept slipping in and out of sleep, and whenever he woke, even though he wasn't lucid, she'd force him to drink some water. Toward dawn, she dozed off and was wakened by chirping birds and bright sunshine.

Guiltily she felt his brow. Though pallor had lightened his dark tan, his fever had broken—which meant she had succeeded in getting out the worst of the poison. She checked the wound, and it showed no sign of infection.

"Guess I'm gonna live, Doc," he said.

"How are you feeling?" she asked, handing him a canteen.

"Like I've been kicked in the head by a horse." He shifted to a sitting position, and she moved his saddle for him to lean against.

"Do you think you can stay alone while I ride back to the ranch to get a wagon?"

"I can ride," he said.

"You'd be better off resting a little longer and getting something to eat to restore your strength."

"Let's just get back to the ranch. I can rest there. I don't even have a fever, so I'll be fine."

"Well, just sit still while I clean up here," she ordered.

Beth drenched the ashes and kicked dirt over them. After saddling up their mounts, she packed the blanket and poncho away and gathered up the rifle and canteens. Then she led Solomon over to Michael and helped him to his feet. He was stronger than she had anticipated, and within minutes they were on their way back to the house. By the time they reached their destination, the ride appeared to have helped him: the color had returned to his face and the luster to his eyes.

Dismounting at the hitching post in front of the house, Michael glanced at the barn. "That's odd. I'm sure I closed that door when we left."

"You go inside the house; I'll take care of the horses," Beth said. She took Solomon's reins and rode to the trough. Unsaddling the Arabians, she let them drink, then led them to their stalls.

The barn door suddenly banged shut, startling her. Shadows bathed the interior, and feeling edgy, she wished she'd taken the time to open both doors. She quickly tossed hay into the stalls, and started to hurry away. Then she suddenly drew up, shocked, unaware of the scream that burst from her throat.

Chapter 17

$\sim\!\!\sim\!\!\varsigma\!\!\varsigma\!\!\infty\!\!\sim$

Michael knew he should take another day to recuperate, but he didn't want to go to bed. Besides, if he isolated himself in the bed, Beth might seek her own privacy in the other bedroom. And he didn't want that. He enjoyed her company. Her constant challenge of him was stimulating and more effective than any rest would be. But he did have to get out of his ragged Levi's, so he headed for the bedroom.

"What the hell!" he exclaimed, stopping in surprise at the doorway. The pillows had been slashed, and there was goose down scattered over everything. He checked the other bedroom, and it was in the same condition. He couldn't imagine who would commit such vandalism. Sure, at times kids might shove over the outhouse or release the chickens from the coop; he had done as much when he was a youngster. But no one had ever invaded the house to do any destruction.

Just as he went outside to check the coop, he heard Beth scream. Hurrying to the barn as fast as his injured leg permitted, he shoved the doors wide open.

"Beth!" he shouted. He saw her at the rear of the

barn and rushed to her side. "Beth, what happened?"

She pointed to the far corner. "Somebody has a sick sense of humor, Michael." He looked and saw what had frightened her: a burlap sack stuffed with straw had been formed into a scarecrow. Wearing her dress and hat, it hung by a rope from the rafters. Disgusted, he cut it down.

"Who'd do such a thing? It scared the life out of me."

"Obviously some vandals. They got into the house, too. Let's get out of here."

They checked the Slocums' house and then the chicken coop. Both places appeared untouched.

"It's strange that nothing in the house has been disturbed except for the pillows in these bedrooms," he said, when they returned to the house. "I suppose it could have been worse."

"It seems personal, to me." Beth shivered.

"Good Lord, Beth, it was most likely a couple of kids being mischievous," Michael scoffed

"Who obviously hold little regard for my taste in bonnets." She smiled, but it didn't reach her eyes. "You sit down and rest, Michael. I'm an expert at cleaning up feathers. Through the years, my sisters and I have had more pillow fights than I can count."

He headed for the kitchen. "I'll get you a broom and put on a pot of coffee."

It took Beth almost an hour to clean up the rooms, and after finishing the task, she went into the kitchen to find Michael sitting at the table. He looked drawn. "It's time you got to bed; you *are* recovering from a snakebite."

"All right. I'll lie down, but not for long."

The fact that he agreed so readily made it clear to Beth that he was still suffering the effects of the bite. He was asleep before his head even hit the pillow.

Beth had bathed and had a light supper started when Michael awoke.

"I found some bandaging. As soon as you clean up, I'll put a fresh dressing on that bite so it doesn't become infected."

"I'm a fast healer, Beth."

"Just the same, I'll take a look. In the meantime, the water's hot, and I hope you like omelettes, because that's what we're having for supper."

"Sounds good to me. Come to think of it, I'm hungry."

"Then get moving."

She sliced strips of smoked ham, and had chopped up peppers and onions by the time Michael rejoined her. The bath and change of clothing appeared to have lifted his spirits, and it was hard for her to believe that only twenty-four hours earlier he'd been flat on his back, fighting a fever.

"How about a game of cards?" he asked, when they finished the meal.

"I shouldn't take advantage of your condition," she teased, "but on the other hand, I'd be a fool to turn down the opportunity. We won't play too long, though—you need rest."

It was after eight o'clock by the time she finished cleaning up the dishes and they sat down for their game. When Michael's pair of tens and fours beat out her pair of aces, he leaned back in his chair, grinning.

"I came here prepared for this win." He went to the dresser and pulled a package out of a drawer. "You're in jeopardy, honey. I want you to wear only this for the rest of the evening." The package contained a red silk combination. "It's much more attractive than those white cotton ones that you wear."

Beth held up the flimsy garment, appalled. "Michael, you can see through this!"

"All the better to see you, Little Red Riding Hood."

"Michael!"

"You have a lovely body, Beth. It's wrong to cover it up with that ugly undergarment you wear. So, yes or no?" he asked. "If you chose to forfeit, I believe the controlling share of stock is mine."

She glared at him. His devilish grin was infuriating, and she was certain that was precisely what he wanted to accomplish—to get her so angry she would refuse the jeopardy. Well, she wasn't going to play right into his hands. He'd certainly reminded her enough times that he'd seen her naked, so this would just be one more time. At least she'd be wearing *some*thing! She snatched up the garment and strode into the bedroom.

She changed into the transparent lingerie and gasped, "Oh, Good Lord!" when she looked in the mirror. The garment clung to her curves like a second skin, the top cut low in front to expose a generous portion of her cleavage. The outline of her nipples was visible, and only a lacy inset at the top of the flimsy material prevented them from being bared to the eye. The pants hugged her hips, but fortunately the deep color of the material prevented a clear view of her most intimate area. She wondered how she could sit wearing it and calmly play cards while he ogled her.

On the other hand, maybe it would be enough of a distraction to prevent him from concentrating on the cards! Why not give him a double dose? She quickly pulled the pins out of her hair and brushed it so that it flowed past her shoulders. Drawing a deep breath, she went to the doorway, leaned an arm on the doorjamb, and struck a pose.

"Well, what do you think?"

Michael glanced up when she spoke, then sucked in his breath. The sight was like a punch to his innards, and he cursed himself for thinking he could remain immune to the sight of her in the sexy red garment. His gaze followed her long auburn hair flowing across her shoulders to where the garment clung to the rounded curve of her breasts. His loins knotted as he watched the mesmerizing movement of her hips when she walked barefoot across the room. Clenching his hands into fists to conceal their trembling, he was so hard he ached.

"You look lovely," he said to her.

"And what brothel did you find this in, Michael?" she asked jokingly as she took the seat opposite him.

"I bought that at a store in Dallas specializing in Parisian intimate apparel."

"The place should be reported to the authorities," she teased.

"I must get you a blue pair to match your eyes."

"My eyes! Who would know?"

"I would. Then every time I looked into them, I'd be reminded of what you were wearing under your dress."

The moment he spoke those words, Beth realized Michael hadn't exaggerated—he *was* obsessed with her. Why not turn that to her advantage? The only way he could actually make her miserable was if she opposed him, fought him—responded to his ploys to get her attention. While in truth, she tortured him with just the bat of her eyelashes or the tenderness of a smile! How could she have been blind to such an obvious fact before? It was much more than just wanting them to be intimate. Mr.

Suave and Sensuous Carrington, entrepreneur extraordinaire and millionaire with the Midas touch, was starved for her attention! For the first time in her soon to be twenty-six years, Beth savored the real meaning of power.

And it tasted delicious!

"I believe it's your deal." With a cunning smile, she pushed the deck across the table.

"What?" he asked with a leery look. "That smile is just a little too crafty for comfort."

"Michael, you remind me of a puppy I once had: it kept yanking at my skirt to get my attention."

"I might admit to wanting to yank *up* your skirt, but I'm anything but a puppy."

"Oh? And how do you see yourself?"

"More like the king of the jungle, stalking his quarry masterfully, confidently."

"Hmmm, interesting. Or maybe an ape, pounding on its chest in a mating call?" She deliberately raised both arms to push her hair back, knowing how it would stretch the sheer fabric tightly across her breasts. "Your deal, I believe?"

"Oh, of course," he said, sounding distracted. He started to shuffle the cards, then suddenly slammed down the deck. "Okay, you win. What would it cost to get you to go to bed with me?"

"We've already established that," she said calmly.

"Dammit, Beth, you know what I mean! I want you so badly, it's ridiculous to try to disguise it. What's it going to cost? And don't tell me you haven't come up with the answer."

"Sounds to me like you've got a tiger by the tail, oh king of the jungle. Is this what you consider subtle seduction?"

Michael banged his fist on the table. "Dammit,

I've paid for the privilege. I don't have to bargain with you!"

"I wondered how long it would take before you got around to that accusation," she said scornfully. "Since you're physically stronger than I am, I can hardly fight you. It will be interesting to see if you honor your word, or if you're the bastard I think you are."

Michael's face contorted with anger. "Don't push me too far, Beth." Shoving back his chair, he strode out of the room.

That night, he slept in the other bedroom.

The following morning, finding no sign of Michael in the house, Beth followed the path to the barn. She found him at Solomon's stall.

"Good morning," she said, as casually as she could manage.

"Good morning." His reply sounded just as guarded. "Solomon's edgy this morning. Sheba's in heat, so I separated them. I don't want her to foal."

She walked over and stood beside Michael. "You miss her, don't you, boy," she said gently, patting the horse's head. When Solomon responded by nuzzling her hand, she glanced at Michael. "Male animals seem so lost and forsaken without their mates."

"Yeah, they say a wolf mates forever," he said.

"I think the human animal should take notice of such an example."

"Some do. Your father never remarried when he lost his wife, did he?"

Her heart swelled. "I believe that after she died, there wasn't a day he didn't think of her. And Giff's mother died when he was born, but remarrying was never a consideration to Buck. In a way, it's very beautiful. I think every woman would like to believe that the man she loved could never love any other woman but her." *At least, I would*.

For a long moment, she gazed pensively into space and thought how wonderful it would be if she and Michael could share such a love. She sighed deeply for what never could be. "What about your father? You told me your mother died when you were young, too."

"I must have been seven or eight the first time I remember hearing my parents argue about my father's infidelities. The arguments continued until she died. After that, he made no effort to disguise his affairs."

Surprised by the bitterness in his voice, Beth turned her head. His misery was so clear that she felt genuine sympathy for him.

To lighten the mood, she said spiritedly, "I think this day is too beautiful for such dismal remembrances. How are you feeling today, Carrington? Back to your cantankerous self?"

Picking up a handful of hay, she threw it at him and tried to dash out of his reach. Michael was too fast for her; he grabbed her arm, and they went tumbling into a pile of hay. Beth came up with a handful and tossed it in his face, then quickly crawled out of his grasp when he released her to dust it off.

"Oh, no, you don't," he said. Grabbing her leg, he pulled her back to him on her stomach, then flipped her onto her back. "You started this, lady— now you're gonna say you're sorry or eat some of this hay."

"Never," she shouted through her laughter.

She came up with another handful and dumped it over his head. Then, squealing, she succeeded in evading his outstretched arm and squirmed away on her back. He dove after her and trapped her under the weight of his body. They rolled together in the haystack, laughing and taunting each other, but Beth's game struggle was no match against Michael's physical advantage, and he managed to pin her beneath him.

Beth was not about to concede defeat, and managed to keep bombarding him with hay until Michael succeeded in pinioning her arms above her head in the firm grasp of one hand. Picking up a handful of hay, he held it threateningly above her face.

"Now tell me you yield, my lady," he warned.

"Never!" she shrieked laughingly as he slowly dropped strands of the hay on her face. She twisted her head from side to side to try to avoid them. "I'm going to sneeze in your face if you don't stop!"

"Do you yield?"

"All right."

"All right *what*, my lady?"

"I yield, I yield!" Laughter bubbled forth from her eyes and voice.

Her laughter died when the amusement in his eyes was replaced by naked desire. After a silence that seemed to go on for an eternity, he said in a husky voice, "Oh, Lord, Rusty, I want you."

She felt a tingling in the pit of her stomach and suddenly became aware of every place their bodies touched. Her heart began to pound with excitement as she realized she wanted him, too.

"Did I not say I yield, Sir Knight?" she murmured in a tremulous whisper. Closing her eyes, she parted her lips in invitation.

At the first touch of his lips, velvet warmth spread through her body. No man's kisses had ever been able to affect her the way his did. The kiss was slow and persuasive as his mouth moved on hers with tender mastery until she was breathless.

Raising his head, he gazed into her eyes. "Can't we put aside our demons for now and take what this moment is offering us?"

Why shouldn't she? She was so tired of this endless battle. Of denying her body the pleasure she knew he could bring to it. How she wanted to lose herself in his embrace, as she once had done.

Hot blood pounded at her pulses and temples when he trailed warm, moist kisses down her neck. "Even now I can feel your body responding to mine," he murmured softly, the huskiness in his voice adding to the bombardment that his kisses were evoking. Releasing her hands, he carried one to his heart. "Feel it, Rusty. Feel what you do to me."

She breathed in tandem with the pounding beneath her fingertips, offering no resistance as his caressing hands worked at her gown, her shoes, her underclothing until she lay naked beneath his hungry perusal. She felt gloriously alive again . . . free . . . womanly—responding to his male demand with passion that had lain dormant for so long. It seemed forever since she'd known the exquisite sensation of his arousing touch on her flesh. Yet memories were a tenacious, unrelenting enemy that battered relentlessly at her mounting passion until she floundered helplessly between denying his touch and the mounting desire swelling within her that remembered the erotic thrill of it.

"Your body's like satin, Beth," he whispered in her ear. "Smooth satin, meant to be stroked . . . caressed."

Closing her eyes, she gave up the fight and surrendered to sensation, allowing herself to drown in the sweet passion washing through her. As his hands and mouth began to reacquaint themselves with the most sensitive areas of her body, all thought of resistance shattered, and with shaking hands she helped him disrobe in her rush to feel his nakedness against her own.

She was wrong to think they were no longer those two people who had explored and charted one another's bodies that long-ago day—for each immediately sought the well-remembered pleasure spots of the other. With touch, kisses, and words of endearment, he aroused her to the glorious heights of that never-forgotten weekend. In uninhibited response, she murmured erotic words of encouragement and elicited his groans of pleasure.

They both intentionally stretched out the moment to the ultimate limit, neither wanting to relinquish one stroke, one kiss, one precious second of the renewed union, certain the splendor of climax would be even more glorious then before—but knowing full well that once it was reached, they would return to the reality of two people in conflict.

"It's incredible how you managed to restrain such passion for so long," Michael said later, as they lay side by side.

"You can take credit for that, Michael. My experience with you taught me not to believe a man's sweet words. I learned they weren't coming from the heart but a completely different organ."

He rolled onto his side and propped up his head in his hand, then began to idly pick strands of straw out of her hair. "If you believe that, then how do you explain what just happened between us?"

"Maybe women don't always think with their brains, either." She sat up and grabbed her underwear.

"I admit I'm fascinated by you, Beth. I can't resist

you. When are you going to admit you feel the same about me?"

She dared not admit it. It would be an admission that she'd accept a relationship that brought no emotional commitment to their bed. Without that, they'd never really have a marriage.

"I'd never settle for anything that shallow. I just wanted you to see the woman within me—the wife you could have had. Things could have been so different if you'd come to me with love in your heart, instead of revenge."

"No matter what you say, you know this will happen again."

"Not if I can help it."

He gently pulled her back and leaned over her, his mouth so close their breaths mingled. "But that's the wonder of the attraction between us, Rusty. Neither of us can resist it," he murmured, just before his lips claimed hers.

Once again she found herself gripped in a heat of passion. Each kiss lengthened, deepened, grew more arousing. A groan of ecstasy slipped past her lips when he took the swollen bud of her breast into his mouth, and the garment she clutched slipped through her fingers as she wound her arms around his neck.

Chapter 18

~~~ ᧰᧲ ~~~

Bright sunshine had brought a radiant warmth to the day when they left the barn.

"How about a swim?" Michael suggested. "I think we both could use a quick cleaning off. There's a great swimming hole nearby, and the water's not real cold."

"Aren't the Slocums due to get back soon?"

"We've got plenty of time. They won't make it back for a couple of hours yet."

They stopped at the house to grab a blanket and towels, then walked the short distance to where the pool was centered in a copse of oak and cottonwood.

Stealing a glance at him as he stripped off his clothing, Beth had to admit that Michael had a beautifully proportioned body: broad shoulders, slim hips, and long, muscular legs. Leery of the water temperature, she kept on her combination.

Michael dived into the water, and his head bobbed back up as he trod water. "Come on in; the water's great."

She tested the water with her toe. "It's cold!"

"It doesn't feel cold once you're in. I see you're back to wearing that ugly white underwear."

She grinned. "I'm saving the red one for our card

190

games. I intend to use the distraction to my advantage."

"You're pretty confident, aren't you?"

"Try to deny it if you can, Michael," she taunted, diving into the pool.

The water felt refreshing and cleansing after their torrid lovemaking in the hay. She lounged in its coolness, enjoying the relaxation. Michael preferred a vigorous swim, and she wondered where he got his energy, considering the events of the last couple of days.

He disappeared under the water and came up grabbing her around the waist. Despite the cool water, his lips were warm as he pulled her against him and kissed her.

"Don't you ever tire?" she asked breathlessly as he took her arms and slipped them around his neck.

"Not that I remember." Treading water, he kissed her again.

"I thought the purpose of this swim was to cool off, Michael," she said, as he trailed kisses along her neck.

"Hmmm. It would appear that's exactly what *you* did." He released her, and Beth swam back and climbed out of the water. Michael followed and sat down on the blanket beside her, where they dried off. "Feel better now?"

"Yes, it was very refreshing. We have a great swimming hole on the Roundhouse, too." She gave him a smug smile. "*It* has a waterfall."

"I think I know the spot you're referring to. I remember seeing a waterfall a little off the road near the depot. Is that it?"

"Yes, that's the one. The water's cool, but we've all gotten used to it through the years." Her voice was heavy with nostalgia. "My sisters, Giff, and I had great times there while we were growing up. It seems like such a long time ago."

"We could go to the Roundhouse for a couple of days when we get back from St. Louis. I have to go there on business, and I want you to come with me."

Beth frowned. "Michael, I have business, too, you know. Business I've been neglecting. I'd prefer not to go with you."

"I'll compromise. I planned on staying here for a week, but we'll go back to Dallas tomorrow, instead. You can check with Dave and take care of any business the following day. Then we'll leave for St. Louis the day after that."

"That's a compromise? You make it sound as if I have nothing to say about it," she said, perturbed. "Making plans that affect me without discussing them first is extremely inconsiderate."

"I made my intentions clear before you agreed to marry me, Beth. Nothing has happened that would cause me to change my mind."

It was clear he was referring to the intimacy they shared. As he had reminded her last night, he'd paid for the privilege.

The day suddenly lost its radiance.

Slim and Martha arrived back shortly after Beth and Michael returned to the house. Their concern was evident after they heard about Michael's snakebite and the vandalism.

"Nothing like that's ever happened as long as we've been here," Slim said. "Kids around these parts usually don't do any damage. I sure don't understand it." He walked away scratching his head.

After dinner that evening, over Martha's protests, Beth insisted she help with the dishes.

"Honey, with all that's happened, you should just sit down and relax," Martha declared as Beth dried the dishes. "It's a shame your first trip to La Paloma had to be spoiled with all them bad goings on." Smiling warmly, she said, "But I knew the minute I laid eyes on you that Jake had picked the right woman for a wife. You're strong, honey, and you'll be good for him. If he'd married one of 'em pampered city gals, it would've destroyed him. No city gal could've saved him from that snakebite." She shook her head sadly. "I worried my heart out what would become of that boy," she said. "Losing his ma and all at such a young age. Now I can see an end to my worry."

Curious, Beth asked, "Martha, what was Mi . . . ah, Jake's father like?"

The woman's brow creased in a frown and her lips thinned into a grimace. "I ain't one to bad-mouth people, especially after they've passed on, but Mike Carrington wasn't the nicest of people. Reckon you could say he was a bitter man. Wasn't too much love lost between him and Jake either. Seems like the boy could never do anything right in Mike's eyes. Jake's ma was a fine woman, though. Sweet and gentle-like. I knowed it hit Jake hard when her and the twins were killed."

"Twins?" Beth almost dropped the plate she was holding.

Martha looked bewildered as she handed her a dripping-wet platter. "Seth and Amy. Jake's sister and brother."

"How did they die, Martha?" Beth asked.

"Didn't he tell you?"

"No, he only mentioned that his mother died when he was sixteen."

"Jake was away at one of them eastern schools when it happened. The twins were only twelve.

We'd had a flash flood, and Amy got caught in a dry riverbed when it hit. She wasn't the best of swimmers, and Seth tried to help her. When Laura heard their cries for help, she jumped in and tried to reach them. All three of 'em was swept away. Took us two days to find their bodies.'' Martha's eyes misted. "Poor Jake just about went crazy when they told him. If it hadn't been for his grandma, Lord knows what might have happened to the boy. His pa sure was no comfort to him." Martha pulled a handkerchief out of her apron pocket and blew her nose. "But they say every blow makes you stronger. If that's so, I reckon Jake's 'bout as strong as Samson now." She smiled and patted Beth's arm. " 'Bout time that he finally gets the happiness that's coming to him. You got a fine man, honey."

As much as the tragic death of his mother and siblings had moved her, Beth had difficulty seeing the boy Martha described in the manipulative, self-serving, domineering man she'd married. A dozen questions flashed through her mind. Was he two people in one? Did he show a darker side to her than he presented to others? How else could he elicit these fierce loyalties from people—even her own family members. One couldn't go through life fooling people all the time. Which side of him was the real Michael Carrington?

When they finished in the kitchen, Martha said good night and went back to her house. Michael had disappeared right after dinner, and Beth wandered outside in search of him. Since Solomon's stall was empty, she knew Michael had gone for a ride.

He'd seemed unusually solemn at dinner, and she thought that perhaps the events of the past few days were finally catching up with him emotionally.

The stars looked close enough to reach up and pluck one out of the sky. With the night too pleasant to waste sitting in a bedroom, Beth continued to stroll. To make sure she wouldn't get lost in the dark, Beth began following what appeared to have once been the channel of a river. After a short distance, it occurred to her that this could be the same riverbed in which Michael's mother and siblings had drowned. It gave her an eerie chill, and she quickly scrambled out of the bed to higher ground. It was then that she saw Solomon's golden coat in the moonlight. Peering around, she made out the form of Michael sitting on the ground with his back against the white trunk of a tree. He hadn't shown her this part of the ranch, and it took her a moment to realize what was different about it—the birch trees. There was a ring of them, literally a circle. Birch had always been a favorite tree, and she hadn't seen any on the ranch until now.

Beth stepped closer, and the new angle revealed what had brought him to this spot: a large gravestone set in the center of a patch of bluebonnets, enclosed by a white picket fence. She didn't have to see Michael's face; his bowed head and the slump of his shoulders told her all she had to know. Not wanting to intrude, she turned to leave, just as he looked up and saw her.

"Beth! What is it?"

"Nothing. I'm sorry I disturbed you. I was taking a walk and just decided to go back to the house."

"I was thinking about returning myself. I'll go with you." He got to his feet.

While he walked over to get Solomon, Beth read the name CARRINGTON chiseled on the stone marker. Below it was carved LAURA ANN 1835–

1869, and the lowest line read SETH JAMES and AMY RACHEL 1857–1869.

"They were entombed together," Michael said, coming up to her. "I guess it was only fitting. Especially with the twins—they always were inseparable. And I'm sure my mother liked it this way, too."

"I'm sure she did," Beth said softly.

They walked in silence back to the house, Michael leading Solomon by the reins. Beth felt awkward and intrusive, at a loss for words. It was too late to offer any condolences, because the accident had happened twelve years earlier. Furthermore, he seemed exceptionally reluctant to discuss any family member—with the exception of his grandfather and grandmother.

"Michael," she said hesitantly, "did you say you intended to sell La Paloma?"

"Yeah. I got a wire from Randy Bowing, my St. Louis attorney, before we left Dallas. He's sold my house in St. Louis and said he has a potential buyer for the ranch: a sheep farmer from Australia."

She glanced at him with surprise. "Sheep!" She understood cattlemen well enough to know that the word was taboo among them.

"Yeah. I'll probably get kicked out of the Cattlemen's Association when they hear of it."

"So you've made up your mind to sell to that buyer?"

"I don't know yet, Beth," he said solemnly. "That's why I have to go to to St. Louis."

"I understand. But, Michael, it's not reasonable of you to expect me to pack up and leave every time you have to go somewhere on a business trip. I have responsibilities, too."

"I believe we've had this conversation before,

Beth. You know my feelings on the subject. I'm not repeating them."

They continued the rest of the walk in silence.

As soon as they sat down to their nightly card game, Beth brought up the subject that had been on her mind from the first time he'd mentioned it. "Michael, I don't think you should sell La Paloma. You have too many ties to this ranch."

"It's hardly something I want to do," he said tightly. "But I have to raise money as quickly as possible to finish paying off the Lone Star."

"Surely you could give your company a note without having to sell the ranch."

"I suppose I could, but I don't choose to. I can't expect the Lone Star to finance my marriage."

"Then the Rocky Mountain Central will lend you the money."

"And where will you get it?"

"I'll borrow it. We've got most of the supplies we need to finish the trunk. Whatever you end up owing your railroad the Rocky Mountain Central will loan you."

"I won't even consider it. Look, Beth, I knew what I was doing when I bought that stock. I'm prepared to make some sacrifices."

"It's one thing to sell a mansion in Colorado or a town house in St. Louis, but the La Paloma is where you grew up. You have family buried here."

"I don't need you to tell me that," he said angrily and began to pace the floor. "I'll just have to live with that knowledge." He riffled his fingers through his dark hair.

"Well, I won't! I don't wish to live with the guilt of knowing that you sold your ranch because of me."

"Why should you feel guilt? It's for damn sure this marriage wasn't your idea."

"It would still weigh on my conscience."

"That doesn't make any sense."

"I doubt the rationale of any person of conscience makes sense to you, Michael."

"Dammit it, Beth, I'm not in the mood for another verbal duel with you. I told you that I'm prepared to live with this, so let it go." He stalked out of the room.

His slamming out in anger was becoming a nightly procedure, Beth thought as she went to bed. Was he going out to ride the countryside like a tortured hero in a gothic novel again? And would he not return, like last night?

"It would appear, Michael, that the tables have turned," she said, fluffing one of the pillows Martha had replaced on the bed. "Your nights are becoming more miserable than mine."

Beth read for an hour and had just extinguished the lamp when Michael came to bed. When he rolled over and began kissing her, she said, "Michael, I have a headache."

"So have I, but I'm not going to let it interfere."

She could smell liquor on his breath, so she didn't have to guess what he'd been doing for the past hour. "I'm not in the mood for this, Michael."

"Relax and I'll get you in the mood." He slid his hand under her gown.

"Michael, I said I did not—"

His mouth cut off her words. She tried to deny the first stirring of arousal as his warm palm slid up her thigh and came to rest on the core of her sex in a stimulating massage. "Open up for me, baby. I want to sink into you, Beth—feel you tighten around me." Passion flared from the double inducements of his hands and mouth, and his erotic whispers of what he intended to do for her fueled that passion with exquisite excitement.

"This is madness, Michael," she moaned breathlessly. But she knew she was beyond the point of no return and allowed him to pull the gown over her head.

"Jake, Rusty. I want you to call me Jake when we make love. I want you to cry it out the way you did the first time we made love."

"I don't remember. It was too long ago."

"Oh, you remember, all right. And you remember this," he murmured, running his tongue down her stomach, stopping just before he reached the spot that throbbed for his touch. "Say it, Rusty," he whispered. "Tell me what you want me to do to you. Beg me like you once did." A shiver rippled her spine when he promised what he'd do for her after she did.

"You want me to believe that I have a side as dark as yours, but I don't."

"Yes, you do. Baby, you want me as much as I want you. You're so hot right now, you can't think of anything but satisfying those carnal instincts of yours, even if it is with me. But you won't admit it—that way a woman of *conscience* like you won't have to feel any guilt."

He kissed her again and again, robbing her of breath, of reason. His teeth tugged at her lips, the pulse in her neck, her hardened nipples, until her head whirled with mindless delirium as a sensual spring coiled within her, winding tighter and tighter, each twist spiraling ecstatic sensation throughout her body. She writhed beneath him, seeking fulfillment, but he raised his head and continued to deny that satisfaction to her, continued his whispered erotica. His promises raised her to a fevered pitch that bordered on sensual insanity.

"Please, Jake. *Please?* Do it! Do it!"

"Do what, Rusty? I want to hear you say it."

The words burst past her lips in an uncontrollable supplication—the earthy expression that reduced the act of love to mere physical lust. And she repeated the cry rapturously over and over again as he fulfilled his whispered promises.

Toward dawn, exhausted and entwined, they fell asleep.

Chapter 19

$\sim$$\bigcirc$$\bigcirc$$\sim$

Michael made little attempt at conversation on the ride back to Dallas the following morning, which was fine with Beth, because it gave her a chance to think about the previous night. She was mortified just thinking about her actions. Until last night, she had always believed that the sexual act was the ultimate expression of love between two people. But last night, love had never entered her mind—only physical gratification. And when they had finished, she had wept at the stark demonstration of this dark side of her nature. Unexpectedly, Michael had held her in his arms, murmuring soothing words of comfort and apology. He'd then made tender love to her, as though she were a fragile, delicate doll that would shatter if touched. Oh, he was a complicated man! She would never understand the multiple facets of his personality. He was a walking, breathing contradiction.

But hadn't last night proven she was, too?

Beth stole a sidelong glance at him. His profile was set in stony brooding. He'd been unusually quiet even before they left. What thoughts were churning through his mind?

To change the direction of her thoughts, Beth

asked, "Michael, if you sell the ranch, what will become of Slim and Martha?"

"I imagine they'll start a small ranch somewhere."

"I would think starting all over at their age would be pretty difficult for them. Especially if they don't have your Midas touch."

"I don't intend to argue about it, Beth." He returned to his brooding silence.

Neither do I, she thought—for she'd just grasped a reality that she'd denied in the past.

He'd often accused her of being a woman of passion—and last night had proven it to her as well. But suddenly she saw beyond that limited definition. Passion meant more than just sexual fervor; it meant carrying that same intensity into her feelings for him: her empathy for the grief he carried within him, the anger he raised in her, the resentment when he taunted her . . . and the love she'd felt for him from the first time he'd kissed her. This passion was all part of her being—not a reflection of a good side or a dark side, but simply that she was a woman of passion.

And the passion in that woman would never let him sell La Paloma—the ranch meant too much to him.

As soon as they reached Dallas, Michael dropped her off at the mansion and went on to his office. Fortunately, Martha's and Slim's warm good-byes were enough to sustain her through James's dour greeting, and as soon as she had disposed of her bonnet and gloves, she hurried to Rachel's room.

"How good to see you back, my dear," Rachel said, as Beth kissed her cheek.

"I missed you, too, Nana Rachel." She sat down on the floor and clasped the woman's wrinkled hand.

"And how are Martha and Slim? Did you find them both in good health?"

"They were both fine. They asked me to extend their greetings to you."

"I'd like to go back there again some day. I haven't seen La Paloma since Laura and the twins were buried." She sighed. "It's such a peaceful place."

"I'm afraid it wasn't quite so peaceful this time, Nana." By the time Beth had finished telling Rachel about Michael's snakebite and the vandalism, leaving out the effigy, the old woman's eyes were misted with tears.

"Oh, how horrible. My poor Jake." Her hands were shaking as she pressed Beth's hand to her frail breast. "And I might have lost him had it not been for you. How can I ever thank you, dear child?"

Beth had never fashioned her role as being heroic and felt the praise was unearned. "Nana Rachel, Jake was the hero there, not I. He would never have been bitten if he hadn't tried to help me."

"You are undervaluing your own courage—he would have died had you not helped him through the night," she insisted in a quavering voice.

"Madam! Madam! What has upset you?" Bertha asked, when she entered the room. Rushing to Rachel's side, the maid gave Beth an accusing glare. "What have you said to her?"

"Oh, nonsense, Bertha; I'm fine," Rachel grumbled. "And stop accusing the dear child. She has done nothing wrong."

"It is time you rest, madam," Bertha declared, making it clear she wanted Beth to leave.

Beth stood up. "I must unpack anyway, Nana Rachel. I'll see you at dinner, and if you'd like, I'll read to you before you go to bed."

A smile of pleasure lit Rachel's face. "I'd like that."

Beth paused at the doorway and looked back. Rachel was brushing aside Bertha's hands. "Saints alive, woman, will you stop that fussing! I don't need any help to get to my bed!"

Once back in her room, Beth began to unpack her clothes. She lifted out the red combination and carried it over to the chest of drawers. When she opened a drawer, a folded piece of paper lay on top of the lingerie there. She knew it had not been there the last time she'd been in the drawer.

Perplexed, she picked up the paper and unfolded it. Her eyes rounded in shock, and with mouth agape she read the words that had been cut out of a newspaper and pasted on the sheet.

get ᵒᵘᵀ or you Will be Sorry

Beth slumped down in a chair. Who would send such a message? Was it meant to be a threat, or a warning? If it was meant as a joke, it was a very grim one. No matter what the intent, it had to have been done by someone in this house. Her first instinct was to blame Stephen Carrington. He hated her enough to try driving her away. On further reflection, the childishness of it might indicate Emily was the culprit. Surely Millicent was too timid to do such a bold thing—but despite his reserve, she wouldn't put it past James.

Determined to find out who was behind the note, she slipped out of her room and walked to the stairway. Leaning over the banister, she heard Millicent speaking to Helga. Normally at this time of day Stephen would be at the office, so she went to the door of their suite and tapped on it. When there was no response, she opened the door and peeked in. The sitting room was empty, so she tiptoed across the floor, gave the bedroom a swift glance, then quickly crossed to the desk and opened the drawer. There were two stacks of stationery: one bore Millicent's monogram, the other was plain. Neither of them matched the sheet in her hand. Closing the desk drawer, she left the room, rapped on Emily's door, and when there was no answer, entered the room. Her inspection ended in the same result—the paper did not match.

Beth had just stepped out of the room when Bertha appeared in the hallway. "May I help you, Mrs. Carrington?" Bertha asked.

Quickly shoving the letter into her pocket, Beth turned around and smiled at the maid. "I'm looking for Millicent."

"Her room is the next one, Mrs. Carrington, but I believe she is downstairs in the drawing room."

"Thank you, Bertha. I'll look there."

As she walked down the stairs, the maid stood watching her. When Beth reached the foot of the stairway she glanced back up, and saw that Bertha had disappeared.

Now that she'd temporarily ruled out Stephen and his family, that left four other people with access to her room: James, Bertha, Helga, and Mary, the cook. She doubted that Mary was a suspect, since she'd never seen the woman after they'd been introduced. It might have been safe to assume that as James's wife, the cook hated her as much as the other servants did, but Mary would never have cause to go upstairs, particularly to Michael's suite. James's quarters would be the hardest to check, because if she was observed, she'd have no excuse for being in that section of the house. The same thing would be true about Bertha's and Helga's rooms. She shouldn't overlook Robert Harris, either, even though he lived above the carriage house. Since she had encountered him and Emily in a tryst, Robert had good cause to try and scare her into leaving. He might have been able to slip into the house unobserved and put the letter in her drawer.

Returning to her room, Beth paced the floor for several moments. Then she sat down, drumming her fingers on the desk. The situation called for some deep thought. If she was caught in the room of someone not involved, she'd look ridiculous. She'd just had a narrow escape as it was. Bertha could have caught her actually coming out of Emily's room. In the future she'd have to plan her movements more carefully—but she doubted there'd ever really be a good time. She'd just have to make the most of any situation when it presented itself. Beth felt exhilarated: this was actually exciting! Too bad Thia wasn't there to help her—the two of them would have had fun solving the mystery. One thing was clear to Beth: finally focusing on a serious problem felt good, requiring her to use her head for a change—instead of her body.

Business detained Michael at the office, so he did not make it home for dinner. The meal, as usual, was not the most cordial affair. Rachel and Millicent were pleasant enough, but Stephen and Emily barely spoke. Beth still refused to rule out Stephen Carrington. The man made no attempt to conceal his resentment of her. Furthermore, he could have used a sheet of paper from the office. She would have to find out from Michael if they all used the same kind, and if so, have him bring home a sheet. She glanced from Stephen to Emily. She didn't doubt either of them would like to see the last of her.

As usual, James and Helga were serving the meal—which put a thought in her mind. If she excused herself, this would be a good time to check James's room. She could go upstairs, use the rear stairway down to the kitchen, and sneak past Mary when her back was turned. The problem was that Bertha was upstairs turning down Rachel's bed for the evening. If the maid caught her sneaking around again, she'd be suspicious, and if Bertha was the guilty one, she'd know Beth was on to her. Well, it was a risk she'd have to take.

"Would you please excuse me for a moment?" Beth said, rising.

"Of course, dear," Rachel said. "You'll be back to join us for dessert, won't you? Mary has made peach cobbler."

"I wouldn't miss it," Beth said, and hurried off. She was certain they thought she was going to use the bathroom.

To Beth's relief, there was no sign of Bertha in the hallway. She slipped down the back stairway quietly, pausing when she heard James's and Helga's mumbled voices. The sound faded as they went back into the dining room. She figured she only had two or three minutes before they'd return to the kitchen. Beth peeked around the corner, and just as she hoped, Mary's back was to her as she washed dishes at the sink. As quickly and softly as she could, Beth raced across the kitchen and dashed into the room. A single lamp glowed on the night stand, and she saw it was a small suite, cozy but sparsely furnished. Quickly riffling through the night table drawer, she couldn't find any stationery, so she tried the chest of drawers. The search produced no results. She dared not take any more time, so she went to the door and put her ear against it to listen. She could hear Mary humming at the sink and opened the door a crack. There appeared to be no one else in the room. Taking a deep breath, Beth dashed across the floor and up the stairway.

She flattened herself against the wall, her heart pounding like a drum. When she finally caught her breath, she cautiously peeked around the corner. Seeing no sign of Bertha, she hurried to the front stairway, then slowed her steps to descend the stairway, winking at the portrait of Jacob Carrington as she passed it.

Returning to the dining room, she took her seat, and James immediately put a slice of cobbler in front of her. "Thank you, James," she said and forked a bite into her mouth.

"Why, Beth, whatever are you smiling about?" Rachel asked. "Are you sure those aren't canary feathers you're chewing, kitten?"

Beth smiled. "Just happy, Nana Rachel."

Stephen's and Emily's disgruntled glances failed to dent her satisfaction. *Five down and three to go!*

Beth had no opportunity to attempt a search of the two maids' quarters that evening. After reading to Rachel, she returned to her room and turned off the light, hoping to give the impression she'd gone to bed. Then she sat at the window and waited in darkness, hoping her hunch would be right. After the house had quieted down for the night, she caught a glimpse of Emily sneaking into the garden.

Beth moved quickly. She went downstairs in the darkened house, lit only by a lamp kept burning in the foyer for Michael.

She stole down the same path she'd taken before, and as anticipated, she spied Emily and Robert in an embrace. Crouching in the concealment of the shrubbery, she stole around them, and when she was out of their sight, she dashed across the darkened lawn to the carriage house.

Burning lamps hung on each side of the door, but Robert's quarters above were in darkness. She climbed the stairway and entered the darkened room. Enough light from below filtered through the window to enable her to get her bearings. After a hasty search that failed to produce anything, she decided to leave. She froze when she heard the door of the carriage house open and realized Robert had returned. She had to get out of there before he came upstairs. In her haste to leave she accidently kicked over the wastebasket, and it banged against the wall. She held her breath and listened, hoping the sound hadn't attracted his attention. Finally, after several seconds, she knelt and began to gather up the spilled contents. As she stuffed them back into the receptacle, she saw scraps and clippings from a newspaper. Her heart seemed to sink to her stomach. She'd hoped Robert wouldn't be the culprit.

Hastily putting the rest of the debris into the wastebasket, Beth left the room. She expected him to appear any moment and fought the impulse to rush down the stairs. Instead, she forced herself to carefully ease down each step without making any noise.

Suddenly the area was thrown into darkness, and she knew he had extinguished the carriage house lamps. With a half-dozen steps remaining, she heard him close the door and knew that at any moment, he'd come around the corner. She swung herself over the stair railing and clamped her lips together to keep from crying out as a shock of pain shot from her ankle to her head. Crouching against the side of the stairwell, she held her breath as he climbed the stairs next to her. Only when she heard the door close above did she raise her head. Hugging the shadows, she set out for the house, her progress impeded by the pain in her ankle. She was a fool and should have just confronted the young man with the evidence of his misdeed. Instead, she now had a painful ankle for the effort. Having gone this far, though, she had no desire to be detected. If she used the front door, he might glimpse her out of his window, so she veered toward the rear of the house.

The moon slipped behind a cloud, casting the night in inky blackness. After stumbling several times, she finally managed to reach the rear door. Much to her relief the door eased open when she turned the knob, and she slipped in, closing it softly so as not to wake James or Mary in the nearby room.

With her eye on their bedroom door, she started to steal across the room to the stairway. Suddenly from out of the darkness a tall figure grabbed her, and her scream was smothered by the pressure of warm lips, awakening her frightened senses to the identity of her attacker. She stopped struggling.

"Michael!" she whispered, still trembling with shock when the kiss ended. "What are you doing down here in the dark?"

"I didn't have dinner, so I thought I'd see what I could find. I didn't want to turn on a light in fear of disturbing James and Mary. But more importantly, what the hell are you doing sneaking around in the dark? I saw you through the window and thought you were a thief. Lucky I caught a glimpse of that red hair of yours."

"I wanted some fresh air, so I went for a walk in the garden."

"Well, you almost got yourself a good whack on the head, lady." He kissed her again, then swept her up in his arms. "I've suddenly developed an appetite for something other than food, Mrs. Carrington."

With that, he carried her up the stairs.

Chapter 20

Kneeling at her feet the next morning, Michael looked up with a worried frown. "How did you do this?"

Unwilling to attempt going downstairs for breakfast, Beth had finally told him about her ankle.

"It was dark in the garden. I stumbled and twisted it," she said, trying not to wince as he gently checked her bruised ankle.

"Beth, why didn't you say something about this last night? I would have put some ice on it to reduce the swelling."

"It feels better than it did. At least it's not broken."

"Nevertheless, I'm sending for the doctor."

"That's not necessary. It only hurts when I walk on it, so I'll just stay off it for a while."

"Beth, this ankle looks like hell. You're not going anywhere today."

"You said we would go to end of track so I could take care of my business. I've been looking forward to it." Beth didn't tell him that another reason for going was that it was her birthday, and she wanted to celebrate it with Thia. "Just wrap it up. I swear, it doesn't even hurt. And please don't say anything to your family about it."

"Why not?"

"Because I feel foolish. It happened because of my clumsiness," she lied. "There's no reason why they have to know." She didn't want anyone in the household to find out she'd been roaming around outside last night.

"They'll know soon enough when the doctor shows up here," Michael said as he strode from the room.

Beth was helpless to stop him.

Dr. Raymond didn't arrive until late afternoon. Beth recognized him as one of the guests who had attended the wedding ball. He quickly checked her ankle and assured her that it was merely bruised but that she should stay off it for a day or two. He then pulled out a form. "I'd like to ask you a few questions about your health for my files."

She answered his routine questions about her age, health, allergies, previous illnesses, and general well-being. Then his questions became more intimate.

"Have you ever had a child?"

"No," she said. The doctor's mien was almost accusing and lacked the gentle and compassionate manner of her Uncle Jim toward a patient. She found his offensive attitude more embarrassing than the personal questions he asked.

"A miscarriage?"

Her embarrassment turned to indignation. "Of course not—as you well know, I'm only recently wed. Really, Dr. Raymond, are these questions necessary?" She gave Michael an exasperated look, hoping he would intercede. He raised his brows and shrugged.

The doctor peered at her over the top of his glasses. "I apologize if you feel the questions are insensitive, but I'm sure you and Michael intend to start a family. I like to know as much about a patient's medical background as I can. I've found it helps to anticipate the possibility of any complications that may arise." He stood up. "This will do for now. Are you sure you wouldn't like a sedative to help you sleep?"

"No, thank you. My ankle isn't that painful, and at the moment, I'm very sleepy."

"Very well. Good day, Mrs. Carrington."

He and Michael walked out to the sitting room.

"How about a brandy before you leave, Richard?"

"Perhaps a small one," the doctor said. Putting aside his medical bag, he sat down. "How is your grandmother, Jake?"

"She's just fine."

"Her health is amazing for her age," the doctor said, taking a sip from the brandy snifter Michael handed to him.

"Yes, it is, thank God. I can't remember the last time she had a sick day. And she won't forgive you if you don't stop to say hello to her."

The doctor quickly downed the drink. "Well, I delivered a baby this morning, so I'm running behind schedule today." He got to his feet and put aside the glass. "I'll go say a quick hello to Rachel right now."

"I'll come with you," Michael said. He came to the bedroom door. "Beth, we'll be right back."

"No hurry, Michael. I'm fine," she said. She preferred privacy, but it would appear Michael intended to hover over her all day. She reached for a nearby book but couldn't read more than a couple of lines before her eyes began to droop.

Beth awoke with a start. A quick glance at the clock indicated she'd dozed off for only a few minutes. Glancing through the open door, she glimpsed a shadowy movement in the sitting room.

"Well, that didn't take long, Michael." When he didn't reply, she called out, "Michael, is that you?"

Gripped by an uneasy feeling, she shoved aside the quilt and crossed the floor to the bedroom door. "Oh, Helga, it's you."

"Vill der be anydink else, Frau Carrington?" the maid asked, struggling with English.

"Nothing, Helga. Thank you." The maid left hurriedly.

"Beth, what are you doing out of bed?" Michael asked, as he and the doctor returned to the room. Hurrying to her side, Michael helped her to get settled back in bed.

"Mrs. Carrington, I instructed you to remain off that ankle," Dr. Raymond scolded, "or you'll aggravate it."

"I won't do it again, Doctor," Beth assured him.

After a hasty glance at his pocket watch, he said, "I must be off. I have other patients. Good day."

Michael followed him out of the room. "Richard, don't forget your bag."

"I never do. Now, what did I do with your wife's medical record?"

"Is this what you're looking for?" Michael asked, retrieving the record from the top of the dresser.

"That's odd," Dr. Raymond said. "I'd have sworn I put it down here with my medical bag." He expelled a heavy sigh. "I'm getting absentminded these days."

Michael chuckled. "Well, in the event you've forgotten the way to the front door, I'll see you out." Their voices faded as they disappeared down the hallway.

Minutes later Michael was back, and he came into the room rubbing his hands together. "All right, what would you like to do? I intend to spend the rest of the day with you."

"Must you?" Beth said, glancing up from the book she'd resumed reading.

He broke into laughter. "Beth, are you implying you don't enjoy my company?"

Actually, she had to admit she enjoyed being with him. But it was all an act with him—his cat and mouse game.

"Surely an important entrepreneur like you *must* have some business that requires your attention."

"Nope. I'd figured that we'd be driving out to Tent Town today, so I worked late last night to finish things up."

"How fortunate that you can take care of *your* business. I wish I had the same opportunity. Instead, you keep me literally a prisoner in this house, or squire me off somewhere."

"Were it not for your accident last night, we'd be in Tent Town by now. Unfortunately, I've already made arrangements for us to leave for St. Louis tomorrow, so you'll have to postpone your trip until we return."

"Oh, I'm incapacitated, Michael, remember? You'll just have to go without me. In your absence, I'll go to Tent Town and stay with Cynthia and Dave until your return."

"That's out of the question," he said.

"Why? It would give me the perfect opportunity to devote my time to my business, Michael."

"This whole issue could be simplified by your setting up an office here in Dallas until the trunk line is completed. Running out to Tent Town every time there's a decision to make is ludicrous. I have a bit of advice to offer, Beth: the successful way to run a business is to hire the right people, whom you can trust to do their jobs. You can't seriously believe Dave Kincaid needs you looking over his shoulder."

"I don't need you to tell me how to run my business," she snapped. "You'll be interested in hearing that Dave and I have already discussed the issue of an office, and we intend to rent one here in Dallas. He even placed a newspaper ad for a ticket seller when we were at the Roundhouse—on that blessed occasion of our marriage!"

"Forgive me for underestimating you, my love."

She smiled sweetly but said through gritted teeth, "Michael, you have no idea how you underestimate me. Now, since most of the day has been wasted already, if you'd get out of here, I'll take a nap."

"How about a card game later?" Kissing her cheek, he left the room. The cunning gleam in his eyes left her feeling uneasy.

What scheme is he concocting now?

Beth drifted into sleep with that challenge in her thoughts, and when she woke later, she drew herself a bath.

She did love Michael's bathtub, which bore the initials of the famous London export house of Silber and Flemming. Obviously custom-made to accommodate his size, the tub was made of sienna japanned marble on the inside with green marble outside, and stood on massive bronze cast-iron feet with a band of ornamental bronze bordering the base. Fed by the boiler in the kitchen shed, the tub had polished bronze hot and cold water valves.

After pouring some perfumed crystals into the tub, Beth sank down in the hot water with a contented sigh, leaned her head back against the bold flanged rim, and closed her eyes. Luxuriating in the jasmine-scented warmth, she felt decadent—like a pampered Roman empress in a pool afloat with rose petals.

"Need any help?"

Her centurion guard had just appeared.

Beth opened her eyes and saw Michael's wide grin. "If that offer is sincere, have a lock put on the bathroom door."

"I have something more pleasant in mind. How about a back rub? Or a taste of this fine wine?" He held a glass to her mouth, and she took a sip.

"Delicious. Now, will you be kind enough to leave? I'd like to get out of here."

She knew it was a mistake the moment she said it. Michael put down the glass, grabbed the towel, and, spreading his arms, held it open for her.

" ' "Come into my parlor," said the spider to the fly.' " The warmth of the towel and his arms wrapped around her when she stepped out of the tub.

"God, Rusty, you smell great!" he murmured, just before he kissed her.

Unlike some of his recent kisses, this one had a slow intimacy, as if he intended his lips not to arouse but more to reacquaint themselves with hers. He tugged lightly at her lips, nibbled at her jaw, and pressed kisses to her eyelids and the tip of her nose, returning often to her mouth, both of them enjoying the pleasure that just kissing brought to them. But under this subtle coaxing, the pressure of each kiss increased and his tongue soon began to probe. By the time he swept her up in his arms, her head and body swirled with passion.

Much to her surprise, he did not carry her to the bed but continued into the sitting room and put her down in a chair at a candle-lit table.

"Tonight I've planned an intimate dinner, complete with candlelight and wine."

"Michael, since you've already succeeded in seducing me, it isn't necessary for you to continue
any romantic pretense. I feel foolish enough as it
is."

"You didn't say that last night when I carried
you up the stairs," he said.

"My ankle was aching. Besides, I doubt it would
have done any good. Remember? Your *appetite*
needed appeasing."

"And let's face it, Beth, my love: we share a taste
for the same food, don't we?"

"Admittedly, I have not stopped you from con-
tinuing this intimate relationship."

"I wonder why?" he taunted. "Could it be because you want one as much as I do?"

"Michael, I like ice cream, but that doesn't mean
I can't exist without it."

"I thought we were over that hurdle, Beth. At
this point, what would be accomplished by going
back to the old arrangement? The only time we're
being truly honest with each other is in bed."

"How can you be certain we're being honest
then? I don't doubt that you take me to your bed
just to prove your power over me—as another way
of humiliating me in your pursuit of revenge. The
honesty will come when you grow weary of the
game and give it up."

"If that's what you're hoping for, Beth, it's not
going to happen. I thought you were smarter than
that. I figured you held out as long as you did to
have your own revenge—that you'd figured it out
the day I offered marriage."

She looked at him, perplexed. "Figured what
out?"

"My obsession for you. I even let that slip then."

"Oh, I figured *that* part out, Michael."

"Then you should realize that all this time that

you've been fretting about my humiliating you, you had me just where you wanted me. Sure, when we first met, I deliberately set out to seduce you. But the whole thing boomeranged. Every kiss, every touch became a memory that I tried to put out of my mind—and the more I tried, the more intense the recollection became. It was driving me crazy. I tried other women, but no one mattered. I had to have *you*! That's when I concocted the scheme to get you to marry me. I even convinced myself that it was all for revenge. I wanted to get even with you for what you were doing to me— even more than seeking revenge for my father. I should have remembered what Scott had to say about a tangled web."

"But Scott said the cause of it was deceit." She shrugged, torn by confusing emotions. "Are we deceiving each other, Michael?"

"I think we're deceiving ourselves. No woman can satisfy me like you do, and you have never responded to another man's kiss or touch. And neither of us can get enough of each other. What does that tell you?"

"I don't know," she said, bewildered.

"No matter how much you claim you despise me, or how often I remind you that you're the object of my revenge, nothing can prevent this physical marvel between us. Why do you try to fight it, Beth? Why not just relax and enjoy it?"

"Because I hate myself for doing so," she answered defiantly.

But he was right. When, in their bizarre relationship, had they lost the ability to resist each other? They were two fools who had dived into the dangerous waters that both believed to be merely physical attraction. But now the current was pulling them deeper and deeper into an emotional eddy from which neither could escape.

With a grim smile, Michael drew a package out of his pocket and put it on the table. "Anyway, this is for you. Happy birthday, Beth."

The gesture caught her off guard. Surprised, she opened the package. A sparkling necklace of blue sapphires lay inside.

"It's very lovely, Michael. But I told you why I'm not comfortable accepting these gifts from you."

"This necklace was not my mother's. I had it especially made for your birthday." He put it around her neck, then stepped back, his admiring gaze on her face.

She felt a tingling in her stomach, and suddenly they were staring at each other in a building web of desire until he finally broke the spell. "I knew it would match your eyes," he said, in almost a whisper.

Nervously touching the gems at her throat, Beth sought the safe refuge of triviality. "How did you know this was my birthday?"

"You told me the date when we first met."

"And you remembered it after all this time," she said, amazed.

At the sudden guilty downward shift of his eyes, Beth was suddenly struck by a thought. She sucked in her breath when the shock of the truth hit her.

"Oh, my God! They were from you, weren't they?" He looked up, then quickly lowered his gaze again. From the brief contact, she knew that she'd guessed right. She sat there, astonished, as it all became clearer to her. "It's been you who's sent me a single rose on my birthday for the past three years. Of all the possibilities, I never suspected you. And Mrs. Mosey would never tell me."

He looked up and grinned self-consciously. "She was well paid not to."

"Why did you do it?"

He looked uncomfortable. "Let's just say that I'm a sentimentalist at heart."

"I think it's more than that."

"What more could it be?" he asked. He cleared his throat. "I . . . ah . . . promised to drop in and say good night to Grannie. If you don't mind, I think I'll forget dinner tonight."

He left her motionless, still puzzled, seeking an answer to a question that raised more confusing doubts about the man she'd married. Then, moving to the bedroom, she withdrew her Bible from the drawer of the night table. Sinking down on the bed, Beth opened the book and with a trembling finger, lightly touched the withered petals of three roses that were crushed between the pages.

Softly she began to read aloud the words that seemed to leap from the page:

> *The song of songs, which is Solomon's.*
> *Let him kiss me with the kisses of his*
> *mouth: for thy love is better than wine.*

She closed the Bible and clutched it to her breast. "Why, Jake? Why?" she whispered. A single teardrop slipped from the corner of each eye and slid slowly down her cheeks.

Chapter 21

Because of the long nap she had taken earlier, Beth wasn't at all sleepy. Slipping on a nightgown and robe, she decided to visit Michael's grandmother and perhaps to read to her if Rachel wished.

"I'm glad you came, dear," Rachel said when Beth joined her. "In fact, I hoped you would. Jake was just here. I haven't seen him this confused since he was a youngster. Do you have any idea what is bothering him?"

"Jake is not one to seek help in solving a problem, Nana Rachel. He has a great deal of self-confidence, and I'm sure if something is bothering him, he'll eventually reach a solution that will satisfy him."

Rachel looked at her with a speculative gleam in her eye. "That's an interesting reply," she said. "Do you mean as opposed to reaching a satisfying solution? I sense you mean he's self-serving."

"Well, it would be naive to believe Jake doesn't serve his own interests first, Nana Rachel."

"Perhaps he often gives that impression, but it can be very misleading. As a child he learned to conceal his wishes, knowing his father would reject them, so he's cautious in revealing his inner feelings. Has Jake ever discussed his father with you?"

"Occasionally," Beth said. She did not mention the bitterness Michael appeared to harbor against his father.

"Jacob and I must take some of the blame for our sons' weaknesses," Rachel said sadly. "Rather than embrace their fathers' strengths, they fled from them: Stephen's father turned to alcohol, and Jake's father found his solace in bitterness." Sighing regretfully, Rachel continued, "We saw it happening but could not stop it. Stephen's poor mother turned to alcohol along with her husband, but Jake's mother tried to offer the love to her children that their father denied them. On that tragic day when Laura and the twins perished, Jake not only lost the loved ones he adored, but the three people who had endured with him the tribulation within their home."

"But you and his grandfather were there for him," Beth said.

Rachel shook her head. "By that time, the scars were carved too deeply, my dear. He was left to a father who had no compassion."

Rachel's story matched what Martha Slocum had told her, but it didn't help to cast much light on her own understanding of Michael. If he was accustomed to keeping his true feelings to himself, how could she know what they were toward her?

Rachel crooked a finger and motioned Beth closer. "Come here, dear." Shifting over to her, Beth sat down on the floor at her feet. "Do you love my grandson?"

Love was the one word Beth had tried to avoid considering in the emotional upheaval she was experiencing. "I don't know, Nana Rachel."

Rachel cupped Beth's face between her hands and stared deeply into her eyes. "I think you do.

And I believe he loves you. Why both of you choose not to admit it is beyond this old woman's understanding.''

"I think we have to admit it to ourselves before we can do it to each other, Nana."

After leaving Rachel's room, Beth still pondered that question. She was becoming more and more confused about her feelings for Michael. They seemed to run the full spectrum of emotions, and it was becoming necessary to remind herself again and again of the motive behind their marriage. She was beginning to suspect that Michael was waging an internal battle over these feelings, too.

Beth paused at the portrait of his grandfather. A wily gleam seemed to sparkle from the dark eyes of the man in the picture. "You know, Jacob Carrington, I don't doubt for a moment that those boots of yours were hard to fill."

Upon leaving his grandmother's bedroom, Michael had come downstairs, and having no stomach for confronting Stephen's family, he closeted himself behind the door of the library. He'd come close to confessing the truth of his marriage to his grandmother, but at the last moment had thought better of it: he knew his conduct would have disappointed her. And Beth—how close he'd come to admitting to her that he no longer understood his own motives. Once it had been so clear, his purpose so absolute. He'd made his dying father a promise, and the good Lord knew he'd devoted the past four years of his life to honoring that pledge. He snorted in derision—where was the honor in a pledge that evoked dishonor?

To make certain his actions were justified, he'd hired an investigator, who had confirmed that his father's accusations had been correct: Matthew

MacKenzie had used bribery to get the government contract.

And that truth would always stand between him and Beth.

He clenched his fists in frustration. Oh, his plan had been brilliant—especially coercing her into marriage. From the weekend they'd spent together, he knew and anticipated that the sex between them would be great—the best he'd ever known. His loins tightened just thinking about it. What he'd not been prepared for was the extraordinary pleasure he felt from just being with her. At such times revenge was the farthest thing from his thoughts, until the two of them broke out in a quarrel. He'd fallen in love with a woman who hated the sight of him. A woman he'd do anything for, except give her the freedom she coveted.

Stephen's family and the household staff had retired by the time he finally left the library. He walked up the darkened stairs and was surprised to see light glimmering from under the door of his suite. His surprise was greater when he opened the door.

The room glowed with the sensual glow of flickering candles. Dressed only in the red combination he'd bought her, Beth sat at the table playing solitaire, her long legs stretched out and resting on the other chair.

His heart immediately thudded against his chest, and he felt the telltale tightening in his loins.

Dammit! How does she always succeed in doing this to me!

"It's about time you showed up," she said. "I thought we had a card game planned for tonight. Are you reneging, Carrington?"

"I don't like what you're wearing," he said.

"I thought this is what you wanted me to wear."

"I have a different ensemble in mind for you."

The faintest suggestion of a smile teased the corners of her mouth—right where he'd like his tongue to be right now. Arching a brow, she asked, amused, "What is it now?"

"Something simpler: that necklace you're wearing, your eyes that match it, and that red hair of yours."

His fingers itched to touch her as he waited for her next move, wondering if she'd tell him to go to hell or just laugh in his face. She stood up slowly, and his heart started hammering again as he waited, hoping—but doubting—she would do it.

Lowering his gaze to her breasts, he saw her fingers had begun releasing the buttons of the garment. With an erotic shimmy of her hips that slammed into his groin like a punch, she slid it down and stepped out of it. His gaze raked down her long, slim legs to her bare feet before returning to the jeweled necklace that glittered against the creamy-white swell of her breasts.

The hot blood surging through him felt like it was burning him alive, licking at his loins, pounding at the pulses of his temples until it almost blinded him. He was so hard he could barely keep from clutching himself and wanted to curse aloud for reacting like a piss-proud schoolboy.

"Is this what you mean?"

He had to swallow to moisten his throat to be able to answer her. "Damn you, Rusty, I'd like to strangle you right now. I had good intentions when I came up here."

"And what are your intentions now?" she asked, in a voice heavy with suggestion.

He crossed the room and swept her up in his arms. Surprise was evident in the sapphire depths of her eyes when he lowered her to the floor, but she said nothing. Candlelight gleamed on the jewels glittering at her breast as she lay waiting, her chest heaving with excitement, her nipples already peaked from arousal.

She was ready for him, just from the foreplay of their locked gazes in the seconds it took him to shed his clothes. When he lowered himself on her, she arched her body toward his and his bare flesh met hers.

Their union was fast, explosive, and divinely satisfying.

Their bodies glossy with perspiration, for several moments afterwards they could only lie trying to gasp much-needed breath into their lungs. Finally, when his heart had settled back to a normal rhythm, he said, "Wow! That sure beats a dish of ice cream!"

Beth threw back her head and laughed, surprising and delighting him. "Don't start, Michael!" she warned.

Chuckling, Michael went into the bathroom to draw a bath. Then he returned and lifted her into his arms. He carried her into the bathroom and lowered her into the tub.

"We both can't fit in here," she protested, when he climbed in after her.

"Of course we can." He maneuvered them around until he was under her and she sat facing him, straddling his hips. "You see, it's just like riding a horse."

"But I always rode mares," she teased.

He squeezed the spongeful of water over her head, cutting off her words. "You were saying, Mrs. Carrington?" he said, trailing the sponge down the column of her neck.

Beth closed her eyes and sighed. "Oh, that feels good."

"You feel good," he murmured.

They began alternating sponging and soaping one another with their bare hands. It didn't take long before the cleansing strokes became caresses, with the warm water an added aphrodisiac. "I knew this tub was built for decadence," she said, running her soap-slicked hands along the slope of his shoulders. "How many women have you brought here?"

"None. This is my grandmother's house. I'd never bring a woman here to do this."

He closed his eyes and leaned his head back against the rim. Her hands were wondrous sensual tools, he thought, as she soaped his chest. He could feel himself swelling.

She slipped her arms around his neck when he pulled her against him and shifted her enough to slide into her. Her mouth captured his, swallowing his groan of rapture when the warmth of her tightened around his hardness, encasing it in the velvet depth of her. Their tongues dueled, their hands fondled, their passion soared—building to eruption until their water-sleek bodies cleaved together in a tumultuous moment of release.

When the water finally turned tepid, Michael carried her to the bed. Neither seemed willing to end the magic spell cast upon them that night.

Was it an enchantment of love or one of sorcery? Beth wondered as they lay side by side, talking in soft tones. Had Rachel's words become a love potion to blind them to the reality of their marriage?

As if reading her thoughts, Michael said, "I had a long talk with my grandmother tonight."

"I did, too," Beth replied.

"Grannie believes we can build a happy marriage, Beth."

"Did you tell her the full story behind our marriage?"

"I tried, but . . ." He faltered, and a momentary silence ensued before he asked, "Did you?"

"No. I couldn't either. She's too dear to hurt. And hearing the truth about us would do that."

"Couldn't we try to salvage a marriage out of this wreckage, Beth?" Perhaps it was only wishful thinking, but Beth detected a wistfulness in his voice.

"I believe there's an adage about closing the barn door after the horses are out."

"If you're going to fall back on cliché, consider the one about not claiming the battle lost until you try fighting it first—or even better late than never."

Not to be bested, she said, "Well, if our argument is going to stand on the words of others, then let me remind you of Dante's warning: 'All hope abandon, ye who enter here.' "

"And you think we entered into Hell when we married, is that it? I don't believe so, unless we make it one. And remember, Dante passed through Hell and found Paradise—maybe we could, too."

Michael grinned. "You know, this is really ludicrous—we spend an hour having the best sex we've ever had and then the next hour dredging up quotes from the past to justify our actions."

"It is pretty bizarre, isn't it?" She started giggling, and soon they both were laughing.

"One more, just one more, I promise," he said. "Actually, it would be more apropos to get down on bended knee for this one, but you'll have to settle for just a kiss." Clasping her hand, he raised it to his lips and pressed a kiss into the palm. " 'Come live with me and be my love . . .' "

"I'm afraid our marriage is anything but the bed of roses that Mr. Marlowe promised in that poem."

"You are a distrustful wench. Like King Lear, I'm forced to say that 'I am a man more sinn'd against than sinning.' "

He was altogether too charming—and she didn't dare trust him. "I doubt that defense would do well in a court that governs by the principle of Malice Aforethought." With that reminder of his reason for marrying her, Beth rolled over on her side with her back to him.

The spell of the evening which had glowed so brightly had burned out, like the candles in the room that had flickered down to nothing but molten wax.

Chapter 22

Michael had planned on taking a Lone Star trunk line northeast to link up with the Santa Fe and go straight into St. Louis. However, they were informed that the Santa Fe workers were on strike and there were no trains running. So they went east to Louisiana, where they left his private car at the train depot and boarded the Mississippi Belle riverboat bound for St. Louis.

Beth found the unexpected change of plans a pleasant experience. She'd never been on a riverboat and was awed by the opulence of the three-decked ship with its ornate columns, lattice-scrolled arches, red and gold carpeting, and painted murals on the ceiling. She wanted to explore the whole ship immediately and pointed to the deck above.

"I want to go up there."

"That's the Texas deck, Beth. You can't go up there."

"Don't tell me you Texans have a deck of your own," she said, disgusted.

He started to laugh. "No, my dear. If I understand correctly, these riverboats used to name their decks after states. And since that top deck has the largest cabins—which are the officers' quarters—

and Texas is the largest state, somehow that connection was made."

"Well, if that doesn't sound stupid to me. Why not just call it the Officers' Deck?"

"I wouldn't know; I'm in railroads, remember? I'd be surprised if you found a single Texan among a ship's crew—we're more comfortable on a horse. Let's unpack, and then we can take a walk."

As soon as the steam-driven paddle wheel started turning, Beth and Michael left their cabin to explore the boat. They started with the lower deck, and although it was wider and longer, Beth saw that the passenger cabins were smaller and less lavish than those on the middle deck, where their cabin was located.

Besides cabins, the middle deck had a room with a large stage that offered a nightly show; that in turn led to a smaller room lined with a long bar and several tables for those who sought the recreation of a card game.

By the time they finished, it was time to return to their cabin and dress for dinner. The dining room was as opulent as the rest of the boat, with crystal chandeliers reflected in mirrored walls and mosaic ceilings, and velvet drapery on windows and alcoves. Ringed by tables, which were covered with linen tablecloths and set with fine china and Waterford crystal, was a dance floor. A five-piece string ensemble offered relaxing dinner music.

"For heaven's sake, there's the Bennetts," Michael said.

Beth's enthusiasm for the trip plummeted when he stood up and waved the trio over to their table.

"What a coincidence!" Carl Bennett exclaimed as the men shook hands. "Jake Carrington, you're the last person I'd ever expect to see on a Mississippi riverboat."

Michael had pulled out a chair for Diane to sit next to him. She looked stunning in a purple velvet gown that accented her full breasts and slim hips. As they sat down, both women's glances swept Beth, and she felt dowdy in the same cream-colored gown she'd worn to the ball.

"How are you, dear?" Caroline asked, then turned her attention back to Michael without waiting for a reply.

Throughout the meal, Beth said little and listened to the other four. Whenever Michael made an attempt to include her in the conversation, the Bennetts somehow managed to steer the topic away from her.

When dinner ended and couples took to the dance floor, Beth declined Michael's offer, claiming her injured ankle as an excuse. He had no recourse but to invite Diane to dance.

Watching Michael waltz past with Diane, Caroline said, "They always make such a striking couple. He so dark; she so fair. Wouldn't you say, my dear?"

It was only the second sentence Caroline had directed toward Beth from the time she'd sat down. "Oh, yes. Striking," Beth agreed. Faking a yawn, she brought her hand to her mouth. "I'm exhausted, and I think I'll retire early. Would you tell Jake I've gone to bed? The devoted man hasn't left my side day or night from the time we've wed, and I insist he remain and enjoy himself with old friends."

"I'm so sorry you must leave, but I understand, dear," Caroline said, making no effort to disguise her jubilation. "Carl, you must escort Elizabeth to her cabin."

"That won't be necessary. It's just a short distance away. It's been a pleasure, Mr. and Mrs. Bennett. Enjoy the evening."

"We will see you tomorrow," Caroline tittered.

"Undoubtedly—it's a small boat," Beth replied.

She was tempted to look back and grin when she heard Caroline declare huffily to her husband, "I can't believe how rude that woman is, Carl!"

Beth didn't go directly to their cabin but chose instead to stroll slowly along the deck. The air was heavy, but an evening breeze fanned her face, and she leaned against the rail.

She was troubled, not by Caroline Bennett's remarks, but by her confused feelings for Michael. Beth knew that the incredible physical relationship they shared kept his attention, but that could only last until the novelty wore thin. And no matter how much she tried to deny it to herself, it did trouble her to see Michael and Diane together. Their agreement was that he wouldn't seek sexual satisfaction elsewhere and expected her not to, either. Was he beginning to regret that hastily made arrangement?

She must separate the physical from the emotional commitment in their marriage; there was a strong division between the two, and she must stop trying to merge them.

She lifted her face, and a strong gust of breeze whipped at her face and freed her hair from the pins that restrained it. It felt exhilarating, and she surrendered herself to the night.

In the moonlight, she caught an occasional glimpse of silvery moss fluttering like spectral wings from the trees that lined the shoreline. She closed her eyes and listened to the sounds of the river: the steady rhythm of the paddle wheel lapping at the water, the slap of an oar from a passing raft. The low hum of a negro spiritual floated through the night, and she glimpsed a circle of figures huddled around a campfire on the shore. It was all so peaceful, she never wanted it to end.

"Did you know your eyes are shinning like stars, Beth?"

Michael's voice jolted her out of her reverie. "Oh, I thought you were with your friends."

"Caroline said you were tired and were going to bed. I was worried when I didn't find you in the cabin."

"What did you think I'd do, jump ship, Michael?"

He moved closer and stood next to her. "If you wanted a late stroll, I just wish you'd asked me to join you."

"It appeared to me as if you had your hands pretty full. And now I am going to bed."

"That's a provocative idea," he said. He brushed back some strands of hair blowing in her face. "Did you know, madam, that I have done a scientific study of your hair color?"

"Really. And just what were the results of your study, Professor Carrington?"

"After extensive observation, I've concluded, madam, that darkness turns it to auburn, sunlight to vivid carmine, candlelight to the color of a rich claret, and moonlight..." He reached out and rolled several of the strands between his fingers. "Moonlight transforms it to glory." Cupping her cheeks between his hands, he gazed deeply into her eyes. "Let's go to bed, Beth."

Beth found herself falling under his mesmerizing spell. But if she kept succumbing to this magnetic charm of his, she'd lose all of her self-respect. She stepped away.

"Go back to your friends, Michael."

A flash of irritation flared in his eyes. "Is that what you prefer, Beth?"

"Yes," she said. "That's very much what I prefer."

"Then I'll say good night." He walked away.

Michael returned to the cabin very late, and Beth couldn't help wondering if he'd been with Diane.

For the balance of the trip, the Bennetts pursued Michael relentlessly. Beth and Michael found little opportunity to be alone, and more and more often, she made up an excuse to return to their cabin just to avoid joining them. And each night Michael would return to the cabin later and later, disrobe, then climb into bed and go to sleep.

By the time the boat docked at St. Louis, the rift had widened between them, and the weight of the world had settled back on Beth's shoulders. She was glad that the Bennetts were going on to Chicago.

Michael's house in St. Louis was as large as the mansion he'd owned in Denver. "I was hoping for something less ostentatious," she commented as they drove up an oak-lined driveway leading to a three-storied, columned white house with an all-around porch and a second-floor gallery.

"Beth, I don't build houses. When I need one, I buy what's available." The sharp rebuke silenced her from making any further comment.

The inside was no less extravagant, with an Italian marble foyer, large upholstered chairs and sofas, Duncan Phyfe tables, tapestries on the walls, heavy red damask draperies with gold tassels at the windows, and an abundance of ornate rococo lamps, bronzed statues, and an actual helmeted suit of armor—complete with lance—standing like a sentinel in the foyer. It was a jarring mixture of tasteful and tasteless.

The whole effect was overpowering, but before

Beth could utter a word, Michael said curtly, "The furnishings came with the house. The only personal items I have here are a few books, some papers, and clothing."

Beth said demurely, "I see."

"Regardless, you won't have to suffer it for long. Randy's found a buyer for the place."

"The Australian sheepherder? The flock should fit right in." She lifted her head and boldly met his dark-eyed gaze. A trace of amusement glinted in his dark eyes as he stared at her, then he burst out laughing. No longer able to control her own amusement, Beth joined him, and the hall rang with the sound of their laughter.

"Come on, minx," Michael said, grabbing her by the hand. "You'll love the upstairs. No expense was spared—the master bedroom even has mirrors on the ceiling over the bed!"

"So what do you think?" he asked a short time late, after they'd toured the whole house.

"May I be frank?"

"Of course. I told you, I bought it sight unseen, so my conscience is clear."

"I think it's hideous. You actually should be paying someone for taking it off your hands."

"Lady, you are showing an unaccustomed lack of imagination. That mirrored ceiling in the bedroom has great potential." After a hasty glance at his pocket watch, he grabbed his hat. "And I'd prove it to you right now if I didn't have to leave. I have an errand to run which shouldn't take more than thirty minutes, so while I'm gone, take a rest and get used to those mirrors. We'll be going out to dinner later, too. I promised Randy we'd join him and his wife." At her distressed look, he said, "Beth, Randy Bowing is my best friend. I think

you'll like him and Jennifer. They're good people."
He was out the door before she could reply.

Following his suggestion, she lay down on the
bed and looked up at the ceiling. She had to admit
there was a certain appeal to seeing herself
stretched out against the counterpane. It didn't take
much imagination to visualize her and Michael naked and entwined. "The man is clearly corrupting
me," she murmured, amused.

Beth got up and unpacked the gown she would
wear that evening. When they returned to Dallas,
she'd have to hire a dressmaker. When she'd left
Denver, she'd thought it was a good idea to leave
most of her dresses behind, but she was getting
weary of wearing the same few gowns to everything she attended.

Barefoot, Beth went downstairs and checked the
kitchen for something to eat. There were several
tins of food on the shelf, among them a can of
peaches. She found an opener and carried the open
can with her, forking slices of peaches as she
walked into the parlor and studied a statue set on
a table. It looked like a cross between a fertility
goddess and a satanic icon. Shuddering, she moved
on to a lovely seventeenth-century wall tapestry.
Perplexed by the varied selections, she abandoned
the inspection when Michael returned. He finished
off the can of peaches and then reached into his
pocket.

"I've got something for you. I wired ahead to
have this made." Smiling, he took her left hand and
slipped a ring on the third finger. "It's about time
for this, wouldn't you say, Mrs. Carrington?" The
ring consisted of two diamond-studded strands of
gold, one yellow and the other white, twisted together into a band. "Now you've got to stretch
your imagination and think of those gold bands

and diamonds as railroad tracks and ties."

Dazed, she stared at her hand. She understood the parallel he intended, but the gold and diamond band seemed to emblazon the reality that she was indeed his wife—another reminder that she belonged to him.

"Michael, it's lovely, but I thought you needed money."

"This isn't a gift; it's a wedding ring. Besides, I won a lot of money on the boat playing poker."

"Poker!" She felt a jolt of unrestrained elation. "So that's what you were doing at night!"

"Of course. What did you think I was doing?" He studied her with curiosity, then suddenly a gleam of comprehension illuminated his dark eyes. "My God! You thought I was with Diane. Didn't you?"

She turned crimson and wanted to sink through the floor. "Nonsense! That was the farthest thought from my mind." He had to be gloating with smugness. Unable to look at him, she turned away.

His hands on her shoulders forced her around and, cupping her chin, he tipped up her face to search it. "Look at me, Beth."

By now she'd had time to compose her features, and she raised her eyes to his probing stare.

"We're at odds about many issues, but infidelity should never be one of them," he said. "I made you a promise when you agreed to marry me. I have no reason or inclination to seek the company of any other woman. I know the Bennetts annoyed you, and since there was no avoiding them, there wasn't too much I could do about it other than respect your wishes to be left alone."

"I felt the same about you, Michael. They were old friends; you enjoyed their company; so I kept out of the picture. I thought maybe you wanted to renew your . . . friendship with Diane, so I wasn't going to interfere if that's what you wished."

"That's the last thing I wanted. *You* are the most exciting woman I've ever known." He began to pick the pins out of her hair, tossing them aside. "In fact, just thinking about how exciting you are— excites me." He lifted her into his arms. "And with the aid of that mirrored ceiling, my love, now's the perfect time to show you just what a seductive, exciting woman you are."

The tall blond man who rose to his feet when they entered the restaurant looked familiar to Beth. She stood silently observing the two men while they greeted each other, then Michael introduced her to Randy Bowing.

He clasped her hand and smiled warmly. "Hello, Blue Eyes."

The instant he said the words, Beth remembered where she'd seen him: he'd been among Michael's friends in the park on that long-ago morning. Every moment of that heartrending scene flashed before her, and she blushed, recalling the humiliation and despair she'd felt. Somehow she managed to muster enough composure to get through the introductions.

Although Jennifer Bowing was attractive, Randy's dark-haired wife's real beauty lay in the serenity she emanated when she smiled at Beth. Her brown eyes were filled with warmth when Michael introduced them, and the sincerity in her greeting soon enabled Beth to relax and enjoy the meal.

Whenever the men's conversation slipped into a recollection of the past, Jennifer always steered it back to the present.

Ultimately the talk got around to the sale of the

house, and the two women giggled with amusement comparing their opinions on which was the most atrocious object.

After dinner, Beth again begged off dancing because of her ankle, but she couldn't help smiling as she watched Jenny laughing on the dance floor as Michael twirled her in a series of fast turns.

"They're having a good time, aren't they?" she said to Randy.

"They usually do. I'm relieved that Jake and Jenny do get along so well. They're my two best friends, and I'd hate to have them at odds." He paused. "Beth, I'm sure Jake wouldn't want you and me to be at odds, either. I want us to be friends. I know you have good cause to resent me, and I apologize for my conduct the first time we met. None of the guys realized at the time what you meant to Jake. We all just assumed that you were another—"

"I remember quite well what you all assumed, Randy," Beth said, embarrassed.

"Jake lit into us and put us in our place, all right."

"It doesn't matter now, Randy. I put it behind me a long time ago."

"Jake sure never did." He shook his head. "He and I did the grand tour of Europe right after we left Harvard, and believe me, Beth, Jake was hurting. And in the years that followed . . . well, all I can say is that he never got over you."

"Randy, you *are* a good friend to him," she said nervously. "I think you might be overdramatizing the situation, though. I can't envision Jake not in control of any situation—especially his own destiny. But if you're sincere about wanting us to be friends, then I'll ask a favor of you. Michael spoke of selling his ranch."

"Yes, I had a possible buyer for it, but the deal fell through."

"That's good—because if he insists upon going through with a sale, I'll buy it, but I don't want you to reveal that to him. He loves that ranch too much to let it fall into the hands of a stranger."

"You're putting me on the spot, Beth. I'd hate to lie to Jake."

"I don't expect you to. Just don't volunteer any names. Besides, he told me he hadn't really made up his mind whether or not to sell it, so the situation may never arise."

"Does Jake have any idea how much you love him, Beth?"

Beth was silent. How could he? She didn't even know, herself.

Michael and Jennifer's return to the table ended any further discussion, but Randy's words weighed heavily on Beth's mind the rest of the evening. Time and again, she found herself staring at Michael and wondering what thoughts were really lodged behind that easy smile of his.

When the time came to say good-bye to the Bowings, she and Jennifer promised to write to each other.

With the riverboat leaving in the afternoon, Beth and Michael spent the next morning crating up his personal belongings. By the time Michael had to leave for Randy's office to finalize the sale of the house, they were through except for several shelves of books, which Beth proceeded to pack in his absence.

Climbing up on a chair, she started removing books from the top shelf. Many were dusty law books, but occasionally she found a title that she hadn't read and looked forward to having the opportunity to do so once they were back in Texas.

As she started to climb down from the chair with an armful of them, her weak ankle gave out, and she lost her balance. Dropping the books, she grabbed for the shelf and managed to prevent herself from falling.

Relieved, she climbed down and knelt to gather up the fallen books. She picked up a sealed envelope that had fallen out of one and was about to replace it when she glimpsed her own name. Intrigued, she sat down on the chair for a closer examination. In Michael's handwriting, the envelope was addressed to Elizabeth MacKenzie at her address in Denver.

How long ago had he written the letter? Why he hadn't ever mailed it was even more baffling. Did she have the right to open it now, or would that be prying? Maybe he'd put the letter in the book and forgotten about it, believing he had mailed it. She decided it would be best to return it to where she'd found it, so she quickly shoved it back into the book. Seconds later, she snatched it out again. The letter was meant for her—it just hadn't been posted yet!

The seal had long since dried and opened easily. With curiosity, she unfolded the sheet of paper enclosed.

Dear Rusty,

I know that as you read this letter you hate the thought of me, and I can't blame you. The unfortunate scene in the park was not of my making or choosing. I swear that I said nothing to any of my friends about our time together.

Regrettably, I do admit I deliberately seduced you, and for that I apologize. My motive was not what

you've been led to believe—but neither is it any more
pardonable. I am sure that one day it will become
clear to you.

I'm not proud of what I did, Rusty. You are a
lovely, loving person, and the pain I brought to those
beautiful, trusting eyes of yours will haunt me in the
years to come—as will the memory of those wondrous
hours we shared last week—the most incredible I've
ever known.

Jake Carrington

She lowered the letter and stared, perplexed, into
space. He had written this a week after she'd fled
from him. She knew now what his motive had
been, but this letter was an apology, remorse for
what he'd done. Why hadn't he mailed it? And
even more puzzling, why had he married her out
of revenge, if he felt guilty for what he had done?
Every time she thought she had him figured out,
she discovered something else.

"How can one man be so complicated?" she lamented aloud.

By the time Michael returned, everything was
crated and ready to be shipped, she was dressed
and packed, and they boarded the Mississippi Belle
for their return to Texas.

The trip had certainly raised more questions in
her already confused mind. Both the letter and
Randy Bowing's words had revealed yet another
facet of the complex personality of this man she
had married.

Chapter 23

Since their return from St. Louis a week ago, Beth had driven every morning to the site of the rented office of the Rocky Mountain Central Railroad. The ticket office had been completed, and the finishing touches were being made to her office at the rear of the building. On Monday morning, the Rocky Mountain Central would begin selling passenger reservations for future travel between Dallas and Denver, or on to the farther connection at Laramie, Wyoming, where they could board the Union Pacific transcontinental railroad that could take them east or west across the United States.

Excitement had begun to mount, and with the track still under construction, Beth had already been approached by businesses wanting freight contracts to ship their cotton and cattle to northern sites.

She'd received replies to the ad David had placed in the newspaper, but hadn't had time to review the responses, deciding to go over them with Michael when he returned from Fort Worth that day. Beth wanted to be sure she was back home when he arrived—as hard as it was to admit it, she missed him and looked forward to his home-coming.

Robert had the buggy harnessed and waiting when she left the house, since Beth found the light-weight rig more comfortable than a buckboard.

"Good morning, Mrs. Carrington," he said politely.

"Good morning, Robert."

Since there'd been no other threatening letters, she'd never confronted him about that issue, but she did remain reserved with him. He seemed equally uncomfortable in her presence—a sign of guilt, as far as Beth was concerned.

She took the reins and was about to drive away when Rachel came out on the porch. "Beth, wait up," she called out. James and Bertha followed on her heels, both of them agitated and issuing protests.

Alarmed, Beth asked, "What is it, Nana Rachel?" She saw Rachel was dressed for an outing, complete with bonnet, shawl, and parasol.

"If you have no objection, dear, I would like to join you this morning. I have business in town."

"Then, madam, I will drive you," James declared.

"I don't need you to drive me. I can go with Beth."

"But, madam, you cannot go alone," Bertha insisted. "I will accompany you."

"Oh, poppycock!" Rachel sputtered. "I'm not an invalid. I wish the two of you would cease treating me like one, just because I can't maneuver on stairs as I once did. I'm tired of being confined to this house as if I'm in my dotage."

Beth couldn't help a slight grin at that remark from the eighty-year-old woman.

Rachel shrugged off Bertha's hands, adjusted her bonnet, and declared firmly, "I shall go to my lawyer's office, and then I hope to have a pleasant luncheon with my grandson's wife, if she is willing."

"I'd be delighted, Nana Rachel."

"You see!" Rachel said with a triumphant smile at the two servants. "So please stop fussing over me; it wears me out. James, tell all the help they may have the day off," she declared, with a royal sweep of her gloved hand. "Now, if you'll assist me into this conveyance, I can get on with my outing."

As they rode through the city, Rachel exclaimed, "Oh, this is so delightful. It feels so good to be free of people hovering over me as if I were helpless. Telling me what I can do and what I can't do. I know the dear souls have my best interest at heart, but if they only knew how oppressive it can feel at times."

"I understand exactly what you mean," Beth said. Rachel was a woman who'd embraced any challenge life offered with courage and a determination to prevail. For others to now consider her dependent on them was probably the hardest adversity she'd ever had to deal with. She wondered how Rachel would react if she knew her beloved grandson had been trying to make Beth just as dependent from the time they were married.

When they reached the lawyer's office, Rachel reintroduced her to Martin Glazer, whose face Beth also remembered from the wedding ball.

"She won't be long, Mrs. Carrington," he said to her. "I just have a few papers for her to read and sign."

Beth sat down and began jotting down a list of things remaining to do before opening the ticket office. Glazer came out and called his secretary into his office, and a few minutes later, all three came out from behind the closed door.

From there Beth drove to her office and enjoyed the delight on Rachel's face when she saw it.

"This is so exciting, Beth. It makes me wish I were young again. Reminds me of the days when Jacob formed the Lone Star, and he and I worked together to get it started."

"Nana Rachel, I have a great idea: why don't I collect my mail and then take the day off. You and I can spend the rest of the afternoon together."

"I'd love that, honey," Rachel said.

Swooping up the responses to the ad, Beth shoved them into her purse. Then, arm in arm, they left the office.

Once seated in the buggy, Rachel declared, "You know, I have a mind to buy myself a new bonnet."

"Then let's do it," Beth said, with a flip of the reins.

"I wonder if that little French milliner near the hotel is still in business?"

"If you're referring to the one I have in mind, I remember seeing it when I stayed at the hotel."

They found the store, and like giddy schoolgirls they tried on every hat before Rachel decided on an elegant bonnet with an eye-catching peacock feather. She decided to wear it in lieu of the one she'd worn to town, and as they left the store, she paused for a womanly preen in the window.

"There's nothing like a new bonnet to lift a woman's spirits," she said as they moved on. She stopped abruptly, and Beth grabbed her, fearing the woman was falling. Instead, Rachel said in shock, "My, my! Will you look at that!" Her stare was fixed on a sheer black combination exhibited against an unfurled bolt of white satin in the window of the next shop. "A bit on the naughty side, I must say." Then she grinned. "My Jacob would've loved it."

Glancing at the name above the door, Beth saw that the shop had a French name and realized this was the very store where Michael had purchased the red one for her. She took Rachel's arm and quickened her step to get past it.

Next they went into a chandlers, and upon seeing Beth purchasing a box of scented candles, Rachel tried to stop her. "Beth, we have plenty of candles left over at the house. Ever since we put in gaslights, we rarely have use for them any more."

"Ah . . . Jake prefers scented candlelight, Nana Rachel," Beth stuttered.

"In heaven's name what for?" Rachel asked.

Blushing furiously, Beth didn't know whether to look at Rachel or the floor.

Suddenly the truth dawned on Rachel, and her face broke into a wicked grin. "Why, that rogue! He's so like his grandfather."

"That he is, Nana Rachel." Beth quickly steered her out of the store.

They spent the next two hours peering into shop windows and buying little gifts: a collar box for James, a pearl-handled crochet hook for Mary. In a perfume store, Rachel bought Helga a box of scented soap and found a satin-covered pincushion for Bertha.

Beth in turn, couldn't resist purchasing a handsomely inlaid mother-of-pearl card case for the nightly card games with Michael. When they stopped in a tobacco store, Rachel bought Michael a box of Havana cigars, and a box of Cosmopolite cigarette paper with gummed edges for Robert Harris.

When they drove up to the hotel, the hostler took their buggy, and the two women ate a tasty lunch of chicken salad on avocado slices, topping off the meal with a lemon tart. Then they continued on with their shopping: this time at a jeweler's, where Beth stood steadfast in her refusal of the gift of an expensive pearl brooch, settling instead on a small folding sewing case for traveling. She in turn bought Rachel a copy of *Ben Hur* at a bookstore, which she promised to read to Rachel in the evenings.

Finally they sat down on a bench in the park to watch an organ grinder with a trained monkey, and Rachel clapped with delight when the chattering little animal jumped up on the bench beside her and held out his cap for a coin.

Beth bought a bag of corn from a street vendor in the park, and as they sat in relaxed companionship feeding the pigeons, Beth decided to disclose a suspicion she'd had since her return from St. Louis.

"Nana Rachel, can you keep a secret?"

"My dear, I have so many secrets in my head that I've forgotten most of them."

"I haven't breathed this to a soul, not even to my sisters, but I believe I'm carrying Jake's child."

Rachel's eyes moistened with tears. "How I've prayed that I would live to hold a child of Jake's in my arms. You couldn't have made me happier, my dear."

"Well, I haven't had it confirmed by Dr. Raymond, but I'm sure I am."

"Why haven't you told Jake the good news?"

"I've been waiting until after my doctor's appointment tomorrow. I'd hate to raise any false hopes."

Rachel clasped her hands. "Thank you for trusting me with your precious secret, dear child, and you can be sure I'll not spoil your surprise with Jake. Oh, Beth, I love you dearly, and I bless the day you came to us."

"And I love you, Nana Rachel," Beth replied emotionally, hugging her. "You've been so good to me."

"Now I think we must bring our outing to a close, Beth, or I'm afraid James will have a posse on our trail."

Beth suspected Rachel was exhausted but too proud to admit it. "I've kept you out too long, Nana Rachel. I hope I haven't overtired you."

With a spunky toss of her head, Rachel declared, "Nonsense, girl. I am tired, but not from boredom for a change."

They returned to the hotel, where the hostler brought them their buggy, and then headed homeward. As they rode through the city, Rachel sat spinning her open parasol like a young coquette as she nodded and smiled at passersby.

After several of the gentlemen returned her smile and doffed their hats to her, Rachel asked with a saucy twinkle in her eye, "Do you suppose it's this new bonnet, dear?"

"I suspect it's those flirtatious eyes of yours," Beth said with a smile.

Rachel sighed with pleasure. "Beth dear, I can't remember the last time I've enjoyed such a day. I shall never forget it."

"We'll do it again, Nana Rachel."

Suddenly a young child dashed into the street directly in the path of the buggy. Beth reined up sharply, and the buggy swayed violently. The sound of splitting wood combined with their screams as the rear of the vehicle crashed to the ground. Rachel was pitched off the seat as the buggy rolled over, and Beth was pinned beneath it.

Dazed but conscious, Beth heard the shouts for help from the people who rushed to the accident.

"Don't try to move, ma'am," a young man cautioned when she attempted to sit up after several men had unhitched the horse and succeeded in shoving the buggy off her.

Through glazed eyes she saw a group gathered around Rachel, who was lying on the road, her outstretched hand still grasping the parasol, the ribs now bent and twisted in a grotesque pattern. Her new bonnet had been knocked off in the fall and lay in the street, the peacock feather flattened and hanging by a few threads.

"Nana?" Beth called, reaching a hand toward Rachel. She tried to hang on, but she found herself slipping deeper and deeper into a black abyss. Her last memory was of the thickening red stain in Rachel's gray hair.

Gradually the blackness turned to a gray haze, and Beth tried to open her eyes, alternating between light and dark when her lashes kept fluttering. They proved too heavy to keep up, so she abandoned the effort. Her head ached, and there was a stinging sensation on her arm. She'd have to open her eyes to see what was wrong with it. Concentrating hard, she managed to raise her eyelids and finally was able to keep them open.

Where was she? Why was she in this shadowy room, lit only by the dim glow of a lamp on a far table? She groped at her aching head and felt a bandage taped to her forehead. Turning her head to the side, she saw Michael in a nearby chair. His shoulders were slumped in dejection, and he sat leaning forward with his elbows propped on his knees, his head buried in his hands. He looked like a man in the throes of grief. She tried to call to him, but her throat was so dry she couldn't speak—so she closed her eyes and slipped back into the darkness.

The next time she opened her eyes, the room was bathed in sunlight, and Michael stood staring out a window.

"Mi . . . Michael," she managed to murmur, barely able to get out the word.

His head jerked around. "Beth!" He hurried over to the bed. "Thank God, Beth."

"Water. I'm so thirsty," she croaked.

Grabbing a pitcher, he quickly poured water into a glass. Wincing, she held up her head. "Sip it slowly, honey," he said, with a supporting hand on her shoulders.

When she finished, she lay back, exhausted, and touched her aching head. "What happened? Where am I, Michael?"

"In a hospital. You were in an accident, Beth."

"Accident? The last thing I remember, I was . . ." Then, horrified, she remembered: the buggy . . . the darting child . . . the shrieks . . . and Rachel lying in the road with blood staining her hair. Ignoring the pain, she shot up to a sitting position. "Nana Rachel! How is she, Michael?"

"Lie still, Beth. Nurse! Nurse!" he yelled. "Dr. Raymond! Somebody come!"

She felt rising panic. "Tell me, Michael—how is Nana Rachel?"

"Beth, please. You must remain quiet," he said, holding her down by the shoulders to restrain her.

"Let me go!" she cried out hysterically. "I want to see her. Where is she?"

"Grannie didn't make it, Beth. She suffered a broken neck in the fall."

"No," Beth cried, staring up at him with disbelief. "Don't say that." She began whimpering. "Please don't say that, Michael."

Dr. Raymond and a nurse hurried into the room. Michael and the nurse held her down, while the doctor injected a tranquilizer into her arm.

Within seconds, the drug took effect, and Beth ceased struggling and lay back. "When is the funeral, Michael?" she asked groggily.

"Beth, honey, we buried Grannie yesterday," he said kindly. "You've been unconscious for three days."

Chapter 24

After one more day of observation, Dr. Raymond was convinced that Beth no longer suffered any effects from the accident. With a warning to avoid any exertion for another week, the doctor released her from the hospital.

As relieved as Beth was to get out of the dismal place, she did not look forward to returning to the house. The servants had been hostile enough toward her before the accident; now she imagined they'd hold her responsible for Rachel's death.

She'd asked herself that question dozens of times while she lay in the hospital. Could she have done something differently? What if she'd refused Rachel's request to come with her that morning? Or what if she'd insisted they return earlier that day? Then they wouldn't have been there when the child ran into the street.

But as always in the past, her deep-rooted faith in the Almighty prevailed: whatever occurred had been meant to happen.

Unconsciously, she spanned her stomach with her hand. She hadn't mentioned her suspected condition to the doctor. If she had lost the child, she'd be bleeding—and there was no such evidence. She knew her baby had been spared. That certainty now took precedence over anything else: Rachel's unfortunate death, the Rocky Mountain Central, and especially any animosity that she felt toward Michael. He was the father of this unborn child, and she'd do everything within her power to avoid raising their baby in an unhappy household. If it meant swallowing her resentment toward her husband, dismissing these pretentious, hostile servants, or turning the reins of the railroad over to Dave Kincaid—she vowed to do it. *So help me God!*

"Do you really feel that grim, Beth?" Michael asked.

"What?" she said, startled out of her musing. She had been so deep in thought that she'd forgotten Michael was sitting beside her and now saw that he'd turned the carriage into the driveway of the mansion.

"You should see your expression. Does coming back to this house distress you that much, Beth? We don't have to live here, you know. We can build a new house if you'd like."

"I hadn't thought about that, Michael—although I admit I don't think I could ever live comfortably around Stephen and his family."

"At least he's gone for now; he took his family to Austin to get away for a short while."

"I confess I haven't given him any thought since the accident. I'm sure he must be suffering the loss of his grandmother, too."

"Yeah, I imagine if he loved anyone, it was Grannie."

When they drove up, she saw a grapevine wreath draped in black crepe hanging on the door. James immediately came out and took the reins. "I trust you are feeling better, Mrs. Carrington," he said, with his usual disdainful reserve.

"Much better, James. Thank you." For what, she was uncertain.

"James, where the hell is Robert?"

"I don't know, sir. I haven't seen him since the funeral."

"Have you checked his quarters?"

"I did two days ago. His clothes are gone."

"And he didn't say he was leaving? That's strange. Take care of the team, James."

"Very well, sir."

Helga was waiting when they entered. She dipped her knees in a slight bow but said nothing. After taking Beth's wrap and Michael's hat, she scurried away.

"Beth! Beth darling!" The shout came from above, and her world suddenly got brighter. With outstretched arms, Cynthia came rushing down the stairway. Beth's floodgates opened—the tears of sorrow she'd withheld in the hospital poured out, and mingled with those of joy at having Thia there. Beth cried uncontrollably as Cynthia hugged and comforted her, wiping away her own tears. Then she was in Dave's arms. As soon as he held her, she felt the quiet strength she'd always drawn from him, and it bolstered her own fortitude.

She couldn't have hoped for a better homecoming. No matter how grim the situation, Cynthia always had the capacity to lift Beth's spirits. Even Michael appeared to have put aside his sorrow—at least temporarily. And with Stephen and his family gone, they were able to sit down to an enjoyable and relaxing meal.

"Dave and I were at the Bonner ranch the day of your accident," Cynthia explained, "so we didn't get Jake's wire until yesterday, or we'd have been here sooner. He sent a carriage for us to come to Dallas to be here when he brought you home."

Turning to Michael, who had been unusually silent throughout the meal, Beth smiled at him with gratitude. "Thank you, Michael."

He grinned, the sheepish grin that she'd come to recognize whenever he'd done something especially nice that he didn't want to claim credit for.

"How long can you stay, Thia?" Michael asked.

"Just until morning."

"Morning! That barely gives us time to even chat," Beth said in disappointment.

"Dave's been away too long as it is. I'll be so glad when the track reaches Dallas. Somehow being this close makes me feel more anxious than when we still had hundreds of miles left to lay."

"Not to mention a bridge or two along the way," Dave added.

"Dave," Beth said hesitantly, "have you ever considered a more stationary job? Something along the lines of President of the Rocky Mountain Central Railroad—working out of an office instead of a caboose, living in a house instead of a railroad car . . ." She glanced around the table and saw that all three of them were looking at her as if she had just fired a shotgun into the ceiling.

"You must have suffered a worse hit on the head than Jake indicated," Dave said.

Beth smiled. "With the exception of Angie, the rest of the Rocky Mountain stockholders are right here at this table. I thought it would be a good time to feel you out."

"Beth, dear, there isn't a person at this table who believes you could seriously give up running the Rocky Mountain. That railroad's like a baby to you," Cynthia said.

Beth almost choked on the bite of beef she'd just taken. She grabbed for her water glass. *Having* a baby was the very reason she wanted to hand over the company reins to Dave.

"It's comforting to hear you didn't say 'lover,' Thia," Michael said.

"Beth, I thank you for the generous offer, but I think this isn't the time to make that kind of decision. You've just gotten out of the hospital, and you and Jake have suffered the loss of someone you both loved dearly. Let's just concentrate on getting that track into Dallas."

Michael picked up his wineglass. "I'll drink to that, Dave." Glancing at Beth, who was still gulping water to clear her throat, he added with a grin, "And so, apparently, will my wife."

As much as she would have liked to visit longer that evening, Beth tired quickly and had to excuse herself to go to bed. She had no idea when Michael came upstairs.

In the morning, while the men loaded the carriage for the return trip, she and Cynthia took a walk in the garden.

"Poor Jake, my heart aches for him," Cynthia said. "He must have gone through hell, losing his grandmother and not knowing if you'd recover or not. I wish we could've been here for both of you. Did he have anyone to help him get through it?"

"He seems to have a lot of friends here in Dallas, Thia. And his grandmother was well loved. But his family is small—and unbearable."

"It must've been hard on Jake. It was probably just as well I wasn't here. I don't think I'd have borne up too bravely having to sit at your bedside for days not knowing if—" She broke off with a sob.

Beth grasped her hand, and they sat down on a bench. "Hey, we aren't going to start crying again, are we? You're the one who's in charge of laughter in this family. Let's think of something cheerful."

"Oh, my!" Cynthia said, "I *do* have some wonderful news: I forgot to tell you that Angie is going to have a baby."

"What! How could you have forgotten to tell me my little sister is going to have a baby!"

"She said she wrote you a letter."

"Oh, I haven't read any mail since before the accident. I'll look forward to reading it. But it's wonderful news!" Beth was tempted to tell Cynthia her own suspicion, but thought she'd wait until the doctor confirmed it and she'd told Michael. "When's the baby due?"

"In four months."

"And she didn't tell us about it until now?"

"After that mishmash last year, she didn't want to rush to judgement."

"And how's Giff taking the news that he's going to be a daddy?"

"Angie said that at first he tried not to appear too excited, but since Uncle Jim confirmed it, he's been walking on air." She hugged Beth. "Can you believe it—we're going to be aunties! It's hard to believe, isn't it? It seems like Giff, Angie, you, and I were all kids just a short time ago. Oh, and speaking of kids—you remember Dave's sister, Sally, don't you?"

"Of course."

"Well, she's just had a baby boy. That's why we were at the Bonner ranch at the time of your accident."

"So what about you, Auntie Thia? When are you and Dave starting a family?"

"The night that damn railroad reaches Dallas. Or maybe we won't wait that long—we might get the little bugger started in the afternoon."

"Oh, Thia, you're incorrigible!" Beth exclaimed.

They got up and arm in arm, started walking back to the house.

As soon as the carriage drove away, the temporary cheer departed with it, and the pall returned to hang over the household.

When Michael decided to go to his office, Beth was left on her own, alone in the house with only the four hostile servants. She couldn't think of a more dismal way to spend a day, so she dressed to go out.

To purposely avoid telling James she was leaving, Beth didn't request a carriage, but walked down the driveway to the street, where she found a hack for hire. She told the driver to take her to the doctor's office.

Dr. Raymond appeared surprised to see her so soon. "I hope you aren't suffering a relapse, Mrs. Carrington," he said as soon as they were seated in his office.

"No, my visit today has nothing to do with the accident, Dr. Raymond. If you remember, before that unfortunate occurrence, I had made an appointment to see you. I believe I'm pregnant."

"Good heavens, madam, why didn't you mention this in the hospital?"

"It was just a suspicion on my part, and I thought my husband had enough on his mind without burdening him with the possibility of losing an unborn child. Since I see no evidence that occurred, I'd like you to confirm whether or not my suspicion is accurate."

She left his office with his affirmation that she was indeed with child. Beth couldn't wait to give Michael the good news.

She went straight to his office, but Howard informed her that Michael had left for home. "I'm glad to see you're well enough to be up and around, Mrs. Carrington," he said.

"I've never felt better, Howard," she said cheerfully, which brought a disgruntled look from Frederick Taylor, who sat at a nearby desk. The German engineer had appeared uncomfortable when she'd appeared and never offered a greeting or word of condolence. Most likely both men misconstrued her reply to mean she was not mourning Rachel's loss, but she no longer gave a damn what any of these people thought about her or her reasons for marrying Michael. The only person whose opinion she'd respected had been Rachel. Beth hailed a carriage to return to the mansion.

"In the future, Mrs. Carrington, I would appreciate it if you would inform me when you leave the residence," James said.

"That certainly was inconsiderate of me, James, for which I apologize," she said graciously. "As my mother always advised me, there's really no excuse for *anyone* to be inconsiderate or rude. Is there, James?"

"No, Mrs. Carrington," he answered hesitantly.

"One could say it might even reflect a very poor unbringing. Wouldn't you agree, James?"

Now he appeared confused. "Yes, Mrs. Carrington."

"Therefore, so there's no further misunderstanding on either of our parts, in the future, James, I would appreciate it if *you'd* remember that I'm the wife of your employer, and expect to be treated with the courtesy that position entitles me. Please inform the rest of the staff of my wishes, as well— or if you'd prefer, you can assemble them now and I'll inform them myself."

Having recognized he'd been cleverly trounced,

he said, somewhat abashed, "I will inform them, Mrs. Carrington."

"Thank you, James." With a serene smile, she handed him her wrap, then walked up the stairway.

Finding no sign of Michael in their suite, she started to go downstairs, then thought of the place he might be. She headed for the left wing.

When she opened the door of Rachel's suite, Michael was slumped in a chair, gazing into space. He glanced up when she entered. "Beth, where have you been? I've been worried about you."

"I'm sorry. I should have left you a note."

He suddenly blurted, "God, I miss her, Beth. I'm so used to coming home and seeing her here."

Beth knelt at his feet, then gently clasped his hand. "I loved her, too, Michael."

He tried to smile, but the pain in his eyes tore at her heart. "I know you did. Considering how the rest of my family treated you, I'll always be grateful for your kindness to my grandmother."

"It wasn't hard to do; I only responded to her gentleness."

"I guess the hardest thing was not being there at the end. I've been trying to remember if I kissed her good-bye when I left for Fort Worth." Tormented, he looked at her. "I can't remember, Beth. I can't remember." He buried his head in his hands.

"Michael," she said gently, taking one of his hands, "she was very happy that day. That was the last thing she said just before the accident." Beth told him about Rachel's new bonnet, her delight in the organ grinder's monkey, and many of the other moments they had shared that day.

"I'm glad for that," he said.

"Middy always told us that the Lord never closes

a door without opening a window. I have something to tell you, Michael, that I hope will be that window for you."

He raised his head and looked at her, curiosity blanketing the wall of misery that lay behind it. "What is it?"

"We're going to have a baby, Michael."

For several seconds his expression didn't change, and she wasn't sure he understood. Then, as if a light had gone on in his head, she saw the exact second he grasped the meaning of her words. His eyes moistened. "Oh, God, Rusty," he said with a reverence she had never believed he possessed. Pulling her up onto his lap, he clutched her tightly against him and held her for a long moment.

"Nana knew, Michael," Beth said with tears in her eyes. "I told her that day. She was thrilled by the news and promised she'd keep the secret until I told you."

He suddenly stiffened and pulled back to look at her anxiously. "But the accident . . . the baby—"

"Is fine. The doctor examined me today; that's where I've been. He's confident we'll have a healthy child in October. You don't think a little bump would hurt our baby, do you? Our son's a tough Texan like his daddy, who can shrug off a snake's bite as lightly as a gnat's."

"Our son."

Michael's warm chuckle pierced the misery that had encased her heart the past few days. She knew that the healing would begin now for both of them, and the expectation of their child would speed that recovery.

"Just what makes you so sure the baby's a boy, Mrs. Carrington?" he asked, shifting her so that her legs hung over the chair's arm and she was leaning back in the curve of his embrace. "I'd prefer a little

redhead with sapphire eyes and a sassy mouth, just
like her mother."

"We'll give that our prime attention after our son
is born."

He kissed her long and gently, then covered her
face and eyes with quick, moist kisses. "A baby!"
he murmured, as if he still couldn't believe it. "Oh,
God, Rusty!" he said, hugging her to him.

Chapter 25

⌒⌒◯◯⌒

"**T**wo pairs," Beth declared triumphantly, laying down her hand.

Michael threw down his cards. "I swear you've got these cards marked somehow."

Two events—Rachel's death and the anticipated birth of their child—had brought a sense of normalcy to their marriage. They had spent a relaxing evening in their suite, enjoying each other's company. Neither of them had been inclined to eat in the formal dining room, so they'd eaten a light supper in their suite and then resumed their game of Truth or Jeopardy.

"By the way, Michael, what happened to my purse and the packages that were in the buggy the day of the accident? I bought us a lovely mother-of-pearl case for these cards."

"It all must be at the wheelwrights—that's where the wreckage was taken. I intend to go there in the next day or two to see if the buggy can be salvaged. Now, what nasty feat have you got in mind for me: a truth or a jeopardy?"

"I'm in a very benevolent mood, Michael. I'm going to make it easy on you: you just have to read me to sleep." She retrieved a thin volume from the night table and handed it to him.

Glancing at the title of the book, Michael's face contorted in agony. "Beth! Love poems!"

"Elizabeth Barrett Browning has always been a favorite of mine."

"But *Sonnets from the Portuguese*!" He groaned. "Is that what you call being benevolent? It's more like torture."

"I remember some pretty poetic words from you on that riverboat." She tapped a finger on her chin. "If I recall, it went something like darkness changing my hair to auburn—"

"I had seduction on my mind at the time."

"That didn't make it any less poetic. But you can always get out of this by handing over a share of stock."

"Why not some Shakespeare? *Hamlet*? *Romeo and Juliet*?"

"Too dreary."

"Okay, then how about Poe? *Murders in the Rue Morgue*?"

"Too grisly."

"Shelley or Byron?"

She shook her head. "Elizabeth Barrett Browning." Faking a yawn, she patted her mouth with her palm. "I am feeling very sleepy."

"You show no mercy, lady."

"None whatsoever, Sir Lancelot," she said, smiling. Removing her robe, she climbed into bed.

For the next thirty minutes Beth lay contentedly as the sensual huskiness of his voice lulled her into drowsiness. Her eyes gradually drooped, and she slipped into slumber.

Michael stood up and put aside the book. For a long moment, his gaze drank in the delicate oval face. This woman had come to mean his life to him. He'd botched it horribly when he tried to tell her that. And those three days when she'd lain unconscious had been the worst hell he'd ever gone through. He'd chosen the wrong person as an object for his father's petition for revenge. How cocky he'd been, believing he could hold the upper hand with her. No matter what his intent, she'd always managed to turn the tables on him—that first weekend they met and now again with their marriage. He'd indeed gotten caught in his own web, and he knew she'd never forgive him unless he released her—and that was the one thing he couldn't bear to do.

" 'How do I love thee? Let me count the ways,' " he whispered, and pressed a light kiss to her forehead.

At breakfast Michael broke the bad news to Beth that Stephen and his family were returning that day for the reading of Rachel's will.

"Martin Glazer has set the reading for two o'clock. You're expected to attend, Beth."

She grimaced. "Why must I, Michael? It's your family's business. I'm not a Carrington."

"You are by marriage, honey, and Martin's letter indicates all family members."

"I hated the reading of my father's will. It's bad enough when you're among people you love, but I think there's something ghoulish about sitting and listening to the effects of the dead being distributed. I think a simple letter to any heir would be the kindest thing to do."

"I can't say I'm looking forward to it myself," he said sadly. "It's like the deceased speaking to you from the grave, and it's hard to distinguish in your mind that the loved one was alive when the will was written."

They'd no more than finished the morning meal when Stephen and his family returned, which drove Beth to the sanctuary of her room until lunch.

As usual, Stephen succeeded in turning the meal into an unpleasant ordeal for all involved. Beth marveled at how Michael managed to keep his temper when his cousin continued to goad him.

"If I were you, Jake, I'd be concerned," Stephen said smugly. "With Grandmother's stock most likely being divided evenly between you and me, you won't have that big voting block she always brought to the table in your behalf. And if she willed some shares to Emily, I'll have my daughter's proxy. You're in trouble, Jake."

"I'll worry about that when and if that time comes, Stephen. Ten percent of Lone Star stock is in the hands of stockholders who aren't Carringtons. You'd still need that vote for a majority."

Stephen smiled cunningly. "I know, Jake. I've been talking to several of them lately."

"Had your own private little board meeting down in Austin, did you? I hope you found your family in good health, Millicent," Michael said pointedly to her. Then he turned back to Stephen. "I never doubted that was the purpose behind your sudden trip to Austin. I'm surprised that you waited long enough for us to bury Grannie before you rushed down there."

"I'm sure you'll be in for more surprises at the next stockholders' meeting, Jake."

"I wouldn't count your votes before they're cast, Stephen. Now, if you'll excuse us."

"Michael, will you explain that whole conversation to me?" Beth asked, once they were back in their suite.

"The Lone Star's voting options are determined by the percentage of stock owned: in other words, ten percent would mean ten votes, twenty percent, twenty votes. Grannie owned fifty percent of the stock."

"Therefore, fifty votes," Beth said.

"That's right. Stephen and I each own twenty percent, and the remaining ten percent is owned by non-family, several of whom are Wallaces—Millicent's family. They live in Austin."

"I see; it's starting to become clearer. So if your grandmother split her stock between you and Stephen, you'd each own forty-five percent, and that remaining ten percent would be critical."

"There are a couple of other stockholders: Carl Bennett, for instance. I imagine Stephen could easily tie up his vote since I've dropped Diane. So if Grannie willed any stock to Emily, it merely fortifies Stephen's position. He'd have her voting proxy because she's a minor."

Beth sighed. "It doesn't look good for you, Michael. I'm sorry. I know the Lone Star means as much to you as the Rocky Mountain means to me."

"Don't count me out just yet. I don't give up any battle that easily."

"Considering our own private one, I'd have to agree."

He slipped his hands around her waist and pulled her into his arms. "*Especially* that battle, Mrs. Carrington," he murmured, just before he kissed her.

"Is that baby of ours tucked away safely?" he asked, his hands skimming down her sides and coming to rest on her rear.

"What do you mean?"

"Where its daddy can't harm it, if he wants to make love to its mother?"

"Of course." She arched a brow provocatively. "Is that what our baby's daddy has in mind?"

"It sure is."

"I think we should give the baby a name, instead of calling it, 'it.' "

"Don't try to change the subject." His hands had begun a tantalizing sweep of her spine which was driving her wild. And before she knew it, he had managed to raise her skirt and slide his hands under it.

"Michael," she gasped when his palm slid between her legs. "We don't have time for this."

"Oh Lord, Rusty, you feel so good. I needed to touch you . . . to feel the heat of you."

She felt on fire. His hands and whispered words were arousing her passion to a fever pitch. "Stop it, Michael. You know I can't think when you do those things to me."

He abandoned the sensual pressure and moved his hands to her neck, then covered her mouth again, feathering her lips with light kisses until she ached for the firm pressure of his lips. By the time he kissed her and slipped his tongue between her parted lips, her heart was pounding so hard she could barely breathe.

When he began to unbutton her bodice, she breathlessly stopped him. "Michael, we *must* go downstairs. They're waiting."

"Uh-huh," he agreed, nudging her backwards toward the bedroom. She closed her eyes, her head swirling in passion as his mouth played erotically with the pulse at her throat.

Seeking closer contact, she pressed against him and breathed in the tantalizing male scent of him. "Whatever you do, don't stop." Sliding her arms around his neck, she fell back onto the bed and pulled him down on her.

Just before entering the library, Beth stopped Michael. "Wait a minute—your cravat. She adjusted the knot, then nodded her approval. "There, that's better."

"Your hair." He smoothed the top of her head. "There, that's better." He winked and took her hand.

Upon entering the room, they were met by a scowl from Stephen and a disgruntled pout from Emily, who was sitting between her parents. James, Mary, Bertha, and Helga sat in a rear row. Beth observed that none of them offered their usual scornful glances at her. She wondered if James had passed on her message to them, or if it was because Michael was with her.

"Do you suppose Stephen suspects why we were late?" Beth whispered, as they sat down in the two remaining chairs in a far corner.

"The thought would never occur to the prig. He wouldn't make love in daylight even to his mistress," Michael replied *sotto voce*.

Martin Glazer cleared his throat. "Now that we are all assembled, I would like to preface the reading of this will with a few words. This was Rachel Carrington's final will, signed and duly executed on the very day of her death. Her assets, with the exception of this residence and her stock in the Lone Star Railroad, have been evaluated by the accounting firm of Jenkins and Crockett, and they estimate the value at approximately twelve and a half million dollars." He picked up the will and began to read aloud.

I, Rachel Louise Carrington, being of sound mind and body, do hereby declare this to be my last will and testament.

As the lawyer read on, Beth remembered her family gathered together at the reading of her father's will. She closed her eyes and could see her sisters, Middy, Dave, and Giff sitting solemnly as Charles Reardon read her father's will to them. Shaking aside the image, she forced her attention back to the present and the drone of Glazer's voice.

> . . . *from which I bequeath the following: five hundred thousand dollars to my great-granddaughter, Emily Ann Carrington, to be held in trust until her twenty-fifth birthday; twenty-five thousand dollars to James and Mary Nugent, who have served me so devotedly through the years; ten thousand dollars to my faithful nursemaid, Bertha Harriet Kaul; five thousand dollars each to the dear wives of my grandsons, Millicent Wallace Carrington and Elizabeth MacKenzie Carrington, both of whom I love dearly, so I hope they'll take this money and have themselves a grand old time with it; one thousand dollars each to Helga Schneider and Robert Harris, who have served my household; one hundred thousand dollars to St. Luke's Hospital Building Fund; ten thousand dollars to Our Savior's Lutheran Church; ten thousand dollars each to the Masonic Orphans' Fund, the Catholic Orphans' Fund, and the B'nai B'rith-Sons of the Covenant-Orphans' Fund. The remainder of my estate, with the exception of my Lone Star Railroad stock, is to be divided equally between my grandsons, Stephen Richard Carrington and Michael Jacob Carrington. As to the division of the house, boys, you're just going to have to fight it out between you.*

The remark was so typical of Rachel that it even brought a smile to the lips of Stephen.

Pausing to take a sip of water, Martin Glazer read on:

*I bequeath my jewelry to my great-granddaughter,
Emily, with the following exceptions: I wish my
pearl ring be given to Millicent Wallace Carrington, my gold locket to Elizabeth MacKenzie Carrington, and my jade cameo brooch, which she so
admired, to Bertha Harriet Kaul.*

*As to the disposition of my fifty percent stock
ownership in the Lone Star Railroad, I bequeath
one-fifth of the shares to Stephen Carrington, one-
fifth to Michael Carrington—*

The distribution was even worse than Michael
had imagined it would be. Beth turned sympathet-
ically to him and squeezed his hand as the lawyer
continued:

*—and the remaining three-fifths of the shares to
Elizabeth MacKenzie Carrington.*

Beth's own gasp was drowned out by all the others.

Recalling what Michael had told her earlier, she
did a hasty calculation and realized that she, Michael, and Stephen would each hold thirty percent
of Lone Star stock. Even with the remaining ten
percent from the other shareholders, Stephen
wouldn't have the majority vote he sought; the
most he could count on would be forty percent
against her and Michael's combined sixty percent.
She looked at Michael, and his wide grin confirmed
that he had reached the same conclusion. Rachel
had willed controlling interest of the Lone Star
Railroad to them.

Stephen had already jumped to his feet, shouting
that he'd challenge the will. "I'll prove that my
grandmother was senile at the time she executed
that will," he continued to rave.

Martin Glazer looked at him disgustedly. "Stephen, you've a legal right to challenge the will, but as her personal attorney for the past forty-five years, I can assure you that Rachel Carrington's mind was as sound as anyone's in this room. I shall further advise you that if you intend to besmirch her sanity in a court of law, I personally shall fight you to the end."

Glazer once again cleared his throat. "In conclusion, as you all know, I acted in accordance with Rachel's request in her will, and her remains were entombed beside her husband."

Michael shook Glazer's hand, thanked him for his help and guidance through the years, and then turned to Stephen.

"*Now* it's time for that stockholders' meeting you wanted. Call it for Monday, Stephen; I'm sure the stockholders would like to meet the new member."

Stephen's malevolent glare sent a chill down Beth's spine.

Grabbing Beth by the hand, Michael literally raced up the stairway. As soon as he slammed their door, he picked her up and swung her around in a circle. "Grannie! Grannie! Grannie! I love you! I love you! I love you!" he shouted joyously. Then he kissed Beth and hugged her. "Did you see Stephen's face, Beth? Oh, what a coup! I've never known such satisfaction." He threw back his head and closed his eyes. When he opened them, he said soberly, "But it was a hell of a price to pay, wasn't it? A lifetime of such moments could never compare to having her back."

Beth felt the rise of tears, and Michael gently brushed them off her cheeks with his thumbs. "Tell you what, Mrs. Carrington, mother of my unborn child: this is our night to celebrate. I want to spend it just with you. We'll put on our best bib and tucker, go to the finest restaurant, eat the best they have to offer, have a waltz or two together, and then I'll bring you home and make passionate love to you."

"Do you think that's what Nana Rachel would like us to do?" she asked gaily.

"Absolutely! Grannie was a romantic at heart."

As they dressed for dinner later, Beth thought about Michael's words. Rachel had spoken often about her life with Jacob Carrington. It was indeed true that she believed strongly in the bond of marriage, and clearly Stephen's marriage was a disappointment to her. But how could she think any differently about Michael's? Rachel knew Beth *had* married Michael to regain the Rocky Mountain stock, yet she held firmly to the belief that they were in love. And the greatest puzzle to Beth was why Rachel would trust Lone Star stock to her hands.

"Michael, why do you think your grandmother willed me that stock? She had no way of knowing I was carrying your child when she made out that will."

"I think it's pretty obvious. It wasn't for my sake or yours—she did it for the good of the railroad, Beth. Grannie knew Stephen would have the advantage if she split the shares equally."

"I don't doubt that, but why choose me? I'm your wife, which tips the scales to your advantage."

"Not necessarily. Grannie was a shrewd businesswoman, Beth, and I'm sure she was thinking more about the future of the Lone Star than pleasing either of her grandsons. I think she trusted you enough to know you have the grit to stand up and challenge me if I show bad business judgement."

"So, you admit that you do show bad judgement at times."

"I said *if* I did." His eyes filled with devilment. "Which is very unlikely."

"Oh, what a swellhead!"

He slipped her wrap around her shoulders, then slid an arm around her waist. "Let's get going, lady: my mind's already on the after-dinner 'dessert.' "

Chapter 26

B eth awoke and stretched languorously. For a few seconds she lay contentedly before turning her head. Michael was gone, but a single red rose lay on the pillow. Purloined from the garden, no doubt, she thought with amusement.

Smiling, she picked it up and breathed in the sweet fragrance and thought of last night. The whole evening had been wonderful. Michael could be so incredibly romantic when he wanted to be— his little gestures that made her feel cherished, the warmth of his chuckle, the devilishness of his grin, his sense of humor. The way his eyes brightened when his gaze found her in a crowd. His kiss, his touch, the male essence of him—those, too, contributed to her feeling for him. Although she had never been intimate with any other man, she knew in her heart that no other could arouse her and lift her to the heights of ecstasy that he did.

But how could any woman with pride fall in love with a man who had married her out of revenge? Rachel's death had forced them into an alliance where adversary became ally, and now they were deluding themselves into believing they were in love.

Enemies couldn't change their loyalties that easily, could they? *Not when that enemy has slandered my father.*

And that was the unscalable wall that would always stand between them, because both held firm to their own belief.

The more she tried to rationalize her feelings for Michael and seek a solution to their bizarre entanglement, the more confused she became. She finally threw back the quilt and climbed out of bed. "Regardless, he's your baby's father, Beth—and that means you're here to stay."

Michael and Stephen were sitting at opposite ends of the table, their heads buried behind the morning newspapers. Millicent and Emily didn't even bother to look up when she came in and sat down.

"Good morning, everyone."

Michael peeked out from behind the newspaper. "Morning, Beth. We didn't wait for you; I wasn't sure if you were getting up for breakfast."

When there was no response from anyone else at the table, she arched a brow. He grinned and winked.

James came in and put a poached egg down in front of her. "I'd prefer a dish of oatmeal this morning, please." At his distressed look she asked, "Is that a problem, James?"

"I'm afraid the cook has prepared you a poached egg, Mrs. Carrington."

Stephen lowered his newspaper enough to peer over the top of it at her. Michael folded his and put it aside. She knew he was waiting to hear how she'd handle the situation.

"The cook? I believe *the cook* has a name, doesn't she? In fact, since she is your wife, you should be quite familiar with it, should you not?"

"Yes, Mrs. Carrington. Her name is Mary."

"In the future, James, I prefer you to refer to her as such. Now, will you please inform Mary that I do not wish a poached egg? Now or in the future."

"Yes, Mrs. Carrington." He picked up the dish containing the egg. "It will take time to make the oatmeal."

"I'm prepared to wait, James. The day is young."

"Really, Beth! We're not in the habit of sparring with the servants in this household," Stephen said, when James departed. He got up and left the table. Millicent and Emily followed.

"Oh, my, it appears I've offended your cousin," Beth said.

"You're enjoying this, aren't you?"

"Michael, perhaps you see this all as a game, but I don't. These people treat me as an interloper who's trying to run off with the silverware. I intend to make it clear to all—whether it's your cousin or the household servants—that I will *not* tolerate their attitudes. They don't have to like me any more than I like them, but if I have to remain in this house and raise my child here, I expect them to demonstrate the civilities they credit themselves as possessing. What the heck are you grinning about, Michael? This isn't funny."

"What I'm hearing is that you're determined to remain here."

Irritated, she declared, "Of course I'm determined. We have an arrangement, haven't we?"

He got up and came over to her. Leaning down, he smiled into her eyes. "I have the impression you'd stay, arrangement or not." He kissed her, then started to leave. "I'll be back for lunch."

She jerked her head around. "Where are you going?"

"To the wheelwright's to check out the buggy."

"I want to come with you."

"Beth, why would you want to come along? It's just a workshop."

"I know what we had in that buggy, so I'll be able to tell you if anything's missing."

"And if there is, it'd be long gone, Beth."

"All right, I'll be truthful: I don't want to remain here alone with all these angry people. They're likely to tar and feather me while you're gone."

Folding his arms across his chest, Michael leaned back against the wall. "Well, why didn't you say that to begin with? After what you said earlier, Miz Susan B. Anthony, I figured you wanted to spend the day marching back and forth out front with a sign declaring this house unfair to suffering wives."

"I hope the others take me more seriously than you do."

"Beth, I am taking you seriously. And if the servants are treating you disrespectfully, I'll get rid of them. You're my wife, and with Grannie gone, you and Millicent are running this household. I doubt *she'd* give you an argument about anything. Now get your hat, honey, and you can come with me. I might even take you to lunch if you promise not to argue with the waiter."

She glanced at him sheepishly. "I can't come right now."

He threw his hands up in frustration. "Good Lord! After all this argument, why not?"

"I have to wait for my oatmeal." Their eyes met for a second, then they both broke into laughter.

Beth had not anticipated the shock to her emotions that hit when she saw the small pile of packages that had been put aside to be claimed. Her heart seemed to twist within her breast when she picked up Rachel's battered hat, and tears ran down her cheeks.

"What are you doing, Beth?" Michael asked gently.

"The peacock feather's supposed to be upright," she sobbed. "I can't make it stand up, Michael."

"The feather's broken, Beth," he said, gently prying her hands away from it and hugging her. "Did you find your purse?"

"My purse? Oh—yes, there it is," she said, when she saw it among the brightly wrapped packages. "And there's your grandmother's, too."

"What about the other things?" he said firmly. "Do you remember how many there were?"

Beth realized he was trying to make her concentrate so she didn't dwell on Rachel's death. She wiped away her tears and reached for the first package; but trying to identify the gifts from memory became a painful procedure that ended up making her recall the laughter and pleasure they'd shared when she and Rachel picked them out.

"To the best of my memory, nothing's missing, Michael."

He nodded, and she could tell from his tormented look that he'd probably have been happier if it all had been lost. Cupping her chin, he tipped up her face and stared deeply into her eyes, which were still moist with tears. "You okay, honey?" he asked.

"I'm fine now. I'm sorry I broke down."

His arm curved around her shoulders protectively, pulling her against his side. "Thanks, Clyde," he said to the wheelwright, who had stood by looking solemn and sad. "How bad is the damage to the buggy?"

"Well, Jake, I reckon it could have been worse," he said, leading them over to the corner of the shop. "Front's in good shape, but the rear got the worst of it. Left wheel's bent and can't be repaired." He took off his hat and scratched a head of salt-and-pepper hair. "Sure curious 'bout something, though. Mrs. Carrington, can you recollect how that accident happened?"

"Well, I remember this child darting into the path of the wagon, and I pulled up sharply on the reins."

"You hit anything when you did?"

"No. The wagon swayed violently for a couple of seconds, then suddenly the rear of the carriage just collapsed to the ground, and we rolled over. Rachel was . . . was tossed out, and I got pinned under it."

"You say the rear collapsed before it rolled over?"

"Yes."

"That means the axle splintered apart before it even hit the ground," Clyde said. "Probably when you said it swayed."

"What happened? Did it lose a wheel?" Michael asked.

Clyde shook his head. "No. If the wheel had rolled off, it wouldn't have been bent from the crash."

"That doesn't make sense." Michael frowned. "There's a metal connecting rod between the front and rear axles. If that broke somehow, then the front and back would have gone down at the same time."

"That's what I figured, too. And that rod ain't broken. That's what got me to thinking, so I checked over that rear axle real good." He knelt down. "Take a look at it, Jake. Them broken-off sides are smooth—too smooth to have splintered in a crash. 'Pears to me like that axle was practically sawed through."

Michael knelt down, and after examining the wooden axle carefully, he glanced up at the wheelwright. "My God, you're right!"

"What are you saying?" Beth asked, her heartbeat quickening.

Michael looked up at her, his eyes hardened with rage. "It means that it was no accident—Grannie was murdered."

She shuddered at the thought and closed her eyes in anguish. "No! That can't be true!"

Michael's arm held Beth upright as her trembling legs buckled beneath her. "Clyde, for the time being, I'd appreciate it if you didn't say anything to anyone. I've got to think some more about this."

"Maybe we're wrong, Jake. There ain't a person alive who'd have wanted to see any harm come to Rachel Carrington. There ain't never been anyone sweeter than her."

"I know. So please hold off on any repairs to the buggy until I tell you to. And thanks again."

Michael helped Beth into the carriage, and they were about to drive away when Clyde came running out.

"Hold up there, Jake. You almost forget these here packages. He put them in the back of the carriage. " 'Bye, folks."

Michael shook his hand. "Good-bye, Clyde."

"Good-bye," Beth said numbly.

This latest development abolished any thought of going to lunch. By the time they reached the house, her trembling had stopped, and she brushed off Michael's hands when he moved to pick her up to carry her up the stairway. "I can walk up myself," she declared.

"Let's try and figure this out," Michael said once

they were seated in their sitting room. "Tell me exactly what happened that morning, Beth."

"We all had breakfast—nothing unusual there. Stephen left for the office, and I went out to leave, too, the same as I'd been doing all week. I was about to drive away when Rachel came out and asked to go with me. James and Bertha tried to stop her, but she was insistent. The first thing she asked to do was to go to Mr. Glazer's office, and then we went to the Rocky Mountain office just long enough for me to collect the mail. From there we went to about a dozen stores."

"What about the buggy all that time?"

"We were in and out of it until I left it with the hostler at the hotel during lunch and for the short time we were in the park."

"That was the only time it was out of your sight for any length of time."

"Yes."

"I think it was unlikely anyone would tamper with it then."

"Michael, the more I think of it, it just seems to be an unfortunate accident."

"I doubt that. The axle had been sawed through enough that just a minor jolt or strain on it would cause it to crack and tip over. Let's go over this again. You said Stephen had already left."

"Yes, and just as I'd been doing all week, I had Robert hitch up—"

"Robert!"

"Of course."

"Robert disappeared the day of the funeral. Don't you think that's a coincidence?" He got to his feet and began to pace. "This is beginning to become clearer. Did you drive that same buggy every day?"

"Yes, I specifically requested it because it was light and easy to handle."

"And since you'd been doing it all week, everyone was aware of your schedule. Grannie going that morning was unexpected. Whoever tampered with the buggy had not anticipated that."

Her eyes widened. "So I was the intended victim."

"I think so, Beth," he said solemnly.

"If that's the case, you've got a whole household of suspects."

"That's true, but Robert's the only one who ran off after the accident."

"Oh, my!" she exclaimed, suddenly remembering the threatening letter. She went to the dresser and dug it out. "I didn't tell you about this," she said, handing it to him.

Reading it quickly, he glanced up, appalled. "When did you get this?"

"I found it in my top drawer the day we returned from La Paloma. I figured only someone in this house could have put it in my room, so I decided to investigate. I managed to check Stephen's, Emily's, and James's rooms. Then I found some newspaper clippings in Robert's room. He almost caught me in the act, and I hurt my ankle escaping."

"My God, Beth, why didn't you tell me?"

"I thought the letter was just a threat to scare me away. I never believed that it was life-threatening."

"Did you confront Robert with this?"

"No. I never received any other letters, so I didn't make an issue of it."

"I can't figure out why Robert would do this. He hasn't even been with us that long. And he wouldn't have any reason to have a grudge against you."

She lowered her eyes guiltily. "There's something else."

"What, Beth? What else haven't you told me?" he demanded in a sharper tone.

"Maybe he thought he did have a reason. I discovered Robert and Emily in the garden one night. Apparently they'd been meeting there regularly. He asked me not to tell Stephen. Also, Emily hates me, and I'm sure she's expressed that sentiment to him. Wouldn't that be enough to try and scare me off?"

Michael took her in his arms. "Lord, Beth, why did you keep all this to yourself?"

"Robert seemed like such a nice young man. It's hard for me to believe he's responsible for Rachel's death."

"Well, I'm going to notify the police. I want him found." He tucked the letter into his pocket. "Let's go together. After I report this to the police, we'll have that lunch we talked about."

At the police headquarters Michael signed a complaint, and he was unusually quiet throughout lunch, clearly preoccupied with his troubled thoughts. Once back at the house, Beth preferred to remain in their suite while he went down to the library to do some paperwork. Shortly before dinner, he came back upstairs.

"How would you like to get out of here for a couple days and take a ride out to Tent Town tomorrow? I think we both could use a good dose of Cynthia."

"I can't think of anything I'd rather do—other than go back to the Roundhouse," she said.

Anticipating the trip, her spirits were high when she entered the dining room for dinner.

"You told them!" Emily accused, jumping to her feet. "Oh, I hate you! You've brought us nothing but grief." Sobbing, the young girl dashed from the room.

Millicent Carrington rose to follow. "Millicent, sit down," Stephen ordered. "By sanctioning child-ish behavior, you only encourage it."

"I'm sorry, Stephen, but our daughter is griev-ing. As a mother, I cannot ignore her suffering."

Though taken aback by Emily's attack on her, Beth wanted to stand up and cheer when the woman placed her napkin on the table and walked out of the room.

Stephen turned his ire on Beth. "Am I to under-stand from Emily's outburst that you were aware of the illicit relationship between my daughter and a stable boy?"

"I was not aware of any such relationship, Ste-phen."

"How dare you lie to me!" Stephen declared with unbridled anger. "Emily's accusation made it evident you knew of the relationship."

"I saw Emily and Robert sharing a kiss in the garden, which I consider to be perfectly normal. An illicit relationship in my opinion is more on the or-der of a married man engaging in an adulterous affair."

Stephen blanched at the pointed remark, then his mouth narrowed into a thin line. "You scheming little whore. How dare you accuse me—"

Before he could finish, he was yanked out of his chair and slammed against the wall. Michael grabbed a fistful of Stephen's shirtfront, and his eyes, black with fury, bored into the startled man. "I normally wouldn't hit a man older than I am, you pathetic bastard, but unless you apologize to my wife, I'm going to wipe up this floor with you."

"Deny it if you can," Stephen mumbled in a frightened falsetto. "All of Dallas knows she only married you to get back her railroad."

"That's between her and me," Michael said.

"And now she's got her claws into the Lone Star, too."

"Stop it, both of you," Beth cried out. "Michael, I don't care what names he calls me."

"I do," Michael said through gritted teeth. "Stay out of this, Beth. This fight's been brewing for years."

"Exactly. And I refuse to allow either of you to make me the focus of your rivalry."

Michael released Stephen, and he slumped against the wall. "This house isn't big enough for the both of us," Michael said.

"Actually, I've made plans to leave."

"Moving in with your mistress, Stephen?" Michael said contemptuously.

"I've only remained this long for grandmother's sake. I didn't trust her being left alone with you. My family and I are leaving, and Bertha will be going with us."

"Oh, you couldn't persuade the others to go, too? Why don't you try another crack at it—James might have changed his mind after this morning when Beth wouldn't put up with his attitude."

Beth felt they both were beginning to sound like children. "Please stop this. We do have serious differences here, and it's obvious we're not compatible, but I think we should try to reach a solution that would be satisfactory to all of us. After all, let's consider Millicent and Emily: this is their home. It might be wiser if Michael and I left."

Stephen adjusted his disheveled clothing. Walking over, he leaned on the table, and his scornful glare fell on Michael. "I'm going to ruin you, Jake. I have support among the other stockholders who didn't like your relinquishing that Rocky Mountain stock back to a rival railroad. Many feel you're considering your wife's interests ahead of the Lone Star's."

"Too bad it won't do you and your father-in-law any good. You can't win, cousin, so don't climb out too far on that limb or you're in for a big fall."

"This time you're the one who's going to fall, Jake. That overconfident attitude of yours is exactly *why* I'm going to win."

"Aren't you overlooking one obvious point, Stephen? Beth and I own controlling shares of the stock—so you don't have a majority to vote me out of the presidency. No doubt Grannie anticipated this kind of move on your part, which is why she willed Beth the stock."

"That may be, Jake, but your wife was bought once—there's no doubt she can be bought again if the offer is good enough. Am I mistaken, Beth?" Stephen asked slyly. "Sam Wallace and I are prepared to make you a very juicy offer."

Michael threw back his head in laughter. "Why don't you tell him, Beth?"

"Tell me what?" Stephen asked warily, glancing from one to the other of them. He had clearly lost some of his previous bluster.

"I'm afraid that as always, Stephen, your timing is bad as your judgement of character. I'm holding what's known as an ace in the hole. No matter how lucrative the offer, Beth would never sell out the father of her child. You see, Stephen—my wife and I are expecting an heir."

Chapter 27

After the unpleasant scene with Stephen, Michael and Beth returned to their suite and ultimately ended up sitting down to a game of Truth or Jeopardy.

Beth experienced an unusual run of bad cards and had to throw in her hand several times. Finally she took a chance on one, and lost.

"Am I looking forward to this one," Michael said, rubbing his hands together and leering villainously. "I've thought of a great jeopardy."

"I'm afraid to ask."

"We're going to play a game. You're a slave girl, and I'm your cruel master."

"Sounds like we're well cast for the roles."

"Unlike the clever Scheherazade, you, my naive little maiden, have tried to keep me entertained by reciting inane love poems. I shall have you put to death unless you can succeed in seducing me . . . by dancing in that undergarment you're wearing, made of the finest silks from the Orient."

His imagination was much wilder than she'd ever have guessed—but a jeopardy was a jeopardy, and she wasn't about to renege.

"How am I expected to dance without music, master?"

"Do you not have a music box, slave?"

"I do, but it plays Bach's 'Air for the G String.' I doubt that would be any more to your liking than my love poems, master."

"It will test your skill, maiden."

"I claim no dancing skills, master, other than a few ballet lessons."

"Your evasiveness has roused my wrath, slave—so now I shall not spare you. If you succeed, I promise a quick extinction in my arms from the burning heat of a *petite morte*—but if you fail, you will be subject to a lingering death under the lashing tongue of Stephen Carrington."

Beth couldn't help laughing. "Both options are pretty grim, but I'll take my chances on the first."

"Aha, maiden, but there's the rub: you must seduce me, first."

"With your appetite!" she scoffed. "Without even touching you, I can have you squirming in that chair by the time the music box runs down."

"And I say you can't. In fact, I'm so sure you'll fail that not only will I spare your life, but I'll *gift* you with a share of Rocky Mountain stock should you succeed. But remember, maiden: no touching—hands or lips." He grinned. "Your master does have his weaker moments."

Beth lit several candles, then extinguished the lamp. Picking up the music box, she returned and handed it to him. After kicking off her slippers, she removed the pins from her hair and shook it out to fall in a coppery dishevelment to her shoulders. Then she knelt down on one knee, the other leg stretched out behind her, and bowed her head.

"Very well, master, wind up the music box."

With the first notes of the melody, she slowly raised her head, her eyes as seductive as the graceful, beckoning movements of her arms. She lithely rose to her feet, the invitation in her eyes drawing his gaze deeper into her own. On the balls of her feet, she moved in light, flowing turns and spins, bending her supple body in coaxing, provocative movements, her legs in sleek, smooth bends, always beckoning alluringly with her eyes and arms.

As the song drew to a close, she raised a leg and put her foot on the edge of his chair.

"Have I pleased you, master?" she asked in an exaggeratedly throaty murmur.

Never breaking their locked gazes, he encircled her ankle and slowly ran his hand up the side of her leg, past her calf, her knee, to the inside of her thigh. She slid onto his lap and faced him, her legs straddling his. He kissed her long and deeply until they were both breathless.

"I'll up the ante if you'll do that dance again," he whispered in a husky murmur.

"Auntie? I'd have thought you'd have given it a more masculine name," she teased with a seductive wiggle against his erection, and slid her arms around his neck.

When Beth and Michael rode into Tent Town the next day, Cynthia was just dismissing her students. She and Lydia Rafferty, the wife of the crew boss, shared the teaching responsibility for the crew's children.

Upon seeing them arrive, Cynthia rushed over joyously, and after the hugging and kissing, she stepped back and took a long look at Beth. "You look radiant, Beth. A far cry from the last time I saw you."

"I have some marvelous news to tell you, Thia: I'm going to have a baby."

"Oh, Beth, that's wonderful! Oh, my—Angie and

you both expecting! That settles it; I'm not waiting any longer," she declared.

"Not waiting for what?" Dave asked, joining them. After a quick handshake with Michael, he gave Beth a peck on the cheek.

"To start a family," Cynthia announced. "This railroad will be completed by the time our baby's born, so we can settle in one spot."

"Cyn, I'm an engineer. I go where the job is. We've discussed this before."

"I tend to agree with Thia, Dave," Beth said. "I suspect the future president of the Rocky Mountain Central Railroad would have to settle down in Denver or Dallas. And my vote's on the latter."

"You and I discussed this before, too," Dave said.

"Yes, but this time there's no question about it: I'm stepping down as president. I'll have a child to raise."

Momentarily speechless, Dave glanced at Michael, then back to Beth. "Well, I'll be damned! Another sister-in-law expecting!" He grabbed her in a bear hug. "I'm happy for you, Beth. And you, too, Jake."

"And in nine months you can expect the same congratulations from them, Kincaid," Cynthia said.

Dave laughed and slipped an arm around Cynthia's waist. "Sounds like my work's cut out for me. Good thing you sent me that assistant, Beth. I'll need him more than ever, now."

"What assistant?" Beth asked.

"Robert Harris. He told me you sent him to help me out."

"Robert Harris is here?" Michael glanced at Beth. "It couldn't be the same Harris. Where is he?"

"He should be in the office."

Michael strode toward the caboose that served as Dave's office.

"What's going on, Beth?" Dave asked.

"Harris may be responsible for the death of Rachel Carrington." She ran after Michael, with Dave and Cynthia close behind.

Robert Harris jumped to his feet when Michael stormed through the door. "Mr. Carrington?"

"You should've run a damn sight farther than this, Harris."

"I don't understand, sir," the startled young man said.

"You know damn well what I mean, you murdering son of a bitch!" Papers flew in all directions as Michael grabbed Harris by the shirtfront and yanked him across the desktop.

"Stop him, Dave, before he kills him," Beth cried out.

"Cool down, Jake," Dave said. Grabbing Michael by the arms, he held him firmly. "Let him go, Jake, and tell me what this is all about."

Michael's expression was menacing, but he released his hold on Harris with a shove that sent him sprawling back onto the desk.

"In his attempt to kill Beth, this bastard murdered my grandmother."

"Murdered?" Harris cried. He stared at Michael, as shocked as he was frightened. "I didn't murder anyone."

"Is that why you ran away?"

"Will someone please explain all this to me," Dave demanded.

"This bastard tampered with the axle on the buggy Beth had been driving the day my grandmother was killed."

"That's not true! I don't know what you're talking about—I never tampered with the buggy."

"Try convincing the police of that," Michael snarled.

Robert turned to Beth. "It's true, Mrs. Carrington. I never tried to harm you or his grandmother."

"What about the threatening letter you sent me, Robert?"

"Beth, don't waste your time listening to this lying murderer," Michael said.

"I never sent you a threatening letter, Mrs. Carrington. You must believe me," Robert pleaded.

"Robert, I found the newspaper in your room that you cut up to use in your message to me."

"What newspaper? What message?"

"What did I tell you, Beth," Michael said. "You're wasting your time. This guy's not going to admit what he's done."

"Is anyone going to fill me in on this?" Dave asked.

"Someone put a letter in my room threatening me to leave or I'd be sorry," Beth said. "It was written in words clipped out of a newspaper."

"Oh, my God!" Cynthia exclaimed.

"I later found newspaper clippings in Robert's quarters."

"I cut out your ad for a ticket seller. That's the only time I ever cut anything out of a newspaper."

"That's a pretty weak alibi, Harris," Dave said.

"I can prove it to you," Robert said. The moment he moved his hand toward his pocket, Michael and Dave both leaped for him. "I just want to get the ad out of my pocket,"

"I'll get it," Dave said. He reached into Harris's coat pocket and pulled out several folded papers. The neatly clipped ad was among them, as he had claimed.

"I didn't want to be a groom all my life," Robert

explained. "So when I read this ad, I thought I'd apply for the position."

"Why didn't you just speak to me directly about it?" Beth asked.

"I thought it'd be better if the Carringtons didn't know I was seeking employment elsewhere any sooner than they had to."

Cynthia, who had been unaccustomedly silent, added her insight. "It wouldn't make sense, Jake, that he'd try to drive Beth away if he hoped to get a job with the railroad."

"How do we know he's telling the truth?" Michael asked. "Just because he kept this ad doesn't mean he's not trying to weasel out of this."

"There's a good way of finding out if he's telling the truth," Beth said. "I stuffed all the responses to that ad into my purse the day Nana Rachel died. They should still be there, and my purse is among those packages we picked up from the wheelwright. I was so upset, I forgot to take the packages into the house. I'll get the purse out of the carriage, and we'll know right away whether Robert's lying about responding to that ad."

"I'll get the purse," Michael said. "Dave, keep an eye on this bastard. He's liable to try and make a break for it."

"I'm telling the truth, Mr. Carrington," Robert insisted.

Dave walked over and drew his Colt from the gun belt hanging on a peg. "I'd hate to have to shoot you, Harris, so don't try anything foolish. Just sit down behind that desk."

Michael came back shortly with Beth's purse. She pulled out the packet of letters and handed them to Harris. "Which of these is yours, Robert?"

The young man quickly sifted through them and

pulled one out of the pile. "This is it," he said, relieved.

Michael snatched the letter from him and ripped it open. After scanning it quickly, he looked up and nodded. "At least he's telling the truth." Michael handed the letter to Beth, who read it as Cynthia looked over her shoulder.

"That still doesn't convince me you didn't tamper with the buggy, Robert," Michael said. "Why would you run off after my grandmother was killed and not tell anyone you were leaving?"

"I didn't run off. Emily's father fired me and ordered me off the property." Michael's surprise showed on his face, and Robert continued, "When Mr. Carrington found out about Em and me, he told me to pack up and get out."

"How did he find out about you and Emily? I never told him I saw you and Emily in the garden," Beth said.

"He said James saw us. I left Em a note telling her."

"Apparently Stephen must have intercepted it, because Emily accused me of telling her father."

"And Stephen didn't bother to deny the mistake," Michael added.

"Did you expect him to?" Beth asked bitterly.

"I admit to meeting Em in secret, but I'll take an oath on the Bible that I never did anything to the buggy."

"How exactly had the buggy been tampered with?" Cynthia asked.

"The rear axle had been almost sawn through, so that any strain would cause it to snap," Michael said. "Which is exactly what happened when Beth had to rein up sharply."

"I didn't do it," Robert insisted. "Them others were always bad-mouthing you behind your back,

Mrs. Carrington, but I had no quarrel with you. You were always kind to me. You didn't even tell Em's father about her and me when you could have. I'd never try to harm you or Miss Rachel. You both were always nice to me. And I'd never try to kill anyone anyway, even if I didn't like 'em."

"I believe you, Robert," Beth said. "Michael, what he's saying makes sense."

"I suppose you're right. When we go back to Dallas, I'll withdraw my complaint. The police chief and I are good friends, and once he hears the truth, you'll be cleared of any suspicion, Robert. I'm sorry." Michael offered Harris a handshake.

"Thank you, sir," Robert said, as the two shook hands. "Under the circumstances, I'd have thought the same thing if I'd been in your place." He looked at Beth. "I hope this doesn't spoil my chances at getting a job with the railroad."

"You'll have to ask Dave about that, Robert," Beth replied. "He's the boss around here."

"And that was a whopper of a lie you told me, Harris," Dave said.

Hanging his head, Robert nodded. "I shouldn't have lied to you, but I was desperate. I needed a job, and I thought that once you saw my work, you'd be pleased enough to overlook my lying to get the job."

"I admit you do a good job, Harris."

"And he wouldn't be the first person who's lied to get a job, Dave," Beth put in hopefully.

"Yeah, Kincaid," Cynthia urged, "the poor boy's been made a victim of love."

Dave groaned. "I might have known little Miss What I Do for Love would interject that argument. Since you are a good worker, Robert, I'll overlook the way you stretched the truth. We'll get out of here now, so you can get back to work."

"Ah, Robert," Beth asked before leaving, "do you plan on trying to see Emily again?"

"I certainly do. If I get a steady job with the railroad, I intend to ask Em to marry me."

"I wish you luck."

"And he's going to need it if he marries that spoiled little twit," she murmured to Cynthia as they walked to her car.

Cynthia tucked her arm in Beth's. "I can't wait to hear this whole story. It sounds so intriguing." She stopped sharply and spun around to face their husbands.

"So if Robert Harris didn't tamper with that buggy, then who did?"

"I don't think anybody did," Beth said. "I think the whole incident was what it appeared to be— an accident. My goodness, we almost had a wanted poster out on poor Robert, and look how that turned out."

"Beth, I think Jake has good reason for his suspicions," Dave said. "If the front and rear axles were attached together by a metal rod, it's illogical that one axle would collapse without the other one, unless a wheel rolled off."

"And the carriage didn't lose a wheel," Michael said.

"Isn't it possible the wood simply splintered?" Cynthia protested.

Michael shook his head. "Not in this case. That rear axle had a cross-grain split almost completely through its thickness."

"Which would reflect a blow from the top from an axe or hatchet," Dave added.

"Or having been sawn through," Michael said pointedly. "And the part of the axle that did actually split apart splintered *along* the grain—with ragged edges. The same piece of wood wouldn't split in two different directions in this type of accident—it wasn't enough of a trauma."

Cynthia's gaze swept their small circle. "Then we're back to the same question—who did it?"

"What the hell is going on over there?" Dave asked, his attention on a cloud of dust billowing above a dozen or so wagons converging on the camp.

To add to the sense of impending drama, a train whistle sounded a shrill clarion, alerting the camp to the early return of the work train carrying the Rocky Mountain crew.

"Jake, I don't like the looks of this," Dave murmured. "Get the gals inside." Then he headed over to the train, which had come to a screeching halt.

"Let's go, ladies," Michael said, hustling them onto the platform of the private car. But both women refused to budge any farther.

Fifty or sixty shouting men climbed down from the wagons, and to Michael's surprise, he recognized the men from the Lone Star crew. Frederick Taylor and Joe Brent, the chief engineer and the crew boss, were among them.

The Rocky Mountain crew jumped off the work train, and the two groups of men squared off against each other as the women in the camp collected their children and whisked them away to the safety of the tents.

"What's this all about, Joe?" Michael asked the man who had been the crew boss for the Lone Star when Michael had worked as a spiker during his school summers.

"There's a strike goin' on, and the men don't like the idea of that Rocky Mountain crew laying rail, Jake."

A chorus of nods and grumbled agreements followed Joe's statement.

"That strike's out east. What difference does that make to you men?"

"Maybe ve go on strike, too," Frederick Taylor said in his guttural accent.

"You men are paid well and work under the safest conditions possible. We don't ask any man to take personal risks, so why would you strike?"

"Ve vant dis railroad out of here."

"Well, it's not gonna be," Sean Rafferty declared from the opposite camp. "We've put our blood and sweat into laying this track, and we're not gonna stop now 'til we get to Dallas."

"We heard talk of a merger," Joe Brent said. "We heard that your wife would get rid of us and bring in her crew."

"If these two railroads ever merged, it would only mean more jobs," Michael yelled, in an effort to be heard above the disgruntled shouting. "Who's feeding you this bullshit? I've got my suspicions."

"You are tryink to protect zer vife," Taylor shouted. "She vant to destroy za Lone Star."

"My wife's never interfered with any decision regarding the Lone Star. She has her own railroad to run."

"Yah! And before ve know, she vill be rippink up our track and layink her own."

Beth had listened to all she intended to. She stepped to the rail of the platform and raised her arms. "I have something to say," she yelled. The hoots and hollers that followed drowned her out. "Please, all of you. Will you please listen?"

"We ain't interested in anything you gotta say, lady," a voice called out. A tossed stone whizzed past her head.

The Irish crew exploded into protective action, and with swinging fists they rushed into the crowd as Michael shoved Beth and Cynthia inside the car, then rushed out and joined the fracas.

Michael ducked the punch of one of the men and backed up into someone. He spun on his heel to deliver a punch to the man, who had turned to do likewise to him, and stunned, looked into the eyes of David Kincaid. With upraised clenched fists, the two men stared at each other.

"Whose side are you on?" Dave asked.

"I was about to ask you the same thing."

"I don't want to hurt you, Jake, but I'll remind you that I did three rounds with John L. Sullivan."

"And I was the boxing champanion of my graduating class."

Suddenly a rifle blast brought everyone to a frozen halt. All eyes turned to Cynthia, who held a smoking rifle pointed in the air. Beth stood beside her.

"Stop it, all of you, before someone gets hurt!" Beth shouted. "I have no desire to get involved with the Lone Star railroad. And I don't know who gave you the idea we'd be ripping up your tracks. We're railroaders here: we lay track—not destroy it. My railroad does *not* present a threat to the Lone Star. This country needs railroads."

"What she says is true, men," Michael said, stepping onto the platform beside her and Cynthia. "There's no stopping the railroads now; it's the travel of the future. Do you think the Rocky Mountain is the only railroad with an eye on Texas? Why, the Santa Fe and the Southern have all gotten grants to lay track in this state. And railroads will do for the fortune of this country what the Texas longhorn did for the cattle business. Within ten years, there'll be so much track crisscrossing this country that anyone will be able to travel to any part of it quickly and cheaply. Now, Joe—get your men out of here. I guarantee that right now all your jobs are secure, but anyone who wants to continue the fight here will be looking for another job. Do you all understand?"

By this time, the fight had gone out of many of the bruised and battered men. They started to climb back into the wagons.

"Should we let 'em go, boss?" Sean Rafferty asked Dave.

He nodded. "Good riddance."

"Who do you think put them up to coming here, Jake?" Cynthia asked a short time later, as she applied a cool rag to a bruise on Dave's forehead.

"I'm sure it was my cousin. Frederick Taylor is a pawn of Stephen's. He's likely to do anything Stephen asked him to do."

Unexpectedly, Beth chuckled and glanced at Michael. "There were enough suspects who wanted to kill me before—now I guess I can add the whole crew of the Lone Star Railroad to those ranks."

Chapter 28

~~~⌒⌒⌒~~~

Stephen and his family were in the process of moving out of the house when Beth and Michael arrived back in Dallas the next day, which led to an exceedingly awkward situation when they all sat down to eat lunch.

Beth nibbled at her meal, her mind not on the plate of food Helga served her, but rather struggling with the question of whether or not to tell Emily about Robert Harris. She also didn't know what to say to poor Millicent, who most certainly was a victim in this rivalry between Michael and Stephen.

And Michael and Stephen made no attempt to ease the unpleasantness. Throughout the meal, the two men didn't even look at each other. Beth took her lead from Michael, who continued to remain silent regarding his suspicions about the carriage accident, so she refrained from telling Emily about Robert Harris, deciding that ultimately it would be wiser to let the young man contact Emily on his own when he was ready.

She felt like an interloper when the meal ended and Stephen's family left for good. Had she driven them out of the house? Despite her dislike for Stephen Carrington, guilt now lay heavily on her shoulders. She'd never had any desire to interfere in the Carrington family, and wished it were she and Michael who'd moved out instead of uprooting the others.

When Michael left to go to the sheriff's office to clear Robert Harris, Beth went upstairs. Never had the big house seemed so empty. To take her mind off the situation, Beth sat down to write Angie a letter.

Her throat felt dry, so she poured herself a glass of water. It didn't help the dryness. Soon her throat felt swollen, and she clutched at it when it became difficult for her to swallow.

Still clutching at her throat, she went into the bathroom and looked in the mirror. Horrified, she saw her face and neck were crimson. She began to feel lightheaded as the rate of her breathing increased excessively. She had to have help.

Beth staggered out of the room and grasping the banister, groped her way down the stairway. She was scared. The only other time she could remember anything like this happening to her was a long time ago, when she'd had a reaction to seafood. But she hadn't eaten seafood since she was a child.

When Beth reached the foot of the stairway, she saw Helga in the foyer and cried out to her. By this time, her throat felt almost completely closed.

The maid hurried over to her. "Yes, Frau Carrington."

"Doctor," Beth gasped. Once again trying to clear her throat, she managed to say, "I need a doctor."

At that moment the front door opened and Michael came in. He immediately rushed over to her, saying, "Beth! My God, what's wrong?"

"She vant doctor, Herr Carrington," Helga said.

Beth tried to speak but couldn't get the words past her swollen throat.

"Are you choking? Is something lodged in your throat?" he asked, stricken. Beth shook her head. "Can you breathe, Beth?" She nodded.

Michael swooped her up in his arms and carried her out to the carriage. Racing the team down the driveway, within minutes he reined up in front of the doctor's office and carried her inside.

Dr. Raymond examined her throat, and after listening to her heart and checking her blood pressure, he put aside his instruments. "Everything appears normal," he said to Michael, who'd hovered in the background throughout the examination. "Your wife's symptoms appear to be an allergic reaction—most likely to a food." He glanced at her medical record. "I see that she's allergic to seafood."

"We haven't had any seafood, Richard. Our cook has explicit instructions not to serve it because of Beth's allergy."

"Do you know what she had for lunch?"

"A chicken salad, the same as I did. I know Beth's had chicken before, so the reaction couldn't be from that."

Beth listened to the two men discussing her as if she wasn't there. It was becoming irritating that neither of them attempted to include her in the discussion even with eye contact.

The doctor prepared a hypodermic and continued to talk to Michael. "This injection will relax those throat muscles to make her feel more comfortable."

Why not give him the shot? she thought, irritated, when the doctor poked her in the arm with the needle.

"Her color should gradually return to normal

within the next couple of days. And it wouldn't hurt to have her drink tea with a lot of lemon juice."

"Doctor, the baby?" Beth asked.

"Had she experienced a more drastic reaction, I'd be concerned, Jake, but there's no reason why this should have an effect on the baby. Whatever she ate, she obviously didn't ingest enough to cause any serious bodily harm."

"Thank the doctor, Daddy," she said to Michael when they prepared to leave.

By the time they got back to the house, the swelling had gone down enough to ease some of Beth's discomfort.

"I'm curious about what was in that chicken salad that caused such a reaction," Michael said. "Did it taste unusual to you?"

"I didn't pay any attention, Michael. I was trying to decide whether or not to tell Emily about Robert."

"Well, mine didn't taste any different than it always did," he said. "I'm going to check it out with Mary."

Michael strode into the kitchen and found Helga alone at the table, drinking a cup of coffee. She jumped to her feet when he entered. "Helga, where is Mary?"

"Dis is da day for dem to be off, Herr Carrington."

He snapped his fingers. "That's right; I forgot. Helga, who made that chicken salad you served for lunch?"

"Mary did before dey left dis mornink. Vhy you ask, Herr Carrington?"

"There was something in it that made Mrs. Carrington ill."

Helga shrugged. "I not know, sir. Is the same as da others and dey not get sick."

"Obviously my wife is allergic to something that was put in the food. When Mary returns, tell her I want to see her immediately."

"Yes, sir. Mrs. Carrington vill be better?" Helga asked.

"She'll be fine in a couple of days," Michael said.

"Dat is goot."

Michael started to leave, and as a last-minute hunch, he asked, "By the way, Helga, was anyone else in the kitchen this morning?"

"Ya. Bertha and Miss Emily vas in here vhen I vas gettink to serve da lunch."

"What was Emily doing in here?"

"She come for glass of milk."

"Thank you, Helga," Michael said, and left the kitchen.

"Well, I didn't learn much," he said, joining Beth in the library. "This is Mary's day off, but she did make the chicken salad before she left. Are you sure you aren't allergic to something other than seafood?"

"I've never had a reaction to any other food," she said. "I certainly don't have a problem with chicken, fruit, or vegetables."

"Maybe Mary used a spice that you're allergic to."

"Perhaps."

"I'll talk to her and find out."

As soon as James and Mary returned, Michael called them and Helga into the study to question the cook on the ingredients used.

After Mary listed the items, it didn't appear to Michael that any special spice had been used. "I made it the same way I always did for your grandmother, and she never complained," Mary said resentfully, folding her arms across her chest.

"All right: this is as good a time as any to settle this issue once and for all," Michael declared, exasperated. "Sit down, all of you."

The three people exchanged surprised glances but sat down awkwardly. "I know how much all of you loved my grandmother, but unfortunately she is gone. I have no doubt you miss her as much as I do, but I wish to make it clear that my wife is now running this household, and I expect you to honor her wishes as you did my grandmother's. Whatever rumors you may have heard, I will not tolerate anyone in this household maligning her character or showing any disrespect. Since she is also carrying our child, her welfare and protection must be given priority over any other consideration. If any of you have a problem accepting this, I insist that you leave. I'll certainly write a letter of recommendation for anyone who chooses to do so.

"And in the future, Mary, I want you to go over the daily menu in detail with Mrs. Carrington every day—*that means every damn ingredient*—until there's no question in your mind as to what is unsafe for her to eat. Thank you, that will be all."

In stunned silence, the three people filed out of the room.

Stretching and yawning, Beth glanced at the clock and saw that it was time to leave and meet Michael. Closing the ledger books, she got up and put on her hat.

Spring had come and gone, and now, in the late summer, she was in her seventh month of pregnancy. She'd kept herself active by running the Rocky Mountain Central office until Dave was ready to take over, but she was looking forward to next month, when Robert Harris would take over these duties for her.

The street was full of people out walking, enjoying the beautiful night, and after locking the door, Beth decided to walk the few blocks to Michael's office. She needed the exercise. Other than the added weight, she felt good, but she'd be happy when the baby was born. It couldn't be soon enough for Michael either. Every day he'd bring home a gift for her or the baby, saying it was for "one of his gals." And every night before they went to sleep, he'd kiss her stomach and say good night to the baby.

He was a far cry from the man she'd married. From the time they'd become intimate, he seemed to have abandoned his threat to make her miserable. He even, through one pretext or another, which she'd always seen through, made up excuses to return shares of Rocky Mountain stock to her.

Beth paused under the gaslight across the street from his office and saw Michael at the window. He leaned out, waved, then called, "I'll be right down, Beth."

She smiled to herself and waved back. When had she fallen in love with him? And did he love her, or was it just an obsession, as he once claimed?

Before crossing the street, she waited for an approaching carriage to pass. Without warning, a figure darted out and slammed into her, throwing her forward. Beth screamed and instinctively grabbed for the lamppost to keep from pitching head first into the street.

Several people came to her aid and helped her to her feet. Suddenly Michael was among them.

"Beth, what happened?"

"I don't know. Someone bumped into me."

"Are you okay?" he asked worriedly.

"Yes, I just had the wind knocked out of me."

"Did anyone see what happened to my wife?" Michael asked the circle of people that had gathered around them.

"I wasn't paying much attention until she screamed," one of the men said. "When I looked over, all I saw was a man running away."

"Did anyone see what he looked like?"

They all shook their heads. "Good thing she grabbed that post, or she'd have fallen right in front of a carriage," a young woman said.

"It's getting so it's not safe for a person to even walk down the street anymore," another woman complained. "You sure you're all right, honey?"

"I'm fine," Beth said. "Thank you all."

"I'll get us a cab," Michael said.

"No, Michael, let's walk. It's such a lovely night."

"After this, I don't want you walking alone anymore."

"Nonsense! Accidents happen."

"You could've been seriously injured, Beth. If you won't think of your own welfare, think of our daughter's."

"Son," she corrected. Laughing, she slipped her arm through his.

In the Truth or Jeopardy game between them that night, Michael extracted her promise not to go walking beyond the garden without him.

For the past week, since the accident, Beth had thought seriously about Michael's words. The baby was due in two months, and Michael was right: it was time to give up going to the office. Robert would have to take over.

When she announced her decision to Michael at breakfast, he reached over and squeezed her hand.

"I can't tell you how relieved I am, Beth."

"Well, I can't see myself knitting booties for the next two months, but I guess it's time I become a lady in waiting, Sir Lancelot. I'll finish up today and close the office until Robert can take over. Dave will probably miss his help, but he'll have to do without it."

"I'll pick you up there tonight, and we'll go out to dinner. You may not have anything to celebrate, but I do, Beth. I've been worried about your health, and as long as you intended to retire, what difference is there if it's a few weeks earlier than you planned?"

Those words played through her mind that evening as she finished the last entry and closed the ledger book. Despite her decision, Beth knew she'd miss all this. As much as she looked forward to motherhood, the Rocky Mountain Central had dominated her adult life, and it was poignant now to end that chapter by closing a ledger book.

Sighing, she stood up and stretched her aching back, then walked to the window. The day had been exceedingly hot, and now steam rose like fog as a cool rain bounced off the pavements. The downpour paralleled her gloom. A sudden bolt of lightning streaked across the sky to reveal a lone woman huddled against the storm as she scurried along the deserted street to reach shelter. The jagged bolt was immediately followed by a deafening boom of thunder. Beth shuddered. She hated thunder storms—they scared the blazes out of her.

She thought of how she and Angie used to crawl into Thia's bed on such nights when they were younger. As the storm raged around them, Thia would hug each of them to her side and proceed to scare them more with a ghost story. She smiled, thinking about her sisters. Angie had had a baby boy last week, and Thia was expecting in another four months. Middy sure got her wish: in a short time the Roundhouse would be abounding with the patter of little feet.

Turning away with a smile, she picked up the ledger books and carried them into the small storage room. Michael called it a glorified closet, because it was only large enough to contain a floor safe and several shelves stacked with office supplies. As she placed the books in the safe, the sound of the rain increased and then declined, as if the front door had been opened and quickly closed.

"I'll be right out, Michael, as soon as I lock up the safe," she called out.

Just as she slammed shut the heavy steel door, the lights went out and the room was cast in total darkness. "Michael?"

When he didn't reply, her heart began pounding in her chest fiercely. Maybe she'd been wrong. Maybe no one had come in. Maybe the wind had blown the door open—and blown out the lamp. She was being foolish.

At the sudden creak of the floor, her heart leaped to her throat. Someone *was* in the office—someone up to no good. What should she do? She had no place to hide, no weapon. And it'd be useless to scream, because no one was on the streets, much less able to hear over the thunder and lightning.

The floor creaked again, and she knew the intruder was right outside the door of the stockroom. Terrified, she groped frantically on the shelves for something to use as a weapon. Her fingers encountered the large bottle of ink. If she could throw the ink in the intruder's face, maybe she could get past him. Her fingers were trembling so hard, she could barely uncap the bottle. Crouching low, she waited, ready to spring. *Please, God, help me.*

Her breathing sounded like a drum to her ears. She sucked in a deep breath as the door slowly swung open and the shadowy figure of a man stepped into the opening.

Beth sprang forward, tossing the liquid at what she hoped was his face. Uttering an oath, he staggered back, and she started to dash past him. He grabbed her arm, and she swung the ink bottle at his head. His grip slipped away, and she heard a thud as he fell to the floor. Beth ran to the door as fast as her condition allowed and dashed out into the storm. Screaming for help, she ran down the center of the street toward the lamp of an approaching carriage.

The driver reined up, and jumping down, he shouted, "Beth! My God, Beth, what's wrong?"

"Michael!" she cried out, and pitched forward into his arms.

Beth awoke to see Michael's anxious face bent over her. She threw her arms around his neck, and he gathered her into the sanctuary of his arms and rocked her as she vented her tears.

"What happened, Beth?"

"I was so scared," she sobbed. "He touched me. I felt his hand on my arm!"

"Who, Beth? Tell me, what happened, honey?"

Dr. Raymond appeared next to Michael, and Beth realized that they were in the doctor's office. Her hand instinctively slid to her stomach, and she discovered her clothes had been removed and she was covered by a blanket. She felt a rising hysteria. Clutching at Michael's shirt, she cried, "The baby! Did something happen to my baby?"

"Try to remain calm, Mrs. Carrington," Dr. Raymond advised.

"No, honey, the baby's fine," Michael assured

her. "Your clothes were soaking wet, so we had to
get you out of them so you wouldn't take a chill.
Now, tell me what happened."

Michael listened grimly as she related the details
of the frightening experience to him.

"And you never saw his face?"

"No, it was too dark."

"Well, I'm sure he's long gone by now, but I'll
go back there with the police. For now, Beth, I'm
taking you home and putting you to bed."

"I wish you'd get the police now and go back,
Michael. The office is open, and my purse is there.
I can't remember if I finished locking up the safe
either. I'll remain here until you get back."

"I guess you're right. I won't be long—but I
don't want you to budge from this spot."

"How can I, wrapped in this blanket?"

After Michael left, Dr. Raymond checked her
heartbeat and blood pressure again, and this time
was more pleased with the results.

In a short time Michael returned and said they
had found wet footprints in the office and some ink
stains on the floor. Everything else was in order.

"From what you described, Beth, it looks like
your aim must have been pretty accurate. The intruder got the worst of it. That was quick thinking,
honey.

Now, let's get you home and into bed. At least
the rain's stopped." Michael picked her up to carry
her out to the carriage. "You are definitely getting
heavier, my love."

"Blame it on your son, Michael."

"Daughter," he said. "Richard, I'll bring your
blanket back tomorrow."

"No hurry," Raymond said. He handed Beth a
package with her wet clothing and shoes. "Do try
and avoid any further incidents at least for the next
two months, Mrs. Carrington."

Chapter 29

As soon as he'd tucked Beth safely in bed, Michael went out to the sitting room. This string of accidents couldn't possibly be coincidental; someone was trying to harm his wife. There had to be some common link between them that would reveal the identity of the perpetrator.

He took a sheet of paper out of the desk and began to list the unusual events that had occurred since he'd married Beth.

1. *The vandalism at the ranch—Beth hung in effigy.*
2. *The threatening letter Beth received.*
3. *Buggy accident resulting in Grannie's death.*
4. *Beth's unresolved allergic food reaction.*
5. *Beth almost shoved into path of carriage.*
6. *Beth attacked in her office.*

Unquestionably Beth was the common link between all of them. Now it was a matter of finding out who else was the common link that could be behind them.

The first thing he'd have to do, though, was to make sure Beth was out of danger—and that certainly wasn't here. As long as she remained in

Texas, her life was in danger. He'd have to send her back to the Roundhouse.

Frustrated, he shoved the paper back into the desk and started to pace the floor. The thought of sending her away was unbearable—but the consequences that might result if he didn't were worse.

He finally went to bed with a heavy heart, thinking of what lay ahead tomorrow and the days that would follow. Stretching out on his side, he leaned on an elbow, cradled his head in his hand, and stared at her face. Serene in slumber, her beauty awed him. He realized that he'd been fooling himself for years, for he knew now that he'd loved her from the first time they'd been intimate. He'd tried to tell himself it was just sexual gratification—but it was love. He reached out and brushed back some strands of hair off her cheek, and she stirred. Dipping his head, he pressed a light kiss to her lips. She opened her eyes and smiled. It was his undoing. God forgive him, but he had to touch her, to feel her warmth in his arms. Once again he lowered his head and reclaimed her lips. They parted and fitted to his. With a stifled groan, he reached for her.

First thing the next morning, while Beth was still asleep and before he became tempted to change his resolve, Michael dispatched James to the telegraph office to send a wire to Dave and Cynthia. Then he went upstairs and began packing her trunk.

"Michael, what are you doing?" She sat up.

"I'm sorry to have wakened you, Beth. I'm sending you away for a while."

Shoving aside the sheet, she sprang out of bed. "What! I think I have something to say about that!"

"Not this time, Beth. My mind's made up. This is for your own good . . . and the baby's."

Ever since the previous night, he'd been fighting an internal battle to keep her with him—to protect her. But he'd sure as hell been doing a miserable job. He couldn't take that risk without knowing who could be trusted and who couldn't. The only way for him to guarantee her safety was to send her back to the people who could be trusted.

"Michael, I understand why you think you must do this, but that's running away—and my father never raised his daughters to be quitters."

"Your father! Like it or not, your father's the one responsible for this whole damned mess!"

"How dare you make that accusation! I'd hoped that in the past months we'd made strides away from that false argument of yours."

"Beth, I'm in love with you. There's nothing more important to me than you and the baby. But I've never changed my belief about your father's malfeasance."

"And what of your father? Where's the honor in a father extracting an oath of revenge from his son? At least Daddy wasn't motivated by bitterness— the railroad was his dream."

"Dammit, Beth, it was my father's dream too! What makes you think *your* father had an exclusive right to that vision!"

"Michael, I've got to know. If you've never been honest about anything with me before, you must be honest now. Do you believe the issue of our fathers will always stand between us?"

"Don't press for answers that I don't know myself," he said, flustered.

"Don't you see that we're no longer those two people who once shared a weekend? For heaven's sake, Michael, I'm carrying your child. If we haven't learned anything from the past, than there truly is no hope for us to reconcile our differences.

Our child would be raised in the same atmosphere as you were."

"I'm not my father!" he lashed out angrily.

"How do you differ from him? You've carried his bitterness into your marriage—and it will affect your son the same way he infected his son."

"I'd never do to you what my father did to me and my mother."

"Nor what my father did to me and my mother," she rebutted.

"What does *that* mean?"

"He loved us wholeheartedly. That's the example he set for his family. I want no less for my child and for myself."

"Then why did you ever agree to marry me?"

"I made a grievous mistake when I made that agreement. I never thought beyond that moment. It was naive of me not to consider that one day I might bear you a child. I see now it was the most selfish, self-serving decision I've ever made. Well, I've come to my senses, and I'm calling off all previous agreements. If you wish, I'll sign my share of the Rocky Mountain stock over to you, but I will not raise my child in the kind of household in which you were raised—a father infused with a bitterness that will destroy him, and parents at odds with each other. I *will* go back to the Roundhouse— and that's where I'll raise my child."

"I don't intend for you to remain there."

"I don't care what you intend. We both have some serious thinking to do, Michael. It's better that we do it apart." She snatched the garment from his hands. "And I'll do my own damn packing!"

They said little to each other throughout the day, but despite their resolve, each of them had begun to dread impending separation.

That night as they lay together, Michael didn't make love to her. Instead, he put his arm around her and held her against his side, wanting to tell her he no longer could imagine a life without her. That her smile, the sound of her voice, her laughter, touch, the scent of her, had all become his sustenance. He wanted to confess that at times he deliberately goaded her just to see her incredible sapphire eyes flare with anger, that he challenged her just to get her attention.

He wanted to say all these things—but he didn't. There had been so many accusations, so many painful scenes, that he understood why she felt as she did. And with the danger to her safety, this was not the time to ask for her forgiveness and beg her to stay. He wanted her somewhere she'd be safe— even if he had to let her go.

When Dave and Cynthia arrived the next morning to take her away, he still couldn't say the words in his heart to tell her his true feelings.

While waiting for Beth, Dave and Cynthia tried to make light conversation with him, but it was difficult for all three to keep up the pretense. None of them seemed able to say what was on their minds, and when Beth came outside, Cynthia paused beside Michael and put her hand on his arm.

"I'm sure you'll soon get to the bottom of this mystery, Jake." She kissed him on the cheek and climbed into the carriage.

Michael went over to Beth and took her in his arms, his misery squeezing his heart like a vise. "Whenever this whole thing is solved and this problem with Stephen is over, I'm coming for you." He kissed her tenderly, then lightly caressed her cheek as he took a lingering look into those eyes that would haunt him in her absence. "I love you, Rusty." He kissed her palm and pressed it to his cheek.

"I love you too, Michael."

Then he helped her into the carriage. "Take good care of her, Dave."

"I will, Jake." The two men shook hands, and then Dave flicked the reins.

Awash with desolation, Michael watched the carriage until it disappeared from view.

Michael pulled out his list of suspects and began to go over it again. In the six weeks that Beth had been gone, he had lost count of the number of times he'd pondered it. But until he figured it out or the police came up with some evidence, it was out of the question for her to return—even if he could persuade her to do so.

He missed her so much that he was nearing his wit's end. At work he tried to keep his mind off her, but at night, wretched and lonely, he'd roam the empty house thinking of her, wanting her. He wrote her often, living for her return letters, and memorizing each word she wrote. Somehow they'd have to put the issue of their fathers behind them for the baby's sake as well as their own. He wouldn't let any ghosts of the past interfere with their future!

Frederick Taylor's voice, raised in anger, jolted him out of his musing. The engineer was arguing with Howard again. The two men had never gotten along, from the time Frederick started working for the Lone Star. Lately their spats had become more frequent. Though Stephen was in charge of personnel, he hadn't put a halt to their bickering.

Michael strode to the door and yanked it open. "Dammit, how is a person supposed to think with the two of you shouting at each other!" Slamming the door shut, he went back to his desk and returned to his list of possible suspects.

Stephen, Millicent, Emily, James and Mary Nugent, Bertha Kaul, Helga Schneider, and Robert Harris all had easy access to the house, where three of the incidents had occurred: the letter, the chicken salad, and the tampering with the buggy.

Recalling the engineer's wrath toward Beth that day at Tent Town, he had included Frederick Taylor on the list as well as his secretary, Howard Gamer. He had even listed Richard Raymond and Diane Bennett, but later crossed out Howard and Richard. He couldn't think of any motive that either man would have to want to harm Beth. Diane, on the other hand, was jealous and vindictive enough to harm anyone who got in her way. But Diane had not been near the house since the wedding ball, so he'd crossed her off.

Even if the street incident and the vandalism at the ranch were simply coincidental—though he doubted that they were—the tampering with the buggy and the attack in her office were intentional. They'd been committed by someone who either followed Beth or knew her schedule.

Witnesses had claimed they'd seen a man running away the night Beth had been shoved, and she had said her attacker in the office had been a man. That would eliminate Millicent, Emily, Mary, Bertha, and Helga, despite their availability to the house. But it certainly didn't eliminate Robert Harris. His alibi about the newspaper clipping did not rule him out in Michael's eyes; and Harris had good reason to resent Beth. In fact, he and Emily could even be cohorts.

No matter what theory he applied, the only one that made sense was that there was more than one person involved: one had to be a male, and at least one of them would've had easy access to the house. Stephen and Millicent? Stephen and Emily? Emily and Robert? James and Mary? Stephen and Frederick?

Stephen was the prime suspect; he had the most to lose because of Beth. But he'd gain nothing from her death other than satisfaction. And despite his personal opinion of Stephen, Michael doubted that his cousin would resort to physically harming Beth.

He buried his head in his hands. He'd go over it again.

This time he eliminated Robert Harris, who would've been in Tent Town the night of the storm. So now it narrowed down to four possible couples: Stephen and Millicent, Stephen and Emily, Stephen and Frederick, or James and Mary.

Howard tapped on the door and opened it. "Mr. Carrington, Sheriff Johnson is here to see you."

Glancing out of the window, Beth wondered if she'd ever get over the misery of missing Michael. She'd once believed that she'd never be happy anywhere except the Roundhouse. But as much as she cherished the ranch and the memories it held for her, she yearned to be with Michael. No matter what she'd said to him, she couldn't live apart from him.

She slid her hand to her stomach. The baby had been active lately. It seemed like the little tyke never slept, but kicked and poked day and night.

"I think you miss your daddy's good-night kiss, little one," she murmured. "So does your mother."

Lately, she'd taken to talking over her troubles with the baby. Somehow it made her feel nearer to Michael.

She turned away from the window when Angie came into the room. Her usually bright face was solemn. "Beth, a messenger just arrived from Uncle Jim. He said Uncle Charles is asking for you; he's not expected to last through the day."

On her arrival home, Beth had been unprepared for Charles's appearance the first time she saw him. His condition had deteriorated drastically from the last time she'd seen him, the day before her wedding. The flesh on his once hardy face and body had shrunk to practically nothing, reducing him to mere skin and bones, and it was clear that the beloved lawyer's days were numbered. Now, faced with that reality, Beth couldn't hold back her tears.

Angie reached for her and they hugged and shed their tears in a shared grief. "Giff's hitching up the team right now. He'll take you," Angie said.

"Aren't you coming?"

"I can't. It's almost time for Matthew's feeding. Giff said he'd drive me in later, when the baby's sleeping. He's going to wire Thia while you're with Uncle Charles. Hopefully she'll get here in time."

Giff popped his head in the door. "Ready, Beth?"

She nodded. "I'll get my wrap."

It didn't take long to cover the five miles to Denver. James Fielding met them at the door. Hugging her, he said sadly, "Charles is very weak, Beth. Don't let him tire himself too much."

"I won't, Uncle Jim."

When she entered the bedroom, Charles lay asleep. Beth choked back her tears when he opened his eyes and smiled at her. "You got that railroad finished?"

The sound of his weakened voice ripped at her heart. "We've reached the outskirts of Dallas, Uncle Charles."

"That's good! Matt and I'll have something to celebrate when I see him soon." She couldn't hide her heartache, and he tried to grin. "Don't grieve,

Beth. I've long been ready to go. Don't think I'll last till that baby of yours is born, though."

"It should be in a week or so, Uncle Charles. I don't know which will come first—my baby or the completion of the railroad. I think it'll be a close race."

This time he managed to chuckle but paid the price with a coughing spasm. "Hard to believe you and Angie with youngsters. Seems like just a short time ago I was bouncing you gals on my knee. Are you happy with Carrington, Beth?"

"Yes, Uncle Charles. I love Michael very much."

"It worried me when he bought up all the Rocky Mountain stock. Never figured he planned on giving it to you as a wedding gift. Lately, I've done a lot of thinking about you girls. I don't have to ask about Angie—I know Giff will take care of that gal. Been thinking about Thia a lot, though. Is she over her restlessness?"

"Long over it, Uncle Charles. She and Dave are starting a family, too."

Tears glistened in his eyes. "That's good to hear. Dave Kincaid's a fine young man. I made Thia my heir, Beth. She's my godchild. I know Angie's got everything she'd ever want right there on the Roundhouse with Giff, and Michael will see that you have anything you'd ever hanker for. Tell Thia I want her to take what I left her and buy herself the biggest house she can find. She always liked big houses. Can't believe she's been content living in a railroad car—don't care how fancy it is."

"You can tell her yourself, Uncle Charles. She'll be here tomorrow."

"Good, I'll be glad to see her. Just in case I miss her, you tell her what I said, Beth."

Tears scalded her cheeks, and he reached for her hand.

"Beth, I'm sorry for what I did—it was reckless of me, but I was only trying to help Matt. I never meant to hurt you MacKenzies. I love you all very much. Only trying to help . . ."

His voice faded as he closed his eyes.

The next afternoon, amidst the family he loved and had served so faithfully, Charles Reardon was laid to rest in the family plot at the Roundhouse.

Thia had not arrived in time for the burial, and even though it was still early, as much as Beth would have liked to wait for Thia's arrival, she was too exhausted to remain at the wake. Excusing herself, she went up to her bedroom, but despite her tiredness she couldn't fall asleep. Her back ached, and once alone, her thoughts continually drifted back to Michael. Charles's death had accentuated the need to be with the man she loved.

She had almost succeeded in dozing off when she heard Matthew crying. Getting out of bed, she hurried to the nursery. As soon as she picked up the tiny infant, the baby began to root at her breast.

"Sorry, little one, but I can't help you," she cooed. "You're going to have to wait for your mama."

Despite her aching back, she walked the floor and gently rocked him, cuddling him to her as she smiled down at the precious little face in her arms.

Gradually she sensed she was not alone. Her heart lurched as she raised her head, but before she even turned it, she knew it was Michael. Their gazes met, clung, and then melted into each other's. His dark eyes caressed her face, stroked her heart—probed her soul.

"Michael." She knew she had mouthed the word, but the sound never carried to her ears.

Returning the baby to his crib, she turned to Michael, and he closed the distance between them. His kiss was gentle but drugging in its passion. Between confessions of loneliness and admissions of love, he covered her face and eyes with sweet kisses.

"All right, you two, there's a baby present," Angie teased, entering the room. "A hungry baby," she added, when Michael ignored her and continued to kiss Beth.

"I think she'd like us to leave, Michael." She took his hand and led him to her bedroom.

"How did you get here?" she asked, when they were in her bedroom.

"I came in with Dave and Thia. I'm sorry to hear about Charles Reardon, honey. But right now, I have to hold you and kiss you." He pulled her back into his arms.

"Michael, we have so much to discuss," she said, leaning back to look at him.

"Do you love me, Beth?"

"You know I do."

"Did you miss me?"

"Intolerably."

"Discussion ended." He pulled her closer and kissed her. Then he pleaded, "Come home, Rusty. Whatever differences we have, we'll work them out."

She gasped at a shock of pain in her lower back. Stepping away, she asked, "Michael, is my Uncle Jim still downstairs?"

"Yeah, I remember he said hello."

"Will you go and get him—and Middy? Unless I'm mistaken, I'm about to have a baby!"

Chapter 30

〰〰〜

Unfortunately, as Michael soon found out, the baby did not come that quickly. And he'd been banished by Dr. Fielding from Beth's bedside. As Beth labored throughout the night, Michael paced the floor below, Dave and Giff offering him their moral support. Each time one of the women came downstairs, Michael would rush over to her anxiously, only to be told, "Not yet." Then he'd follow her to the stairway and watch helplessly as she hastened back upstairs carrying towels or sheets, basins or hot water.

"I'm a bastard!" he cursed, after twelve hours of this exercise in futility. "I'll never forgive myself for putting her through this!"

Giff chuckled. "I wouldn't advise going near her right now, pal, or she'll probably agree with you."

"And to think I have this to look forward to in a couple of months," Dave said. "Why don't you sit down, Jake, before you wear out the floor."

"Why is it taking so long?" Michael asked. "Do you think there's a complication?"

Giff shrugged. "I'm not a doctor, but I've seen my share of mares foal. Sometimes it can take a long time."

Dave poured Michael a drink and handed it to

him. "Jake, you started to tell us that Frederick Taylor was responsible for the accident that killed your grandmother. Why don't you sit down and tell us the whole story? How did you discover it was him?"

Michael knew that Dave was trying to get him to take his mind off what Beth was going through, and he appreciated the two men sitting up through the night with him. Their support, their camaraderie... this was family. What affected one of them affected all. Family was what the MacKenzies were all about—that's what Beth had meant about raising a child in a loving household.

He swallowed the whiskey, then sat down. "Actually, the sheriff discovered a jacket and shirt stained with ink in Taylor's room, when he answered a complaint from the landlady that Taylor'd been drinking heavily and she wanted him out of her rooming house. Taylor admitted under questioning that he'd sawn the axle on the carriage but said he hadn't intended to harm anyone—certainly not my grandmother. And he claimed he only intended to scare Beth into leaving when he vandalized the ranch and hung her in effigy."

"Was he the one who attacked Beth in her office?" Dave said.

"Yes, he admitted to that, and also to trying to shove her in front of a carriage."

"Wonder what he'd have tried if he *intended* to hurt her," Giff scoffed.

"Actually, at that point he *was* attempting to harm her. He had also planned for me to have a fatal accident down the pike, but first he had to dispose of my wife and any possible heirs of mine."

"What was his motive?" Dave asked. "What would he gain from this?"

"With me gone, and no heirs, my cousin Stephen would gain control of the Lone Star."

"You mean your cousin conspired with this Taylor?" Giff asked.

"No. Stephen knew nothing about it, but he liked Frederick and did a lot of complaining to him. He even convinced Taylor that Beth intended to take over the Lone Star, kick him out, and bring in a new engineer by the name of Dave Kincaid. That's when Frederick thought of the whole scheme to protect his position and do Stephen a big favor at the same time. Besides scaring the hell out of Beth, that bastard was responsible for the death of a wonderful old woman." His bitterness sounded in his voice.

"I'm sorry, Jake," Dave said.

"Yeah. I guess you could say some good did come out of it, though. Stephen was appalled when he realized that he'd been indirectly responsible for his grandmother's death. My cousin's got a lot of faults, but he did love our grandmother. It seems to have changed his attitude. He's now feeling guilty—and very humble. We had a long talk and made peace with each other. He claims he's giving up his attempt to discredit me as the Lone Star's president. He'd never have succeeded in that attempt anyway, but at least he bowed out graciously. I'm not holding any great expectations of how long this will last, though. He and I have always been at odds." He took another drink of whiskey. "But at least Taylor's in the hands of the police now, and I can get my wife back again." Michael perked up suddenly. "Did you hear that? It sounded like a baby crying."

"It could very well be Matthew, Jake," Giff said.

Michael slumped in despair. "Oh, yeah. I forgot there is a baby in the house."

This time a baby's wail sounded louder. Giff frowned. "That doesn't sound like my son's cry."

"Do you think that maybe . . ." When Angie came down the stairs carrying a baby, Michael's hopes plummeted—until he saw Cynthia at the top of the stairway, also holding a blanketed bundle.

"Congratulations, Jake, you're a father," she said.

"Hey, that's great news!" Giff said, hitting him on the back.

"Congratulations, Papa!" Dave exclaimed.

Michael could only stare dumbfounded at them.

Cynthia came down the stairs and put the baby in his arms. "Jake, may I introduce you to your son."

Giggling, Angie stepped forward. "And may I introduce you to your daughter." She put the blanketed bundle she'd been holding into his other arm.

Mouth agape, Michael stared from one sleeping little face to the other.

"Wow! Twins!" Dave said as he and Giff crowded around him to see the infants.

The others began laughing at his befuddlement as he continued to stare back and forth at the two infants. Finally he broke into a wide grin. "Yeah, twins!"

After a good look at the babies, the two couples finally went to bed, and Michael carried his son and daughter upstairs to Beth's room, where a grinning Middy put them back in the crib.

Jim Fielding shook Michael's hand and congratulated him.

"When can I see Beth?" Michael asked impatiently.

"She passed out before the second birth, so she

doesn't know she delivered a girl, too," Fielding said.

Alarmed, Michael asked, "Is she okay?"

"She appears to be just fine."

Michael sat down at Beth's bedside and clasped her hand. "She looks so pale, Doctor. Are you sure she's okay?"

Fielding chuckled. "Cut her a little slack, son. She just labored for over twelve hours and delivered a healthy set of twins. No complications. Heartbeat's good—blood pressure, too. If Matt MacKenzie were alive, he'd declare that a damn good day's work." He patted Michael on the shoulder. "I don't know about you, but I'm going to take a nap. Wake me if you need me."

"Thank you, Uncle Jim," Michael said, grinning.

Without turning around, Fielding gave him a wave and continued down the hall to Angie's former bedroom.

Michael remained at the bedside, holding Beth's hand and waiting for her to wake up. Middy came over with a basin of warm water to sponge off her forehead and face. "I'll do it, Middy," he said. "You get yourself some sleep."

"Reckon I'll go and stir up some vittles for everybody when they wake up. This is a great day for this house." She shuffled out of the room.

Tenderly he sponged Beth off, then gently smoothed her hair. She opened her eyes.

"Hi," she said sleepily.

"Hi, love. How are you feeling?"

"Tired. I'm sorry about the baby."

"Why should you be sorry? You did a wonderful job, my love."

"I know you wanted a girl. Next time, Michael."

Grinning, he went over to the crib and picked up his son. Beth reached out. "Oh, let me see him."

Michael laid the baby in her arms. "Oh, he's so precious. And he's so beautiful!" Absorbed in admiring the infant, she didn't pay any attention to Michael when he went back to the crib.

"You've got your son, love—and I've got my daughter." He put the baby in her other arm.

"Oh, Michael!" she said, smiling up at him through her tears of joy. "Oh, Michael!"

He'd hold that image in his heart forever.

Finally, when she could barely keep her eyes open, he took the infants from her arms and returned them to the crib.

"Come and lie down," she said, patting the bed beside her. He joined her and put his arm around her. "What do you think we should name the babies?"

"Well, now, let me see . . . Why not name our son Rocky after your railroad and our daughter Star after mine," he said, tongue in cheek.

"Not on your life, Carrington!" She yawned, and her eyelids began to droop.

"You mean you'd rather name her Lone? Hmmm . . . Lone Star Carrington. It does have a good Texas ring to it."

"Better than Jacob Michael and Rachel Elizabeth?"

"Honey, I think you're onto something," he managed to say, right before they both drifted into sleep.

The next morning the issue of the children's christening arose, and who would sponsor whose children. Not knowing how to resolve the problem, the three couples decided upon a double set of godparents for each child and for any future children.

The following Sunday, Elizabeth and Michael Carrington and Cynthia and David Kincaid watched proudly as their godson, Matthew Peter Gifford, was given the sacrament of baptism. Immediately following, Cynthia and David Kincaid and Angeleen and Peter Gifford presented their godchildren, Jacob Michael and Rachel Elizabeth Carrington, to receive the same sacred rite—thus strengthening the woven threads of their ever widening circle of family love.

That evening, when all were gathered in the parlor, Beth and Cynthia presented the deed for the Roundhouse to Angie and Giff.

Flabbergasted, Angie shook her head. "You can't do this. The Roundhouse belongs to all three of us."

"Look, Pumpkin," Cynthia said, "Beth's home is in Texas, and Dave and I have found a house in Dallas that we like, too. With the inheritance Uncle Charles left me, we can easily afford it now."

Angie's chin began to quiver. "Does that mean you're all moving out?"

"Honey, the Roundhouse is your and Giff's home," Beth said gently. "It always has been, and it's only right that you and Giff own it exclusively."

"Your offer is very generous, but we can't accept it," Giff said. "Tell you what: we'll buy you gals out."

"We've already talked it over with our husbands, and they both agree with our decision. The ranch has been signed over to you and Angie."

"You can't do that!" Angie declared, with an emphatic toss of her curly head. "The terms of Daddy's will clearly said the ranch couldn't be sold unless we all agree to it. Well, I don't agree!"

Cynthia grinned. "We didn't sell it; we simply transferred the ownership to you and Giff."

Angie turned helplessly to Giff. "Isn't there some

way we can stop this?" Sobbing, she ran into his arms.

"I don't know what to say," he said. "I wish you'd all reconsider. At least let us give you something for it."

"Giff, you have a child now," Beth said. "This is little Matthew's home and that of any other offspring you may have. Michael and I have a house in Dallas and a ranch where we'll raise our children. They have to know where they call home. The same is true for Thia and Dave. Do you understand what I'm trying to say?"

Giff nodded. "We understand, Beth. Don't we, Angel?"

"You'll come home ... I mean come here ... to visit, won't you?" Angie asked, trying to hold back her tears.

"Of course, we will, Pumpkin," Thia said. "The Roundhouse will always be our old home—but as Beth said, there has to be a place our children can recognize as their home. A place that one day they can look back on, and think of home as we've been able to do."

"And the best thing about the whole situation," Dave interjected, "is how easy it'll be for any of our children to climb on the Rocky Mountain Central and come visit the place where their mothers grew up."

"Anytime they want to," Giff said.

"The door will always be open," Angie added, smiling through her tears.

Beth and Thia ran over to her, and with laughter and tears, the three women huddled in a shared hug.

Middy interrupted the moment by entering the room carrying a lit birthday cake, and all eyes turned to Michael with a chorus of "Happy Birthday."

Surprised, Michael tried not to show his pleasure. "Who told you it was my birthday?"

Beth walked over and slipped her arms around his waist. "Do you think you're the only one who remembered?" she said. "I may not have sent red roses, but I never forgot." She kissed him before her sisters converged on him with their hugs and kisses.

When they finished, Beth presented him with a large, flat package. "Happy birthday, Jake," she said, kissing him again.

He looked at her and grinned. "You understand, folks, this *is* truly a special occasion for Beth to call me that."

"Open your gift," she said.

He ripped off the wrapping paper, and his laughter stilled as his mirth turned to wonder. He looked at her, then grabbed her and hugged her. "Oh, God, baby," he murmured.

"Angie painted it," she said. Holding her, he looked again at the large framed portrait of his grandmother and grandfather. "I think it'll look wonderful hanging right over the fireplace at the ranch."

"But how—"

"The locket Nana Rachel willed me had a picture of them inside. My talented sister supplied the rest."

"This is the most thoughtful gift I've ever received. I love you, Beth." After kissing her, he went over and did the same to Angie. "You're a gifted artist, Angie. Thank you; you've captured their expressions beautifully."

"Don't tell my sisters," she whispered, "but you

know that picture of Daddy in the library? I'm going to copy it for each of them."

"That's a wonderful idea," he said.

"Hey, what are you two whispering about?" Beth called over to them.

"I was just telling her how talented she is." He winked at Angie and walked back and clasped Beth's hand.

Packing up the rest of their clothes was a tearful event for all of them, but the day finally came when they left the ranch to return to Texas. Beth couldn't speak for Cynthia, but it didn't seem possible to be saying good-bye to the Roundhouse, knowing she would be a houseguest the next time she came back. As she dabbed at her eyes, Michael came out and joined her on the observation deck.

"Michael, do you mind if I don't want to go back to Dallas? I'd like to stay at La Paloma until the babies are on a regular schedule."

"If that's what you want, Beth. You'll need some help, though. Do you want me to send Helga to help you with the babies?"

"That won't be necessary; Martha will help me out. Besides, there isn't a bedroom for Helga. Do you still plan on selling the ranch, Michael?"

"No. My inheritance from Grannie has solved my financial problems."

"In that case, why don't we enlarge the ranch house? I'd like to spend more time there, than in Dallas. And once the railroad is finished, it'll be simple to get back and forth between Dallas and the ranch."

"That's not a bad idea, Beth. I'll talk to James Burke. He's a good architect.

For the rest of the trip they decided upon what additions they wanted to make to the house, and when they reached Tent Town, instead of going to Dallas, they went to La Paloma.

Slim and Martha were as excited as grandparents when they saw the twins, and it didn't take long for Martha to pull out cribs, blankets, diapers, and even a couple of nursing bottles.

"Whatever are those for, Martha?" Beth asked, as she nursed the babies while watching Martha sterilize the bottles in boiling water.

"The little darlings need water, too, you know," Martha told her.

"Uncle Jim said they'll get everything they need from my nursing them."

"Shucks, don't pay a doctor much mind, honey. You'll see that with both of them suckling, they'll be times when you'll need something to put in one of their mouths. I remember when Miz Laura was nursing Seth and Amy. The bottle was a godsend to her."

"I'm glad you're here, Martha. I'm so new at motherhood, I've got a lot to learn."

Martha patted her hand. "Don't you worry, honey. I've been waiting a long time for Jake to bring home a young'un. I'm gonna enjoy every minute of it."

Michael left for Dallas the following morning with a list of supplies to bring back. He promised he'd return the following day and stay for a week. As much as she hated to be separated from him for even a night, she knew she'd be happier here with Martha than back at that big house with those aloof servants.

Upon returning to Dallas, Michael informed the servants of the birth of the twins and told them that Beth would be staying at the ranch for a few weeks. After dispatching Helga to the store to get the items

Beth had requested, he bathed, dressed, and went into the office.

Sitting down at his desk, he picked up the stack of mail. He felt good. He hadn't felt this happy since before his grandmother died. For a while it had seemed like everything in his life was going wrong: Grannie's death, raising capital, Beth's life threatened and having to send her away, the fight with Stephen. The loss of his grandmother would always leave a void in his life, but all the other problems had been resolved. Of course, there still was the issue of their fathers between him and Beth, but it hadn't been raised since the twins were born. And those twins! He missed them already. Lord, his life had been blessed! He meant it when he'd told her he'd never do to her and the children what his own father had done. He'd devote the rest of his life to Beth's happiness and the children's.

Whistling, he opened his desk drawer to pull out the letter opener and saw the list of suspects he'd made. Picking it up, he was about to toss it away, then stopped. In the excitement since the twins were born, he hadn't given the situation much thought. Seeing the list reminded him of his earlier theory. There were still a couple of unexplained incidents—the threatening letter and the chicken salad. Frederick Taylor had not confessed to either of them—but he hadn't even been questioned about them.

He started to shove it back into the drawer when a name suddenly seemed to stand out on the sheet. Why hadn't he seen it before? Helga *Schneider*. *Schneider* was German for "tailor"—and Taylor was an English variation of the word tailor. Coincidence? Unlikely! There had to be a connection. He grabbed his Stetson and headed for the jail.

At first Taylor denied any connection between

him and Helga. But finally, after a steady hour of questioning by the sheriff, Taylor broke down and confessed that Helga was his sister but that he'd encouraged her not to get involved.

Michael didn't wait to hear any more. The sheriff accompanied him home to arrest the maid.

However, James informed them Helga had never returned from the shopping trip.

"Oh, my God! Beth!"

Within minutes, Michael was on horseback, galloping toward the ranch.

"Who the devil's raisin' all that dust?" Slim Slocum said as he stood in the doorway of his cottage and watched the wagon racing up the path toward the house.

Martha came to the door and squinted at the woman driving the wagon. "Ain't nobody I know. Must be a friend of Beth's. She sure can't handle a team, though."

They watched the woman rein up and climb down from the wagon, then Martha turned away and returned to cooking.

Beth had just fed the twins and put them down for a nap when she heard the rapping on the door. Since everyone on the ranch used the kitchen entrance, she couldn't imagine who would be at the front door. Her surprise was even greater when she opened it to Helga Schneider. The woman carried a huge picnic basket.

"Why, Helga, come in. Whatever are you doing here?"

"Mr. Carrington sent me vit supplies." She started to open the basket.

"Oh, it wasn't necessary for you to drive way out here, Helga. Mr. Carrington could have brought them tomorrow when he comes. Sit down, Helga, you must be tired after such a long drive."

Beth turned to lead her into the parlor, and never anticipated the blow from the bottle that Helga brought down on her head.

"That gal sure didn't stay long, Mar," Slim said, when he saw Helga rush out of the house, carrying the basket she'd come with.

"Probably Beth ain't up to company. Them two young'uns keep her pretty busy. 'Taint polite for people to come uninvited, anyway. Especially after the poor gal just delivered twins. 'Stead of nosin' at others comin's and goin's, Slim Slocum, how about shellin' these peas for me?"

"All right, Mar," he said, giving her a playful pat on her rear end. "But the way she rode off, hell-bent for leather, that gal sure can't handle a team."

Chapter 31

〜 ○◯○ 〜

"Shet!" Billy Bob Walden grumbled, when his stomach growled like a hungry bear cub. He wuz hungry, all right. It'd been prit' near a week since him and the boys had put a good meal under their belts, and that weren't much more than a rabbit Curly'd cut up fer stew. He wuz the boss and the brains of the Billy Bob Walden Gang, and the boys wuz lookin' to him for guidance. So he'd have to figure out somethin'.

That sheriff in Fort Worth had no call to be runnin' him and the boys out of town jist 'cause them bad losers threatened to tar and feather him for dealin' off the bottom of the deck. When yuh come right down to it, men sure lost their good natures when it cum to cards and women! Shet! All him and the boys meant to do wuz get enough money to buy some grub, put down a couple drinks of likker, and have a diddle in one of the whorehouses. No worse than any red-blooded man wud do!

Billy Bob leaned back and squinted one eye shut. He'd have to do some deep thinkin'. It wuz time to come up with a new secret plan. He still wuz hard put to believe there weren't no gold in that mine! He'd paid that fella in Denver a gold eagle for that map to that mine—ten hard-earned dollars! The sorry part of it all wuz that they hadn't got the money robbin' freight trains or ranches—the boys had earned that money with the sweat of their brows, workin' in that there lumber mill in Denver. And that dad-blamed hombre had sold him a map to a gold mine without even an ounce of gold in it—but so full of rattlesnakes that him and the boys had to skedaddle out of there afore one of 'em rattlers got their fangs into 'em. A man wuz hard put to know who he could trust these days!

Billy Bob crossed his arms over his burly chest and stroked his long mustache. Yep, the time had come for William Robert Walden to do some serious thinkin'. He lay back, tucked his hands under his head, and closed his eyes.

"Yuh sleepin', boss?"

Billy Bob woke up with a snort and opened his eyes. "The hell yuh say, Curly! Can't yuh see I'm thinkin'?"

Removing his hat, Curly Ringo scratched his bald pate, then plopped the battered felt back on his head. "Cain't always tell, boss, 'ceptin' when yer mouth's open and yer catchin' flies like yuh wuz jist now."

"Whatta yuh want?" Billy Bob said gruffly, sitting up.

"The boys are hungry, boss, and they wanna know how yer plannin' on gettin' us some vittles. We ain't had nothin' but beans fer a week, we ate the last of the hardtack two days ago. And I've boiled 'em same grounds so often, the coffee tastes like piss warmed over."

Suddenly Jeb Bloomer let out a loud holler and pointed excitedly. "I see a wagon."

"The hell yuh say!" Billy Bob squinted in the di-

rection Jeb was pointing but couldn't see anything.
"Yeah, that's a wagon all right."

"Maybe we kin hold up the driver and get
money to buy some food?" Stew Potts said hopefully.

"All right, mount up, boys," Billy Bob shouted,
and swung his short, bowed legs and dispropor-
tionate bulk into the saddle. "The Billy Bob Walden
Gang rides agin!" With that battle cry, he galloped
away, leading the charge, until Hank Withers
caught up with him and guided him in the right
direction.

The woman driving the wagon had whipped the
horses into a lather. She reined up in a balloon of
dust when the gang rode up with pistols drawn—
albeit empty.

"Hold up there, lady," Billy Bob shouted in a
belly-bottomed growl.

"Yuh plannin' on runnin' 'em horses to death,
lady?" Hank asked. "If yuh do, we're hungry
enough to eat one of 'em now."

"Vat you vant?" the woman grumbled.

"Oh, a furinner, huh?" Billy Bob said. "Since yuh
can't talk good English, I'll tell yuh. This is a
holdup, lady. We want yer money and jewels."

"I got no money or jewels," she snarled.

"Yuh must think we're dumb, lady," Billy Bob
said. "Jeb, jump up in that there wagon and see
what she's carryin'."

Jeb did as told and after a quick inspection, said,
"There ain't nothin' back here but a basket, boss.
Looks to be like one of 'em there picnic baskets."

Stew Potts perked up. "That means somethin' to
eat!" He climbed down from his horse. "Give it
here, Jeb."

Jeb handed the basket to Stew and was about to
jump down when the woman whipped the reins

and the horses bolted forward. Jeb let out a yelp as he somersaulted off the back of the wagon and tumbled to the ground. He stood up, rubbing his rear end. "Now why'd she go and do that fer? That was downright mean. I coulda broke my neck!"

"No call to be chasin' her," Billy Bob said. "We got all she had, anyway."

Rubbing his hands together, Stew knelt down to open the basket. "Sure hope there's a fresh-baked pie inside."

"This ain't the place to find out," Billy Bob said. "Grab the basket and let's get out of here afore that lady comes back with help."

After several miles Billy Bob called a halt, and they gathered around him expectantly as he prepared to open the basket.

"Boy, I kin taste that pie already," Stew murmured, salivating.

"Maybe there'll be a chocolate cake," Jeb said.

Billy Bob opened the large basket and stared pop-eyed at the contents.

Curly scratched his head.

Jeb gaped.

Hank frowned.

And Stew looked on the verge of crying.

"Sure don't look like no home-baked pie or chocolate cake to me," Billy Bob lamented, as they all stared at the two sleeping infants.

"Might of knowed from the way she whupped 'em horses that woman wuz no good. What kind of mother rides off and leaves her babies to the likes of us?" Hank grumbled.

"Whatta we gonna do with 'em, boss?" Jeb asked.

Billy Bob pursed his lips and slowly stroked his mustache. "Reckon we're jist gonna have to find a ranch house and leave 'em."

"We ain't seen a ranch house for two days, boss," Jeb said.

"And iffen we do, are we jist gonna ride up, knock on the door, and tell 'em we found the babies on the side of the road?" Hank snorted, and spat a spray of tobacco juice against a rock. "They hang yuh here fer stealin' a horse. Whatta yuh figure they'll do to us fer stealin' a couple of kids?"

They all started shouting, trying to be heard above one another, and the babies woke up, crying.

"Now look what yuh done," Billy Bob complained.

"What should we do, boss?" Curly asked.

"I gotta think on this." Billy Bob shuffled over and sat down under a tree, thinking for all he was worth. After several minutes he shouted, "Ain't one of yuh gonna try quietin' them babies? How's a man s'pose to think!"

"We don't know nothin' about quietin' babies, boss," Curly said.

"Shet, yer dumb, Curly! Yuh jist pick 'em up and rock 'em." He stomped over to the basket. "What in tarnation is this?" he asked, holding up a small bottle with a nipple on the end.

"I knowed what that is," Stew said. "It's fer a sugar tit."

"Watch that dirty talk around the babies!" Jeb snapped sharply, nodding toward the basket.

"When my ma wuz nursin' me, she said she had to feed me a sugar ti—" He glanced guiltily at the babies. "A sugar teat 'cause I wuz always hungry and she cudn't keep me in milk. Bet them babies are hungry. That's what's makin' 'em cry."

"How'd yuh go about makin' this sugar teat?" Hank asked.

Stew shrugged. "Reckon yuh jist mix some sweetin' and water together."

"We got any sweetin', Curly?" Billy Bob asked.

"Some." Curly dug the remains of a bag of sugar out of his saddlebags and poured part of it into the bottle, then added water from his canteen. He handed the bottle to Stew. "Reckon yer the one with the know-how, Stew."

The men huddled around the basket and leaned over it as Stew held the bottle to one of the infants' mouths. For the first few seconds the baby sucked it voraciously, then turned its head away and resumed crying.

"It don't like it," Hank observed.

Stew shrugged to hide his confusion. "Makes no sense to me at all. Mama said I always liked it."

"Shet, Stew, yud eat anything," Billy Bob said, disgruntled. "Try the other one, Stew. Maybe it'll take better to that sugar teat."

Once again the men leaned over the basket as Stew stuck the nipple in the other baby's mouth. The baby sucked about three or four ounces of the sweetened water, then closed its eyes.

"Yeah, yuh did good, Stew," Billy Bob said. Redeemed, Stew grinned with satisfaction as the others patted him on the back.

Young Jeb picked up the other infant and cradled it in his arms. The baby stopped crying and stared up at him with round, blue eyes. "Yuh gotta drink somethin', li'l maverick, or yuh'll start feelin' puny." He rocked it gently and began to softly sing a long-remembered lullaby as he put the nipple in the baby's mouth. This time the infant began to drink, staring up at him with wide-eyed curiosity.

The sugar teat was a fleeting solution, though, and throughout the night one or the other of the babies awoke crying as they dropped in and out of short naps. All the men stayed awake, hovering over the infants and taking turns rocking or walking them.

Near dawn, Jeb made a suggestion. "Boss, this here baby's pants are mighty wet. Maybe if we took off them wet pants they're wearing, they'd be more content."

"That's a good idea, Jeb boy," Billy Bob agreed. "We ain't been givin' yuh no credit for yer common sense."

"Well, I'll be goldarn! One's a boy and one's a girl," Curly exclaimed, when they unpinned the diapers and removed them. "Here all this time I've been thinkin' they wuz twins, and they ain't."

"Sure are," Billy Bob said. "They're a spittin' image of each other. They're twins all right."

"How kin they be twins when one's got a dinger and one ain't!"

Billy Bob rolled his eyes heavenward, slapped his forehead, and wiped his paw down his face. "I swear, Curly, it's a wonder yuh ain't died of dumbness by now!"

" 'Taint fitten to let this one lay here buck-naked. She's a girl and we're fellas." Jeb picked up the discarded diaper.

"She's jist a baby, Jeb, boy. She ain't gonna know the difference."

"It wud hurt her feelin's."

"That baby don't have feelin's, Jeb. She's a mite too young."

"Jeb's right," Curly said. "Everybody's got feelin's. Some jist don't show 'em as easy as others. Yuh think it don't hurt me, boss, when yuh call me dumb?"

Billy Bob clamped his big fist on Curly's shoulder. "Yuh knowed I don't mean nothin' by that, Curly."

"Anyone got somethin' clean I can use?" Jeb asked.

Hank opened his saddlebags. "I've got a bandanna I've been savin' for a special occasion. Reckon this is special enough." He handed Jeb the scarf, and they all watched as he folded it into a triangle and put it on the tiny girl.

"Careful you don't catch her with that pin, boy," Billy Bob warned.

When Jeb finished the task, he cradled the infant in his arms. "Bet that feels better, li'l darlin'," he cooed, then kissed the top of her head.

Later, as Jeb and Hank walked side by side rocking the infants in their arms, Hank said to him, "You know, Jeb, you've got a real feelin' fer fatherin'. Yuh still young. Get out of this gang, find yerself a woman, and settle down and have some children. Don't waste yer life like the rest of us."

"I'd never leave the gang. I'd miss you fellas too much."

"Ah, we gotta think of givin' up outlawin' soon. Billy Bob's eyes have given out on him, and it's gettin' so he kin hardly swing one of 'em bowlegs of his over the saddle."

"What'll happen to him iffen he gives up outlawin', Hank?"

"Jist don't know, Jeb," he said sadly. "Jist don't know."

Pat O'Hara brought Clementine II to a grinding halt where the five people waited next to the track. When the door of the freight car opened, Luke, Flint, and Cleve MacKenzie stared down grimly at the five people waiting anxiously. Dave and Michael hoisted a ramp in place, and the three men led their saddled dun horses down it to where Beth and Cynthia waited with Slim Slocum.

The greetings were somber, as none knew what to expect if Flint succeeded in picking up the trail of the five outlaws who had the twins.

"The Rangers tried to pick up their trail, but I think they were following a cold one." Michael grabbed a stick and marked a spot in the dirt. "This is where we are right now—about five miles west of where Helga Schneider said the outlaws hit her while she was heading north. That's about twenty miles from my ranch. Helga said she took off and never looked back, so she doesn't know in which direction the outlaws rode away. I don't think the bitch would tell us even if she knew," he said. "The Rangers followed a trail due west from this spot but didn't find anything."

"Let's get moving before we lose the daylight," Flint said.

Michael nodded. "Dave and I are coming with you, and I've brought along two pack horses with whatever we might need." He came over to Beth and took her in his arms. "Don't worry, sweetheart—we'll find them."

"Michael, I want to come with you."

"That's out of the question, Beth. Thia, take her back to the house, and, Slim, you stay close to the house."

"I will, Jake. You fellas take care, yuh hear?" Slim said.

"We'll get your babies back, Beth," Cleve MacKenzie said.

Luke nodded and hugged her. "Don't you worry, Beth."

The reticent Flint looked down at her from the height of his saddle. "We'll find 'em, cousin."

Cynthia clearly tried to disguise her anxiety as she said good-bye to her husband. "David Kincaid, you watch your back. I don't want you coming back full of holes, or I might be tempted to trade you in for a younger model."

"No, you won't, Miz Sin. You're too crazy about me."

"Oh, you're right as usual, Kincaid," Cynthia said, throwing her arms around his neck. "Be careful. You almost got killed the last time you rode off with my cousins. No heroics, promise?"

"Promise, Miz Sin," he said. He kissed her goodbye and then climbed onto his horse.

Cynthia and Beth watched the five men ride away. Neither spoke their anxiety aloud but said it eloquently through their clasped hands.

As soon as they arrived at the site, Flint got off his horse and examined the trail carefully. He recognized that many of the hoofprints had been made by the Rangers and studied the tracks where they had ridden off in a westerly direction.

"Can't we be of some kind of help to hurry this along?" Michael said impatiently when Flint returned to analyze a trail of prints that led northeast.

"Jake," Luke said calmly, "Brother Flint has scouted for the army and wagon trains, and he can read Indian signs as well as the best of 'em. But he's a lone wolf. He doesn't like traveling with the pack."

"What Luke is trying to tell you, Jake, is that Flint prefers doing it alone," Cleve interjected. "That way his instincts and judgement won't be influenced by others. We're accustomed to his habits and we leave him on his own."

"I'm sorry," Michael said. "I'm just anxious to get going. I feel so helpless waiting here."

"And I'd be the same in your boots, pal. It may seem like a slow process, Jake, but it'll save us a lot of time in the end by not ending up following the wrong trail like those Rangers did."

Dusk had shadowed the trail by the time Flint returned. "I'm pretty sure I've found their tracks," he said. "There's a trail leading off toward the northwest. One of the horses 'pears to have a split in its left rear hoof. I didn't see that sign on the trail the Rangers took or among any of the other tracks leading away from here. My guess is that's the trail we should follow. We'll set up camp right here for the night and move out at first light."

Sleep was out of the question for Michael. He sat up drinking coffee and feeding wood to the fire— and reliving the nightmare of the last couple of days: Those anxious hours as he galloped to the ranch only to discover that he'd been too late to prevent another attempt on Beth's life and that his children had been snatched by the deranged Helga Schneider. He'd caught up with the fleeing woman, was told that five outlaws now had his children, and he'd turned Helga over to the Rangers. But they'd failed to pick up the outlaws' trail, so he'd taken Beth's advice and sent for her cousins. With Dave and Cynthia's help, they'd used the Rocky Mountain Central to get the MacKenzie brothers to them as quickly as possible. God willing, they weren't too late to be of any good.

Dave Kincaid woke up, poured himself a cup of coffee, then sat down next to him.

"I thought sitting up the night the twins were born was bad enough," Michael said. "But this waiting is driving me crazy."

"We'll find them, Jake," Dave said. "I was with these fellas when they were tracking a cougar that had killed one of the horses. Flint MacKenzie can follow a trail like no man I've ever seen. You've gotta trust him, Jake."

"I do—implicitly. But I keep wondering if my

babies are okay—I can't help but believe they're in danger. What would a gang of outlaws want with two infants on their hands? They should have just left them on the trail where they'd be found immediately."

"Would you abandon a couple of newborn infants, Jake?" Dave asked.

"No, of course not." Michael buried his head in his hands. "I'm just not thinking straight." He raised his head and said cynically, "Would you believe that yesterday morning I sat at my desk in Dallas thinking that I was the luckiest man in the world? A man can take just about anything except his family being threatened."

"What's still confusing to me is why this Helga Schneider kidnapped the twins. Did she intend to ask for ransom?"

"I don't think she took time to really think the whole thing out. It was pretty spontaneous on her part after she heard we had twins. She was bitter over her brother's arrest, and I believe she would have killed them. She denies this, of course, and claims she took them to make Beth and me suffer as she was suffering. She told the Rangers that when her brother finished his prison term—whatever it would be—she intended to return the twins to us. I don't believe a word of it. She did admit to sending the threatening letter to Beth and putting lobster in Beth's chicken salad. She'd read Beth's medical report." He shook his head. "Why in hell did I insist Beth come home with me, without making certain she'd be safe?"

"Jake, don't start blaming yourself. We'll find them." He patted Michael on the shoulder. "Why don't you try to get some sleep."

"Yeah, I will . . . later." But he didn't.

They broke camp as soon as it was light enough

to follow a trail. The going was slow and cautious until Flint broke into one of his rare grins and pointed to two discarded diapers.

"Thank God!" Michael said, feeling relief for the first time. Apparently the outlaws had not harmed the children.

Michael's spirits were buoyed by the knowledge that they were on the right trail, but when they stopped to rest their horses, Dave said, "Flint, I'm not trying to tell you your job, but I noticed we've turned southeast. We're heading right back in the direction we came from."

Flint nodded. "Yeah, that's kind of sticking in my craw. 'Pears these fellas are riding in circles. Looks like they have been for days. There was a spot where their tracks even crossed. It don't make sense, unless they're trying to cover up their tracks by doubling back."

"What sense would that make?" Dave asked.

"None to me."

"They must know they'd be followed," Luke said. "Why would they leave diapers in plain sight?"

"It's not only that," Flint replied. "I've seen tobacco juice on the trail and even a spat-out wad."

"These guys have gotta be the dumbest outlaws in existence!" Dave exclaimed.

"Either that, or they just plain want to be caught," Cleve added judiciously.

"You don't suppose a couple of them are laying clues just to throw us off the track?" Michael asked.

Flint shook his head. "No. They're still all together. I make it out to be five riders and no pack animal. They're traveling light—everything they're toting is in their saddlebags. But we're closing on them. The tracks are getting fresher." He mounted up and moved on.

They found no more discarded diapers, but there were signs of tobacco juice and fresh horse droppings. As Michael looked around him, the terrain became increasingly familiar. His suspicions were confirmed when they ended up at the same spot they'd originally started from.

"I'll be damned!" Flint cursed. "This is the craziest thing I've ever seen!" After another inspection, he pointed toward the south. "Now they're turned straight south."

"Which will take them directly to the ranch house!" Michael exclaimed. He goaded his horse to a gallop.

"My God!" Dave said.

The others raced after him.

By dusk the outlaws had run out of sugar.

"We jist gotta git them babies some milk, boss," Curly said. "They cain't go another night without eatin'."

"I thought by now, we'd of found a ranch house fer sure," Billy Bob replied. "No sense in making camp tonight. Them babies don't let us get no sleep, and there's nothin' to eat nohow. Might as well jist keep riding."

In a short time moonlight cast enough light to enable them to remain on the bumpy path they'd stumbled upon, hoping it would lead to a house or town.

"Is that a light, Hank?" Jeb suddenly asked, peering ahead through the darkness.

"It damn sure is!" Hank exclaimed. "Let's go."

"Wait up," Billy Bob shouted. "We can't jist go galloping up in the dark—that's a good way to get full of buckshot. We gotta be smart and use our heads. Scout it out first."

"Yer right, boss," Curly said.

"This is what we'll do: Hank and me's gonna ride up and introduce ourselves while the rest of yuh hang back aways. That way nobody will start throwin' lead at us."

"Why don't we jist leave the babies on the porch?" Stew said. "Nobody's gonna throw lead at babies, and they're sure to feed 'em."

"I ain't leavin' 'em with no strangers," Jeb announced. "We don't know what kind of people they are. They could be real ornery or even murderers, fer all we know."

"Jeb's right," Hank agreed. "Billy Bob's got the best idea. Let's do it."

With the others in the concealment of some trees, Billy Bob and Hank rode up to the hitching post of the ranch house and dismounted.

"Now remember what I said, Hank. Act real friendly-like and polish up to the lady of the house if there's one. Ladies always have softer hearts."

"Yeah," Hank grumbled. "Especially the one who wuz drivin' that wagon."

As Billy Bob stepped up on the porch, he tripped and fell, crashing against the door. It flew open, and he tumbled head first into the room.

"Don't shoot," Hank shouted to the man with a rifle trained on him. "We don't mean yuh no harm."

"Then you better start grabbing some air, stranger."

Hank raised up his arms.

A feminine voice broke into the conversation. "Well, if it isn't Mr. Billy Bob Walden and Mr. Hank Withers! Small world, isn't it?"

Billy Bob raised his head and looked into the barrel of a shotgun in the hands of Cynthia MacKenzie Kincaid.

Chapter 32

With drawn Colts, the MacKenzie men sprang through the front and kitchen doors to discover five of the most motley-looking men they'd ever encountered seated at the kitchen table, as Cynthia put down a huge platter of flapjacks and bacon in the center of it.

The gang all threw their hands up in the air. "Don't shoot! Don't shoot!" Billy Bob shouted. "We ain't packin' no iron. Miz Martha made us hang up our gun belts outside."

"Put down those weapons," Martha ordered indignantly from the stove, where she continued to flip pancakes. "These boys are heroes." Her smile embraced the seated men. "More coffee, boys?"

"The babies?" Michael asked frantically, sliding his Colt back into the holster.

"Your son and daughter are in their bedroom, most likely having their dinner," Cynthia said.

Michael shoved past everyone to get out of the kitchen. He opened the bedroom door and froze at the sight of Beth sitting in a rocking chair, holding a baby to each breast.

When she saw him, her chin began to quiver, and he rushed across the floor and knelt before her, hugging them all in his embrace. He never wanted

359

to let go. "Are they okay?" he murmured, and kissed away her tears.

"They're perfect, Michael. They were hungry, thank goodness! It feels so good to get rid of that milk! The little darlings are exhausted, though. They've both fallen asleep. Will you take Rachel?"

He stood up and lifted the infant out of her arm. Holding the precious little bundle as if the slightest touch would crush her, he gently placed his daughter in her crib. Then he took his son and put him in the other crib.

Beth came over, and Michael slipped an arm around her shoulders, drawing her against his side. For a long moment they gazed lovingly at the beauty of the sleeping infants.

"It's over now, love. It's finally all over," he whispered. He drew her into his arms and held her, unaware of the tears that slid down his cheeks.

Later in bed, Michael and Beth lay talking, and Beth brought up the matter of the five outlaws. "Thia said she recognized them on sight. They call themselves the Billy Bob Walden Gang, and tried to raid Tent Town once in New Mexico. She said they even held up the freight train once."

"The freight train? What was it carrying—gold?"

"No, just rails and ties."

Michael chuckled. "Well, how many rails did they ride off with?"

"Thia swears she also saw Hank Withers at the Roundhouse barbecue last spring. Small world, isn't it?"

"Guess there's no escaping them," Michael said, amused.

"Michael, we *are* indebted to them. How are we ever going to repay them? They're like children. If we give them money they'll squander it, and within a year they'll be as bad off as they are now."

"You're working up to something, Beth. What's going on in that fascinating little head of yours?"

"Well, I suppose I could ask Dave to hire them on the crew."

"I thought you liked Dave," Michael said, chuckling. She poked him in the ribs.

"Michael, they're adorable misfits, and we owe them so much. They did bring our children back to us."

"And if they hadn't taken them, we'd have had the twins back sooner. Remember, I caught up with Helga."

"They didn't take them intentionally. The poor dears thought they were stealing something to eat. At least when they discovered their mistake, they brought them straight back."

"Honey, you can ask the other fellows—those guys were plumb lost. They stumbled on the ranch by accident."

"Now you're nitpicking, Jake."

"Jake!" He rolled over and stared down at her. "Why, you devious little minx. You're trying to work me, aren't you?" Devilment purled in her eyes, along with laughter. He dipped his head and kissed her. "All right, we'll keep them here on the ranch."

"I thought you liked Slim and Martha," she said, failing miserably at suppressing a giggle.

Lying back, he clasped his arms under his head. "I'll buy some more cattle, and we'll start running a herd again. I can only hope this Billy Bob Walden Gang doesn't keep running the damn cows right into Mexico!"

She rolled over and leaned across him to gaze into his eyes. "I love you, Michael Jacob Carrington." She settled back, and he slipped his arm around her shoulders and drew her closer. She cuddled against him and laid her head on his chest, and he kissed the coppery top of her head.

"I love you, too, Rusty. I love you, too."

Out in the barn, Billy Bob glanced contentedly around the hayloft. He had a hot meal under his belt, and this was the best place they'd had to bed down since they'd left that shack in Denver. One by one, the boys climbed up and spread out their blankets to settle down for the night.

When they were all together, Billy Bob said, "Boys, I've been doin' some serious thinkin'. Time you knowed what it is."

"Yuh mean yer gonna tell us yer secret plan, boss?" Curly asked.

"Yep, Curly," Billy Bob said. "I'm thinkin' we oughta give up our outlawin' fer good and settle down right on this here ranch."

"But we ain't ranchers, Billy Bob," Stew said.

"Didn't know much about robbin' trains or rustlin' cattle, but we learned, didn't we?"

"Cain't say that fer sure, boss," Curly declared, in an untypical contradiction of his leader.

"But, boss, yuh said yuh hated MacKenzies. This here ranch is full of 'em," Hank said.

"Yep, reckon little Jacob and Rachel's got MacKenzie blood, same as Miz Beth and Miz Cynthia—and I sure don't want nothin' to happen to none of 'em. I've been givin' this some serious thinkin'. You know, boys, feudin' is really dumb. I ain't got no call to hate MacKenzies. Sure, they killed my brothers—but Charlie and Beau were mean. Real mean." Billy Bob bowed his head. "I've got a confession to make to yuh fellas. I told yuh that I rode with Charlie's gang, and that wuz no lie. But I never took part in the killin'. I never had the heart fer it. When Charlie raided a ranch, I'd hide 'til it wuz over. Somebody had to stop him and Beau, or they'd still be rapin' and murderin' innocent women like Miz Beth, Miz Cynthia, or Miz Martha—little kids like Jacob and Rachel.

"When Charlie raided the MacKenzie ranch, the men were off fightin' the war. There weren't nobody but an old Mex, two women, and a young boy. I helped the old man get away with the boy, but there wuz no way I could help them two women. The men had already started rapin' 'em, and the whole gang, including them Comanche that rode with us, had their way with 'em before they killed 'em. Them MacKenzies did right to gun down my brothers after what Charlie did to their women." Billy Bob brushed a tear out of his eye.

"Charlie wuz teched in the head—plumb loco— and Beau wuz near as bad. They had no souls." He shrugged his shoulders, then lowered his head again. "I ain't got no good memory of either of 'em. Truth is, you boys are more like brothers to me than Charlie and Beau ever were. And I think we should stay here together and see that nothin' more happens to little Jacob and Rachel. They wuz sent to us for a reason."

"Zat so! By who, boss?" Jeb asked, bewildered.

Billy Bob squinted at the young man fondly and tried not to show his impatience. "Well, it sure weren't the Dev'l, Jeb, boy. I figure them babies are our re-spons-i-bility now. That's why we gotta stay here. So, that's my secret plan. 'Ceptin' it's no secret now that I told yuh."

"I'd like that real fine, boss," Curly said.

"And that Miz Martha sure is a durn good cook," Stew said, nodding his approval.

"Maybe I can find me a wife in town and we kin hire out right here," Jeb said, grinning.

"What are you thinkin', Hank?" Billy Bob asked. He had long recognized that Hank was the best thinker among the gang—maybe even better than Billy Bob himself, and he braced himself for one of Hank's steely-eyed glares.

Hank Withers thought deeply, then spat his chaw of tobacco out of the loft door. "I'm thinkin' that's the best secret plan yuh ever had yet, boss."

Billy Bob's eyes glistened with moisture, and his toothy grin stretched to his ears. "Yep, boys, from now on MacKenzies can sleep peaceful in their beds—'cause the Billy Bob Walden Gang ain't gonna ride agin!"

The following morning, after saying good-bye to the Kincaids and MacKenzies, Michael assembled the gang together and offered them a job on the ranch.

"If you're interested, we can clean up the old bunkhouse and get you fellows settled in. What do you think?"

The four desperados looked to their leader. Billy Bob cleared his throat. "That's a right generous offer, Mr. Carrington."

"We don't stand on formalities here, Billy Bob. Just call me Jake."

Billy Bob puffed up like the only rooster among a passel of hens. "Jake, the first time I laid eyes on them babies, I knowed it wuz a sign from God. And there weren't a dad-blamed thing that cud keep me from gettin' them young'uns back to the lovin' arms of their mama. That's why we high-tailed it straight back here, 'cause I knowed good wud cum from it!"

"But yuh didn't know about this place, boss," Jeb said.

Billy Bob turned red and rolled his eyes.

" 'Course I did. That wuz my secret plan, Jeb boy."

"But yuh said yer secret plan wuz—"

"My *old* secret plan," Billy Bob declared, squinting impatiently at the young man.

Michael changed the subject by asking, "Have you fellows been around cattle very much?"

"Reckon a time or two, when we rustled—"

"Hustled!" Billy Bob shouted, with an elbow jab to Curly's ribs. "He meant when we *hustled* them to market. Poor Curly jest ain't got the hang yet of the English language."

"Well, do you boys know anything about branding cattle?"

"We sure do," Stew spoke up proudly. "Best to try changin' the brand before sellin' the steer."

Billy Bob's eyes bugged out of his head. "Ole Stew meant to say—"

"Never mind." *Good Lord, Beth! What have you gotten me into!* "Just tell me, boys: has any one of you robbed a bank or killed someone?" His glance swept the circle of heads shaking their denials. "Okay, that's good enough. Let's get to fixing up that bunkhouse."

Chapter 33

❧ ‿‿ ⚬⚬ ‿ ❧

A month later, the population of Dallas awoke to an ambiance of festivity. The streets surrounding the railroad depot had been cordoned off for the celebration of the arrival of the Rocky Mountain Central Railroad. Offices, shops, and warehouses were draped in red, white, and blue bunting, and at first light, street vendors had begun laying out their wares in hatched stalls. Hurdygurdy operators were testing their equipment, and concessionaires were setting up tables and preparing food varying from Mexican tortillas to Scottish scones.

Ten miles outside the city limits, Pat O'Hara and Tim Harrington had polished Clementine II until she shone brightly, so she'd look her best on her arrival in town.

With only two hours to go before the official opening ceremony, Beth and Michael returned to the city accompanied by the Billy Bob Walden Gang, who, despite recent shaves, baths, haircuts, and new clothing, still managed to appear like a suspicious-looking, disreputable gang of outlaws.

By high noon most of Dallas had congregated at the site, waiting for Governor Roberts to arrive from Austin. The Lone Star stockholders had assembled on the dais, Beth and Michael among them. The rest of the Rocky Mountain Central's dignitaries were due to arrive on the train.

A murmur passed through the crowd when a contingent of mounted horsemen approached the flag-draped stage.

"I know that brand," one of the cattlemen on stage murmured. "That's the Triple M riding in."

"Who are they?" Emily Carrington asked, mouth agape.

"I don't know, dear," her mother replied, equally awed. Even the normally austere Stephen Carrington appeared impressed.

They looked magnificent, Beth thought with pride, as she watched the approach of her cousins and their families.

Luke and Honey led the contingent, with nineteen-year-old Josh, a younger version of his handsome father, catching the wistful eye of many of the young female spectators as he rode beside his mother. A wagon carrying the MacKenzie children followed the trio, driven by a vaquero with eighty-year-old Maude Malone seated beside him on the box, holding Cleve's youngest offspring.

Flint and Garnet flanked the right side of the wagon; Cleve and Adriana rode on the left. Cleve's beautiful Spanish wife sat astride a powerful black stallion that drew murmurs of admiration from the spectators.

Rays of sunlight bounced off the elegant, silver-adorned saddles and trappings of Adriana's father, the distinguished hidalgo Don Alarico Carlos Ramon Fuente, as he and six of his vaqueros followed the wagon.

"My God, who are they?" Stephen asked.

"Those are the MacKenzies," Michael said. "Rather a formidable army, aren't they? I should add, Stephen, that they're Beth's cousins—in the event you're planning to resume warring against my wife."

The celebration continued throughout the day, capped off by a spectacular display of fireworks which illuminated the Dallas sky with a shimmering, colorful incandescence that officially ended the celebration.

Beth observed that James managed to maintain his austere composure as the whole MacKenzie crew trailed into the house, laughing and calling out to one another.

When all had been given rooms and their children were bedded down for the night, the adults converged downstairs in the parlor.

Beth smiled as she watched James pass among them with trays of tasty canapés prepared by Mary and glasses of sparkling champagne. She followed him on one of his numerous trips to the kitchen for refills.

"James, it's been a long time since my family's been together, and this could be a very late night. It's not necessary for you and Mary to stay up. We can help ourselves."

"It's our pleasure, madam."

"That's very nice—" She suddenly stopped, struck by the enormity of his words. "James, you called me madam!"

"Yes, madam, I did."

"I'm flattered, James—but I know you reserved that title for Rachel Carrington, and I don't expect you to change on my behalf."

"I have been negligent until now, madam."

Beth smiled and said teasingly, "Does that mean I've finally met with your approval, James?"

"Madam, I find this very embarrassing."

"Forgive me; it's not my intention to embarrass you. Knowing and loving Rachel as you did, James, do you think she would approve of my sisters and cousins?"

James caught her completely by surprise when he grinned broadly and said, "Madam, the moment those tall Texans walked through this door, she would have been delighted."

Smiling with pleasure, Beth returned to the parlor in time to hear Cynthia declare, "Don't even think it, Cleve MacKenzie. You may rest assured, cousin, that this baby will be as much MacKenzie as Kincaid."

"Well, I can't speak for my brothers-in-law," Michael said, "but I've lived with the MacKenzies in one way or another for the past four years, so I figure I'm as much MacKenzie as I am Carrington."

"Hear! Hear!" David agreed, nodding. "They've sure as hell become my family."

"Well, you aren't gonna hear any different from me," Giff spoke up. "I was raised with MacKenzies. Heck, that makes me one of you, doesn't it?"

"Gentlemen, you have reached a reality that my brothers and I concluded about our wives years ago," Cleve remarked. "And I'd like to say that—"

"Oh, no!" Flint grumbled. "Sounds like you're gonna make a speech again, Little Brother."

"Just a toast."

Luke groaned. "You're right, Brother Flint. He's gonna make a speech."

"Quiet, folks!" Michael cried out. Laughing, he tried to stifle the good-natured groans among the assembled. "Let's hear what Cleve has to say."

"Thank you, Jake. You're a man of impeccable character and taste. I must compliment my cousin for her extremely good judgement in choosing you as a husband."

"I didn't choose him," Beth protested. "He chose me—so I'm going to have to agree with your opinion regarding his impeccable taste."

When the laughter quieted down, Cleve said, "All joking aside, I propose a toast to these remarkable women whom we were fortunate enough to marry."

"I think you should include those remarkable men we women were fortunate enough to marry," Beth said, "who, by the admissions I just heard, are MacKenzies all."

"Too long, too long," Cynthia complained. "Remember, in my condition, I need my rest. So let's get on with this toast so I can get to bed. Besides, my arm's tired from holding up this glass."

"Thia's right," Michael said. "And she's reminded us that we're overlooking the remarkable children these remarkable women and remarkable men have produced—among whom, if I may refresh your memories, gentlemen, Beth and I produced *two* in our first attempt." To drive home his point, he raised two fingers in the air.

Naturally, the comment produced a chorus of moans and groans as well as threats on his life, which dissolved into laughter. Still chuckling, Michael slipped an arm around Beth's shoulders. "So as pompous as this may sound, let's simplify it." He raised his glass. "To the MacKenzies."

"The MacKenzies!" all shouted, echoing the toast.

The sound of laughter and voices followed Beth up the stairway as she slipped away to check on the twins. She peered into the sitting room. Open-mouthed and snoring, the babies' five self-appointed godfathers were stretched out on floor and chairs. She picked her way carefully across the floor, trying to avoid disturbing the vigilant guardians.

Jacob was sleeping soundly, a little arm with an open palm framing each cheek on the pillow. Marveling at how he could remain sleeping through the cacophony of loud snorts, hoarse inhaling, and wheezing exhaling, Beth smiled tenderly at the infant.

"You're just like your daddy," she whispered lovingly. Bending down, she kissed his cheek, then moved to the other crib. Rachel lay awake, cooing contentedly.

"So, little one, you're awake," Beth murmured softly. The baby stared wide-eyed and curious in response. "You're too smart to sleep through all of this, aren't you, little love?"

She began to gently rock the cradle back and forth, and soon Rachel's blue eyes closed, her long, dark lashes sweeping her cheeks.

"She sure is purty, ma'am," Jeb Bloomer said softly at her side.

Beth smiled. "Thank you, Jeb."

"You jist go back to yer party, ma'am. Nothin's gonna happen to 'em while me and the boys are here. Yuh kin be sure of that, Miz Beth."

"I know that, Jeb." She felt tears misting her eyes, for it warmed her heart to know that his words were sincere and from the heart. And as bumbling and unlikely protectors as the Billy Bob Walden Gang might appear to be, as long as there was breath in any one of those lovable misfits, she knew her children would never come to any harm. "Thank you—but you and the others can leave now. You'll find plenty of pillows and blankets in the quarters over the carriage house. I'm sorry we kept you up so late."

Jeb glanced around at his sleeping comrades. "Shucks, ma'am, don't give it a never-no-mind. Weren't no trouble at all. Yuh sure yuh don't have no more need fer me and the boys tonight?"

"No. Get some sleep, Jeb. We'll be heading out to the ranch tomorrow."

Jeb woke his companions, and with nods and head shakes, the five men shuffled out of the room.

As Beth opened the top drawer to get a handkerchief, the sealed letter from her father caught her eye. What better time to read it than now? Her life could never be happier than this moment.

Carrying it over to the desk, Beth lit the lamp and sat down, pausing to touch the small sculpture of the Betsy. Her fingers trembled as she withdrew the letter from the battered envelope. For a brief moment, she felt a stab of pain in her heart as she recognized the familiar script. Then, forcing back her tears, she began to read.

My dearest Beth,

I've saved this letter for last because it is the most difficult one for me to write. In watching you these past years, I knew without asking that you would do everything within your power to continue my dream for the railroad. And now, with my end so near, I can see how unfair I have been to you. Why should you dedicate your life to fulfilling my dream? What about your dreams—your visions, my dear? When will you have the time to pursue your own happiness? To find love?

One can never acquire greater wealth than the gift of love—can never know a greater force than the power of love. And there can never be a greater ful-

*fillment than the peace and contentment in the arms
of the man you love, knowing he returns that love.*

*By encouraging you to live my dream, I have de-
nied you the chance to experience that exquisite happiness, Beth. And alas, dear child, my guilt is
increased tenfold by the confession I must make to
you. I not only have done an injustice to you, but I
have been a party to a dishonorable act in the effort
to achieve my aim.*

*Therefore, I give you this tiny replica of the Betsy
as a reminder of a better day—a finer hour.*

*I hope by the time you read this letter that Charles
has told you the truth. But I cannot go to an eternal
rest without this confession: that an act of bribery
was committed to gain the railroad contract for the
Dallas trunk line. Charles did not inform me of his
actions until after the fact, but I did nothing to correct the misdeed. It would have meant the incarcer-
ation of a dear and loyal friend, who, like you, had
been dedicating himself to the fulfillment of another
man's dream. And that silence has led me to deceive
people I love dearly—my daughters and David Kincaid.*

*That is why I beg you, Beth, not to sacrifice your
life on the altar of a man unworthy of that devotion.
Seek your happiness, my dear, and let an old man's
dream be buried with him. Only then will I find a
peaceful sleep, and you will be free to pursue your
own happiness.*

Forgive me, my dearest Beth. I love you.

In a state of shock, Beth sat back in the chair. So
Michael's father had been right: there *had* been
bribery involved when the Rocky Mountain Central got the railroad contract. Charles had tried to
confess this to her before he died, but she had
thought he was talking about the stock. And trag-

ically, it had not only affected Charles's and her father's lives, but Mr. Carrington's, Michael's, and her own. How differently their lives might have been played out had she and Michael known the truth.

She picked up the tiny replica and clutched it to her breast. "Oh, Daddy, I love you so much. You'll always be a man of honor to me, because you're a man of conscience." She half-smiled, wondering what Michael's reaction would be to that remark. "If only you could have lived to see this day, Daddy." She pressed a kiss to the small facsimile of the first engine of the Rocky Mountain Central.

"So here you are," Michael said from the doorway. "I've been looking all over for you. What are you doing—?" Seeing her stricken look, he hurried over to her. "What is it, honey? What's wrong?"

She handed him the paper. "I just opened the letter my father wrote me before he died." As she watched Michael read the letter, she wondered if his reaction would be the same as hers. She felt emotionally drained, as if she'd been crying for days. "I owe you an apology. Your father was right," she said, when Michael finished reading it.

Kneeling down, Michael grasped her hand. "Honey, he may have been right about the bribery, but he was wrong to ask me to carry out his revenge—and I was wrong to do it."

"No, you weren't. Were our roles reversed, I'd have done the same thing," she said, admitting aloud for the first time the truth she had wrestled with for the past year.

She lovingly caressed his cheek. "When I think of all the cruel things I've said to you . . . We came so close to destroying our own lives for the sake of the dreams of others, just as Daddy said. If only I'd opened his letter sooner."

"What difference does it make, Beth? Now, at least, we can put the past behind us—wipe the slate clean. No more guilty feelings on either of our parts. All the mistakes, misguided motives, and heartaches are behind us forever."

"I doubt it's that easy."

"But it is, honey. Hadn't our love gotten us past the worst of it even before you opened that letter? So now, being people of conscience," he said with a loving grin, "neither of us has to look back in guilt. We can go back to the beginning and start over."

"Wouldn't that be wonderful, Michael! How I wish we could," she said wistfully. "Looking up and seeing you for the first time . . . our first kiss."

He cupped her face between his hands and smiled down into her love-filled eyes. "We can, my love. We begin with:

"Hi, I'm Jake. I bet with that hair of yours, you're called Rusty . . ."

A fantasy, a love story, a summer of change...

The China Garden

&

By LIZ BERRY

"Like a jewel box with hidden drawers and compartments, this finely crafted, multilayered novel holds many secrets...richly laden with mystery and suspense, in which the ordinary often masks unexpected interconnections and the extraordinary is natural to the story's wildly imagined terrain."
—PUBLISHERS WEEKLY ☆

Dear Reader,

So many of you have been patiently waiting for Lori Copeland's next Avon Romantic Treasure, so I'm thrilled to say you don't have to wait any longer! Next month, don't miss *The Bride of Johnny McAllister*—it's filled with all the wonderful, warm, western romance that you expect from this spectacular writer. Johnny McAllister is on the shady side of the law, and never in a million years would he believe he'd fall for the local judge's daughter. But fall he does—and hard. You will not want to miss this terrific love story.

Contemporary readers, be on the look out—Eboni Snoe is back, too! Your enthusiastic response to Eboni's last Avon contemporary romance, *Tell Me I'm Dreamin'*, has helped build her into a rising star. Next month don't miss her latest, *A Chance on Lovin' You*. When a stressed-out "city gal" inherits a home in the Florida Keys, she thinks that this is just what she needs to change her life...but the real changes come when she meets a millionaire with more than friendship on his mind.

Gayle Callen is fast becoming a new favorite for Avon readers, and her debut Avon Romance, *The Darkest Knight*, received raves. Now don't miss the follow-up *A Knight's Vow*. And sparks fly in Linda O'Brien's latest western *Courting Claire*—as an unlikely knight in shining armor comes to our heroine's rescue.

Don't miss any of these fantastic love stories!

Lucia Macro
Lucia Macro
Senior Editor